*To dear (
with love
Barbara .*

Barbara Kendall-Davies

TRUTH WILL FIND
A WAY

Limited Special Edition. No. 17 of 25 Paperbacks

Barbara Kendall-Davies is the author of the seminal, two-volume biography *The Years of Fame* and *The Years of Grace* of the French singer, composer and teacher Pauline Viardot Garcia, published by Cambridge Scholars Publishing, as well as a family history, *The Food of Love*, set at the beginning of the Second World War and an esoteric exploration of life after death entitled *Life Is Everlasting*. The latter two books are published on Amazon Kindle under the name of Barbara K Davies.

Truth Will Find a Way is her debut novel.

Dedicated to Chris, Giles, Kate, Charles and Lawrence.

Barbara Kendall-Davies

TRUTH WILL FIND
A WAY

AUSTIN MACAULEY PUBLISHERS™

LONDON • CAMBRIDGE • NEW YORK • SHARJAH

A CIP catalogue record for this title is available from the British Library.

ISBN 9781528913843 (Paperback)
ISBN 9781528913850 (Hardback)
ISBN 9781528913867 (Kindle e-book)
ISBN 9781528960649 (ePub e-book)

www.austinmacauley.com

First Published (2019)
Austin Macauley Publishers Ltd
25 Canada Square
Canary Wharf
London
E14 5LQ

To all the writers who have inspired my work to the present day.

Cast List

Dr Guy Giffard, art historian and TV personality.

Dr Sally Wentworth, lecturer at Courtauld Institute of Art and intimate friend of Lady Monica Montford.

Lady Monica Montford, owner of the Gayton Art Gallery in Mayfair.

Sir Douglas Montford, diplomat, husband of the above.

Marcus McIver, Earl of Drumlomond, brother of Lady Monica

Sir Conrad Beight, successful artist.

Polly Parsons, wife of the above, artist, teacher at St Martin's School of Art.

Imogen Beight, daughter of the above: apprentice auctioneer at Sotheby's.

Lord Patrick McIver, homosexual son of Marcus McIver, Captain in the Royal Signals Regiment

William Wilcox, merchant banker, lover of the above

Daniel Brewster, artist, protégé of Lady Monica and former student of Sir Conrad.

Jane Partington, TV producer, lover of Marcus, Earl of Drumlomond.

Brigadier General Arnold Partington, estranged husband of Jane Partington.

Sylvia Delavere, former actress, PA to Jane Partington.

Ranu Gupta, Indian industrialist and entrepreneur.

Emma Simson, aspiring actress and mistress of the above.

Bernard Daubigny, French art historian.

Tom Giffard, Viscount Torrington, elder brother of Guy Giffard.

Ginny Giffard, wife of the above

Toby Giffard, son of Lord Torrington and his wife.

Helen Giffard, daughter of Lord and Lady Torrington.

Paul Dainton, estate manager, husband of the above.

Martin Morson, private secretary to Sir Douglas Montford.

Miranda Pointer, young artist, protégé of Lady Monica.

Nancy Lolongo, successful actress.
Piers Gambourne, archivist.

Synopsis

This novel is basically set around the Mayfair area of London, and the Art Gallery and apartment of Lady Monica Montford. She is married to the British Ambassador to France so spends her time between Paris and London. Her London venue is a central meeting place for her aristocratic, academic and artistic friends, some of whom live in the Midlands but regularly visit London.

Lady Monica and Dr Sally Wentworth, an art historian who teaches at the Courtauld Institute of Art, met at Cambridge and have enjoyed a satisfying sexual relationship over the years.

Monica introduces Sally to her friend, Dr Guy Giffard, and they are immediately attracted to each other.

A few days after meeting Sally for the first time, Guy invites her to Sunday lunch at the Dower House on his family estate. He has heard rumours about her and Monica, but is not sure if they are true. He seduces Sally, but she does not resist him. Afterwards, a wall of silence comes down and they never mention it. Sally does not tell Monica about her unusual encounter.

Guy's niece, Helen, has been made pregnant by Paul Dainton, the estate manager of West Bridge Hall, the family seat. She is 18 and is a student at an agricultural college. Tom, Guy's elder brother, tells him that although Toby is his son, Helen is the child of Sir Conrad Beight, but Conrad does not know. Tom confesses that he is impotent and that modern medicine has not cured him. Tom does not know that his wife, Ginny is also involved with Paul, but admits that she is too young for a life of celibacy. Helen plans to keep the baby and a wedding is arranged.

Ancient documents are found during renovation at the Hall, and Sally and Piers Gambourne are keen to investigate. Sally becomes interested in the question of the Shakespeare authorship. There is also the story of a haunting at the Hall and though the family do not believe it; Sally finds evidence of a killing made to look like a suicide at the time of the Civil War.

Guy goes to France to gather material for his new TV documentary series, then to Germany. Jane Partington, the mistress of Marcus McIver, the Earl of Drumlomond and brother of Lady Monica, is Guy's Executive Producer. She was married at 18 to a man who is now a Brigadier General, Arnold Partington, but she ran away from him on her wedding night because she discovered he was a brute and has never lived with him since then. However, he has converted to Roman Catholicism and has become a religious fanatic. He is vindictive because she humiliated him and will not divorce her so that she can marry Marcus, who is a widower with a homosexual son, Captain Lord Patrick McIver.

Relaxing in his hotel room at Versailles before turning in, Guy sees an episode of a film on TV about Charles II and realises that the girl playing his mistress, Barbara Villiers, is Sylvia, who is now working as Jane's PA but was formerly an actress. She sometimes models for Sir Conrad, with whom she is secretly in love. Lady Monica represents him at her gallery and they are great friends, though not lovers. There are rumours that he has committed incest with his daughter, Imogen because he has painted nude studies of her but few people give credence to the rumours. His wife, Polly, is a highly sexed, flighty woman, with artistic talent and the couple have an open marriage.

Although Sally has her suspicions, she has no proof that Monica is bedding her young protégé, the artist, Daniel Brewster. Under Monica's patronage, Daniel is becoming a fashionable painter though he is undecided about his sexuality and suspects that he is bi, as is Monica.

Ranu Gupta, a wealthy Indian entrepreneur, is one of Monica's best customers for contemporary art and has become a good friend. He has a wife and children in India to whom he often returns, but prefers to live in the West. He has a mistress, an aspiring actress, named Emma Simson, who was at drama school with Sylvia Delavere. In the course of the book, Emma moves to Hollywood and Ranu contemplates taking a young artist, Miranda Pointer, under his wing. Miranda is Monica's latest protégé but Monica does not know about her incestuous relationship with her brother, who later committed suicide, leaving her alone in the world, as their parents are dead. She has a house and studio in Bourton-on-the-Water in the Cotswolds, and has been left financially secure by her dead relatives. However, she is a dedicated painter and has ambitions to make her mark in London.

Sir Douglas, Monica's husband dies suddenly in Paris, and she discovers that he has a young mistress who already has two children by him and is expecting a third. Monica befriends her.

Now free to live permanently in London, Monica meets Nancy Lolongo, a beautiful Afro Caribbean actress who is making a name for herself. They fall in love but Nancy already has a lover, an influential theatre director, Thea Constantine. Thea, however, now has another young actress in her sights, so is relieved that Nancy has found a new love, leaving the field free for Thea to seduce the girl. Despite a fifteen-year age gap, Daniel has asked Monica to marry him but she is not interested, though she wants to keep him in the fold as his paintings are proving to be a money-spinner.

Since the hidden documents were found, Sally often stays at West Bridge Hall, but Guy is occupied with his documentary. She accepts Monica just as she is and has no illusions about her complex sexual life. When finally transmitted in the UK and the States, Guy's documentary is successful and he is asked to start working on another one straight away. Sally's expertise is in the English Renaissance and her forays at the Hall into the Elizabethan world are proving very fruitful so Guy asks her to collaborate with him on the new series.

Due to her researches at the Hall, Sally, who is secretly clairvoyant, has become aware of past lives and now knows that Monica was her mother in the 17th century. Guy was her lover at the time but she was not allowed to marry him. Her father was a Puritan tyrant and killed Hannah when she refused to marry the elderly general he had chosen for her. However, he forced her mother to help him drag her body up to an attic and hang their daughter on a beam to make it look like suicide. The mother could not forgive him for his callousness and denying Hannah a Christian burial. She writes a secret report of the murder for posterity. Jeremy, Hannah's lover (now Guy) was a Cavalier who was killed in battle. Sally now believes that she responded willingly to Guy's seduction soon after they met, because it was a subconscious memory of their love in a former lifetime.

Emma Simson, Ranu's mistress is in Hollywood, making a film about a female terrorist. Ranu accompanied her there but then went to see his family in India. He is very fond of Emma but realises that she now wants to stay in the States. Monica has signed up Miranda Pointer, who is living and exhibiting in the Cotswolds. She takes Ranu to see Miranda's work and he thinks he has found just the girl to take Emma's place. However, Miranda is unaware of his intentions. She is still coming to terms with her brother's suicide.

Conrad Beight has won the Turner Prize, but his wife, Polly, has been in Italy for a sabbatical from her teaching and has fallen in love with Emilio, a couturier. When he goes to Vienna to open a new branch, Polly is at the Biennale in Venice with Daniel. While there, she receives news that Emilio has been arrested on money laundering charges. Instead of going to Vienna to join him, she flies home with Daniel.

Polly tells Conrad she has been crazy and wants to resume their old life. Conrad agrees. However, she soon begins an affair with a postgraduate Spanish student, Pedro Gonzales. One afternoon, she takes a group of students into St James's Park to paint but on the way back, they are hit by a heavy lorry driven by a terrorist, and Polly and three of the students are killed instantly, while others are badly injured.

Conrad and Imogen are devastated, and while waiting for the inquest, they sail to the Isle of Man to get away from all the publicity. They live an isolated life but find catharsis in painting in a new environment.

Sylvia and Conrad were seeing a lot of each other while Polly was in Italy, but when she returned, Sylvia sought pastures new, and has been living and working as a PA at the Royal Shakespeare Company in Stratford-upon-Avon, and having a fling with her boss, David Thornton, the artistic director, who happens to be an old friend of Marcus McIver. When she hears of Polly's death, she gives up her job and goes back to London. She has never been able to get over Conrad and now proposes that they should marry after a suitable length of time has elapsed. He agrees.

Imogen is enjoying her training to become an auctioneer at Sotheby's but is naturally at a loose end in her private life with her mother gone and her father soon to marry Sylvia. Also, though she and Daniel have always been great mates, she has not seen much of him lately. Monica refused his offer of marriage and now he has become intimate with William Wilcox, Lord Patrick's long-term lover.

Patrick is an officer in the Intelligence branch of the Royal Corps of Signals and is at present on a six-month assignment in Cyprus. His duties mean that he and William are separated which puts a strain on their relationship. However, they mean to marry when Patrick leaves the service. Daniel and William find they have much in common but had not meant to end up in bed together, though it happened.

In Cyprus, Patrick and another young officer go to the beach on an afternoon off duty. At first, they swim, but then some sexual activity takes place in a cave. They fall asleep and are cut off by the tide. For two days, they go missing, having supposedly drowned but show up at the base having been rescued by a fishing smack. A young ghostwriter, Petra Dubrowska, comes to the base to gain local colour for a book she is said to be ghosting for a retired general. Patrick is appointed to escort her and answer questions. They get on well, but he begins to suspect that she is a Spook. She is and was recruited by MI6 while an undergraduate at Cambridge. He cannot think why she would target him, apart from his homosexuality but that has always been kept under wraps as far as the Army is concerned. However, he discovers that the book she is supposed to be writing is a dossier on Arnold Partington and as his estranged wife is Patrick's father's mistress, it is thought he may have some inside information as it is suspected that Arnold is involved with a Neo Nazi group trying to infiltrate the British military.

Jane Partington's estranged husband has a close connection to a renegade Catholic priest and because of him, is suspected of links with an extreme right wing group. Arnold has always had a tendency to violence but his irrational behaviour is becoming a serious concern. When Jane was in Paris, he visited her at the Embassy and tried to strangle her. He causes increasing concern, and is sectioned and sent to a military psychiatric unit. Finally, in assaulting a medical orderly, he has a seizure and dies. Jane is free at last to marry Marcus. He is concerned that Patrick is unlikely to father an heir for the next generation so is thrilled when shortly after he marries Jane, she gives birth to twins, a boy and a girl.

Monica decides to buy the New York gallery where Guy once worked and Nancy is on Broadway in the play Arcadia. Conrad is now married to Sylvia and he prepares for a solo exhibition of his latest paintings at Monica's new gallery. Patrick and William make up their differences; marry, then go to Scotland to administer Marcus's Scottish estates.

Tom, Ginny and Piers Gambourne, archivist at West Bridge Hall, settle into a warm working relationship, and Paul and Helen have their third child.

Toby, Tom's son gives up his Theology course at Edinburgh, having had a close run thing with drugs and switches to a course in Estate Management nearer home.

During all this time, Sally and Guy are becoming closer through their work but finally Guy decides to throw caution to the winds and asks her to marry him. She says she doesn't know why it has taken him so long to get around to it because, after all, they have been engaged ever since the 17th century, so it is time he made an honest woman of her.

Chapter One

Sally Wentworth could not credit that at the age of 40, she found herself standing half-naked looking out of a first floor window at the home of a man she had only met a few days before. Of course, she had long been aware of Dr Guy Giffard, the eminent art historian, successful writer and presenter of popular TV documentaries but did not know him personally.

She was no naive miss to be taken advantage of, but a highly respected art historian who lectured in postgraduate studies at the Courtauld Institute of Art in London. She had been introduced to Guy during a private view of an exhibition of work by Daniel Brewster, a twenty six year old up and coming artist, which was held at Lady Monica Montford's prestigious Gayton Art Gallery in Mayfair.

After the viewing, Lady Monica had invited a group of friends, including Sally and Guy, to dinner at Le Caprice, a fashionable restaurant in Albemarle Street, just behind the Ritz Hotel. When the guests settled around the table, Sally found herself sitting with Guy on her left and Ranu Gupta, an Indian industrialist and entrepreneur on her right. He was one of Monica's most valued customers and had also become a good friend. Soon, he and Monica were deeply engrossed in conversation so Sally was able to give her whole attention to Guy.

She thought that he was about the same age as herself; a tall, darkly handsome man with humorous brown eyes and personable charm.

"I'm sorry," said Guy, "but there was so much noise in the gallery that I didn't quite catch your name when Monica introduced us."

"It's Sally Wentworth," she said, revealing her attractive smile as she spoke. "Of course, I know who you are because I am a great admirer of your work. My own field is the English Renaissance but I find Enlightenment France equally fascinating."

"Indeed, it is," he returned. Then added, "Monica tells me that you teach at the Courtauld; do you enjoy working there?"

"Yes, I do when I have enthusiastic students," she laughed. "However, if I am honest, I prefer doing research. I envy you and your ease before the camera; it seems to come so easily to you whereas I am sure I would be tongue tied because I am happiest working behind the scenes."

"Well," said Guy. "I suppose, it is a case of horses for courses. I was a curator at a prestigious art gallery in New York and had written a couple of books when I was head hunted by a TV executive. Everything happened so quickly and I soon found myself presenting arts programmes. I felt as if I had been born in front of a camera and the rest is history."

Sally was not usually at her most comfortable with men, but to her surprise, she found Guy immensely attractive. She had always assumed that loving a man was dangerous and up to now, her sexual experiences had been with women, principally, Lady Monica. Early in life, she had been put off a conventional relationship, as her father was a bully and a brute whose behaviour forced her mother to run away from him, taking four-year-old Sally with her. They were sheltered by her mother's great friend, Rachel Connolly and her parents eventually divorced. Her father settled in Thailand with a second family and she never saw or heard from him again. Her mother and Rachel brought her up, and showed her that strong women do not have to rely on men in order to survive. As a child, she was academically precocious and after graduating in Fine Art at Cambridge, she quickly became independent, and developed a successful career as a teacher and lecturer.

Her relationship with Lady Monica began at Cambridge and was still going strong, although Monica was married to Sir Douglas Montford, a highly placed diplomat. As the daughter of an Earl, she was titled in her own right and had a substantial private income, inherited from her mother. Sally, however, had to work for a living.

"How do you come to know Monica?" Sally asked.

"Oh, we go back quite a long way," replied Guy. "As my brother was at school with her brother, Marcus, though I did not see either of them for many years because after Oxford, I did post grad at Harvard, then made my career in the States. It's good to have made contact with both of them again and of course, Jane Partington, Marcus's girlfriend, is the executive producer on my TV shows.

I think that Monica is an exceptional woman, highly intelligent and attractive, but she is also a pragmatist with a steely core, who never lets emotions or sentiment get in the way of her ambition. How did she come into your life?"

"Oh, we met in our first week at Cambridge and have been close friends ever since. We were both studying fine art, though she went on to specialise in Islamic art and culture, and as she spoke fluent Arabic and French, she was a decided asset to her husband. I often stayed with them during the long vacation when they were resident in the Middle East, but at present, of course, as Sir Douglas is British Ambassador to France and resides in Paris, I see Monica more often."

Indeed, Lady Monica now commuted regularly between London and Paris in order to administer the Gayton Art Gallery, in Mayfair, which she had inherited from her grandfather. The gallery had long had a fine reputation, but Monica's emphasis on contemporary art had made it one of the most fashionable establishments in the UK and its international reputation was steadily growing, thanks to the Internet.

Sally enjoyed platonic friendships with men, notably Monica's brother, Marcus, the Earl of Drumlomond, and his son and heir, Captain Lord Patrick McIver, an officer in the Intelligence branch of the Royal Corps of Signals, as well as his great 'friend', William Wilcox, a Merchant Banker in the City.

She was a feminine creature but never entered into emotional relationships with men; her need to give and receive love was satisfied by her relationship with Monica, and her absorption in her work meant that sex per se, did not overly concern her. Now, though, with Guy, she was confronted by a dashingly handsome man whose sparkling dark eyes lit a twinkle in her own and whose physical proximity had an alarming effect on her libido. A large part of his charm, however, was that he gave his total attention to whomever he was talking to and Sally was soon captivated by him.

He had first noticed her from across the room at the private view when she was talking to Imogen, the young daughter of Sir Conrad Beight, a highly successful artist who was represented by Lady Monica. Now Guy was conscious of her serenity and subtle sense of humour. She was a good looking woman of medium height, slim yet curvaceous, whose crowning glory was her mass of Titian hair and perfect complexion, free from the freckles that often accompany such colouring. Her slightly crooked smile enhanced her rather serious countenance and sitting close to her, Guy realised that her looks owed little to artifice as she wore hardly any make up. Her eyes were naturally hazel but the kind that changed colour, according to what she was wearing. Tonight, as her dress was emerald green, so were her eyes. Their expression was arresting and Guy said, "You know, I have the impression that we have met before, but cannot think where it can have been."

"Well, you seem familiar to me because of your TV appearances, but I don't think that we have actually met before tonight. How long have you been back in England?"

"I returned about eighteen months ago when my mother became ill. A lot of my work was centred in Europe so it seemed sensible to base myself in the UK. My elder brother, Tom, and his wife and children live on the family estate in Oxfordshire, and my mother lived at the Dower House, so it was decided that I should go and live with her. She had a couple of nurses but though she had Alzheimer's, it was pneumonia that killed her six months after I moved in. Now I live there alone but I have a housekeeper and gardener who live in a cottage on the estate. I do a lot of work at home so it is a convenient arrangement and London is within easy commuting distance."

Sally was less inclined to talk about herself, but was a good listener and Guy found this trait singularly appealing. Most people, he found, preferred to talk about themselves and it was unusual to find a natural listener. He liked to talk, not so much about himself as about his work which was the main spring of his life. Soon, Sally learned that after Harrow and Oxford, Guy had taken up post graduate studies at Harvard then made his career in the States; first as a Research Fellow at Cornell University and finally as Senior Curator at a well-known art gallery in New York. Though he was not boastful, she read between the lines, and realised that his books, original approach to art history and attractive personality, were the reason he soon came to the attention of television 'head hunters', and awards duly followed.

She asked about his family, and he told her that his elder brother, Tom, Viscount Torrington and his wife, Ginny, with their two teenage children, Toby and Helen, lived at West Bridge Hall, a large 16th century mansion which had been in their family since 1580. His mother had moved into the Dower House on the death of her husband five years before. Guy had not known his mother very well as her place in society meant that nannies and nursemaids had more to do with the rearing of young children than did their mothers. Molly, Guy's late mother was a butterfly, iridescent and fascinating, but what is known as a high maintenance woman. Like his elder brother, who was eight years older than Guy, he was sent away to school at the age of eight and as Molly enjoyed a jet set lifestyle, they rarely met. However, he accepted the status quo; after all, other boys at school were in the same boat. Sally could easily imagine that he had been a happy, humorous, optimistic little chap who enjoyed school because as well as being artistic, he was an athletic, good at cross country running, cricket, tennis and rowing, so was popular with his peers. Indeed, even in his youth, he was blessed with confidence, and made the best of his opportunities during his school years and at University. To Guy, the glass was always half full, rather than half empty.

He enthusiastically described the Dower House to Sally and told her that it had been built fifty years after the Hall. Sally admired the architecture of the period and said, "Oh, I should like to see it, it sounds absolutely unspoiled."

"Yes, it is," said Guy. "Mainly due to the fact that the family fortunes fluctuated over the decades so there was little money to spare for 'improvements' which has turned out to be a good thing. Sally sensed that her companion was very proud of the family home and was pleased when he said that he would be delighted to show her round whenever she wished.

Over the meal, he and Sally discovered that they had much in common, and they exchanged opinions about the private view they had attended earlier that evening; secretly admitting that they did not much care for conceptual art, but liked to know what was happening on the contemporary art scene.

Sally was so occupied with Guy that she hardly glanced at Ranu on her right, but as he was otherwise engaged, it did not matter. The artist in question was Lady Monica's latest protégé, Daniel Brewster. Monica was the same age as Sally, a tall, fair haired, sophisticated woman who exuded sexual allure which magnetised both men and women. One might say that she was born for sex. Sally was devoted to her, accepting her faults and foibles without a quibble, as simply part of her undeniably attractive personality. The fact that she never tried to change Monica probably accounted for the longevity of their loving relationship.

It was as if Guy had read Sally's thoughts when he said, "Between ourselves, do you think there is more than a business relationship between Monica and her young painter? No, please forget I said anything, it was very cheeky of me and not my business," said Guy apologetically.

"Well," chuckled Sally. "You picked up my train of thought, so I am cheeky too. I wondered if it was just Daniel's undoubted talent that had brought him to Monica's attention, or his youthful good looks and devil may care attitude. He was a Barnardo's Boy, you know and has had to make his own way in the world. However, his talent was noticed from an early age and meeting Monica has been a great stroke of luck for him."

Guy agreed then changed the subject and asked when she intended to write another book. She said that she was open to suggestions but there was nothing that particularly grabbed her at present. Having been so deep in conversation, they had paid little attention to their food and now it was time for coffee.

Ever since Monica had agreed to represent Daniel at her gallery, Sally had wondered if there was a hidden agenda. Of course, Monica was too good a businesswoman to back a painter just because she fancied him but if he was talented and attractive, that was a bonus. Her husband, Sir Douglas, who had always turned a blind eye to Monica's peccadilloes, seemed to cope with them as long as Monica was discreet. However, he also had his own sexual secrets.

Monica was on her own in London as her husband was embroiled in a diplomatic row in Paris and she was staying at her duplex apartment above the Gallery, off St James's Street. When Sally arrived early for the private view, Monica took her aside and said, "Sally, darling, as I have the flat to myself, why don't you stay the night? I know you are only a stone's throw from your own apartment, but we have a lot of catching up to do, so please say you will stay. I have nothing planned for Sunday, so we could enjoy a lazy day together."

"I'd love to," smiled Sally. "I don't have anything planned either, so it would be lovely to just chill out and not to have to watch the clock for once."

When Monica's guests took their leave at the restaurant, Guy asked for Sally's telephone number and gave her his in return then he walked down the steps leading to Park Place, where his club, the Royal Overseas League, was situated. It was a convenient place to stay when he was in London and also an ideal place to meet friends. He had planned to return to Oxfordshire after breakfast the next day but an old girlfriend of his, Mandy Pryer, was in town and had invited him to lunch. She was now married, with a child, but lived in South Africa, so they rarely met. Guy's relationships with past girlfriends usually failed through work and logistics but he remained on good terms with most of them, even if only by email, Christmas cards, or the occasional phone call.

Sally and Monica cut along Bennet Street then turned into St James's Street, and made for the side entrance of the gallery that led up to the apartment. Of course, just exchanging numbers meant little, but Sally hoped he would remember his invitation for her to visit his house as a trip out of London would be welcome.

Monica had married Sir Douglas, who was ten years her senior, shortly after leaving Cambridge. She liked him but was not actually in love. However, her family approved and she knew that his career would enable her to travel the world. Sally, though, was not consulted about Monica's proposed new status and there were many nights when she cried into her pillow at the thought of losing her dearest friend.

Fortunately for her, the relationship continued because during summer vacations, Sally would stay with Monica and Sir Douglas at whichever embassy they resided. Happily, Douglas liked Sally so she always found a warm welcome, though as an intelligent man, he suspected that there was a sexual element to her friendship with his wife. Nevertheless, he was used to turning a blind eye and accepted the status quo.

With Monica's relocation to Paris, of course, there was only the Channel to separate them and travel was easy with Euro Star. Monica brought a tray of coffee into the bedroom and on putting it down warmly embraced Sally, who responded lovingly.

"O God, Sally," said Monica. "It's been weeks since we had time alone together. Drink your coffee, my sweet, then let's go and take a shower. I do hope you're not too tired?"

"I'm fine," replied Sally, "but you have had a lot of people to deal with today, so you must be whacked."

"No, never too tired for you, darling Sally. Come on."

She began to unbutton Sally's blouse and her own, then little by little they undressed each other, kissing and caressing as they fumbled towards the wet room. They wallowed in the warmth of the water, spreading sweet aromatic oils over each other, stroking and fondling before they washed away the oil with fragrant soap then dried off with fluffy towels before pleasuring each other on Monica's expansive bed.

Sally was so happy that she gave no thought to Daniel and what he might or might not mean to Monica, over and above their professional arrangement at the gallery. It was late but as they lay entwined in each other's arms, they discussed Daniel's paintings and the people at the private view, as well as Monica's dinner guests.

Her friend mentioned Sir Conrad Beight but said she had only ever passed the time of day with him because somehow, he made her feel nervous. Monica laughed and said, "Oh, his bark is worse than his bite." But added that anything in a skirt was fair game to him.

It was pretty generally known that he and his wife, Polly, were up for any sexual lark, and Sally could not resist asking, "Has he ever harassed you?"

"No," answered Monica. "He knows better than that. Anyway, I know too much about him, though I hear he is dynamite in the sack, virtually giving off electrical charges; however, he is also rather rough and that, as you know, my darling, is not my style at all."

"Who told you this?" asked Sally.

"Oh, one picks up these things on the grapevine nonchalantly," replied her friend.

Monica said she had noticed how well Sally and Guy were getting on at the meal, and Sally told her that he was indeed an ideal dinner companion. Monica admitted that though she found him very attractive, surprisingly, they had never had a romantic encounter. She thought for a while then said that she supposed either she was not Guy's type, or he was too principled to dally with a married woman. However, she thought it was unlikely that he was aware of her bi-sexuality. Somehow, it always seemed easier for a woman to conceal her sexual preference for women than men their preference for those of their own gender.

Sally asked about Ranu Gupta who struck her as being a very exotic personality. "Yes, he is," Monica admitted. "He is a delightful chap and we enjoy each other's company, but without any sexual connotation. He is very wealthy and has a passion for modern art which makes him a very valued client."

"How does he make his money?" asked Sally.

"It started as family money with his grandfather but Ranu and his late father expanded their business portfolio in Europe as well as India, as industrialists and entrepreneurs, and the wealth goes on increasing."

"Is he married?" asked Sally.

"Yes," replied Monica, "but he is very upfront about his lifestyle. He has a wife and two children in India, and an English mistress, an aspiring actress named Emma Simson in London. His wife is happy in India and Ranu returns often, but he does not want to live there. He has a large flat near Regent's Park and a small country house in Hertfordshire. He jokes that his wife orders him home whenever she wants another baby."

"Now," said Monica, "enough of Ranu Gupta. It is late and time we were settling down." With that, she put out her bedside lamp and Sally did the same then they turned inwards, each delighting in the warm proximity of the other.

It was coffee time when they awoke next day. They enjoyed a delicious, continental breakfast of croissants, strawberry compote, thin slices of ham and cheese, with crusty bread and butter, washed down with large breakfast cups of steaming, creamy coffee. "I reckon," said Sally, "that this will suffice as breakfast and lunch," and Monica agreed.

After showering and dressing, they sauntered over to the Royal Academy to see an exhibition of paintings from a Russian collection. En-route, they bumped into Guy who was on his way to his lunch appointment.

"You're going in the wrong direction for the station," Monica informed him.

"I'm not getting the train yet," he volunteered. "An old friend has asked me to lunch with her family so I only need to walk up to their hotel," said Guy, giving them a friendly wave, then continuing to walk towards Piccadilly Circus, while they went across the spacious courtyard into the venerable 18th century building, home to some of the most delectable paintings in the world.

Later that day, when Sally arrived back at her service apartment in Northumberland Avenue, there was a message from Guy on her answering machine saying that he would ring again when he reached home. It was around 9 pm when Sally received his second call and this time she picked up the phone. He said how much he had enjoyed the previous evening and as she had shown interest in seeing the Dower House, he wondered if she would like to come to lunch the following Sunday?

"How very kind of you," she said. "That would be delightful."

"Right," he answered. "Shall we say, 12.30 for one? Oh, by the way, do you have any food allergies, or things you avoid?"

"No, I enjoy most things, so whatever you offer, I am sure it will be fine."

"Good, till Sunday then," and with that he rang off.

Over the week, she often thought of him and as he had already mentioned his present project, a book and TV documentary series about European baroque and rococo art and architecture, she felt there would be a good deal to talk about. He told her that he was principally concentrating on four women and the influence they had on the styles of their eras. He had decided to call the series 'Four Gracious Ladies' as it was to feature Henrietta Adelaide, Electress of Bavaria; Mme de Pompadour, mistress of Louis XV, Wilhelmine, Margravine of Bayreuth, the sister of Frederick II of Prussia and Marie Antoinette, the wife of Louis XVI. This was only a working title so it might change but for the moment, he thought it very apt. Though Sally's specialist field was earlier than Guy's, she thought his project sounded a great idea and was sure it would be very successful, particularly in visual terms.

Chapter Two

Early on Sunday morning, Sally drove in an open topped hire car to Oxfordshire. She did not keep a car in London, as parking is so difficult. Fortunately, the day was fine and so warm that she opted for a halter neck sundress with a pretty green, yellow and blue floral print on a white background, and took a white, fluffy jacket with her, in case it got chilly on the way back. Her shoes were comfortable white sandals with wedge heels and on her lustrous Titian hair she wore a straw hat with a large brim and a band of material in the same colours as her dress. Looking as fresh and natural as an English rose, she appeared far younger than her forty years and wondered what the day would bring when she met her new acquaintance again. Strangely enough, she felt an inexplicable excitement, but had no idea how special her visit to Guy's home would be.

The drive from central London to West Bridge Hall, situated in countryside between Oxford and Banbury, was pleasant, as contrary to her expectation, traffic was very light. The rolling Oxfordshire scene, bathed in bright sunshine was a sight to gladden any heart, and she was once again struck by the wondrous natural beauty of the English landscape and the amazing variety of architectural styles found in a relatively small geographical area.

West Bridge Hall, Guy's ancestral home, was open to the public, so was well sign posted and as she turned into the impressive drive with Georgian lodges on either side of the main entrance, she spotted the roof of what must be the Dower House, in a deep incline, some way from the main building. As she drew up to the front of the attractive golden coloured stone building in the typical conglomeration of styles that signified English Renaissance architecture, the heavy oak front door opened, and there stood Guy wearing a pale yellow shirt and light grey cotton trousers. A lock of dark wavy hair fell over his right eye, and he pushed it aside as he came to open the car door for her and lead her into the house.

"Before we go in," said Sally. "I just want to look at the exterior; it is certainly a most handsome building and you are very lucky to own such a delightful home. As I told you the other evening, this is my favourite type of architecture and I never get tired of exploring such marvellous country houses."

"Well, I am glad it meets with your approval," smiled her host, "but come inside and see what you think of the interior." Thus saying, he led her through the vestibule into the inner hall, where her senses were assailed by the smell of old oak, freshly cut flowers and beeswax, transporting her to an earlier age and reminding her of what she knew not.

"Oh, Guy," she enthused. "This really has the wow factor and no mistake. What a beautiful hall and there is no sign of modernity, no TV or computer to be seen. I am sure you have them cleverly tucked away but it is good to see the place in its proper period furnishings."

"Yes, I suppose I am a bit of a purist at heart, but I use modern appliances like anyone else. However, I have a study upstairs so consign them to where they cannot generally be seen."

There was no sign of a staircase but Sally assumed that it was beyond the tall-carved oak screen at the far end of the room.

The floor was paved in large stone blocks, with Persian rugs strategically placed and in the centre of the opposite wall was an elegant Jacobean stone fireplace. The centre of the room was occupied by a large, dark oak refectory table around which were several oak dining chairs with seats embroidered in red and gold wool in a 17th century zigzag design. The walls were panelled in limed oak and heavy wool, olive coloured curtains hung at the double height window.

"I feel a bit dusty after my journey so, if you don't mind, I would like to freshen up before we have lunch," said Sally.

"Yes, of course," nodded Guy, guiding her towards a downstairs cloakroom concealed by a curtained alcove. When she reappeared, she had removed her hat and combed her hair, and Guy thought she looked truly delectable. However, he made no comment. It was a bit dicey these days to compliment women, so he played it safe and said nothing. He offered Sally a sherry before lunch, but she said that as it was so hot, she would prefer a soft drink. She actually drank very sparingly and never in the daytime. However, she didn't say that.

Mrs Thompson, the housekeeper, had already laid a cold lunch on the long table before going home to spend the rest of the day with her family. The food was just the thing for a hot day, starting with cold Gazpacho soup, followed by Salad Nicoise, with potato salad, crusty bread, a selection of cheeses and farmhouse butter, rounded off by Summer Pudding and cream. Guy drank pale lager and Sally opted for Elder Flower Cordial of which she was particularly fond.

After they had eaten, Sally helped Guy load the dishwasher then he made coffee and carried a tray through to the beautifully appointed drawing room with its boudoir grand piano in one corner. Most of the furniture was of oak, though some pieces were made of mahogany and dated from the eighteenth century. Guy had very cleverly blended a mixture of styles with a truly expert eye and the end result was in fine English country house style.

The ceiling was ornately plastered in Elizabethan strap work and there were French windows leading to the garden, actually a clever 1920s addition; and several large blue and white porcelain vases with fresh flowers which made the room very fragrant. The wide planked wooden floor was highly polished and covered with Oriental rugs so one had to be careful not to slide on them. Despite its size, it was a cosy room, with several small tables with lamps and an elegant stone fireplace over which hung a dramatic John Piper painting of a ruined baroque church. In addition, there were bookshelves and a cabinet containing 18th century china. Two deep armchairs looked eminently comfortable, as did two sofas covered in a blue and white print fabric, along with two French bergère chairs in rose coloured brocade; and a large coffee table, possibly from the 1920s, completed the picture.

Guy poured coffee and Sally relaxed in one of the deeply padded chairs. The warmth of the day and a hearty lunch made her feel quite sleepy so she asked Guy if he minded if she kicked off her shoes and curled her feet under her. "Not at all, what a good idea," he returned. "There is no standing on ceremony here."

As they sipped their drinks, Sally was fully aware of Guy's undeniable attraction, enhanced by his seductive, mellow baritone voice, which had the merest hint of a transatlantic accent, picked up, no doubt, during his years in the States. He was certainly a good-looking man, but it was his whole persona that was so engaging. His very body language was appealing and his face was so alive with good humour that she wondered, not for the first time, if she had been wrong to keep men at arm's length all these years. Might it not be interesting to experience love making with an attractive male for once? Well, if the opportunity arose, why not see where it led? She, of course, was unaware that Guy had overheard a remark at the private view insinuating that she and Monica were more than just good friends, or that he wondered if it were true.

He had realised at the restaurant that Sally was averse to talking about herself; she was much more interested in other people and now as they relaxed in Guy's lovely drawing room, they discussed Monica, and Guy said, "I really admire her, because she has succeeded so well in running the Gallery, making it a must for anyone interested in contemporary art, as well as a popular meeting place for her friends. The fact that she spends time in Paris as well as London must make it pretty exhausting."

"I think she thrives on it," said Sally. "She has always been a very energetic woman and is a great delegator. She does not do everything herself but has built up a really solid team around her."

"I wonder she hasn't set up a gallery in Paris, though," countered Guy.

"Oh, I reckon she has enough to deal with as it is," replied Sally. "However, I think if the opportunity ever arises, she would like to establish herself in New York."

They chatted about Daniel whose work had so impressed Monica when she first saw it in a mixed exhibition by alumni at the Slade and Guy said, "I have to admit that I am not usually much taken with contemporary art, but I think he is really original and Monica has done well to put him on her books. What do you know about him?"

"Oh, he was a former pupil of Sir Conrad Beight and she saw his work at a Slade exhibition of alumni. Beight had invited her to see his work and she immediately took him under her wing."

"I may be wrong," said Guy, "but it seems to me that the fashion for Brit Art is on the wane. People are getting fed up with concepts and want paintings that they can hang on their walls. For a long time, drawing has been neglected at most of the major colleges of art, but now it is once more on the agenda. However, the irony is that the Royal Academy has appointed a conceptual artist as Professor of Drawing and her own efforts leave a lot to be desired."

"Yes, I agree," said Sally, "but Daniel has real talent. He recently returned from Florence as a result of a scholarship he had won to study traditional Italian academic painting techniques, the kind that has largely been out of fashion for well over a century in Britain. It will be interesting to see how well his paintings sell at the Gayton Gallery because they relate back to a lost art, yet speak to our own age. This, however, makes them avant-garde in relation to the former avant-garde that has become old hat. If Monica continues to represent him, it is pretty certain that he has a fine career ahead of him." However, in her own mind, Sally, who had no illusions about Monica, wondered what price he would pay for her friend's patronage.

When they had finished their coffee, Guy suggested that Sally might like to see the garden, but as the sun was strongly beating down, she said she would appreciate a tour of the house first because it was quite cool indoors.

Guy led her up the broad flight of oak stairs at the foot of which were two carved Newel posts, one of which still held a cannon ball from the Civil War, while on the walls hung portraits of his ancestors. The first floor landing was long and narrow, with doors on either side leading to bedrooms, and a narrower staircase ran up to the attics on the top floor, but Guy said they weren't worth looking at as they were full of lumber. He remarked that there was a story at the Hall of the ghost of a young woman who had refused to marry the man chosen for her and had been locked in an attic by her furious father, where she hanged herself. He laughed at the notion of ghosts, and said he had been brought up at the Hall and had never been aware of any haunting. While, as for the Dower House, he denied that there was anything spectral there and Sally agreed that his home had a delightful ambience, particularly on such a bright, sunny day.

She had always been sensitive to atmosphere due to the fact that from her early childhood, she had been naturally clairvoyant, though she had always kept this a secret, even from Monica. Quite early on, she had realised that not everyone was the same, so it was unwise to speak of such things because people who knew nothing of spiritual gifts would assume you were crazy. Most people, of course, were frightened of the unknown, so it was not good to talk of such things, as no one wanted to be thought unhinged. Sally had a theory that many people who were consigned to psychiatric units because they heard voices or saw things that were not there, were unconscious clairvoyants or had a gift of clairaudience, but she reckoned it would take some time before orthodox psychiatry caught up with such theories.

This was the reason that Sally was such a quiet person, one who kept her own counsel, as her mother had always advised her to do. Things were changing though and even some scientists, particularly those working in quantum physics, were beginning to explore the possibility of other dimensions and creative mind energy. The trouble was that even serious documentaries portrayed the paranormal as spooky, so the general public were given the wrong impression about things that were really a part of nature. To

31

paraphrase the writer of Shakespeare, who knew a thing or two: "There are more things in heaven and earth than are dreamed of in our philosophy," and also, "we are such stuff that dreams are made on." Even the mention of the word occult usually conjures up visions of the dark arts, yet the word only means hidden, and can easily apply to radio, X-ray and TV waves as much as to anything of an esoteric nature. Sally, however, kept all this to herself but told Guy that she had taken to his house straight away as it was very welcoming, and she loved its smell of old polish and the scent of flowers through the open windows.

Two of the guest bedrooms had modern en-suite bathrooms and in addition, there was a family bathroom. All the bedrooms had oak beams and white washed walls, colour being supplied by Kilim rugs, patterned curtains and cushions, as well as hand embroidered counterpanes made by elderly females of the family during the 1920s and 30s. Finally, they reached Guy's master suite, with a large bedroom, which had a distinctly masculine air and a four-poster bed in the centre of the room, hung with heavy linen curtains embroidered with colourful crewelwork in a Jacobean design. There was also an en-suite bathroom and a large dressing room which doubled as Guy's study, complete with plasma screen TV over his desk. On the far wall of the bedroom was a mullion window, with curtains of an Art Deco geometric print, overlooking the garden, and beyond, the splendid rural view of the rolling Cotswold Hills with picturesque old churches and villages tucked away among forests and meadows.

As Sally stood looking out of the window towards West Bridge Hall, a vast conglomeration of sugar twist chimneys, large windows and classical ornamentation illustrative of the mixture of styles that represent Elizabethan and Jacobean architecture, she was transfixed by the beauty of the scene, exclaiming at the marvellously colourful herbaceous borders in the extensive garden, while Guy stood behind her, savouring the fragrance of her perfume and longing to take her in his arms. Finally, unable to resist temptation, he bent his head, gently lifted up her hair and surreptitiously kissed the nape of her neck, then daringly released the fastening at the top of her halter neck sundress. He guessed that she could not wear a bra with that style of dress and sure enough, the bodice fell to her waist, revealing her curvaceous breasts with their blushing pink tips. Guy cupped his hands around them causing Sally to experience a frisson that went right down to her toes. As she made no murmur or attempt to stop him, he turned her around planted kisses on her neck and shoulders then her nipples, whereon she practically swooned.

It was beyond her ken though, that a man she barely knew should take such liberties and anyway, he knew nothing about her sexual history. Difficult as it was to believe such a thing about a woman of her age, he would have been amazed to learn that she was technically a virgin, as she had never experienced sex with a man.

There is a saying that one should be careful what one wishes for and Sally had to admit that when she first saw Guy on TV, she had wondered what he looked like naked and what kind of lover he was. She was aware he had a reputation as a womaniser but knew nothing of his private life, only his professional reputation as one of the most knowledgeable and admired historians of his generation. Of course, it was very unusual for her to have fantasies about a man, though she let her imagination run riot where women were concerned. Very few people were aware of her predilection as she was the most feminine of women and strenuously protected her private life. If anybody cared to wonder why the attractive Sally Wentworth had no man in her life, they put it down to her academic ambitions and deep involvement with her career. She was an independent woman, earning a good living and apparently, thoroughly enjoyed the life she had created for herself.

Her tormentor continued his exploration, his tongue finding hers, giving her no opportunity to remonstrate; nevertheless, she felt she ought at least to show some feminine resistance, so she weakly pounded his chest with her fists, but the sensuousness of the moment as his hands stroked and caressed her, weakened her attempt to show disapproval; she dropped her hands and threw caution to the winds because she really longed for more.

The feel of masculine hands on her skin was so novel that, despite her slight misgivings, she was enjoying the experience. His skin and hair smelt delightful, and he was obviously very skilful in the art of love making, so she decided to let nature take its course and willingly gave herself to him.

He picked her up as if she was as light as a feather and placed her on his bed. He unbuttoned his shirt, revealing a lightly tanned, muscular torso with a slight covering of hair then he pulled her dress down over her legs and feet, fingered the tiniest of lace panties; pleased to see that she did not shave that erotic area. To him, a woman who shaved her pussy looked like an oven ready chicken. He slipped off his trousers and Sally saw that his pants already had a decided bulge in them. Lying beside her on the bed, he lent down and opened the drawer of the bedside cabinet from which he took a packet containing a gossamer sheath. *So,* thought Sally, *he is a good boy scout, always prepared.* However, rather than being jealous of any other women he entertained; it simply made her feel even more randy than she was already.

By this time, Sally was as rampant as Guy obviously was. Usually, she and Monica indulged in a fair amount of foreplay, but Sally, wondering if she had gone mad, desperately wanted him to penetrate her. He did not disappoint her and though it was initially painful, miraculously, they both achieved orgasm at the same time; then, all passion spent, they lay back on their pillows savouring the sensuousness of their first sexual encounter.

Sally had her eyes closed but as Guy leant over and kissed her, she opened them and smiled at him. She suddenly felt so free; she was a woman, truly a woman because she had been deflowered by a man, though one she barely knew. Why had she never realised that such bliss could be found in a heterosexual relationship? She had always assumed that men were just after one thing, too impatient for foreplay and it was 'wham, bam, thank you, ma'am, or lie back and think of England.' She had been so much in the moment with Guy that it was as if Monica had never existed. However, if it had not been for her, she would probably not have met him.

Sally just wanted to lie beside him and not ever move away. Could you actually fall in love with a man simply because he had pleasured you? In some strange way, it was as if she had always been waiting for him. She didn't want to break the spell by talking but Guy knew that she was not angry with him because she had such a seraphic look on her face. "You beautiful, darling woman, why has it taken me so long to find you?" he queried. She just brushed his lips lightly with her own, as they cuddled and stroked each other. Feeling dearly cherished, they soon fell asleep and it was late afternoon when Sally awoke. She had arranged to meet Monica, her brother, Marcus, Sir Conrad Beight, his wife, Polly and their daughter, Imogen, for dinner at the Ritz so she needed to make a move.

She rose quickly, though rather stiffly and switched on the shower in the en-suite bathroom. Guy awoke and went to follow her but she had locked the door. He quickly shot into another bathroom; washed, dressed and went down to the kitchen to make tea. When Sally, now in her sundress again, came to look for him, she declined a cup as she was already late and hoped that she would not meet much traffic on her drive back to town. Never having visited Guy before, she had happily accepted Monica's evening invitation as it gave her a good excuse to leave if she wanted to get away. Now she was sorry that she had an appointment, as she would have liked to stay longer. Guy was disappointed too but tried not show it.

"Oh dear, you never saw the garden," he sighed, "but I trust that there will be a next time." Sally said that she hoped so and Guy went on, "I will ring you because I will be in London all next week so, hopefully, we can meet."

With that, he pulled her towards him but suddenly embarrassed, she said, "Sorry, must go," kissing his cheek as she reached for her handbag, then with a smile and wave of her hand, she swept out, opened her car door, switched on the ignition and roared up the drive.

Chapter Three

As Sally sped through the lush Oxfordshire countryside, it was as if she was on autopilot. All she could think about was her surprising afternoon with the one and only Dr Guy Giffard, who had well and truly deflowered her. Did he treat all women in such a way when he was alone with them? Surely not, but maybe he had heard rumours about her and Monica, and being a very macho chap, had seen her as a challenge to his masculinity. Yes, that must be it. Well, she couldn't blame him because she had been very willing and she had to admit that she felt elated.

However, she was in a strange state of mind. Should she feel guilty because she was being unfaithful to Monica or should she consider that all these years, her lesbianism had been an aberration, and that sex with Guy was just as it was meant to be, a union between a man and a woman? She was really not at all certain, however, she knew that she loved Monica but now she felt that it would also be possible to fall in love with Guy. In fact, she began to wonder if she had started to fall in love with him over dinner at Le Caprice. Could one love two people equally? Well, some people did, though most folk expected to have just one love interest at a time. In many cases, inappropriate love affairs and infidelity lead to a great deal of trouble. However, neither she nor Monica had ever been prone to jealousy and a good thing too. Even if Daniel and Monica were having a sexual relationship, that was their business; Sally didn't believe that Monica would love her any the less, even if she was bedding Daniel. In loving two people of different genders in a totally sexual way though, well, what was that all about? Sally had never questioned that she might be bi-sexual rather than purely lesbian, but now began to think that she must be. Otherwise, surely, she would have been repulsed by Guy's advances, but on the contrary, she found it all very exciting and in her heart of hearts, hoped that she would enjoy other delightful experiences with him. However, only time would tell.

She thought of Monica and wondered how she would react if she knew what Sally had been up to. Possibly, she would think it a good joke and anyway, Sally was not throwing herself in the path of an idiot; any woman would be over the moon having caught the eye of the delectable Guy. However, she was determined not to mention anything to Monica about this new adventure in her private life. She would merely tell her that they had had a pleasant afternoon at his picturesque old house. If she knew the truth, of course, Monica would think it very strange of her to let him go the 'whole hog', not just because he was a man, but because she hardly knew him. Sally had just discovered hetero sex for the first time in her life and had to admit that it had been an amazing experience. However, she did not intend to be just another notch on Guy's bedpost.

Nevertheless, she could not stop thinking about him, and mentally relived the astonishing afternoon and the sensuous feelings he arose in her.

She was very relieved though that he had used a condom because she was not on the pill; indeed, she had never needed to be but perhaps, now she should consider doing something about it, because she was aware that she was not a woman who would be able to cope as a single mother.

Back at the Dower House, Guy was feeling rather dejected as Sally had left so quickly, without hearing any explanation on his part. What explanation could he give, though? Maybe, she was promiscuous, used to one night, or in this case, one afternoon stands. No, she couldn't be because, amazing though it was, she had been a virgin when she entered his house, though she was certainly not when she left it. How she could have remained in that pristine state for possibly forty years was an enigma to him. She was far from frigid so it was a decided mystery. Also, she probably thought he always acted like that as he had a packet of condoms close to hand. Of course, she may have heard silly rumours about him being a womaniser. It had all started as a joke with male friends in New York and once it got into print, it was often trotted out in the media. Lots of people had taken it seriously and it stuck, though truly, Guy was no more of a womaniser than any other heterosexual, virile, single chap. In reality, he had a great respect for women and, anyway, had always been far too busy with his chosen career to have time or energy to deflower maidens. Of course, he sometimes took women out to dinner, to the theatre, concert hall, or to an exhibition, but apart from a little dalliance, they were perfectly safe with him, as he never wanted emotional strings attached, nor had he envisaged himself as a family man.

Not having made love to a woman for some time, when Sally came into his orbit, he was immediately attracted to her, not just for her looks but for her quiet, serene personality and her unusual ability to listen in a really interested way. It was, perhaps, inevitable that his manly ardour overcame him when he found himself alone with her but had she not been willing, he would have desisted. However, she was obviously as ready for sex as he was and had proved a willing partner. Well, what was done was done, but he hoped that she had enjoyed the encounter as much as he had. He was not sure of his next move though because afterwards she had acted as if nothing had happened and had simply departed for London without a word of reproach or even a 'thank you!' Certainly, there was a lot for him to discover regarding the mysterious Sally and he realised with a start that he had never before made love to a virgin; she had not made a fuss when it was initially painful, but he hoped that he had been gentle enough not to inflict more discomfort than was usual in such a situation.

The beautiful late afternoon sun cast a rosy glow over the land, so he decided to walk up to the Hall, and beg dinner from Tom and Ginny. He knew that the staff always had Sundays off so was not surprised when Tom opened the door. Guy had a key but rarely used it as there was always someone at the Hall, but anyway, he did not like to walk in unannounced. Tom usually looked pleased to see him, but on this occasion, greeted him perfunctorily. Guy could hear raised voices and going into the inner hall, saw Ginny, Helen and Paul Dainton, the estate manager, in some sort of wrangle. They stopped when they saw him and Guy, realising that he had come at an inopportune moment, turned to go, saying, "I'm sorry to barge in, I should have rung."

Ginny was the first to recover her composure, and coming towards him took his hand and said, "Not at all, dear Guy, it is good to see you. Come through to the drawing room and have a drink."

"No," cut in Tom. "You carry on. I will take Guy through to the library."

With that, he abruptly strode off and Guy followed him to the far end of the house where the book-lined room was situated. There were cosy armchairs, a large desk and occasional tables with lamps; a place of retreat where Guy felt completely at home. Tom offered him a whisky, but he declined, though Tom took a large measure for himself then sat down facing Guy. "Well, old chap," said Guy. "I gather there are storm clouds brewing. What's it all about, or would you rather not say?"

"Well, you will find out anyway," said his brother. "To put it frankly, Helen is pregnant and Paul Dainton does not deny that he is the father."

"Good lord, I had no idea," cried Guy. "I didn't even know that Helen had a boyfriend. Of course, she is a very attractive girl but she is so young. Heavens above; Paul is no callow youth and could have used contraception."

"Of course, he should," declared Tom. "Helen is not experienced in such matters, though she must have known that it is essential, not only to prevent pregnancy but for safe sex. However, passion, particularly among the young, can overtake even the most sensible of creatures. There is also laziness, I suppose, though you would think that in this day and age, with the growing amount of sexually transmitted diseases, prevention is better than cure. After all, they have only known each other for a short time and I doubt that Helen knows much about Paul's sexual history. He thought I would sack him when I found out, but he is too good a manager to lose; anyway, he needs to stick by Helen. I gather that he was engaged but it was broken off shortly before he came here and he caught Helen on the rebound. I trust that he has told her about that engagement. However, he was taking a chance on bedding his employer's daughter. I was tempted at first to throw him out, but it takes two to tango and Helen is old enough to know better, but she needs him, and Ginny and I will do our best to support them."

He went on, "I should have been more aware but I thought she had settled in well at the agricultural college and would make friends there, but apparently, she missed Paul so much that when she came home at weekends. Well, the inevitable happened and this is the result."

"Poor little Helen," declared Guy. "How is she taking all of this?"

"Oh, would you believe it, she is as happy as a pig in muck. She thinks it is great. She wants to marry Paul as soon as possible. Have the baby, leave it here with us, go back to college during the week and come home at weekends. Of course, she is relying on Ginny to look after the child in her absence, though naturally, we will employ a nanny and a nursemaid as well."

"So abortion is not on the cards?" queried Guy.

"I should think not," replied Tom. "That is something never countenanced in this family: you should know that. Rather the opposite, we have had more difficulty supplying the family with new life, rather than stamping it out.

There is something that I should have told you a long time ago, Guy, but I was too embarrassed so I have kept the truth well hidden for most of my life. The fact is that I have always had a low testosterone count and although there is medication for it these days, it has not helped me to overcome impotence. Also, as I grew older, I lost all sexual desire and you can imagine what a strain that has put on our marriage. Ginny is a damned attractive woman, so naturally, she deserves to be sexually active as she is in her prime."

"My God, yes, it must be awful for both of you, but what about Viagra?" asked Guy.

"Hasn't done a thing for me," sighed Tom. "So I have to be philosophical. I have always loved Ginny, so it has caused dreadful frustration being unable to give her a satisfying sex life. Toby is my child, thank heaven, but his conception was a one off and something of a miracle. However, Helen is not my biological child."

"I can't believe it," responded Guy. "Who is her actual father then?"

"It is Conrad Beight," replied Tom.

"What?" exploded Guy in total amazement.

"Of course," Tom went on, "I am the registered father on her birth certificate."

Guy was speechless and it took him at least half a minute to take in this extraordinary news; he was not simply shocked that Ginny had played Tom false, but left wondering how, once she was married, she had found the opportunity to go to bed with Conrad, that most notorious of womanisers.

When he was able to speak again, Guy asked, "Does he know?"

"No, Ginny never told him. She had modelled for him in Paris as a student and being the way he is, they had had a fling. However, they met again in London two years after we married, and as the poor girl was like tinder, she fell into his arms again and Helen was the result. Of course, Helen does not know either, and we would prefer to keep it that way because to all intents and purposes, I am her father, and there is no point in stirring the pot."

"I can see that," answered Guy. "And you can rely on my total discretion."

"Thank you," said Tom. "I trust you, otherwise I would not have told you." He went on, "Of course, you know that Ginny's family and ours have long been connected. Hers, though of long standing were untitled, but a lot richer than ours and she has never had to worry about money. As she was keen on art, when she was seventeen, she was sent to Paris to study. Some of her fellow students modelled because they needed to earn money but Ginny had no need to do that. However, Conrad Beight was a particularly engaging young pedagogue, whose sexual allure made the girls go weak at the knees. He had recently married a fellow student, Polly Parsons, but she had gone back to London to have their baby, Imogen. Although he had a reputation for taking advantage of his models, his charisma was so potent that they fell for him like ninepins, ignoring well-meant advice to give him a wide berth; consequently, he became like a Pasha with his harem. Ginny was also keen to model for him, and says he is the most exciting lover, very curious about sex and always ready for a new adventure. Polly, it seems, is pretty rampant too. Despite their various partners, as far as they are concerned, as long as safe sex is practiced, their marriage benefits because they are never bored; though how Conrad finds the time and energy while working so hard as a painter is beyond me."

Chapter Four

Guy was about to get up to go, but Tom was in full flow and had a more sensational item to relate, saying, "There have been rumours circulating for some time about Conrad and his daughter, Imogen, who is five years older than Helen. It seems he has painted her in the nude several times and it has caused talk because she is his daughter. In his latest painting of her, she is naked, but it appears even more erotic because she is wearing a quantity of jewellery like a concubine. Apparently, he was inspired by a painting that Ranu has of a voluptuous Hindu Goddess.

Ginny does not think that anything of an incestuous nature has taken place, and of course, some artists, notably Henri Labesque and Lucien Freud, have painted their daughters at various ages in the nude, but without, as far as I am aware, being accused of improper behaviour.

Eric Gill, however, was actually guilty of incest with his two teenage daughters whom he painted and sketched in nude poses, which, incidentally, are very beautiful, so it is difficult in the current climate to present his work to the public without the taint of incest, or sexual abuse. Apparently, it never bothered the girls though, as they adored their father and denied that they had ever suffered abuse."

"I have never heard of Gill," retorted Guy. "Who was he?"

"Oh," responded Tom, "a very fine artist and woodcut engraver; he set up a workshop and printing press, and was highly regarded as an artist but his unconventional sexual life has spoiled his posthumous reputation."

"It strikes me," said Guy, "that the creative artist has a larger measure of libido than the average fellow, so it must be difficult to deal with."

"Well," countered Tom. "I reckon you're right, there are many prime examples, old and new, such as Picasso, Augustus John, Auguste Rodin, Duncan Grant and Lucian Freud, to name a few, but there are many others, I am sure."

As Tom continued talking about Ginny and Conrad Beight, Guy reached for the whisky decanter, and poured out a small amount for himself. He had been totally surprised by what his brother had told him; but Tom went on, "As Ginny was so young and inexperienced, she fell into the trap as others had before her. She was besotted with him but thankfully, she didn't get pregnant while she was in Paris. When her parents learned what was going on, though, she was forced to return home in disgrace. They were keen to get her married off before her reputation was damaged and fortunately for them, I came along at the right time.

As our parents were friends; I had always known her, but when she returned to England, I fell in love with her and asked her to marry me. I was not at all experienced with girls, though I did not think I was homosexual. Like a lot of kids at boarding school, I had fumbled a bit with chums, but did not realise that I would have sexual problems as an adult. However, that became apparent soon after we were married."

"Why didn't you confide in me?" asked Guy.

"I was too shy. One's masculinity, or lack of it, is not something one easily discusses; also, you were eight years younger than me, so I didn't think that you would understand. Of course, everyone was delighted when we announced our engagement, but Ginny was only eighteen and did not feel ready to be a mother. She had enjoyed Paris so much and the thought of being buried in the country did not please her, especially when it became apparent that she had a husband who could not pleasure her, as a man should. We could have spent more time in London, but then Father died, and I inherited the title and estate, and there was so much to sort out, not least Death Duties and sales to raise funds, so we had to spend all our time at the Hall.

However, there were advantages for Ginny as she acquired a title and a beautiful stately home. A year later, her unmarried aunt died and left her a sizeable inheritance, so on the face of it, we were a very privileged couple, at least materially. However, few people know the intimacies and intricacies of someone else's marriage. I never told you this, either, but when I was sorting out legal documents after Father died, I came across a box of letters which Mother had kept. They were between her and father, and also some concerned Howard, Dad's Army friend. Mother and Father had been married for a couple of years, and I was born just before Fav was sent to the Far East as a peacekeeper. There he met and befriended Howard whose young wife had been run over in Piccadilly Circus, and killed a year before Howard left England. His life was turned upside down and he didn't know whether to regret not having children, or if it was a blessing that none had been born. He said that Fav virtually saved his life, as without him, he wouldn't have cared whether he lived or died.

After the men returned home, Fav invited Howard to visit and he stayed at the Hall for a couple of months, during which time, he fell in love with Mother. She loved Fav but it seems that she was also very attracted to Howard. She missed him dreadfully when he left, as did Fav, so they invited him to make his home with them. You were conceived shortly after he settled here and though I don't wish to rake over old coals, I've often wondered if he had anything to do with your arrival, or if Fav really was your father; however, with Molly, who knows. Still it's too late now to churn things up. I have an heir and soon, Helen will give birth to a boy; yes, the scan shows that it is a male child she is carrying."

"Don't worry about me," said Guy with a shrug of his shoulders. "As a second son, I never expected to inherit the estate or title, so it makes no odds. Anyway, I don't envy you being tied to the West Bridge. I have freedom and that is what I value. I don't have to tell you what a millstone these old houses can be and now they are more of a commercial interest than family homes. I believe that Death Duties are utterly wrong, as a lot of houses have fallen into ruin because of them. As I see it, a family does not really own a historic property, they are trustees for the future, and I think you and Ginny are martyrs to West Bridge. Really, such houses are owned by the nation whether they are National Trust or not and need to be well preserved for posterity. I am glad that you have taken on the family mantle so courageously, and I cannot thank you and Ginny enough for what you are doing. I just hope that Toby and whoever he marries will be half as successful when their turn comes."

Tom returned to the theme of his parents and their friend, stating, "Howard was a very different character to Fav; a dreamer, a poet and a musician. Molly was quite seduced by his playing of Chopin, and it seems that Fav cared for Howard so much that when he realised that he and Molly were in love, he did nothing to stand in their way. In fact, reading between the lines, I think they often had threesomes and as Fav apparently had voyeuristic tendencies, he enjoyed seeing Molly and Howard together. He also liked Howard to watch when he made love to Molly." He laughed, then remarked, "What a kinky family we belong to; I am surprised that you are as straight up and down the wicket as you are, dear Guy.

44

Anyway, as you know, when Fav died, Molly moved into the Dower House and Howard went with her."

"Why didn't they marry?" asked Guy.

"I don't think they were bothered," countered his brother. "They were happy as they were. It wasn't as if they were likely to have children at their age. Also, Molly didn't want to give up her title and become a plain Missus. They enjoyed their life and their social whirl, going up to London and having forays abroad. That, of course, came to an end when Howard was diagnosed with Alzheimer's. Molly, butterfly that she was, nursed him devotedly, but when he died, all the sparkle went out of her and, as you know, she faded fast."

Guy nodded and said, "I am glad that I was able to spend the last few months with her. I never felt I knew her very well, but all the same, I did love her."

"Two years after Toby was born," said Tom, "Ginny was reading the Telegraph one day and discovered that the pedagogue from Paris was now living in London. He had a studio in town and was represented by Lady Monica Montford at the Gayton Art Gallery in Mayfair. We knew Monica through her brother, Marcus and when Ginny got in touch, Monica invited her to the private view of her latest artist's work, and offered her a bed for a night or two at her apartment above the Gallery. Ginny was all of a tremble at the thought of meeting the now up and coming artist again. Apparently, he was proving to be an enfant terrible of the art world, but was considered a genius by the cognoscenti; his name, as you will have guessed, was Conrad Beight."

Tom carried on with his narration and said that the exhibition was a sell out within three days, and Conrad received a lot of publicity, interviews on TV and radio, articles in glossy magazines and newspapers, and a good deal of attention all round. Credit had to be given though to his PR team, engaged by Lady Monica, because they worked overtime to promote him. His Parisian reputation as a lady-killer did not do him any harm either, it just added spice. His parents were Viennese but he was born and educated in England before setting up his studio in Paris. He was never conventionally good looking, but had sexual magnetism in spades and women ate out of the palm of his hand in London, no less than in Paris.

Soon, celebrities were queuing up to be painted by him and within ten years, he was on his way to Buckingham Palace to be knighted for his services to art (and many added, to women as well).

There were lots of sour grapes, of course, among artists who considered that they had more right to receive a title, but there was no gainsaying his level of celebrity, and the more fair minded acknowledged that he was highly original and a complete master of his craft.

Conrad, though by no means a snob, had always enjoyed meeting titled ladies, and Virginia, Lady Torrington, was also an attractive woman, so having been introduced by Monica, he invited Ginny to lunch at the Ritz and dazzled her with his seductive charm. He did not realise, however, that they had been intimate for a short time in Paris but Ginny, feeling that she had the upper hand, played her cards well and gave no indication that she already knew him. She was well aware of his peccadilloes and did not intend to easily fall into his snare.

He was beginning to paint allegorical and mythological scenes but with a modern twist, and celebrities vied to be painted by him. He used the nude bodies of models, male and female, but painted celebrity faces onto them. Some people thought it scandalously bad taste but others rushed to his studio to become part of an ancient scene. His prices were already high but proceeded to climb higher and his diary was filled for the next couple of years, at least. Monica had certainly reaped her investment in him so laughed all the way to the bank.

Unfortunately, Ginny's good intentions went out of the window when she came under Conrad's spell again and she soon succumbed to his blandishments. "However," declared Tom. "I cannot find it in my heart to blame her; she was young and had been denied a legitimate sex life because of my short comings. The beauty of it is though, that because I have never criticised her, Ginny has always been perfectly frank with me. She realises now that she must have subconsciously wanted another child and when he begged her to pose naked for him, she didn't have the will power to refuse. After each session, the inevitable happened and despite hating herself on my behalf, she left walking on air. Consequently, when she came home, she felt sure that his seed would germinate within her.

Sure enough, nine months later, Helen was born though Ginny did not, at first, tell me who the father was. Of course, I knew very well that the baby was not mine, but if I did not know the name of the real father, I could pretend and I determined that I would be the best father ever to 'my' little girl. Naturally, I prayed that she would never know the truth of her conception any more than I did, though later on, Ginny confessed that Conrad had impregnated her which meant that Imogen, Conrad's legitimate daughter was Helen's step sister."

As Ginny could not have a conventional sex life with her husband and as she did not want to gain a reputation for taking male lovers, she courted women friends, and though not really a lesbian, she did find a couple of good friends to pleasure her in their own way, as she did them. Ginny actually found Guy very attractive, but he was in America most of the time and anyway, she wouldn't be foolish or unkind enough to have sex with her brother-in-law; that would have been beyond the Pale. As for Tom, it was not his fault that he was unable to give her what she needed. However, he made up for it by being a good husband and father, as well as a true friend. In fact, sex apart, they made a good team and their marriage was held to be a successful one. Ginny also learned that she was not alone as it is not uncommon for men to suffer from impotence at some point in their lives. There are few wives, however, in that situation, particularly younger ones, who can resist taking lovers, though there are exceptional women who, because they love their husbands, uncomplainingly accept the hand that fate has dealt them. Sadly, Ginny was not one of them.

Chapter Five

Nevertheless, Ginny did her best to make Tom feel loved and cherished, and daily counted her blessings; however, she was still young and had to admit that she was sexually frustrated. She was naturally heterosexual and loved men's company so her little dalliances with female friends, though enjoyable, were, for her, second best. Thus, when tall, broad, muscular, Paul Dainton came on the scene, Ginny fell for him, hook, line and sinker.

He lived alone at The Grange, a tied property on the estate, with just a daily cleaner. He liked Ginny, whose husband was his employer, but it was eighteen-year-old Helen who caught his eye.

Paul was twenty-eight, several years younger than Ginny and though she was still an attractive woman, Helen was a nubile young thing, who was ready to be swept off her feet by a virile, mature man who had seen something of the world. By the time Paul had settled into his new job and environment, Helen had begun her three years of study at agricultural college. She had always loved animals and the land, and acquiring a degree was her present ambition.

Toby was reading Theology at Edinburgh which his father did not consider helpful because as the heir to the estates owned by the family, he would be expected to give his life to administering his inheritance. He was in his final year and had to decide if he wanted to go on to post graduate studies. He had initially embraced student life enthusiastically, so only came home during the holidays and even then, he often stayed with friends. Helen, on the other hand, was within easy reach of West Bridge Hall and as there was now the attraction of Paul Dainton at home, she came back from college every weekend. Although she was a typical teenager, rather immature in many ways, her figure was that of a mature woman and Paul was itching to bed her. She was more than willing to lose her virginity and the pair had every opportunity to indulge their sexual desires, as The Grange was a convenient place for a lover's tryst. They were a randy couple and took little heed of safe sex; so inevitably, Helen soon found that she was pregnant.

Guy was no prude, but he was naturally amazed to discover what had been going on with his relatives, past and present, virtually under his nose; although he was not aware that Ginny, as well as Helen had fallen in love with Paul. Nor had he ever before been faced with the suspicion that Howard might have been his father.

He was desperately sorry for Tom who had borne his burden so bravely. Guy understood Tom and Ginny's wish for a wedding to take place as soon as possible so that the pregnancy did not become public knowledge too soon. However, many young people forgo marriage these days. Nevertheless, with a child on the way, a secure family base was the ideal as far as Helen's parents were concerned but Guy hoped it would not be a case of 'marry in haste, repent at leisure'.

The bans were put up for Helen and Paul, and an intimate family wedding took place at the village church as soon as the three weeks had passed. It was not what Ginny and Tom had wanted for their only daughter. People in their position usually made a big showing in London and members of society were invited, which resulted in a large number of wedding presents, though there were often lots of duplicates among them.

At such a time, Ginny could not help thinking of Conrad, who had never known that he had a daughter by her. The sad thing is that though Conrad had been very happy to indulge his sexual appetite with Ginny, he had not remembered her from France, nor did she remind him. She presumed that he probably had illegitimate children all over the place, though he only had one legitimate child, Imogen, who was the apple of his eye.

Now Ginny was infatuated with Paul and felt she was making a great sacrifice in letting the marriage with her daughter go ahead. The French painter, Berthe Morisot, was in love with the married Edouard Manet, but married his brother, Eugene, in order to remain close to him. It was the same for Ginny who banked on seeing Paul every day, though this could be as painful as it was pleasant, knowing that it was Helen who had the legitimate right to his bed. What his and Ginny's subsequent relationship would be, and how his marriage to Helen would fare, remained to be seen.

Tom told Guy that he was philosophical because old families such as theirs had often had to resort to underhand tricks in order to keep the line intact. If the truth was known, there were lots of secrets hidden within such families. Now though, with the advent of DNA testing, it is harder to keep secrets hidden.

Although the wedding was a quiet, intimate one, it was delightful, especially as the sun shone all day. The couple drove to North Wales for their honeymoon as Paul intended to do some rock climbing in the Llanberris Pass, although it was not advisable for Helen to join him. However, they had booked into a comfortable hotel nearby and if the weather kept fine, she could enjoy some attractive walks and they would enjoy cosy evenings together.

At the due time, she gave birth to a boy who was named Montague after Tom's grandfather. She was young to be a mother and soon realised that her place at agricultural college was important to her, so it was decided that she would continue to remain a student during the week but come home at weekends. In the meantime, a nanny and nursemaid were engaged, and Ginny would oversee the welfare of her grandson.

However, being thrown together a good deal in the normal course of a day, Ginny and Paul developed a close relationship, and with him missing his physical relationship with Helen during the week and Ginny needing someone to supply what was missing in her marriage: once more, the inevitable happened and the couple found themselves in bed at The Grange one cold, rainy afternoon. They were not religious so did not consider that they were committing adultery, though it rather tickled Paul to remember that he was making love to his mother-in-law. However, she was a cosy armful so he was not complaining and anyway, he thought, *forbidden fruits are sweetest*. Naturally, Helen was ignorant of this state of affairs. The couple were so discreet that Tom was also totally unaware of where his wife was receiving her 'jollies'.

Tom had an excellent estate manager in Paul, and a superb team of staff and volunteers to oversee the running of the Hall, so he decided to work on his family history. He now had a grandson as well as a son, so it was important for him to pass on knowledge of their ancient lineage. He had always envied Guy being a scholar but now decided that he didn't have to be the only one in the family. The library was full of ancient volumes and documents, and as the Hall possessed a large number of family portraits and prints, there was a lot of material to sort through.

As the archives had long been neglected, Tom was delighted to have Piers Gambourne to remedy matters. He was thirty-five years old, unmarried and had previously worked at the British Library, but was now ready for a change of scene. Unknown to Tom, Piers was homosexual. He had left the British Library in order to get away from unpleasant memories of his colleague, Duncan Mackie, with whom he had been having an affair for the past five years. Although unsuspected by Piers, Duncan was promiscuous, not only with men, but played the field with women as well. Piers did not understand why Duncan refused to have sex with him and wondered what he had done to make Duncan fall out of love with him. However, Duncan's uncontrolled sex life had eventually caught up with him because he was diagnosed with HIV. Sadly, his condition quickly worsened and he died of Aids. Immediately, Piers, who, thankfully, was not infected, had a nervous breakdown. He could not believe that he had been naive enough to remain in ignorance of Duncan's true nature but now he understood that Duncan had indeed cared for him and by his sexual abstinence, had saved Piers from a devastating illness. Now all he wanted to do was put the past behind him and make a new life for himself at West Bridge Hall.

Before Guy went off to London, Tom told him what he planned to do and he was delighted, not only because it would give Tom a lot of interest but also because it was important to the family and would supply more fascinating historical information for the visitors to the Hall.

Fortunately, Piers and Tom found they had a lot in common, and soon, Tom was able to call Piers a true friend, rather than an employee and thus began Piers recovery from heartbreak.

Chapter Six

In London, Guy had his nose to the grindstone, but after a while felt the need for some respite so he rang Sally, who was also in London and asked if she would like to have lunch at Fortnum's in Piccadilly then go across the road to the Royal Academy to see an exhibition of Watteau drawings. She said that she was free on Wednesday afternoon and would be delighted to join him.

He was coming along Piccadilly as she alighted from the bus and they walked to Fortnum's together. He had spent a large part of the morning in Waterstone's and Hatchard's browsing through books on various aspects of 18th century style. Fortnum's was buzzing as usual as they entered its venerable interior, decorated in soft turquoise blue, with its splendid food hall and delightful products. Fortunately, there was a vacant table in the restaurant and their ordered lunch arrived promptly, then Sally listened enthusiastically as Guy told her about his forthcoming trip to France.

He had originally played around with various ideas but was now very happy with the shape of his new project, which had received official approval as 'Four Gracious Ladies' by the production company. He had researchers working in Germany as well as France and had already embarked on the book of the series. Filming was planned to begin within three months' time in Paris, Bavaria, Bayreuth, Potsdam and Berlin but tomorrow he would board the Euro Star with his producer, Jane Partington, her PA, Sylvia Delavere, Nigel Walters, the cinematographer, and Ben Braden, the production manager, in order to recce various sites and select hotels for the TV crews.

In turn, Sally told him about her own current interests. For some time, she had doubts about the authorship of the Shakespeare plays and had now embarked on a search to discover the truth. She told Guy that a few weeks ago, she had attended a seminar in Stratford-upon-Avon led by the lecturer and writer, Penny Langstaff, which included a performance of 'Love's Labour's Lost' and 'The Tempest'. Penny admitted that her theories were unorthodox, but she was by no means the only one harbouring them. She had become interested in sacred geometry and the work of the 16th century Magus, John Dee, which led her to Sir Francis Bacon: his brother, Anthony Bacon, and several other writers of the time, including the Earl of Oxford, Christopher Marlowe, Ben Jonson, the Earl of Southampton and Lady Pembroke. For some years, she had been a member of the Francis Bacon Research Trust, and was the author of books on Shakespeare, Bacon and allied esoteric subjects, several of which Sally had recently acquired.

"Of course," she told Guy, "vested interests protect the accepted hypothesis and are determined that the truth should stay buried, as it has been for five hundred years." Guy agreed and warned her to tread warily; after all, many careers had been founded on disinformation and Stratfordians would not thank her for rocking the boat. She went on, "It is true that there was a William Shakespeare who went to London where he worked as an ostler before getting involved in the theatre. However, it is most unlikely that he was the author of the plays, having simply been paid to lend his name, which one might call a 'brand name', to cover a group of writers, led by Sir Francis Bacon. It is believed by some scholars that the Earl of Southampton gave William a thousand pounds to go back to Stratford and keep quiet about the deception. When he bought a splendid house there, the townsfolk assumed that he had made a fortune in London and had come home to spend it. She added that not much was known about him, as there was not much to know; the accepted facts being mostly the creation of Sir David Garrick, the 18th century actor, for the Jubilee celebrations. Sally now had the bit between her teeth and when she did; she was like a Rottweiler who would not let go. Guy was fascinated by the theories but he had never really given the matter much thought though he knew that many people over the centuries had doubted the authenticity of the authorship. Nevertheless, he felt that the plays were the important thing, rather than who had actually penned them.

"Yes, I know that's what many people say," said Sally, "but I am interested in the truth and I am willing to bet that there is an even deeper story behind the plays but it is too complicated to go into now." She admitted that all her life, she had accepted the usual story about the lad, Will, who was considered to be a humbly born genius. However, the more she learned, the more the scales dropped from her eyes and what had previously been a mystery became eminently logical. Now she believed that it was important to know the truth

53

because the plays and, even more particularly, the sonnets, would be more easily understood.

She added, "Nevertheless, if it could finally be proved that Shakespeare was merely a pen name, contrived to cover the canon of plays which were consciously designed to illustrate the human condition, it would be ironic that a country lad who could barely write his name, had been designated the 'Bard', and considered to be Britain's greatest dramatist and poet."

Sally knew a thing or two about esoteric matters, so said that the main difficulty in getting people to recognise the truth was that a thought form, based on the myth of the lad, Will, had built up in the collective mind over the centuries and was now practically solid, so impossible to disperse. It might even be said that the populace had been brain washed to believe a lie. She added, however, that that was not the only myth that was still being taught in schools, but said that she only had time and energy for one thing at a time.

She alleged that some non-Stratfordian scholars believed that the plays owed their existence to more than one hand but thought that the editor in chief was Sir Francis Bacon. Guy paused for a moment then said, "Well, in a way, it makes sense; after all, Renaissance artists had their studios with several apprentices and assistants working for a master, so writers could have created the same system." Sally agreed that it was more than likely, rather like the set up in the film world today. Another bit of evidence was that Sir Francis founded a papermaking factory and employed several writers whom he called his 'Good Pens'. It is also alleged that he left an autobiographical document in code. Ben Jonson certainly knew the truth as is hinted in his preface to the First Folio, where he called Shakespeare the man behind the mask.

Guy agreed with her that there were good reasons for secrecy in those very dangerous times as subversion was cruelly dealt with and simply printing a text to which certain authorities objected could result in a printer losing a hand, or a writer his head.

Sally sighed and said, "Well, whoever 'Shakespeare' actually was, there is embedded in the plays, an intimate knowledge of the Court of Queen Elizabeth I, and other foreign courts, notably those of France and Navarre; a knowledge of languages, derived from a classical education, a profound knowledge of the law, a familiarity with foreign literature and other cultures derived from visiting those countries. None of these things applied to the lad from Stratford, however clever he was thought to have been."

They were both aware that there was little literacy among the general public in Tudor times and education was mainly in the hands of the clergy. Dr John Dee had probably the largest library at that time, comprising some 3,000 books but for the majority of people, they were rare and costly, and as few could read anyway, the plays were a clever device to advance learning and provide entertainment at the same time. Without films, TV, radio, or Internet, drama was an ideal way of telling stories, though writers had to tread warily for fear of offending the establishment. In any autocratic society, the first targets are always the intelligentsia because they can change public consciousness.

Sally and Guy, as scholars, were well aware that in Tudor times, the best organs of news were pamphlets, and word of mouth played its part, of course, though most people spent their lives within a small radius of their homes and travel, as we know it, hardly existed. However, Sir Francis Bacon had been a prodigy, who from the age of nine, translated ancient texts from Greek and Latin into English, was enrolled at Trinity College, Cambridge at the age of 12, and was sent by Queen Elizabeth with the English Ambassador to the Court at Fontainebleau in France at the age of 15, where he became acquainted with eminent poets and men of letters. His brother, Anthony, lived for twelve years at the Court of Navarre and it is thought that he may have been the author of 'Love's Labour's Lost', or closely connected with it because it is set in the court which he knew so well. Both men, like others of their class, were cryptographers. However, it was not considered respectable for a nobleman to be a writer.

Guy told Sally, "You have certainly whetted my appetite, but why does it mean so much to you."

She answered, "It is purely that I value truth above all things and I think it iniquitous to laud one man for work he hadn't created, while ignoring those who have." However, she had to admit that the original writers had succeeded brilliantly in spreading disinformation which made it extremely difficult for present day historians to sort out fact from fiction.

Having, for the time being, exhausted her subject, Sally then asked Guy to tell her about his own family background in that era and he answered that, of course, until the dissolution of the monasteries, Roman Catholicism was the national religion but afterwards, it became very dangerous to profess the former faith. Guy's family soon ditched it and proclaimed themselves Protestant to keep in with the dictates of Henry VIII. However, during the reign of Mary Tudor, the King's fanatical daughter, Catholicism was back on the agenda and many Protestants were proclaimed heretics; tortured and horribly executed. However, Guy's family managed to stay out of trouble, and with the accession of Elizabeth I, Protestantism was restored so, once again, Catholics had to watch their backs.

Guy acknowledged that in the early 17th century, many people became Puritans, a fanatical form of Protestantism and his ancestors also succumbed to the cult. Nevertheless, some of the important Oxfordshire and Warwickshire families defied the Reformation, and continued to celebrate Mass, though it was on pain of death, and houses such as Baddesley Clinton at Knowle, near Birmingham, Compton Wynyates and Coughton Court, near Alcester, home of the Throckmorton family, still have priest's holes in their hidden depths. Other families such as that of Lord Saye and Sele, at Broughton Castle, near Banbury, stood against Charles I, and four sons fought on the Parliamentarian side at the Battle of Edgehill, thus it was pretty certain that it wasn't only West Bridge Hall that held secret papers.

Sally and Guy had been so immersed in conversation that they hardly noticed the time, or what they ate. After coffee, they sauntered across to the Royal Academy and spent two hours enjoying the Watteau drawings. They were right up Guy's street, but many of them were new to him though he was very well acquainted with most of Watteau's paintings,

After looking in on the gift shop and buying some postcards, they had a cup of tea in the cafe then went their separate ways. Sally would like to have invited him for a meal at her flat that evening but he had already said that he was hosting a dinner party for some of his male London friends at the Royal Overseas League.

He was due to leave for France the following morning, so Sally was disappointed at parting with him so soon, especially as he would be away for a couple of weeks. However, it gave her the opportunity to get on with her reading. She was eagerly looking forward to immersing herself in Peter Dawkins's 'The Shakespeare Enigma' which she had just acquired. She had not published anything of her own for some time but her newfound interest acted as a spur for her to get down to work on her own account. Meeting Guy had given her a new lease of life and as she walked along Piccadilly, then across Leicester Square en route to her home in Northumberland Avenue, she had a spring in her step.

Guy had only a few yards to go from the Academy to his club. He wrote some emails and texts then relaxed over a pot of tea before going up to his room to shower and change for dinner, while catching up on the TV news.

Chapter Seven

Although the club has a buttery, a restaurant in the basement and a cocktail bar, Guy thought it would be more relaxing to hire a private room for his guests, and was delighted when he was told that the Mountbatten Room, named after the last Viceroy of India, was available. His Lordship's portrait had pride of place and Guy was aware that it was the 70th anniversary of Indian Independence, but observed that the road to hell is paved with good intentions.

Indians had long wanted to be released from British rule but the partition was not dealt with wisely and caused mass movements of people from areas where they had lived at peace with neighbours for centuries, only to be shunted to regions many miles away. Everyone was on the move but there were massacres and bloodbaths between warring Muslim and Hindu factions, while Sikhs, Buddhists, and those of other faiths were caught up in the violence. Even today, trouble soon flares again and the question of Kashmir has not been solved.

After Guy made sure all was in order for the dinner, he went down to the entrance hall to greet his guests. The first to arrive was Marcus, the Earl of Drumlomond, Lady Monica's brother, then his son, Captain Lord Patrick McIver and his friend, William Wilcox. Soon, they were joined by Sir Conrad Beight and his former student, Daniel Brewster. The last to join them was Ranu Gupta, a new acquaintance of Guy's.

Although Marcus's primary estate was Drumlomond Castle, near Crianlarich in Scotland, he also had a more modest home in Warwickshire, and he and Guy often met, either there or at Guy's Dower House. Patrick was in London for a few days which gave Guy the idea of the dinner party and while some of their other friends were also in town. William worked in the City, and had a flat in the Barbican but Marcus and Patrick used the family mews house off Devonshire Place when they came to London. Patrick and William had been close friends since their school days, and their secret ambition was to marry, once Patrick left the Army.

It was a convivial evening, with a hearty meal, a lot of wine, chat and gossip, and although they enjoyed the company of women, it was relaxing to be in all male company once in a while.

They teased Ranu about how he coped with having a wife living on another continent and he made them laugh by saying that it was a good thing for a happy marriage, as you couldn't be nagged if your wife was based in another country. "Seriously, though," he said. "I am content with the arrangement and my wife is very accepting of our life style. She has two children already and is keen to have a third, so that is my task on my next visit."

Everyone laughed but Daniel asked, "What happens if you can't perform?"

"Oh, that has never happened yet, and as long as I keep my health and strength, I doubt I shall have to worry. I am a pretty lusty fellow, you know."

"Boasting again," grinned Marcus.

"Aren't you afraid that she will take a lover in your absence?" queried Conrad.

"Not at all; you see, we have a different view on marriage to that of the West. I always knew that a marriage would be arranged for me."

"Yes, but you live in the West and have had a Western education; does it not irk you that you were given no choice in the matter?"

"Not at all; the couple must not only think of themselves, we all belong to an extended family and tradition is important to us. After all, many of our arranged marriages are very successful but you cannot say that all your marriages for love work equally well, else why would there be such a high divorce rate? No, I feel it is all the luck of the draw," countered Ranu.

"You are in a privileged position though, Ranu, because you are a rich man; you can travel and you can have a mistress, or mistresses, if you wish. What about women though, surely, they are not allowed to have lovers? What do they do for sexual satisfaction when husbands are away?" Conrad asked.

"That is no problem; where there is necessity, the women can pleasure each other, as they have always done in harems. Hindus do not cut their young girls as in the Muslim tradition, so our women are free to enjoy sex as much as their men folk do."

"I have never understood," said Daniel. "Why such cruelty is inflicted and so unnecessarily."

"Oh there is much in religion that is cruel, even in the twenty-first century," answered Ranu. "It is not so much to do with religion, but with control. It has become tradition in some regions but was originally ordained so that women would not find pleasure in sex, so would not stray. It is akin to the Medieval Knights who locked their women into chastity belts so that they could not fornicate while their men were absent.

However, when the men returned, the women were unlocked. The tragedy for Muslim women is that the cut cannot be reversed and they must suffer horrendously when giving birth or having sex, because husbands still expect to penetrate them."

"It must be pretty miserable for husbands though, having a wife who cannot enjoy sex with them," said Daniel. "Maybe that is why unscrupulous men target English girls and groom them for sex against their will."

"Until fairly recent times," continued Ranu, "there has been no substitute for a husband when a child is wanted but now, thanks to our clever scientists, even that is changing."

"Yes, what about IVF?" asked Daniel.

"What about it when the natural way is more convenient and delightful?" laughed Ranu.

Sir Conrad told him, "You were very lucky, Ranu, with the bride chosen for you. She is a most voluptuous, adorable creature." The others looked surprised and asked how he knew that, as he had never met her. "Oh, Ranu showed me a photograph of a beautiful painting he has of her."

"Yes," agreed Ranu. "She is as delightful as a statue on a Hindu temple, but personally, I appreciate a Western girl with a boyish figure, like my Emma." Guy, Conrad and Marcus were surprised at this admission, as they were fully heterosexual, and liked girls to look like girls. However, Patrick and William, being gay, could see Ranu's point of view. As for Daniel, well, he wasn't quite certain, yet, which side of the wicket he played, though he was becoming pretty sure that he was naturally bi-sexual. Although Sally was unaware of the exact nature of his relationship with Monica, they were indeed having sex and Daniel found that Monica was a great educator.

"What about lady boys?" asked Conrad. "I've always thought they must be fun and I would love to paint a nude study featuring one."

"They can be very beautiful," said Ranu. "Often they pass for girls because they usually have a female bosom, lovely faces and luxuriant hair. However, it is common for them to have a fully developed penis and testicles as well. In truth, they are androgynous, and are regarded in my country and other Eastern countries as a third sex. We do not consider them transgender but complete in themselves. In the West, anyone who has both male and female aspects in one body is urged to undergo surgery to comply with the 'norm'. There is now more openness about such matters but there is still a lot of unhappiness around transgender issues and though it is not considered PC to talk of it, there are several cases of patients deeply regretting reassignment surgery and wanting it reversed."

Finally, after a very convivial evening, the friends made their way down the splendid, sweeping staircase to the ground floor. Marcus held back then whispered to Guy that he would like to talk confidentially to him. After bidding goodnight to the others, Guy took him into the cocktail bar and ordered two martinis. There was only one couple in the room and they tucked themselves away in a corner so that they would not be overheard. "Any problem, old man?" asked Guy.

"Not a problem exactly, but several things that I need to mull over."

"Fire away," said his friend.

"Well the thing is that I have known for a long time that Patrick is a 'dyed in the wool' homosexual but I hoped that he would change. Or, at least, become bi-sexual for the sake of the inheritance. As you are aware, we are a very old family and we now have so few members.

When Paula gave birth to Patrick, it was wonderful to have a male heir first time round. I know a spare is welcome too, but Paula had such a bad time with Patrick that the doctor said she wasn't to have another child. It was a disappointment but we were grateful to have a son. Now he says it is physically impossible for him to father a child, as he cannot bear the thought of being intimate with a woman. He wants to marry William and William wants to marry him. How will that be on our escutcheon?"

"I see your point," said Guy, "but things are changing fast and it is now possible for a female to inherit if she is first born."

"Yes, I know that male primogeniture has been squashed with regard to royalty, but it is not yet cut and dried for everyone else, and really, if you think about it, it is not the answer. Women marry and names change, estates go into another family.

We have had a good line of descent for six hundred years and I don't want to be the one to break it. If I was an ordinary chap with just a house as a home, it would be a different matter, but I own several large houses and estates, and must have a son to hand them onto. My father was an only child, so am I, as is Patrick, so it would be a very distant cousin who would take over when Patrick goes."

"Why did you not marry again when Paula died?" Guy asked. "You were young and could easily have fathered another son."

"Yes, I know, but I have been in love with Jane Partington for years and she is married to that wretched husband who will not countenance divorce even though she continues to give him cause. He is quite batty, of course, because he says a divorce would compromise his eternal soul."

"What on earth are you talking about?" laughed Guy. "You can't be serious."

"Indeed, I am; the man is a Catholic convert of the darkest hue, quite fanatical.

Jane is now 38 and deeply involved with her career as you well know, and even if she was free, I am not sure that she would welcome motherhood. I know women produce children at a later age now, but it doesn't happen that way for everyone. I had a chat with Conrad at Monica's before we came here and he floored me by saying that he thought Imogen had a soft spot for me. Well, she is much younger than me, but it got me thinking. Should I consider a younger wife who would be ready to give me children, or is that too cynical? I know such things have been done in our sort of families over the ages to secure the line, but I am not sure I could sink so low, as I love Jane and even if I pushed myself into marriage, I would still want her as my mistress. God, you must think me a rotten cad; what about the young wife; what would be in it for her? Though, I suppose if she was a worldly type, she might welcome a title, and several houses and estates with staff, and a nanny for the children. Oh, goodness, I don't know why I started this, Guy. It sounds awful. Let's forget I ever mentioned it.

It is wretchedly inconvenient but Arnold Partington comes back from France tomorrow, just as Jane is leaving with you for the Continent. She needs to have a serious talk with him face to face to see if he can be persuaded to change his position, but by the time she gets back, he will probably be returning to France."

"I am sorry, old chap," said Guy, "it is an awful business, and so hard on you and Jane. I wish I could help, but your future, it seems, is in the hands of an incorrigible fanatic."

"Well, you're a good friend, old chap, and it's always helpful to have the ear of a sympathetic listener. I haven't said anything to

Monica as I wanted to talk to you first, as man to man, but the thing is, do you think I should take Imogen out while Jane's away and see how we get on?"

"I'm not with you," said Guy, rather surprised at the change of tack. "What do you have in mind? You have implied that Jane is the love of your life so why upset the applecart by taking Imogen out?"

"It was just a thought, but I suppose it wouldn't do. You see, if Monica had had children, they, or their grandchildren could have come into line after Patrick, though even that would not be ideal; but I cannot see her having any now, can you?"

"You never know, but I think it's unlikely," said Guy.

Marcus thought for a moment then said, "It would be great if Arnold met someone he wanted to marry then all could go with a swing; at least I hope it would."

"Look, old man," said Guy. "Shouldn't you be having a talk with Jane about all this?"

"Well, with things as they stand, there doesn't seem to be much point, because unless she can persuade that swine of a husband to release her, time will pass and we will lose our chance. If we were any couple, we could simply live together and have as many children as we liked, or if not, adopt, but I have to have a legitimate heir. Well, yes, of course, I have one, but he is not going to secure the succession, well, barring miracles, that is. I want to marry Jane: I truly love her and have waited for her all these years, but whether my devotion will ever be rewarded is in the hands of a maniac."

"Why not just enjoy what you have, my dear friend?" asked Guy. "Looking to the future too much is not wise because you miss the present. You have so much to be thankful for; so forget posterity for a while and let things just take their course."

"You're right, of course; well, thanks for listening, old man," said Marcus. "Don't forget to send out a prayer for us. You know, it is, thanks to Princess Diana, that we chaps can now talk more openly; before her death, we were emotionally buttoned up, but now many people let it all hang out and it's quite normal to express one's feelings."

"I've noticed that," said Guy. "But even so, it's not easy to talk about intimate matters even in confidence. Anyway, good luck; let me know how you get on."

"Oh, by the way," Marcus turned to Guy. "Don't say anything about this to Jane."

"Of course not; in any case, everyone will be too occupied with work for any personal stuff," Guy assured him. "Night-night."

Chapter Eight

Despite going late to bed, Guy was up early next morning, took a quick shower, ate a Continental breakfast in the buttery, paid his bill and took a cab to St Pancras to catch the Euro Star, where he met Jane Partington, his executive producer, along with Ben Braden, production manager, Peter Hale, cinematographer, Tim Trufford, sound engineer and Sylvia Delavere, Jane's P.A.

They settled into a first class compartment with tables and their laptops, and began work. Their first port of call would be Versailles as Mme de Pompadour, the mistress of Louis XV and Marie Antoinette, the wife of his grandson, Louis XVl both lived there at different times. Although they were from very different backgrounds, both women were influential on the styles and fashions of their day, and Guy looked forward to filming in the glamorous environment of the palace and its grounds, as well as having access to portraits and paintings of the period.

When he was last in Paris, he had found some erotic prints at a second hand bookstall which illustrated the scurrilous rumours surrounding Marie Antoinette and her ladies, notably Mme de Lamballe, the young widow of the Prince de Lamballe, alleging that the two women enjoyed a lesbian relationship. Whether this was true or not, the accusations did a great deal of harm to Marie Antoinette when she became Queen, and provided her enemies with ammunition to bring her, her husband and the French monarchy down. Marie Therese de Lamballe stayed loyal to her to the end and was one of the first casualties of the Terror, being butchered in the street by a Parisian mob in September 1792.

It is said that there is no fuel without fire and discovering the full facts of Marie Antoinette's marriage could account for the way the salacious gossip started. Although she was married at the age of fourteen to the teen age Dauphin, the marriage was unconsummated for seven years. The fact that Louis was incapable was a well-kept secret, so it was the poor Dauphine who came in for criticism when she failed to become pregnant. If she and her ladies did indeed indulge in lesbian acts, it is understandable. Things did not improve when Louis inherited the crown on his grandfather's death, but finally, the Queen's brother, Joseph II of Austria arrived in France to find out what was the cause of their marital trouble. He learned that Louis needed to be circumcised but as there were no anaesthetics at that time; he had never found the courage to undergo an operation. Joseph told him that he had no choice so the operation went ahead and his recovery resulted in the Queen giving birth to a girl. There was disappointment that the child was not the longed for heir but the couple were young and later, the Queen gave birth to two boys, though the eldest son died at the age of seven.

Nevertheless, mud sticks, particularly when it is in print, and she was to suffer the slings and arrows right to the end of her short life. Guy was now hoping to redress the balance and to show that when Marie Antoinette first came to France, she was an untried young girl, lively and full of fun, forced into celibacy because of her husband's incapacity, but was not the scheming harpy that her enemies declared her to be.

An appetising lunch was enjoyed on the train and the time passed quickly. When they arrived at the Gare du Nord, they hired two cars and drove to Versailles. Having unpacked at a small, but comfortable hotel in the town, the group took a walk before dinner in order to get their bearings. Guy, however, had been invited to dinner by an old friend, an eminent professor of French history, Count Bernard de Daubigny.

Bernard lived at the quaint little hill town of Jouy-en-Josas, near Versailles. He was emeritus professor of the Sorbonne and was a member of the prestigious Académie Française. Although he no longer taught, he was in demand as a consultant and adviser on French cultural affairs. He and Guy had collaborated before, and Guy valued his friendship and the warmth of his amusing personality. He was now in his seventies, but had not lost his youthful spark.

Guy drove up the little lane to the top of the hill and came to a high wall with a stately gateway. He rang the bell and the doors opened, leading into a courtyard. On the right was a large early 18th century house and on the left stood the Petite Maison, with a climbing vine on its venerable old stonewalls. Bernard came out of the smaller house and warmly greeted him. "Come in, come in, my dear fellow, it is so good to see you," he purred, as he led the way into the small interior hall. His English was perfect, the result of post graduate study at Oxford. Though aged, he was still tall and straight, and as alert and energetic as ever.

He had formerly lived in the big house, but had gifted it to his son and his family, and moved into the Petite Maison after the death of his wife. His daughter-in-law, Marine, was an interior decorator so the little house had received the benefit of her skill. It was furnished in Louis Quinze style, with modern comforts, of course and he had a delightful study where he spent most of his time.

The larger house, which had always been in his family, was occupied by German officers during the Second World War, but they were responsible men who had treated it with respect. Luckily, before they arrived, the antique contents had been spirited away by faithful staff and were returned intact at the end of the war. On the opposite side of the lane, behind a high wall, was the house where Mme Blum, the widow of the French politician, had once lived.

Bernard's small dining room still had its boiseries which were painted pale duck egg blue and the furniture, which had been selected by Marine from the main house, reflected the style of the building. The upholstery materials were reproductions of earlier designs and the Toile de Jouy fabric was well represented. Guy wanted to talk to Bernard about this design which was created at Josas during the period when Mme de Pompadour was the reigning mistress of Louis XV.

At that time, Oriental fabrics were highly popular but as they had to be imported from the Far East, they were very expensive. However, the French had the notion of producing fabrics from printed wooden blocks. One of the first results was the Toile de Jouy design which was then taken up in courts across Europe. A mono colour, such as red, or blue, was printed on a white background depicting pastoral scenes, as in paintings by Watteau and Pater. The popular colours were blue, red and green but purple and brown were also produced, and the design is often seen in contemporary decor. In fact, Sally had previously told Guy that her bedroom was papered in the blue design on a white background. He was keen to find out what part, if any, the Pompadour had played in the creation and promotion of the original pattern.

Marine came over to greet Guy and to make sure that all was in order for the dinner. She had lent André, her chef, for the evening and Guy had no fault to find with the excellent French cuisine. Fortunately, he was not a vegetarian, because such a concept is quite alien to the French. There were thin crepes rolled around a mixture of prawns and white crab meat in a béchamel sauce to start with, succulent lamb cooked with Rosemary, Duchesse potatoes and green beans, and for dessert, a delicious fruit tart with clotted cream, followed by salad and cheeses. The repast was washed down with fine wines, coffee and brandy then, having eaten their fill, the two men settled down in the pretty salon, furnished in Empire style, for a chat about Guy's book and the TV documentary but first of all, he wanted his friend to tell him about the origins of the Toile de Jouy. Apparently, Bernard's family had gone into fabric manufacture when the Toile was first produced, creating fabrics for domestic use and for the couture trade. They exported their products to Britain, and many of their designs are sold at Colefax and Fowler in the West End of London, as well as other prestigious outlets in Britain and further afield. Consequently, Bernard had never had to rely on his earnings as an academic. His son was now head of the firm and was proving to be a fine entrepreneur.

Guy wondered what they thought about Britain leaving the EU and admitted that he was in two minds about it himself, but Bernard said he could understand the feelings of the British people. That surprised Guy, but Bernard said that many French people also had their doubts about the way the Common Market had developed into an autocratic dictatorship. "We French have always been proud, rightly or wrongly of our identity and revere Marianne, the spirit of France. Also, I think the majority of French people are more interested in politics than the British, so it was surprising that a large number of people bothered to vote in your Referendum. Of course, politics often gets us into trouble and it is a fact that within my lifetime, we either could not form a government, or keep one in office for more than a few months or even weeks.

As you are well aware, we have had several revolutions but the British only experienced a Civil war and the so-called 'Glorious Revolution' of 1689, a supposedly bloodless revolution. However, many people lost their lives, including the hapless Duke of Monmouth, an illegitimate son of Charles II." Laughingly, he said, "You see, Guy, I am not only versed in French history." Then went on. "After the execution of Charles I, the British gradually instituted parliamentary democracy and it has served them well; it has also been an excellent model that has influenced the world. Quite honestly, I think that your Brexit is inevitable; it is evolution; much better than revolution and those who try to hold it back, are acting like King Canute with the tide."

"It's interesting," replied Guy, "that you mention Marianne, implying a spiritual dimension, because a friend of mine, Sally Wentworth, spoke about the spirit of Britain. She awoke one morning about a fortnight before the Referendum with the phrase,

'Britannia is rising' in her head and wasn't at all surprised when the majority voted to leave. She sensed that Britain has a global, not just European role to play, which will be of benefit to many nations. At one time, Britannia really did rule the waves and she has the experience of Empire, so hopefully, the good things will prevail and lessons will be learned from mistakes made in the past. The die is cast and though the 'remoaners' can cause a lot of disruption, they are backing the wrong horse. Well, this is what Sally gathered; it will be interesting to see if she is right or not."

"I think it is a pity that the original plan was politicised," said Bernard. "For most people, it seemed a good idea when it was first mooted as a common market for European trade. The world was recovering from a devastating war and trade was a way of getting things moving in the shortest possible time. However, I believe that there always was a hidden agenda and that the real project was political. The only people laughing now must be Louis XIV, Napoleon and Hitler, who planned to take over Europe in just such an autocratic dictatorship. Tony Blair had much the same idea, I reckon, because he always fancied himself as Permanent President of Europe; he probably still does as he is pushing his way in again. However, with his track record, the British would do well to stop him from meddling. I may not live to see it, but once the dust has settled, I think Europe will respect individual nation states, but in a kind of Commonwealth, like the British Commonwealth of Nations. Mind you, I am not a politician, nor a prophet, merely a historian with a rather longer perspective than many people. However, I see the kind of dangers ahead because the situation is becoming similar to that of the thirties with certain ideologies vying for power. Democracy is hard won but Stalinist tactics are never far away, nor are Neo Nazi factions, both are toxic and unleashed could lead to disaster. History reminds us that vigilance is always needed."

"I feel the same," replied Guy. "Politics have never been my bag, but I am an interested observer and politics concern us all, whether we like it or not. Anyway, I am delighted that I do not have to solve the problem. My current task is to discover what I can about my 18th century ladies."

"What are you planning to do here, Guy?" asked his friend. "We are choosing locations and plotting cinematography, which is usually a logistical nightmare; then we have to arrange travel, hotels, catering etc. for all those involved in the filming. Everything depends on first-rate preparation and as well as Versailles, we will be filming in Berlin, Potsdam, Bayreuth and Munich. However, with the best will in the world, we cannot foresee things such as accidents and strikes. It is all in the lap of the gods and it is always a great relief when everything is successfully in the can. Viewers sit back and take everything for granted, of course, but have no idea about the blood, sweat and tears involved in the whole process.

"I wish you well," smiled Bernard. "You have certainly chosen a difficult occupation for yourself; however, as you know, I am at your disposal, so don't be afraid to ask if you need me."

"I certainly will," answered his friend. "Please thank Marine and her chef for the most delicious dinner, and thank you for your hospitality."

With that, he drove the short distance to his hotel and was soon tucked up in bed. However, although he had had a long day, he turned on the TV for a little while before settling to sleep and found an episode of a series about Charles II in exile before the Restoration. He was notorious for his raunchy way of life as Prince and King, and the scene reflected his sexual appetite. With him was a nubile young courtesan, whom he had undressed and was passionately caressing. It struck Guy that the girl bore a striking resemblance to Jane's PA, Sylvia, as they were like two peas in a pod, although he had only seen Sylvia fully clothed. Guy put it down to coincidence; turned off the TV and his bedside light, and was soon sleeping soundly.

The next morning, he and the team met Laurentia Bridgeman, an expert on Versailles and its inhabitants, and Pierre Longue, the head of the French TV team. Laurentia, although a Scot, had been resident in Paris for many years, and was a mine of information as she had made Versailles and other Royal palaces of the Bourbons her life's work; periodically producing excellently researched books. Guy, of course, knew her work well, but was delighted to receive the fruits of her knowledge at first hand.

Chapter Nine

After a week, the British team set off for Germany, travelling by air to Tempelhof Airport, Berlin. They had arrived early at Charles de Gaule Airport so Guy and Jane enjoyed chatting over coffee while they waited for their flight to be called. They were very happy with the way things had gone in Paris and felt confident that Pierre would assemble an excellent technical team. Changing the subject, Guy told Jane that he had seen an episode of the Charles II story on French TV and was convinced that the young actress playing a courtesan was really Sylvia Delavere. He asked Jane what she knew of her background and she confirmed that indeed Sylvia had been an actress. She had won a place at the Central School of Speech and Drama, but to help pay her way, she had become an artist's model, principally for Sir Conrad Beight and his wife, Polly, who taught at St Martin's School of Art.

Just, then Sylvia, who had been to buy a paper, came along and Jane asked her to join them.

"I hope you don't mind, Sylvia," said Jane, "but we were just talking about you and the fact that you gave up acting."

"I was puzzled," said Guy, "that you gave up so early in your career, because I think you had definite talent, so it would be interesting to know what happened."

"Well, I qualified from Central after three years then found an agent, Danny Bouter and looked forward to making progress in my chosen profession. However, the first audition he sent me for was not at all what I expected. I had learned two speeches, one classical and one modern, and thought I did a good job but then was asked to undress. This was totally unexpected and I blamed Danny for not warning me. The panel consisted of three men, the director, the casting director, the scriptwriter and a female PA."

"As Sylvia said," cut in Jane, "she was used to nude modelling, but resented being asked to disrobe at an audition. Her agent had made no mention of any nudity so she felt exploited."

"I was as green as grass, of course," Sylvia admitted. "Though I was aware that sometimes young actresses, or actors, are obliged to, in common parlance, 'get their kit off' for a particular scene. However, when I found that I was obliged to improvise a sex scene with a young actor, also nude, I was angry because I had not been warned in advance. I suspect that Danny probably thought that I would refuse to audition if I had been warned so kept quiet and let things take their course.

Not wanting to lose face, I somehow managed to play the scene then I quickly threw on my clothes and fled. I wanted to be taken seriously as an actress, but the fact that I was young and pretty, and had a good figure seemed to work against me. Modelling for an artist or even a group of students is quite different to acting a nude scene with either a male or even a female actor, whom you have never met before, in a studio with other actors looking on and a plethora of technicians, is really daunting. Also, stills photos often appear on social media sites to be gloated over and not at all what I wanted after studying at a reputable establishment for three years. I know that my friend, Emma Simson, has experienced the same kind of thing but Emma has a rich sugar daddy so doesn't have to accept every part that comes along. Mind you, she told me that there is a plan afoot to include classes in sex scenes at drama colleges now. It seems that things have gone full circle, because in the early days, actresses were not considered respectable because they often doubled as prostitutes. Nevertheless, many later actresses fought hard for respectability, but now it seems that the distinction is becoming blurred. Mind you, prostitutes ply their trade behind closed doors whereas modern actresses are expected to reveal all in public."

Sylvia admitted that she was obliged to earn her own living, but had no intention of accepting any sleazy part just in order to pay the rent. She went on, "Directors always tell recalcitrant actors that such sexual scenes are necessary for the plot, but there is a lot of exploitation. Apparently, experienced actresses are canny enough to ask for a no nudity clause in their contracts, but even when there is no sexual scene in the original script, unscrupulous directors will try to insert one, to arouse the punters. An actress is then badgered to take part in such a scene but if she still refuses, a body double will be used. However, it will be a black mark against her and she may find herself labelled as 'difficult', something to be avoided at all costs."

She continued, "I admire Emma for her common sense and the fact that she realises that her sugar daddy might not always be around, so she invests the money he gives her for clothes and jewellery. He is married but his wife lives in India and he makes no secret of his relationship with Emma. He loves to show her off, and wants her to have jewels and fashionable clothes. Even so, although she always looks glamorous, she is not extravagant, so never wastes money."

By this time, Guy had realised that Emma's sugar daddy must be Ranu Gupta, whom he had first met at Le Caprice and whom he had recently invited to dinner at his club.

Ironically, although Sylvia did not want her audition to be successful, she was offered an important part in the Charles II film and her agent persuaded her to take it because if the series was successful, and it should be as sex always sells, he thought it would put her on the map. She was not enthusiastic because, as she suspected, she spent most of the film with her clothes off and had to undergo several scenes of simulated sex.

Cynically, rather than enhance her career, it just brought her more offers of the same kind of role, including one whose 'reputable director' wanted actual intercourse from his leading actors, not just simulation. That was beyond the pale for Sylvia and she never worked with the man. "Well," said she, "although with misgivings, I accepted the TV series but after it was in the can, I rethought my life. I invested some of the money from the film, then enrolled on a course of business studies; learning to type and use a computer. I didn't want to hang around hoping for better acting jobs because I had decided that I was not cut out for an actor's life, hustling for work, being humiliated and coping with financial insecurity. Instead, I wanted to make a good career as a back room girl and that is how I came to be Jane's PA."

With that, their flight was called and they enjoyed an uneventful journey to Tempelhof, from where they were soon installed in their hotel in the Kurfurstendam, a cosmopolitan street full of expensive shops and restaurants, though with the shell of a former church still standing as a reminder of the horrific bombing undergone during the Second World War. The Tiergarten in the middle of the city was a welcome oasis of greenery where citizens relax and children play without worry of traffic. In fact, the team found that reconstructed Berlin was a delightful city with opera houses, theatres and the Olympic Stadium where giant shows were enjoyed by several thousand people at a time. The dreadful wall separating the Western side of Berlin from the East was long gone, but the Brandenburg Gate that now leads to the rebuilt Reichstag; modern art gallery, hotels, shops and offices, is a constant reminder of Checkpoint

Charlie, and the fear and misery engendered by the Cold War and the menace of Soviet Communism.

Apart from the beautiful Palace of Charlottenburg, on the edge of the city; the TV team were focussed on Potsdam, a town made famous by Frederick the Great, the brother of the Margravine Wilhelmine, where he built the splendid Margravine Palace, with its delightful terraces and in the garden, the circular teahouse surrounded by golden Oriental figures. It was a short distance from Berlin and easily accessible by public transport, situated on the banks of a large lake. Crossing the Glenicke Bridge brought further recollections of the Cold War as it was often used for the exchange of agents from East to West and vice versa, as for instance, in the film, 'The Man Who Came in From the Cold' with Richard Burton.

They spent only a day in Potsdam, as their main filming regarding Wilhelmina would be at Bayreuth where she lived after marrying Frederick of Brandenburg-Bayreuth in 1731. In 1735, he inherited the title of Margrave and together with his wife, began making Bayreuth a miniature Versailles, restoring the Opera House, building a summer residence, and constructing a Baroque gem of a theatre in the Sans Souci Palace where ballet and operas were frequently staged. They completed several other expensive projects but practically bankrupted the Treasury by over stretching their resources.

Though a woman, Wilhelmina's artistic influence was more significant than that of her spouse. Emulating her brother, she invited artists and intellectuals of note to come to Bayreuth, including Voltaire. However, at the start of the Seven Years War, she turned to diplomacy, though her meeting with Maria Theresa of Austria caused a rift between her and her brother, although they later made up their quarrel. She died in 1758 and ten years later, Frederick built the Temple of Friendship at Sans Souci in her memory. When Guy first had the idea for a documentary about these women, he was aware of Wilhelmina but the more he discovered, the more enthusiastic he became and was very glad that he had chosen to feature her. He knew not much more about Henriette Adelaide when he began because there is very little about her in English, but trusted that he would discover more as he followed her footsteps in Munich.

He and his team were keen to see more of the superb Bavarian scenery with its mountains and lakes, so opted to travel to Munich by train. They were making good time and had outlined the schedule for filming with the various TV teams who would be working with them when filming began.

They found Munich a thrilling modern city, though it had been completely razed to the ground during the Second World War. However, plans of the original buildings had been preserved and as soon as hostilities ceased, rubble was cleared from the city (it was later the foundation for the Olympic Village), and plans were made to reconstruct former buildings such as the State Theatre, the Residenz, churches and the exquisite Palace of Nymphenburg on the outskirts of the city. Present day Munich was a mixture of the old and new with up to date industries on the perimeter, and a picturesque centre, with parts of the old city wall and gateway into the pedestrian area. The team found shops full of merchandise appealing to all tastes and pockets: there were first-rate hotels and more than thirty of the finest art galleries in the world so they looked forward to a cornucopia of delights.

Guy and his colleagues were booked into the Königshof, a splendid hotel on the Stachus, right in the centre of the old town, and ideally placed for walking. In fact, walking was best, as traffic was so fierce that even a few hundred yards took ages to cover by car. However, there was also the first rate Metro system, as well as bus services serving out of town areas.

The woman they had come to research, Henriette Adelaide, the granddaughter of Henry IV, the first Bourbon king of France, was born a Princess of the House of Savoy and was an ancestor of Marie Antoinette's dear friend, Mme de Lamballe, who had been born into the same ancient, royal house, some eighty years later than Henriette Adelaide.

Adelaide, as she was known, was only fifteen when she was married to Ferdinand Maria, heir of the reigning house of Wittelsbach, who became Elector of Bavaria the following year when his father died. Though very young, she was passionate about art, architecture and music, and introduced the Italian opera into Bavaria, along with a multitude of Italian artists, architects and musicians.

At that time, the Residenz in Munich was the main home of the royal family but Adelaide was keen for them to have a summer residence in the countryside close enough to the city for convenience of travel, but in rural surroundings, so founded the Palace of Nymphenburg. Originally, it was a simple central block in baroque style with formal gardens in the French manner of formal parterres and pathways, but was further developed after her death in 1676.

She and her husband had daughters but the longed for heir took his time to arrive. When he finally appeared, Adelaide founded the Theatiner Church opposite the Residenz in thanks to God. Sadly, she died at the age of forty, yet, in her few short years she put the style of Bavarian Baroque on the European map. Her eldest daughter, Victoire, married the French Dauphin, but died young. Her son, Max Emanuel, was involved in the Seven Years War against France, which, at that time, was the equivalent of a world war, in which Wilhelmina and her brother Frederick II of Prussia were also embroiled.

Guy and his team thoroughly enjoyed their tour, but perhaps, the visit to Munich was the most special because they learned about an extraordinary woman who is little known outside Bavaria, though her artistic influence spread throughout the German States several decades before the beginning of the 18th century Age of Enlightenment.

They flew back to London from Munich, armed with a mass of information and the promise of some beautiful cinematography for their film. Guy had already begun his book but now needed to finish it in order for it to be published in time for the transmission of the documentary.

When Nancy Mitford first ventured into writing her historical books which were full of illustrations, she was criticised by those who resented a non-historian coming onto their territory. However, the books were well written and well researched so became very popular with the public. Guy admired her work and used it as a template for his own, which was the foundation of his documentaries for TV. The visual aspect mattered a lot to Nancy and TV is all about pictures, so Guy took her work as inspiration, and intended to include a good many illustrations from the periods of Louis XV and his grandson, in his forthcoming book of the series. The picture researcher, Torry Watkins, was on hand to help him find suitable material and they started at the Mary Evans Picture Library in Blackheath then moved on to other picture libraries. He also had picture researchers working in the European cities that were to feature in the film. This was one of the aspects he most enjoyed because he believed that portraits and the places where his subjects had lived, gave a truer impression than the spoken or written word alone.

Chapter Ten

While Guy was away, he received a message from his brother, Tom, telling him that when workmen set about clearing an attic to deal with dry rot, they found a hidden compartment which contained a cache of very old documents, some in Latin and a diary that appeared to be in code. Guy suggested that Tom contact Sally Wentworth and ask her to come to the Hall, as they would be right up her street. Tom said he and Ginny would be happy for her to stay, if she was interested, so would contact her straight away.

Thus when Guy returned to London, Sally was in Oxfordshire. Before he went away, he purchased two tickets for the Royal Opera House at Covent Garden in the hope that Sally would accompany him. However, now that she was fully occupied at West Bridge Hall, he needed to find someone to take her place. At first, he thought of Jane Partington but she wasn't free, so she suggested that he invite Sylvia Delavere, her PA.

He liked Sylvia and had enjoyed her company, both professional and personal, over the past couple of weeks, and of course, he had literally seen a good deal of her in the film he had inadvertently come across on TV in his hotel room in Paris. In fact, he had thought quite a lot about Sylvia as he found her sexually alluring and a very entertaining personality. She was artistic but not academic or intellectual; however, he found her a breath of fresh air. While they were working together, he treated her as a fellow professional and did not make advances to her of a personal nature. This meant that she was comfortable with him because she did not fear sexual harassment.

However, unknown to him at that time, Sylvia had been having an affair with Conrad Beight, on and off, ever since she had first modelled for him. She was also a friend of Conrad's wife, Polly, for whom she had also modelled. The couple had always had an open marriage and as Conrad rarely concealed his casual affairs, Polly knew that Sylvia was one of the notches on his bedpost.

Guy rang Sylvia to see if she would like to go to the opera, but her flatmate said she was staying with Imogen Beight in Holland

Park, as Imogen's parents were in New York. Guy rang the Beight house, spoke to Sylvia and arranged to meet her at the Opera House in time for a drink before the show.

The area around the venerable old building had changed considerably while Guy had been in America. It was originally right in the middle of Covent Garden Market but the market had long gone and the area had been given an extensive facelift. It had become a focal point for tourists, even if they never went into the theatre, and the Floral Hall had been retained and was now a splendid restaurant with bars. Sylvia was already waiting for him at the entrance to the foyer, looking very pretty in a mid-blue taffeta evening coat over a matching cocktail dress. She wore high-heeled shoes of the same colour and carried a clutch bag. Her dark brown hair was long but she had taken it up into a chignon for the evening to show off her elegant pearl drop earrings. The style suited her admirably and she felt confident that she was properly dressed for such a swanky evening. She had never seen Guy in a dinner suit with black tie before and thought he looked even dishier than usual.

He had missed the original production so was glad that it was being revived, as it was an opera that was now very rarely performed. The 19th century French composer, Ambroise Thomas, had set the Hamlet story and it was a treat to have the opportunity to see it on the stage, rather than hear it in a concert version.

They went up to the Floral Hall, which was, as usual, crowded before the performance; had coffee, then booked their drinks for the interval. Guy had chosen seats in the Dress Circle as he thought they would have a better overall view of the stage than from the stalls.

Sylvia had never been to the opera house before and looked around admiringly at the very grand auditorium, decorated in crimson, cream and gold; with boxes on either side of the proscenium arch, which was curtained in heavy crimson velvet, festooned with gilded ornamentation.

Sylvia settled down for a very special evening with Guy sitting beside her, reading his programme. She was particularly keen on handsome men in evening dress and she would not have been offended if Guy had held her hand. However, he did not. In fact, though fully aware of Sylvia's allure, he treated her simply as a valued colleague.

The conductor appeared to polite applause and the orchestra struck up the introduction to the opera. The melodic tunes were very appealing and the audience was full of anticipation as the curtains opened, but Guy groaned when he saw the brick walls of the stage, which was utterly devoid of scenery, furniture or props. When Hamlet appeared, he was dressed in the kind of combinations worn as underwear in the Victorian period by both men and women. The other characters wore dingy, tatty coats and only Ophelia wore a decent dress. There was nothing to suggest a royal court, not even a banner or throne and little stage movement to match the music. Thus, when it came to Ophelia's Mad Scene, which is full of vocal gymnastics and where she is meant to run around throwing flowers at the courtiers, she was laid down upon a couch, an actual piece of furniture at last though wholly inappropriate for the vital music. Guy could not believe it and ironically asked, "Is the Royal Opera so hard up that it could not run to some decent scenery for heaven's sake?" At least, the stage was well lit, which is unusual these days when the fashion seems to be for a gloomy stage setting, even when the action is meant to be in daylight.

Guy felt thoroughly ashamed of the artistic team and agreed with the couple in front, obviously French, who were shaking their heads in disbelief. The sad thing was that the production was being spoilt by poor decor, whereas the soloists were superb as were the chorus and orchestra. He remembered a friend who sang at the opera in Bordeaux telling him about the General Administrator who, on seeing the dress rehearsal of a Wagner production, was so appalled at the abysmal staging that he called a halt to the whole thing, sacked the director and commanded the opera to be performed in a concert version. To the surprise of the company, it was actually a great success.

Guy told Sylvia, "There are many opera buffs who know what a production should be like, but now at live opera, they often sit with their eyes closed, which is a waste of money because they could stay at home and listen to a recording."

In the interval, as they sipped their drinks in the Floral Hall, Guy apologised to Sylvia because her first operatic experience was a travesty. He told her that he loved opera because it contained all the arts; music, singing, drama, decor and costumes, requiring real team work, but directors and designers were still brain washed by the concepts instigated fifty years ago by Eastern European directors. It is no longer Avant-garde, but old hat; the real Avant-garde nowadays would be to perform works as their composers and librettists intended.

"Of course," said Guy, "the real problem is that there are not enough new works suitable to become part of the standard repertoire, so the same operas are trotted out again and again, and directors try to make their productions different. However, that is not the answer." He said that he considered American musicals the real operas of the 20th century, particularly those of Richard Rodgers, Jerome Kern, Irving Berlin, Cole Porter and Leonard Bernstein, because they were based on melody so were ideal for singers. However, many so 'serious' contemporary composers decried melody, as they were still in thrall to atonality or minimalism, which did not appeal to the general public.

"Indeed," he declared, "appropriate, well written works from the musical stage, should have their place in opera houses. Operetta, too, of course, is very attractive, but apart from the 'Merry Widow' such works are not often seen on the English stage."

On the last night in Munich, Guy and Jane had seen a performance of 'Der Rosenkavalier' at the Stadt Oper and Guy told Sylvia that it was a pity that she had not been with them because it was just what an opera should be. It was created by the matchless team of director Otto Schenk and his designer, Rudolph Heinrich, and although it dated from 1972, it is still considered definitive, so there is no plan for a new production to replace it. The decor and costumes are simply renovated from time to time.

Guy added, "Of course, there have been many cast changes over the past forty years, but the basic production remains the same. Better to keep something superb, even if old, than to go to the expense of a new, but inferior modern production."

He went on, "Ballet and drama have not suffered as opera has but sometimes productions are so weird that the story does not make any sense at all, and those who are seeing the work for the first time, leave the theatre totally confused. For instance, who can make sense of such a perversion as a previous production of the delectable 'Cosi fan Tutte' at Scottish Opera where instead of a garden overlooking the Bay of Naples, there was an underpass with a load of dumped scrap metal: insanity, or what?"

Sylvia was a novice, so she did not fully understand Guy's point of view but he explained by telling her about a conversation he had had with a German girl who was studying stage direction. She said that one must find a concept: he assured her that the composer and librettist had already created the concept, but she argued that you were not doing your job if you did not create your own concept. He disagreed and said that all one had to do was read the score to discover how to stage the work. In fact, he had seen an old interview with Maria Callas on TV and she said that if you needed to find the right gesture, you had only to listen to the music. Guy said, "The sad thing is that the girl didn't understand what I was talking about so when her turn comes, she will join the long queue of operatic abusers."

"Of course," he declared, "being controversial means that the names of directors become known, even if for the wrong reasons." He laughed at himself, then apologised for getting on his high horse but said it was something he felt very strongly about. During his time in New York, he went frequently to the Met and he promised Sylvia that when there was another HD Met transmission in a local cinema, he would take her; but first, he would make sure that it was a production worth seeing.

Sylvia said that despite Guy's disappointment, she had thoroughly enjoyed the evening because the music and singing were wonderful, and she looked forward to her next visit to an opera. As they said goodnight, she reached up, kissed him on the cheek and thanked him for introducing her to a magical world. He grinned ruefully, but said he was glad that she had enjoyed herself and thanked her for being such a delightful companion. He still had the music spinning in his head, so although he had to blank out the awful stage picture, at least that was something.

Chapter Eleven

When Guy returned home next day, he popped into the Hall, and found Sally and Tom wading through a pile of documents. Sally's eyes were glowing with the thrill of discovery and she told Guy that she now intended to write a book based on her findings.

It was Sally who had suggested that Tom should engage Piers Gambourne, as archivist and Tom followed her advice. Piers was indeed proving to be an excellent choice because he was expert in reading ancient handwriting and could translate Latin texts into English. He was also a noted expert in unravelling Elizabethan codes and had already begun work on what appeared to be a substantial diary, though he was not yet aware who had written it or when. Tom told Guy that he had applied for a heritage grant because the papers could be in the national interest and would also bring more visitors to the Hall when the documents were published.

Guy invited the three scholars to have lunch at his house the next day, as he was keen to hear and see what they had unearthed. Sally thought that was a good idea because although the Hall was not yet open to the public, it was noisy and chaotic due to all the renovation work taking place at the time.

She may have suspected that Ginny and Paul were sleeping together, but she was the soul of discretion and after all, it was no business of hers. At weekends, Helen was back with her husband but there was also the nanny and the nursemaid, who cared for baby Monty, to take into account. Ginny had a lot to cope with as there was so much going on at the Hall, but she was as happy as the situation allowed. She adored her grandson and never got tired of playing with the chubby little chap. Tom loved being a grandfather but was also very taken up with his genealogical research whenever he managed to slip away to the library.

Helen appeared to be content with her double life because she enjoyed her time at college; then at home, she was free to make love to Paul and play with their baby. All in all, things were going quite well for all the family, even for Ginny, who enjoyed her stolen time with Paul while Helen was away. As Paul's mother-in-law, she had a good cover for being in his company so often and also, of course, she was the wife of his employer, so fortunately, as they were discreet, they avoided gossip. It was natural, of course, that Ginny should feel guilty as she was not only deceiving her husband, but also her daughter. However, for her and Paul, the risk of being discovered simply added spice to their illicit affair, although they took every precaution not to get caught.

Tom was not stupid so suspected that something was going on between his wife and son-in-law but he was very practiced in turning a blind eye, and had no intention of rocking anybody's boat. With Helen, it was a case of ignorance is bliss and Ginny was happy, so that was enough for him. He could not live other people's lives for them. In fact, he began to wonder just how lily white were the relationships of some of his friends, or how many were harbouring secrets, even from their loved ones. Not for the first time, he suspected that many lives were lived behind masks. Nevertheless, with modern technology it would become increasingly difficult to keep intimate activities hidden behind closed doors.

Guy worked hard the next morning, then welcomed his lunch guests. He had looked forward to seeing Sally again, and she didn't disappoint him as she looked delightful in a three quarter length turquoise silk dress and high-heeled, cream shoes, with her lustrous hair framing her pretty face. Recently, he had been so taken with Sylvia that he had almost forgotten just how delectable Sally was. Although she was undoubtedly a blue stocking, she didn't look at all stereotypical, whatever that was meant to be and Guy congratulated himself on having such delightful women in his life.

She had not had a chance to see him alone since he returned from abroad but was keen to learn how things were progressing with his book and the documentary. He, on the other hand, was interested in her recent discoveries. Although she was usually reluctant to talk about herself, she was always ready to talk about her work and she was particularly enthused about the documents which had been hidden for so long at West Bridge Hall.

It was well known that the present house had been built on land formerly occupied by a medieval convent which was partly demolished at the Dissolution; the land passing to a branch of the Alconbury family, but lacking an heir, the estate was given, on the orders of Elizabeth I, to Sir Tolly de Giffard, Guy's ancestor, who had been active in assisting Robert Dudley, Earl of Leicester, to entertain the Queen and her large retinue at Kenilworth Castle in Warwickshire. By this time, the de Giffard family had made a considerable fortune from wool, so built West Bridge Hall in the new English Renaissance style, which caused a great deal of curiosity among the local gentry as it was totally different to the Gothic architecture which had been popular for so long.

Piers, of course, though well versed in history, was keen to learn as much about the old pile and its historic family as possible, and the effect that the various upheavals over the centuries had resulted on its fortunes. Tom said that with the accession of Charles I, early in the 17th century, political disputes grew so serious that it was inevitable that they resulted in a ferocious Civil War that set family against family and led to the King's execution in 1649. Tom and Guy's ancestors were fully aware of the undoubted danger in which they stood because no one knew which side would win so, in order to safe guard important documents, they constructed a hidden room, off one of the attics and stored papers that had been rifled from the convent, as well as their own family archives.

Although the house was besieged by Royalist troops, little damage was done as they were quickly put to rout by Parliamentarians. As time passed and members of the family died off, the documents were completely forgotten until a few weeks ago when builders had accidentally uncovered the hiding place.

Sally told Guy that she was enjoying herself enormously investigating his family history, and she felt that she, Tom and Piers had become a good team. "Though," she admitted, "you never know what might be uncovered in a family's hidden history and there is always a chance that it could be unsavoury."

"Well," declared Guy, "that is a chance we will have to take but it could make the family more interesting.

"Indeed," said Piers, "as it happens we have just turned up some alarming material about the owner of the house during the Civil War; one Sir Hubert de Giffard, a Protestant who became increasingly fanatical in the Puritan cause and was certainly a most unsavoury type. For his valour and loyalty, however, he was rewarded by Cromwell with further lands and possessions, though he was considered a traitor by those who had upheld the Royalist cause. Many of them, of course, had had to flee and were exiled on the Continent until the Restoration in 1660. Charles II did not want further trouble so largely refrained from proscribing those who had fought against his father. He felt that it was time to show tolerance, and allow life to become more relaxed and enjoyable after all the hardships."

"Cromwell, like many who become radicalised," said Guy, "had banned many things that the populace had previously relished, such as music, singing, dancing and the theatre, and with his welcome demise, England became 'merry' again. Mind you," he joked, "if the new Labour leader got into Number Ten, shades of Cromwell might rise again, or even Stalin, heaven forbid."

Sally reminded Guy that he had told her about a ghost at the Hall when she had first visited him. He had treated it as a joke but she said, "Ghost or not, it does have its origins in a true event. Apparently, Sir Hubert had a pretty young daughter named Hannah, whom he planned to marry to one of the Puritan generals. He was twice her age and as boorish as her father, so she resisted with all her might. Earlier, she had been promised to Jeremy Manville, the young son of a neighbouring landowner. However, his family supported the Royalist side, so there was now no question of a marriage to unite the two families, as originally intended, before religious and political dissensions reared their ugly heads. The young couple were deeply in love, so their parting was painful in the extreme.

We found a document which must have been written by the girl's mother but hidden away until now. I gather that Hannah was a feisty, courageous girl so did all she could to make her father change his mind, but he was adamant and there was a terrific row, in which he picked up a heavy candlestick and struck Hannah on the temple. She died instantly. Anna, her mother, was well aware of her husband's hot temper and brutality, but this time, he had gone too far, forcing her to help him carry Hannah's limp body up to an attic where together they hung it on a beam to make it look like suicide. Many people knew about the cancelled wedding so the story was put about that the girl had taken her own life while grieving for her lost love.

Of course, Anna was frightened of her husband and horrified by his callous behaviour, especially as he was supposed to be very religious. Nevertheless, he cold bloodedly condemned his daughter to a suicide's grave. The truth, of course, was buried with her and Sir Hubert threatened that he would kill his wife if she ever disclosed what had really happened. Anna did not share her husband's extreme piety, but she believed in God and every day, she prayed for Hannah's soul. However, she secretly wrote an account of what had happened, but left it for posterity to find."

"What happened to Jeremy?" asked Guy.

"He was killed in battle shortly after Hannah died. His father fled to the Netherlands, then his family were spirited away to join him. They did not return until the Restoration. Their estate had been given to a Puritan family, but it was restored to them by the King when he regained the throne," stated Sally.

She and her little team had spent time putting pieces of the jigsaw together, but even more to her delight, she found interesting documents suggesting the real authorship of the Shakespeare plays. There was a lot of work to be done, of course, but she believed that she was on the right track.

Guy thoroughly enjoyed his afternoon with the scholars and all they had to tell him. Sally was obviously thrilled with their discoveries and was quite happy to stay on at the Hall, just going up to London for her two days teaching at the Courtauld each week. Strangely, neither of them had ever spoken about the sensuous afternoon they had enjoyed when she first visited the Dower House. It was as if they had taken a vow of silence, though Guy wanted to explain to her that his behaviour had been quite out of character. He still knew so little about her but the more her saw of her, the more he liked her and as well as being intellectually on a par, their encounter had shown that they had sexual affinity too.

Though a man of the world, he was quite unsure of how to deal with Sally. Jane Partington had dropped the odd hint about her liking women and he knew that from time to time, she stayed with Monica even though she had an apartment nearby, but he could not believe that she was indifferent to men.

He was attracted to two delightful women, yet, he was unaware that he had competition. He did suspect that there was a strong link between Sally and Monica, and knew that Sylvia occasionally modelled for Conrad, but he had no idea that she had been his mistress on and off for quite a while. In fact, although he enjoyed Conrad's company, he knew that he had a reputation as a womaniser and that Polly had her own adventures. However, he mused that when it came down to it, how much did anyone know about other people's sexual predilections or intimate history? Guy was as sexually normal as a chap could be, but had scant curiosity about what other people got up to behind closed doors. He was no prude, but he would certainly have been surprised, had he known what went on within his small circle of friends and colleagues.

Chapter Twelve

It was necessary for Guy to go to London again for a few days, so he booked into his club and was walking down from Oxford Street to Piccadilly the day after he arrived, when he bumped into Lady Monica who was on her way to Sotheby's. She was pleased to see him and suggested, if he had time, he might like to go with her to see the European paintings being put up for the next sale. He often bought out of date catalogues at Sotheby's as they were as well presented as coffee table books and very much reduced in price after an exhibition was over.

After seeing the pictures, he bought a couple of back catalogues, then they retired to the cafe to rest their feet, enjoy a coffee and catch up with news. "I suppose you know that Sally is staying with my brother and his wife at the Hall?" he ventured. "Yes, she texted me and said she is having the time of her life, wading through old papers."

"She is, indeed and came to lunch a few days ago to tell me all about her exciting findings," remarked Guy.

"Forgive me for asking, Guy," said Monica, "but are you and Sally having an affair?"

"Good lord, no," he laughed. "Whatever gave you that idea?"

"Nothing really, it is just that she seems to mention your name an awful lot these days."

Guy smiled, "Well, you know how it is with art historians, we cannot get enough of each other."

"Stuff and nonsense," chuckled Monica. "We all know that academics are more likely to scratch each other's eyes out."

"Oh, not Sally, she is the mildest creature in the world. But joking apart, Monica, she is an enigma and I don't really know anything about her other than her academic reputation. She says so little about herself and I would like to know how she ticks."

Monica thought for a moment then said, "On the surface, she is quiet and uncomplicated, but she is like the proverbial swan, elegantly floating on the surface of the water, but paddling like crazy underneath. Oh, yes, there are hidden depths to our Sally and she is not what she seems. However, I am not suggesting that there is anything sinister, far from it; she is a truly good woman; the most harmless person in the world. In fact, that is her maxim; 'Do no harm'."

"I have to admit, Monica, that she fascinates me because she is mysterious."

"Well, you will have to dig deeply to find the clues," she replied. "I have known her since we were students at Cambridge but Sally does not easily give up her secrets."

"I think you are two of a kind," smiled Guy. "You are a pretty canny bird yourself, dear Monica. I don't think I have ever met a more discreet woman."

"Oh," she laughed. "Don't you realise that that is the secret of my success?"

They walked back to Piccadilly together and Monica invited him to have supper with her at her apartment that evening. He was on his way to the London Library and said he would be ready for a relaxing evening when he finished for the day.

Monica's sitting room was large but comfortably furnished with an Adam fireplace as the focal point. One wall was lined with bookshelves containing a huge collection of art books, exhibition catalogues, dictionaries, directories, and the indispensable 'Burke's Peerage' and 'Who's Who'. There were two long windows facing the street, hung with swag curtains and pelmets, and a large Aubusson carpet covered the parquet floor. The pine-panelled walls were painted soft dove grey, providing a neutral background for colourful contemporary paintings. Guy flopped into a comfortable armchair by the fireplace, and Monica brought in a tray with a bowl of salad and a platter of cold meats, accompanied by crusty bread, and unsalted butter. Guy stood up and pulled out a folding table while Monica said that she hoped he would excuse the informality. He smiled and assured her that it was just what he liked at the end of a busy day. Monica laid plates, cutlery, condiments and napkins on the now upright table, and asked Guy what he wanted to drink with the meal. Like Sally, Guy usually drank very little alcohol so opted for Elderflower cordial, while Monica had white wine.

"Gosh, this is cosy," said Monica. "I am so used to hosting parties here for a crush of people so it is really nice when I can just have a tête-à-tête with a friend.

I suppose Jane Partington told you that she stayed with us at the Embassy when she was in Paris last week?"

"Yes," answered Guy. "She sent me a message saying she had gone over to kill two birds with one stone; more recce for the Pompadour programme and to see her husband."

"Well," said Monica. "She saw him, alright, but little good it did her. I fear for that wretched man's sanity. Really, he should not be in charge of military affairs; heaven knows what horrors he could perpetrate in his deranged state of mind."

"Surely, it's not as bad as that?" queried Guy.

"You don't know the half of it, but she keeps her own counsel, so I am sure she has not discussed it with you. Marcus is beside himself on her behalf. He has wanted to marry her for years but that terrible man, in his deluded religious mania, will not free her. He says divorcing her would endanger his eternal soul. Marcus thinks it is more likely that he hates the thought of sharing his wealth and property with her in a divorce settlement."

"Poor woman," declared Guy. "She always seems so cheerful and upbeat, and she is a consummate professional. Her organisational abilities are first rate and I thank my lucky stars to have her producing the documentary."

"Well, she is a typical Agrimony type," replied her friend.

"Sorry," said Guy, "but I don't know what that means."

"Oh, put simply, there is a system based on thirty nine flower remedies, invented in the 20s and 30s by Dr Edward Bach. He reckoned there are twelve basic types of individual. The remedies are vibratory medicine, not chemical, so have no side effects and you cannot overdose. They are very subtle and affect the body's own healing mechanism. They are not painkillers though, nor do they work on symptoms; one might say that they touch the soul so bring about healing at the deepest level. It is a pity that they are not used by the NHS as they could save thousands of pounds and alleviate many ills, especially for those suffering with addictions and mental health issues."

"I see, but what actually is Agrimony?" asked Guy.

"It is principally for a person who always puts on a good face, even though suffering agonies within. The extreme is someone who commits suicide and leaves everyone totally mystified as they always seemed so cheerful."

"Oh lord, I can see we will have to look out for Jane and make sure she doesn't become too stressed," said a worried Guy.

"Well," replied Monica, "if you ever get the chance to suggest the remedies, you could mention Agrimony and tell her to take it regularly, just four drops in a drink, four times a day. Some health shops sell the remedies and you can also order them from the Bach Centre at Sotwell but actually, it is better to consult a practitioner, if you can find one. However, the Rescue Remedy, which I consider the first port of call, is stocked by most chemists. Mind you, the one who truly needs a remedy is Jane's husband, who should be taking Vine for his controlling, unreasonable, nature.

Have you seen Jane since she returned from Paris?" asked Monica.

"No, I have been writing in the country so we only spoke on the phone or texted."

"Well," continued Monica. "Her husband is seriously out of control and should be sectioned, because he attacked Jane while at the Embassy. He went to her bedroom, became violent and tried to strangle her."

"My God," cried Guy. "I had no idea the poor woman was under such stress."

"Well, there is usually a back story," declared Monica. "Not that I am saying Jane is in any way to blame. He was always a difficult man, but it seems that his conversion to Roman Catholicism has turned his brain. Apparently, he got into the clutches of some priest or other and is obsessed by the man."

"Did you manage to keep the thing under wraps or did it reach the press?" asked Guy.

"Oh, Douglas was called and he managed to get Arnold out of the room, and calmed him down. Jane, of course, was very shocked and upset but Douglas assured her that he would have a word in the right quarter, so that Arnold would be closely monitored. Jane is made of stern stuff, so she put on fresh makeup and wore a high-necked blouse to cover the bruises on her neck. We wanted her to go to hospital to be checked out but she wouldn't and I can understand why. However, as usual, dear old Rescue Remedy came to hand and by the evening, you wouldn't have known that anything unpleasant had happened to her. It must take its toll though, because even when he is out of the country, his dark presence looms."

"Some people can deal with religion but many can't," said Guy. "A friend who suffered a breakdown and was a day patient at a psychiatric unit, said that he was amazed at the number of people suffering from religious mania, and not just from one religion but all kinds. Of course, these are the people who want categorical answers, but don't get them. I have another friend who jokes that there should be a mental health warning over the doorway of every religious establishment. Mind you, it is not a joking matter as religion is still causing the majority of conflicts on the planet. The crucial thing is that nothing can be proved. All religions begin as manmade cults but through weight of numbers become authoritarian, each group proclaiming that they are the only purveyors of truth. Have you heard that joke about the devil and his friend walking down the street?" Monica shook her head. "Well, on the other side, they see a man bend down and pick up a piece of truth. The friend asks the devil if he is worried but he laughs and says, 'now watch him organise it'."

"There is so much misunderstanding," Guy continued, "and so much ridiculous dogma in all orthodox religions so it is hard to make out what is to be believed. I find it difficult to understand why those who get hooked on religion go towards the dark side. The Kabala, the Tree of Life, has Severity opposite Mercy, yet, so often, religious fundamentalists focus on Severity, creating a demon instead of a god, calling for death, destruction and cruelty. Can you credit, for instance, that Sunnis and Shias are still at war with each other over a disagreement going back to the death of Mohammad, fifteen hundred years ago? To me, it just beggars belief and I think all States should be secular, with no orthodox religions at all. Everyone needs faith or a philosophy of some sort, but it should be private.

I think that humanity is actually spiritually based, but religion has muddied the waters. Nowadays, you can understand why intelligent people are voting with their feet and becoming free thinkers or Humanists. After all, we have been taught that God is within. Thank goodness, unless we let the fanatics take over, toleration holds sway; otherwise, many of us would be going to the stake as heretics. And on that note," smiled Guy. "I think I should wend my way. Thank you, Monica, for a delightful evening. I can't believe though, how serious we have been. Still, it is not with every friend that one can explore such subjects. I am truly sorry for Jane and for Marcus, and do hope that there can soon be a solution to their problem."

Chapter Thirteen

The shrill ring of the landline telephone beside her bed shocked Monica out of a deep sleep and she fumbled with the receiver, trying to get her bearings. The voice at the other end was that of Martin Morson, her husband, Sir Douglas Montford's private secretary. He apologised for waking her so early in the morning, but said he couldn't leave it until later because, unfortunately, Sir Douglas had been found in a coma and rushed to hospital.

He assumed that she knew that her husband had recently been diagnosed with Type One diabetes and the medics were still trying to find the right medical regime for him. Monica could not believe that he had not told her, but apparently, he wanted the whole thing kept secret as he thought it might damage his career. He was only fifty-two and expected to stay in office until his retirement but ill health might cut short his time at the Embassy.

Monica said it was foolish of him to think his condition could be kept under wraps, after all, the British Prime Minister was diabetic and had to inject insulin five times a day, yet, it did not preclude her from public life.

Martin said that he was at the hospital and would keep her informed, but she said that she would catch the Euro Star and go straight to the hospital when she arrived in Paris. Fortunately, she had excellent staff at the Gallery, so texted the curator, Andy Tomlin and told him that she was leaving for Paris but did not know how long she would be away. Among her many talents, Monica was expert at delegating and now had a reliable staff who could act on their own initiative in her absence.

When she arrived at the hospital, she was met by Martin Morson, who looked pale and drawn as he had been up all night. He introduced her to the senior consultant, Monsieur Delaunay and she was taken into a side ward where he told her that, unfortunately, Sir Douglas had died a short time ago, without regaining consciousness. Monica was usually an unflappable woman but she was utterly floored by such unexpected news. She had had no idea that Douglas was so ill, but Martin said that he had been struggling over the past few weeks, though he never neglected his duties and was always his charming self, so no one suspected that he was in danger of sudden collapse. The doctor expressed his deep sympathy at Monica's loss, and told her that, sadly, there would have to be a post mortem and an inquest. He assured her that she would be kept abreast of all developments. She was allowed to see Douglas and confirm his identity then, still in shock, Martin drove her to the Embassy.

As usual, there was a lot of traffic in central Paris and hold ups were inevitable, so Monica encouraged Martin to tell her what had been happening while she was in London. He said, as if she did not know, that Douglas was the strong, stoic type of Englishman, who would not admit needing medical help until the last moment. Monica had to agree that his work came before everything and he never spared himself, however he was feeling.

"Of course," said Martin. "I think it will be found at the post mortem, that the previously untreated diabetes damaged his heart and it simply gave up the fight." He added that, as ever, Douglas just got on with things, though he often looked terribly tired and sometimes his speech was slower than usual. His own doctor had urged him to rest but in a busy embassy that was easier said than done. He was a highly experienced diplomat who was used to dealing with complex affairs but lately, he had taken the state of the world more to heart than previously. Seeing the plight of refugees, particularly the children, from war torn areas, had really played on his mind, as the situation was so widespread that it seemed utterly unsolvable. In addition, the planet was being shattered by extreme weather cataclysms and man's inhumanity to man appeared to have no bounds. The fact that there was so much bombing, particularly in the Middle East, sending god knows what into the atmosphere, at the same time, as underground missile and nuclear tests were being activated, put great strain on the Earth's crust, triggering earthquakes in the most vulnerable regions.

Monica began to feel guilty; perhaps, if she had been with Douglas more often, his illness might have been contained. She could have monitored his treatment and taken some of the responsibility of entertaining guests off his shoulders. She had always comforted herself with the knowledge that the Embassy staff was highly efficient, ensuring that the place ran like clockwork. Martin told her how two days before, Douglas had admitted to having a giddy spell, which resulted in him falling down some steps and twisting his ankle. He was shaken but did not want the doctor to know. An elastic bandage was applied to the injury and he carried on, greeting the Indian ambassador as if nothing had happened. Monica knew that Douglas hated fuss, but that evening, he went to bed earlier than usual, leaving his deputy to host a dinner for members of the Israeli diplomatic corps.

After the post mortem which held no surprises, Monica went to see her husband whose body was now in a Chapel of Rest. Before identifying him in the hospital, she had never seen a corpse before and it shocked her to the core to see her husband, usually so full of life and vigour, as just a stone cold statue. Where had that life gone? Surely, it could not just have been puffed out? Some people believe that everyone has a soul and that the body is just the instrument for its use: while others deny any such thing, claiming that it is a case of dust-to-dust ashes to ashes, then oblivion.

For the first time in her life, Monica considered the matter but thought that if proof was needed that the body did indeed hold a soul, it was in observing a corpse and realising that the soul had flown, though goodness knows where it had gone. As she looked at Douglas, she felt guilty that she had never fully appreciated him. He was a fine man and she realised that she had been selfish to live her life as she had. Well, it was no time for regrets, that part of her life was already written. Instead, she hoped that Douglas had enjoyed his life and had found comfort, one way or another.

She admitted to Martin that she lacked a religious faith and now regretted it because it made death harder to handle. "Well," said the young man. "As far as I can see, when it comes to death, even the most religious are at a loss to explain what it means."

"What are your thoughts then?" queried Monica.

"I was brought up C of E," replied Martin, "but my parents were not religious, it was just complying with the form; being christened, going to Church occasionally and R E at school. I actually became quite interested in comparative religion and read a lot, finally coming to the conclusion that Theosophy has more answers than most of the traditional religions."

"What is that? I have never heard of it," said Monica.

"It is an amalgamation of several schools of thought, many of them of Eastern origin. It is really more of a philosophy than a religion but relies heavily on a belief in reincarnation. Not the daft idea that people can come back as animals but the fact that like all other aspects of nature, we are recycled and appear on earth in different guises in different eras. You know, as Shakespeare says, 'all the world is a stage, and the men and women merely players.' Certainly, we can now see that Sir Douglas's form is an empty shell,

93

but I do not believe that death is the end; it is purely a transition to another dimension of life. If you think of quantum mechanics where a particle can jump from one dimension to another; why not a human soul? Really, there is no such thing as death; it is just a change of form into another level of being. People do not disappear, they merely become invisible to us in this dimension. It is said that we have several subtle bodies but each one is on a finer vibration than the one before it and we already have the one in place which we will use on the next dimension, but it is not visible to the human eye, although we feel through it because it is called the sensation body and is the one pushed aside when we have an anaesthetic. Our physical vibrations are slower than the subtle ones. Imagine an aeroplane propeller. Well, when it is static, it is seen in solid form, but when it spins, ready to take off, it is so fast that the form is lost. The phrase 'dust to dust, ashes to ashes' is true, but it does not mean oblivion for the soul, which indeed, I do believe is a reality. No, the soul moves on but the body has served its purpose and does return to dust, blending in with the clay from which it came."

"How old are you?" queried Monica.

"I am almost twenty seven."

"Well, you certainly seem to have an old head on your shoulders," she told him. "I am ashamed to say that although I am almost forty-one, I have never given such matters any thought at all. I live in a totally material world, never having contemplated theological issues. However, I have a friend whose husband is suffering from religious mania and religion has given him no comfort at all."

"Yes, that is the danger," said Martin. "The more one questions, the fewer answers one finds in orthodox religion, so some people end in despair; others turn to drink or drugs and seek oblivion, while lots give it up entirely, just living for the day."

"What is your maxim?" asked Monica. "What philosophy do you live by?"

"My maxim, as you call it, is simple; I believe in the Life Force which some people call God, and I try to love my neighbour and pray for my enemies. After all, the latter need our prayers so that they turn away from their evil deeds. I suppose the Sermon on the Mount is as good as anything because it provides us with a formula for social ethics and does not have to be complicated by religious dogma."

Not long after they arrived at the Embassy, Daniel Brewster, whom Monica had texted before leaving London, came over to support her. She was naturally delighted to see him and they went into lunch together. Although Monica had not eaten for hours, she just pushed her food around her plate. Daniel had never seen her so vulnerable, having always assumed that she was made of Teflon. He was hungry after his journey but felt quite guilty tucking in to the delicious food while his friend was bereft of appetite. She did not relish wine either, but asked for a large pot of coffee, which Daniel shared with her.

Afterwards, she spent time with Selwyn Broad, Douglas's deputy and Martin Morson in Douglas's office. As expected, there were messages of condolence arriving by the minute from around the world, including one from the Queen and the Prime Minister, while newspapers, radio and TV stations badgered the Press Office for information. It was bedlam and soon gave Monica a headache. She just wanted to lie on a bed with curtains drawn and sleep. However, Daniel thought she needed air so took her walking in the Luxembourg Gardens on the Left Bank of the Seine. He was up to his eyes in commissions so Monica was very grateful to him for taking time out to be with her. He hoped that making love to her would bring comfort, but she was not in the mood and anyway, she did not want the embassy staff to find out that they were lovers. After two days, he had to return to London and Monica was relieved to be on her own as his bright, jaunty personality was rather too much for her in her present state of mind.

With the post mortem completed, undertakers were now in charge and it was necessary to decide where Douglas should be buried. Monica said that her husband's family originated in France and their name was actually de Montford. Douglas's great grandfather, Count Rohan de Montford, had settled in England but retained a house in the Forest of Fontainebleau, and Douglas had previously told Monica that if he died in France, he wanted to be buried in the ancient family vault at the cemetery of Montmartre, though, of course, there would also be a memorial service at St Margaret's, Westminster, when she returned to London.

Strangely, Monica had never been to the house in the forest. She imagined that it might be a ruin by now, or it might have been let for many years. When Douglas's private affairs were investigated, it was found that there was indeed someone living at the house, but there was no sign of any rent being received, though rates and taxes were regularly paid by Douglas's bank. Monica decided to go there to see for herself how the land lay. She could do little until the French equivalent of probate was granted so a trip to Fontainebleau,

Seine et Marne; within easy reach of Paris, would be just the thing to clear her head and get her away from the frantic life of the Embassy. She also thought it might be interesting to stay a night at Barbizon, close to the forest, where many famous artists had painted in the late 19th century, notably Rousseau, or Le Douanier, as he was called, due to his occupation as a customs official.

The next day, she was allotted a car from the Embassy pool and drove herself to the forest. She booked into a small hotel at Barbizon and managed to eat some lunch then set off to look for Douglas's family house. It was a delightful day and amid the giant stones for which the forest is famous, she found the house she was looking for. It was in Louis XIII style, so had been built in the 17th century, though it could have had earlier foundations. It was a medium sized stone chateau, situated at the end of a long drive flanked by lawns. It had several long windows with small ornate iron balconies and had pale blue shutters. The roof was pitched with slate tiles and there were tall chimneys at each gable end, and in the centre of the roof, one of which showed a thin curl of smoke indicating that someone was at home.

Monica rang the metal bell pull at the side of the front door and heard it peal within. After a couple of minutes, footsteps on a stone tiled floor indicated that someone was coming. The door was opened by a young woman who was obviously pregnant. She looked quizzically at Monica and waited for her to speak. Monica addressed her in French and the woman replied that she had always expected her to come to find her. This puzzled Monica, who wondered how she knew her, but before she could ask, the woman, who said her name was Clothilde, added that she had seen her photograph so knew who she was. With that, she invited Monica in and led her through a wide hallway into a plain, but comfortable sitting room on the left hand side. She offered her coffee and Monica accepted; more to give her time to look around, while the woman was in the kitchen rather than because she wanted a drink.

When Clothilde returned with a tray of coffee and biscuits, Monica took a better look at her. She appeared to be in her late twenties and though she was decidedly pregnant, she didn't wear a wedding ring on her right hand, as is usual on the Continent. However, she had a pretty dress ring on the third finger of her left hand.

She was of medium height, and had light brown hair and hazel eyes. Her complexion was that of a countrywoman and her only make-up was a pale lipstick. Monica thought that she had never seen such long, lustrous eyelashes in her life, but they were certainly not false and gave her the appearance of a beautiful Jersey cow. Although one could not proclaim her a beauty, she had a certain attraction, despite her obvious bump.

At first, the sophisticated, cosmopolitan Monica was unusually lost for words but thankfully, Clothilde spoke first. "I presume you know who I am as you have found me," she began.

"No, I have to admit that this is all a mystery to me. I came to see the house but assumed it was probably a ruin by this time as no rent appeared to have been received, though I gather that rates and taxes were paid. I know many old French houses are abandoned, then sold and restored, usually by foreigners."

"No, I am living here gratis."

"By whose permission?" asked Monica.

"By my protector," she answered.

"And who may that be?" queried Monica.

"I am not at liberty to say," Clothilde blushed.

"No problem," Monica countered. "I believe it is Sir Douglas Montford and you have guessed that I am his wife." As she said it, Monica suddenly realised that she was actually his widow but had to tread warily as she didn't want to shock this pregnant woman with the awful news that her lover had just died.

"I will be frank with you, my dear," said Monica. "Until just now, I was totally unaware of your existence. I admit that Sir Douglas and I have led rather separate lives for some years, and though I would say that we were happily married, we did not intrude on each other's secrets. I have always been independent, and do not believe that a husband and wife should be joined at the hip. Would you mind telling me how long you and my husband have been associated?" As she said it, Monica realised how formal it sounded, so smiled at the girl, hoping to encourage her to tell her the truth.

Once Clothilde started, the words poured out as though it was a great relief to talk about her relationship with Douglas. Apparently, she was nineteen when she first met him. She had just left business school and was engaged as a temp at the Embassy. She came into contact with Douglas every day, and he was delighted by her efficiency and standard of work. Though her family were country folk, she was an educated girl, could type well, had excellent spelling and was reliable, so she was given a permanent position as a secretarial assistant, dealing with Sir Douglas's diary.

Apparently, it had been common knowledge at the Embassy, at that time, that he had a mistress, the Marquise de Valaumondry, a woman in her thirties, very soigné and sophisticated. Although Monica had never been certain, she had suspected that there was a close relationship between this woman and Douglas. However, she was married and when her husband was posted to Canada, she accompanied him. Thus, when Clothilde met Douglas, he was feeling rather neglected. Their affair began very casually, but soon, they were both in love with each other, despite the age gap; Douglas being twenty-five years older than Clothilde. However, at that time, he was a fit, still handsome man, with a fine figure and full head of hair, and the girl was swept off her feet. Sheepishly, she told Monica that he was very kind to her and proved to be a skilful lover. This was news to Monica who had always found him rather lacking in that department. Oh, well, no doubt different women brought out different aspects in a male.

Monica was a highly sexualised woman, and experienced romantic episodes with men and women. Sally Wentworth had long been one of her lovers and now Daniel Brewster was a decided fixture in her life. She had always liked Douglas but had never been in love with him, though he had initially been swept off his feet by her. They met after she graduated from Cambridge and he was madly keen to marry her. Her parents were then alive and encouraged her to accept his proposal. They were old fashioned enough to believe that though a woman might be educated, her real duty in life was to marry and have children. Monica warned Douglas, though, that she was keen to have a career. She had just inherited the Gayton Art Gallery from her grandfather and was keen to take over as artistic director. Douglas agreed that there was no reason why she should not carry on as her grandfather had. The gallery was highly successful and made a lot of money so that Douglas, who was a rich man in his own right, appreciated that Monica wanted to be financially independent, as so many women do these days, even if they are married.

Finally, Monica was won over and agreed to marry Douglas. She was twenty-two and actually in love with Sally Wentworth, but though Sally was upset at the thought of her marriage, Monica convinced her that it would not affect their relationship. However, Douglas was meant for great things and was soon appointed ambassador to Kuwait. Later, he was posted to other Middle Eastern countries. He and Monica were both Arabic and French speakers so for once, a diplomat and his wife were ideally placed.

It was too far away for Monica to administer the gallery so an assistant director was engaged and thankfully, turned out to be an excellent choice. The gallery went from strength to strength, especially when Conrad Beight was put under contract.

Now Monica was brought back to the present by Clothilde telling her that she had become pregnant within the first year of knowing Douglas. He was delighted when a son was born, whom they called Rohan, a de Montford family name. He was now seven years old and at a good local school, his fees paid by Douglas. When Rohan was three, Clothilde became pregnant again and this time gave birth to a little girl, Rosemarie, who was now at kindergarten. The latest baby was due in three months' time and a scan showed that it was another girl.

At first, Clothilde's parents had been appalled by her lifestyle but such affairs were not unknown in France and gradually, they came around when her son was born. She said that Douglas was a wonderful father, even though he could not spend much time with them. There were times, of course, when he was away from the Embassy and many suspected that he had a new mistress. He was very secretive, though the French are not as prurient about such things as the British tend to be.

He had the forest house renovated and Clothilde moved in. She made the house so warm and comfortable that he relished the times he was able to spend with her. Clothilde told Monica that they were very compatible and their relationship was happy; though he made it clear to her that he would never divorce Monica, despite the fact that his children were illegitimate. However, he assured Clothilde that there would be no barrier to his legitimising them at some point.

A maid was employed for Clothilde, as well as a daily cleaner and a nursemaid when the children were born. There was also a chauffeur/gardener in her employ. Over all, she had a very pleasant life, though she missed the company of adults, as she kept a low profile.

Nevertheless, her parents and her two sisters often visited, and the children knew their father. In fact, contrary to many fathers with illicit relationships, Douglas was registered on their birth certificates. It seemed that it was only Monica who was in the dark.

Now she had the sad task of telling Clothilde about Douglas's sudden death and trusted that she would find the right words. As she received the news, Clothilde gave out a long shriek then appeared about to faint, but Monica held her in her arms and they both wept together. All her sympathies were with this young woman whose only crime was to love a married man. She had done no wrong; indeed, she had made Douglas happy and had given him two delightful children. He was looking forward to the birth of the third baby and as he had so much to live for, his untimely demise was truly cruel.

Monica called to the maid who was outside hanging up washing and told her to ring for a doctor. Clothilde said she also needed the priest as she had to confess. Monica told her that would not be necessary and would only bring unwanted publicity. The quieter she kept, the better. She assured her that she would make sure that she and the little family would be financially secure as she was sure that Douglas would have left provision for them in his Will. In the meantime, she would see that Clothilde's bank account was regularly serviced.

She decided to stay for two more days at Barbizon, and took Clothilde and her children for rides in the Embassy car, visiting the quaint little town of Provins where she bought toys for the little ones at a delightful shop, full of goodies. They also visited several other delightful spots within easy distance, and she told Clothilde that she would keep in touch when she returned home and that if she needed anything, she only had to contact her.

When the Will was read, Monica was relieved to find that Douglas had indeed made excellent provision for Clothilde and the little family. He was already a rich man when he married Monica, but over the years, even after the banking crisis, his investments had trebled so that he left all his dependents well provided for. Monica, of course, was wealthy in her own right and did not need money for herself; however, it was good to have something extra to draw on so that she could set up more art scholarships. Apart from her grandfather leaving her the gallery, she had inherited property and investments from her mother. Her brother, Marcus, of course, as head of the family, had inherited the Earldom, and the bulk of his father's wealth and property.

Chapter Fourteen

A simple, private funeral ceremony was held in Paris and Monica made sure that Clothilde was invited; introducing her as a friend of the family. It was a short but sensitive service and Douglas was laid to rest with his ancestors in the cemetery of Montmartre. His French lawyer, M. DuPont, was well aware of the situation and Monica was able to assure Clothilde that when the time came, she and her children would also be entitled to be interred there. That pleased the girl enormously; she had a simple religious faith and was delighted that Douglas was buried in Paris so that she could take flowers to his resting place, and the children would grow up knowing about their father.

It made Monica weep at the service because she realised that Clothilde had loved Douglas more dearly than she ever had and her heart went out to the bereaved girl. However, she had her children and would soon give birth to another one. Monica had already made provision for her to go to a private nursing home for the confinement when the time came, and for the children to be looked after by Clothilde's parents and sisters.

It had taken some time for the shock to register with Monica as there had been so much to do, so many people to contact and business to negotiate, but finally, all was in the process of being settled and she was free to go home again.

Her friends were concerned about her, but as usual, she coped and made preparations for a memorial service at St Margaret's, Westminster. She was supported by Marcus and Patrick; Daniel, Sally, Guy, Jane Partington, Ranu Gupta and his girlfriend Emma Simson, as well as Conrad Beight and his wife and daughter, and many other friends and acquaintances. Members of the diplomatic corps and officials of the Foreign Office, as well as members of the House of Lords, MPs from both sides of the house and government ministers, led by the Prime Minister, did Douglas proud, and everybody said how delighted he would have been with such a splendid send off.

Afterwards, Monica and her bosom friends adjourned to a private room in the Ritz for a buffet lunch. Few of them knew Douglas very well as most of his career had been spent abroad but were keen to support Monica. She had hoped to have a tête-à-tête with Sally, but there was no opportunity. However, Sally told her that she would be at West Bridge Hall for a while yet and as Monica said she was going to stay for a few days with Marcus at Milton House, his Warwickshire home, they agreed to meet there.

In the meantime, Daniel Brewster intended to stay with Monica until she went to Warwickshire. She was quite exhausted by the time she said goodbye to everyone and let herself into her apartment. If she was honest, she would have preferred to be alone, but thought it was kind of Daniel to want to look after her. Now that she was free from her marriage, she felt a sense of relief. She had enjoyed a good deal of freedom for a married woman, yet, there was always some nagging guilt at the back of her mind, as she had to admit that she was not an ideal wife for a highly placed diplomat. Of course, ambassador's wives were expected to be unpaid adjuncts to their husbands; good at entertaining and keeping up standards at the Embassy.

Well, Monica had learned to delegate and now she was free to enjoy her life unhampered by guilt. However, unusually for her, at present, she was lacking in energy and initiative, and had no idea what she wanted to do with the rest of her life as a single woman. She hoped that staying with Marcus would encourage her to pick up the reins once more and looked forward to seeing Sally again.

Daniel made a cup of tea for them both; then ran a bath for Monica. When she came out, draped in a towel, she found he had turned down the bed covers and was ready to take her into his arms. It was some time since they had made love and as Daniel embraced her, she found her lethargy slipping away. Both of them were more than ready for a romantic encounter and when Monica fell asleep, her dreams were more peaceful than they had been for some time. It was early evening when she awoke. While she slept, Daniel had produced a cold supper for them both, after which they settled down to watch television together.

Monica's concentration came and went as her thoughts kept returning to the events of the past week, and the hope that all would be well with Clothilde. Sadly, everything on TV channels seemed to be gloomy so Daniel put on a DVD of Peter Sellers in the first 'Pink Panther' film and despite Monica's low mood, she was soon laughing out loud. It was thus on a happier note that they went to bed together and slept the sleep of the just.

Next morning at breakfast, Daniel told her that he wanted to discuss their future. It was all rather soon for Monica but he said that he had waited long enough, and he proposed to her there and then. She thought of Sally and wondered how she would react to her marrying again so quickly and to a man fifteen years younger. "Please, Daniel," she begged. "Don't pressure me; I just want time to think and to work out what I want to do now."

He sighed, but said he understood her feelings and hoped it would not be too long before she could give him an answer.

After they finished eating, he went off to his studio and spent the day working on a portrait of the actress, Emma Simson, the girlfriend of Ranu Gupta. In the evening, he returned to Monica and though she found him rather grumpy, she was too caught up in her own emotions, to bother with his moodiness. They had a meal on a tray and she said that she planned to go to bed early, and thought it better if he went back home for the night. He was not at all pleased, so angrily flung out of the apartment. She was beginning to have second thoughts about Daniel and decided that she would rather not have to pander to anyone. Daniel was a delightful bed companion, but there was more to a relationship than sex.

It would evidently be wiser to keep their friendship on a professional, rather than a personal basis. He tended to be unpredictable and, at present, she wanted a quiet life. Also, because he was so much younger, she could see trouble on the horizon. No, she would have to admit to him that she was not interested in marriage, though she hoped they would remain good friends and that he would be happy to continue with the Gallery's representation of his work. There was also Sally to be considered and to see if their relationship would resume its former intimacy. Strangely enough, though Monica had no reason to think anything had happened to spoil their relationship, she picked up vibes and felt that in some subtle way, Sally had changed.

Unknown to her, Daniel was following in his teacher Sir Conrad Beight's footsteps and sometimes bedded women he painted. However, Conrad was the quintessential hetero male, who doted on women, while in Daniel's case, it seemed that he was trying to convince himself that he was macho, because he was sometimes aroused by members of his own sex. After he put down his paintbrushes for the day, he enjoyed a pleasant dinner with Emma who was feeling lonely because Ranu was in India. She was an attractive girl with a boyish figure and a vibrant personality. She was well aware that Ranu had returned to India, to give his wife a third child, which meant that she felt quite justified in seeing Daniel in his absence. She was a delightful creature, but had the typical temperament of an actress who knows that she is desirable to men and it had to be admitted that her budding career owed as much to her sexuality as to her talent. Ranu was bats about her, but he travelled a lot and realised that he could not cage her as if she were a beautiful bird. He was wise enough to know that if he wanted to keep her, he had to turn a blind eye to her occasional lapses from grace. After all, he was married and there was no way he was going to be unmarried. It was as much for the benefit of both families, as for his wife and children, that he would never countenance divorce. However, he was devoted to Emma and was prepared to indulge her every whim to keep her happy.

Monica and Daniel had enjoyed their time together over the past year or so, and despite any misgivings Daniel might have about gender issues, he appeared to please Monica. At present though, she needed to be alone to have time to think. Although Daniel professed that she was the only woman in his life, she wondered if he was the man for her. She was now a widow and a very wealthy one, who was also instrumental in bringing him to international prominence after promoting him at the Venice Biennale. She had been too occupied recently to worry about what Daniel might get up to in her absence, but even before Douglas's death she had begun to wonder about other girls in his life, notably Imogen Beight, his former teacher's daughter.

She knew that he had a lot of work on his plate, so hoped that he would not be distracted by emotional issues. Nevertheless, he had tons of youthful energy and had once confessed to her that when a painting was going well, he had a surge of sexual energy that had to find release. It was the same for Conrad Beight whose name was a by-word for promiscuity even though he was happily married to Polly, his wife of long standing. Apparently, in the nineteenth century, when the French painter, Auguste Renoir, interviewed female domestics, he told them that as well as their household duties, he would expect them to model for him, dressed or undressed. If they were willing, they were engaged, if not, they were sent on their way. In his autobiography, his son, Jean, said that even as a young boy, he was used to seeing models in the house in various stages of undress.

After having a talk with her gallery staff, Monica caught a train to Coventry, where her brother had arranged to pick her up. She didn't feel like reading so spent the journey looking out of the window, taking in the pleasant scenery as it flashed by, and reminiscing about her life and what the future might hold. Daniel was a lusty chap and they had a lot of fun in bed, but she feared the novelty was wearing off as far as she was concerned. In her youth, Monica had considered herself a Lesbian and her relationship with Sally confirmed this, but later, she began to be interested in men as well, so presumed that she was naturally bi-sexual. Daniel appeared keen to wed her but she suspected that he had not thought it through. She had turned forty so if he wanted children, he would be better off with a younger woman. Of course, older women did give birth nowadays, but she was not maternal, nor did she think that Daniel was father material.

She came from a long line of aristocrats, but Daniel was a Barnardo's Boy who had made his way in life by his undoubted talent as a painter. Of course, she had played her part in his success too but she hoped that he did not see her as a mother substitute. She would talk it over with Marcus and see what he had to say. However, she smiled to herself as she could already hear him saying, "It is your life and up to you to decide what you want, I would not presume to interfere." Nevertheless, just talking it over with someone she trusted would be helpful in making up her mind, though she feared that her doubts were already making the outcome pretty certain.

As students, she and Sally had once had a very erotic relationship but although they were still devoted friends, their sexual needs of each other had cooled considerably, largely due to circumstances. They were mature now, of course and both of them had interesting lives. Monica reflected that the leisured classes have more time and opportunity for sexual pleasures but she and Sally were fully occupied with their professional activities, so did not look for sexual satisfaction all the time.

Daniel was a passionate young man, but Monica wondered if she could keep up with him as she got older. She was very happy with her life as it was and had not been looking for change. However, with a young husband, much would have to change and although she loved having friends to stay, she was not sure that she could cope with living with someone full time. Of course, she sometimes got lonely, but who didn't? It was just one of those things, but the more she thought about living with a husband, or lover, for that matter, the less she liked the idea.

She wanted time to enjoy her single status. Even at the most intense period of their relationship, Sally had not put any pressure on Monica and that suited her. Although Sally had good friends, essentially she was a loner, enjoying her own company, reading, researching, writing and for relaxation, she would paint; all pretty solitary activities.

Sally had said nothing to Monica, but her friend couldn't help noticing that since she had met Guy, she had become less available to Monica, and now with her research based at his family home, she and Guy were naturally thrown together a good deal.

Chapter Fifteen

Marcus met his sister at the station and drove her home. Jane Partington was staying with him but had gone to do some work with Guy at the Dower House. She would be back in a couple of days though. As they sat over tea and a plate of Muffins, the siblings talked about Jane's difficult marriage. Marcus appreciated the fact that Jane had not wanted to court adverse publicity in Paris; one had to be even more careful nowadays with so much media coverage, however, it was obvious that she must not be alone with her husband again. Arnold's suspicious behaviour was causing concern in military circles, especially after he assaulted another soldier and it had become apparent to his fellow officers that his drinking problem had got out of hand. Like many alcoholics, he was crafty, lied easily and denied that he had any problem at all. He had first begun secretly drinking when he was in the sixth form at school and it had become a way of life. After so many years, it was now taking a serious toll on his health and temper, so his commanding officer insisted that he was examined by a senior psychiatric consultant. His conclusion was that Arnold's mental health was seriously jeopardised so he immediately asked for him to be sectioned and sent to a military hospital in Wales. It was a great relief to Jane to know that he was not likely to come knocking on her door again, but it didn't solve her ongoing predicament.

Before Jane returned, Monica consulted Marcus about Daniel's proposal. As she had suspected, he did not offer advice, simply let her talk which helped her to put things into perspective. She had lived alone on and off for years, and even in Paris, she and Douglas were hardly ever together.

"The trouble is, Marcus," said Monica. "It is the trivial things that can irritate when living with someone; boredom can also be destructive, though I don't think Daniel would bore me; it could be the other way around though, and he could become bored with me and seek a younger woman.

I have always suspected that he has a soft spot for Imogen Beight, whom he has known for several years through her father.

You know, thinking seriously about all this, I reckon it would be better to stay as friends and enjoy each other's company without strings. I have to admit that when I first met Daniel, I was the one who took the initiative. It began with flirting and I think he was flattered but then he became infatuated with me. I suppose, if I am honest, I have always been the huntress rather than the hunted."

Daniel admitted that he liked women so Monica had never suspected that when he painted male models in the nude, he easily became sexually aroused. He also admitted to himself that he was attracted to William Wilcox, Patrick's boyfriend, though as they were obviously devoted to each other, he couldn't imagine that he would stand a chance with William.

Marcus simply let his sister ramble on but when she appeared to have come to the end of her narration, he asked, "Do you love him?"

Monica looked nonplussed and felt rather like Prince Charles when on his engagement, he was asked if he was in love and said, "Whatever love means." Now Monica realised that Marcus was not saying, "Are you in love?" but, "Do you love him?" and her answer had to be that she wasn't sure. In fact, she wasn't sure that she had ever truly loved anyone, except Sally. It really gave her pause for thought and though Marcus had not given advice, he had led her to the conclusion that marriage to Daniel would be a disaster because though she was fond of him, she didn't love him enough to spend the rest of her life with him.

Jane came back saying that she and Guy had had a fruitful time working on the TV documentary. His book was about to go to press and now he could begin working on the script. The whole project was a complex logistical exercise and putting everything together was like a giant jigsaw, especially as it would be filmed in two countries. At least, they had now decided on the locations, and French and German TV teams were planning the filming schedule, while the location managers booked flights, trains and hotels for the various crews. As Executive Producer, all of this came under Jane's jurisdiction, but she had an experienced English team with whom she had worked before, and she trusted that the French and German teams would be equally competent.

She and Guy, sometimes, had their little differences but by and large, they agreed on most things. Like Guy, Jane had a trained eye and was intuitive, which complemented Guy's historical knowledge, and both of them had acquired technical know how over the years.

Monica was enjoying a time of rest at her brother's home, a large delightful, white stucco Georgian house with five reception rooms, ten bedrooms and five bathrooms set in an extensive park surrounded by farmland. She had never been an emotional woman; in fact, most of her success was the result of her pragmatism. Never one to cry over spilt milk, or difficulties; she adopted the Iron Duke's maxim that if things went wrong, you simply tied a knot in the rope and carried on. However, Douglas's death, and the discovery that he had, what was virtually a common law wife and children, had affected her more deeply than she would have thought. She could not blame him for deceiving her because she had never been faithful to him. Nevertheless, she would stay in touch with Clothilde, and do whatever she could for her and her little family.

Although she was a striking looking woman, she had a good measure of masculine traits within her feminine nature. She was five foot nine inches tall, slim, though with a well-shaped figure and dressed expensively in a deceptively simple, classic style. In fact, she was sophistication personified, with naturally pale blond hair, straight and cut to touch her collar. Her skin was pale and her forehead high but it was the steady gaze in her penetrating, deep blue eyes that was her most arresting feature. Her make-up was always impeccable, and she had a generous mouth with well-defined lips and good teeth. A French acquaintance once called her a fragrant woman and, indeed, her Vera Wang perfume, though subtle, was noticeable. Even now, in the country, she was as well groomed as in town; her light fawn trousers, beautifully pressed, worn with a cream silk blouse and a pale coffee coloured cardigan, thrown carelessly over her shoulders, pronounced her a woman of taste. Like all her footwear, her pale tan shoes were handmade.

It was good to see Jane again and as Marcus was occupied with his farm manager, the two women set off for a walk around the estate. It was a pleasant day, though not overly warm so they dressed appropriately and wore Wellington boots, as it had rained during the night.

They had not had the opportunity for a tête-à-tête for some time, but both had recently undergone critical changes in their lives. Monica with her bereavement, which everyone knew about, though she had kept the news about Douglas's illicit family a secret and hoped that the media would not get wind of it. Jane, of course, had suffered in silence for a long time due to her unhappy marriage. Only Marcus knew the full story. Now, with her husband sectioned and incarcerated in Wales, it was only time before the media came running.

There was an attractive summerhouse surrounded by trees in the grounds, which had electricity, so they decided to sit there for a while, as it had a very pleasant outlook towards a small lake. Jane turned on the electric fire and put the kettle on to boil, then opened a cupboard where they found coffee and a tin of biscuits, while in a small fridge there was fresh milk. Berber matting covered the floor making it warm and cosy; attractive prints hung on the walls, and Rattan furniture, with upholstered cushions in a delightful floral fabric of roses and peonies, completed the scene. Out of date magazines were strewn on the coffee table, which they thumbed through as they drank deliciously hot coffee and tucked into chocolate biscuits.

Jane thought it was a good idea for them to talk in the summerhouse. She had lately become rather paranoid and feared that Marcus's house might be bugged because she stayed there so often. Monica thought that a bit far-fetched, but unknown to both women, Arnold was being investigated, not only due to his mental condition, but because he was suspected of having extreme Right Wing views, fuelled by his sinister priest friend, who was known to belong to an outlawed Neo Nazi group in France, though he had not yet been charged with anything.

The fact is that prior to Arnold being removed to Wales, the body of a young Algerian man had been found, bound, gagged and badly beaten in the Forest of Compiègne in Northern France. It had recently been discovered that there had been infiltration of extreme Right Wing elements into the British military and it was thought that the body might have been a victim of a racial attack. However, no real evidence had come to light and this information was at present under wraps.

After a little while, Jane put down her magazine and began to talk about her husband.

For years, she had kept her own counsel, apart from confiding in Marcus, but now she felt she had a sympathetic ear in Monica and began to unleash past frustrations. "You see," she said, "from the beginning of our marriage, he was an enigma. He never spoke much about his childhood but I reckon that there were some dark events which had made him as he was.

We met through friends of my parents, when I returned from a finishing school in Switzerland. I was just eighteen and rather

110

impressed by a Guards officer who was seven years older than me and a man of the world."

"Was it his apparent maturity or his looks that attracted you?" asked Monica.

"I don't really know, though I suppose going out with such a chap would make me feel grown up. I was pretty green, you see and I just wanted to be noticed. He was tall, well built, with dark chestnut hair and had a decided air of confidence which I liked. I was rather shy and immature for my age, so I admired people who were outgoing. As he was stationed in London at the time and my parents had a house in Bentinck Street, he often took me out for meals or drives."

"Yes, I can see that being taken out by a presentable man would have been enjoyable, but did you fall in love with him?"

"No," said Jane. "I don't believe that I did; it was more a case of having someone to escort me and show me the town. I also met his fellow officers and went to various army functions, so it was a novelty for me.

At that time, I was not sure what I wanted to do in life so my busy social life saved me from having to make up my mind. I am reasonably intelligent but without any specific talent, other than having a good eye for colour. However, I wanted to work, so an introduction to a well-known interior decorator led to a job at Osborne and Little, and a part time course in decor. Later, a job in television came my way and I knew that I had found my metier.

Arnold, it appeared, did not approve of independent women; he was old fashioned, and thought that women's task was to marry and have children. Naturally, I wanted to see something of the world before I was tied to one man. However, I liked being seen out with a man in uniform and Arnold had bags of swank, but, no, I was certainly not in love with him. However, both his family and mine were keen for us to marry, and persuaded me that as the wife of a soldier, I would have lots of opportunities to travel, so when Arnold proposed, I was encouraged by my parents to accept him. They were rather materially minded, and as he had a handsome jointure as well as his Army pay and had inherited a charming house in Surrey, they considered him a good catch and warned me that I might not get a better offer so should grasp the nettle straight away. With hindsight, I realise that his parents; knowing his propensity for unruly behaviour, hoped that marriage would improve him. Of course, we knew nothing of this at the time."

"So, what happened?" asked Monica. Jane admitted that as she was an innocent young girl, she was pleased to find that he appeared gentlemanly, treating her with great respect, and never did more than hold her hand, or put his arms around her and plant a goodnight kiss on her cheek. She had received little in the way of sex education and she had always been too shy to discuss such matters with her mother or school friends, though she heard some pretty hair-raising stories from some of them. Nevertheless, she treated them as fantasies and did not take them seriously.

"Like most of our class," said Jane, "we had a fashionable society wedding and Arnold arranged for us to be married at the Guards' Chapel, after which, we set off by road for a rented cottage in Scotland, spending the first night at a hotel in Stamford in Lincolnshire.

It is difficult for me to relate what followed and apart from my parents, I have not confided in anyone else, other than a doctor and a lawyer, so please treat what I am about to tell you in strict confidence, as not even Marcus knows the full story. On arrival at the hotel, we had dinner, and chatted about the wedding and the guests, then went upstairs. I was surprised to find that the room had twin beds, hardly a bridal suite. However, I was rather relieved, never having slept with a man before. There was an en-suite bathroom and Arnold said that I could use it first. I had dreaded that he might suggest showering or bathing together, but he didn't so I locked the door, showered, and put on a pretty pale blue nightdress with matching negligee and brushed my hair out, and I suppose that without makeup, I looked even younger than my nineteen years. By the time Arnold returned from the bathroom, I was in bed, dipping into the Gideon bible I had found in the drawer of the bedside cabinet. I was not particularly interested but was filling in time and wondering what would be expected of me by my new husband."

"I suppose, it was rather daunting, as you were inexperienced," said Monica sympathetically.

"I'll say," replied Jane, "but I little knew what I was in for."

She told Monica that seeing her already in bed, Arnold said he wanted to sleep that side and seemed so set on it that, without demur, she switched to the other one. He picked up the Bible and said how pleased he was that she was religiously inclined. She had to admit that she was no such thing as she hardly ever went to church as she found it boring, though she loved church buildings and was quite happy to sit in an empty church with just her own thoughts. Arnold, on the other hand, said that church attendance was crucial to him and he was fundamentalist in his Christian beliefs.

He had never talked like this before and Jane was rather put out. Although she too had been brought up in the Christian tradition, there was a lot that she found sinister, particularly the focus on the cross, which, to her, was an instrument of torture, not something to worship. She also thought it was rampant audacity to say that God condemned his 'only begotten son' to suffer on the cross for humanity's wicked deeds.

"No," she declared, "it was men who put Jesus on the cross and making God a scapegoat was blasphemy; well, in my opinion," she countered. She also told him that she loathed medieval religious art with its sado/masochistic obsession but welcomed the Humanism of the Renaissance.

"Young as I was," she told Monica. "I was a free thinker and believed that humanity has the choice between right and wrong, and an individual is responsible for making reparation for their sins or crimes. Of course, this kind of talk is resented by the clergy, and I don't believe that any priest could take someone by the hand and lead them into Paradise. That has to be earned and even the Bible said that one had to show the light (good deeds) in their bushel. I suppose I was asking for trouble but I was only speaking what I truly felt. As for Confession, I think that is utterly futile, but I suppose it is another way of the clergy controlling the laity and though it is meant to be confidential, I think that it could be used for subtle blackmail. However, I soon realised that there was no point in getting into a theological dispute with a confirmed fundamentalist so I tried to drop the subject."

"You must have been mad to goad him," said Monica.

"Well, at that time, I did not know he would react in such a way, because we had never discussed such things before," sighed Jane.

Monica encouraged her to go on with her story and she said that Arnold, by this time, was incensed by her philosophy, and wanted to show her that he had the upper hand. Rather than gently wooing her, he picked up a hair brush on the dressing table, then threw her onto the bed face downwards, pulled up her nightdress and with the back of the brush; whacked her hard on her bare buttocks. She cried out in pain, but he put his hand over her mouth to silence her. He whacked her again, getting highly excited in the process, and the more she squirmed and tried to get away, the more he crowed with delight.

"Oh, my god, I have married a sadist," she groaned to herself and she told Monica, "He was very clever as he never gave me any indication of his real nature while we were courting and I thought gosh, what have I done? Later, I learned that the only way he could get an erection was either to be whacked himself or to whack his partner. I reckon, he chose me because I was young and docile, and he thought he could mould me to his devious ways as I wouldn't know any better. Well, I may have been ignorant, but I was not stupid."

She said that in a high state of excitement, he turned her over again and thrust himself into her, delighting that she was indeed a virgin. She sobbed uncontrollably, but it made no difference. Later, when he had calmed down, he apologised for his roughness, but said she should not have insulted his religion. She was in pain and as she was quite beyond accepting any apology, she turned out the light on her bedside table, and ignoring him, tried to get to sleep.

Arnold also turned off his light, but lay listening to Jane's gentle breathing. He knew he had hurt her but there was cruelty in his nature; there had always been, and as a boy, he had delighted in ill-treating insects and small animals who could not escape him. He knew it was wrong but could not help himself so became adept at keeping his penchant secret. At school, he was a bully, but so cunning and intimidating that he got away with it, and even became head boy. He was an enigma even to himself because he was deeply religious, but his religion was not that of a god of love but one of domination.

By the time he awoke, Jane had already made her escape as she had quietly packed her bags then climbed out of the bedroom window onto the fire escape. Fortunately, the hotel was in the main street, lined with delightful golden stone Georgian buildings that, in happier times, Jane would have been pleased to explore. However, like a fugitive, her one thought was to get as far away from Stamford as possible. She found a taxi and asked to be taken to the nearest railway or bus station. Finally, she arrived in London and took a taxi to her parents' house. However, she had forgotten that they had gone to stay with friends after the wedding reception. Thankfully, she had a key so let herself in and took a shower. There was milk in the fridge, so she made a cup of tea but did not feel like eating. She spent the rest of the day lying on a sofa, sometimes watching TV, but mostly thinking of her predicament and dozing when it all became too painful to contemplate her future.

If she expected sympathy from her parents when they returned, she was disappointed. They were appalled by her behaviour, especially as she had not left a note for Arnold. What a fool he must feel when before breakfast, he discovered that his wife was missing and found that no one had seen her.

Actually, her parents were deeply worried. Their fear for what their peers would say had momentarily overcome their concern for their only child. As Jane would not say what had happened to cause her to fly so precipitately, they could only assume that the wedding night had come as a shock to her. How on earth had she remained in ignorance when nowadays sex was so ubiquitous in books, films and in the media? However, they had not realised how sensitive Jane was, and how she had held romantic notions about love and marriage, gleaned from the novels of Jane Austen, Georgette Heyer, Daphne du Maurier and Barbara Cartland. Of course, Marion, Jane's mother, had also been influenced by them in her teens, but now she knew that they were nothing like real life, only pleasant escapism.

Finally, Marion persuaded Jane to tell her exactly what had happened and naturally, she was incensed that Arnold could have been so boorish and brutal, especially on his wedding night with an untutored girl. Jane was too embarrassed to confide in her father but Marion explained to him. He told her that Arnold was, no doubt, just being playful, but things had probably got out of hand before he realised. Although he did not say anything to Marion, he was a man of the world and knew that many men had less than noble traits when it came to matters of a sexual nature. Most of them kept such things from their wives, which is why prostitution was still such a lucrative profession. In fact, while Marion was in the last stages of pregnancy with Jane, he had enjoyed the services of a high-class call girl. Marion never knew, of course and he would have been devastated if she had ever found out. He did not believe that honesty was always the best policy; people could get hurt, so white lies did little harm and more serious things were better swept under the carpet. Jane would have been horrified to know that her father held such beliefs as she had always considered him the most honourable of men.

Poor girl; she was at a loss to know what to do, but her parents were keen that any scandal should be avoided. They rang Arnold and explained that Jane was with them. She was unwell and needed to see a doctor, so would be staying with them for the time being. They made no reference to the fact that Jane was unwell because of the beating and rape. He said he would carry on to Scotland as he was looking forward to some shooting and fishing, and Jane could join him when she was well enough. In two weeks though, he had to return to his regiment.

Jane's home was close to Harley Street, so an appointment was made with a consultant gynaecologist who saw Jane straight away. He was sworn to secrecy and assured her that everything she told him was in strict confidence. When he internally examined her, he was convinced that she had been raped. He said that if Jane wanted to press charges against her husband, he would give evidence. However, that was going too far for Jane and her parents who dreaded adverse publicity. Apart from public prurience, they could not face their friends if the truth came out.

The consultant assured Jane that with rest, her body would heal itself but said that her father needed to have a serious talk with her husband. He prescribed Rescue Remedy for the shock and pain incurred, and advised that as soon as she was healed, she should return to the work she enjoyed, and hope that her husband would behave better in future. In the meantime, Arnold would be in Scotland and if Jane did not return to him, he would go straight to his regiment so she need not see him. Without revealing the full truth behind their enquiry, her parents put the case to a lawyer friend of theirs who said that if there was evidence of domestic violence, there should be no difficulty in obtaining a divorce.

Jane dreaded ever having to see her husband again, much less be touched by him and hoped that the Army would keep him out of England for a considerable time. It was not only his blatant physical cruelty to her, but something deeper, almost psychic about the sinister nature of his persona that disturbed her and even though she was not in his physical presence, she feared his infiltration into her dreams.

Monica was absolutely open mouthed with horror as Jane recounted her terrible story. "What happened when you saw him again," she asked.

"Oh, I made sure that I would never be alone with him. Fortunately, tours of Afghanistan and Iraq soon came up which took him away for a couple of years, and when he had leave, he stayed away from us as, by that time, he had lost interest in me. However, I had caused him to lose face and no doubt, there was gossip in the mess because his bride had bolted on the wedding night. You may imagine that his vindictiveness knew no bounds. My mother thought he probably found himself a professional dominatrix and though he would have resented paying her, she would likely have given him what he wanted."

"What I don't understand," said Monica, "is why he wouldn't let you divorce him, surely you had grounds enough?"

"I know I did, especially with the doctor as witness to my injuries, but that was the problem. Arnold is a proud man, and has his military career and reputation to uphold. He did not wish to marry anyone else so why should he go through all the trials, tribulations and expense of a divorce? But even more crucially, there was always the religious aspect. No, he is nasty at the core, and wanted to make me suffer, not physically any more, but emotionally and mentally. I did manage to get a separation on the grounds of incompatibility, but he has spoilt my life as Marcus and I have not been able to marry. He is my dear friend and we love one another devotedly, so I just count my blessings. I have also been able to study and gain the qualifications I needed to have a successful career and I really love my work. I am also financially independent of Arnold and, as an only child, I inherited a fair amount of property from my parents, even after Inheritance Tax was paid. I feared that Arnold would interfere when he learned that my parents had died and I was an heiress, but as he is well provided for himself; thankfully, he did nothing to get his hands on my money."

"What do you think happened to bring about his present collapse?" asked Monica.

"Well, his Commanding Officer came to see me, so I learned things I had not known before. Apparently, he had been suffering from religious mania for some time but kept it under wraps, then about five years ago, he became friendly with a Catholic priest, Father Xavier, who had a great influence on him, to the extent that Arnold converted to Roman Catholicism. Rather than bringing him comfort though, it made him worse as he became even more fanatical. He hated everything and everybody, and attacked two of his comrades in the mess for no reason. It seems that his behaviour became so extreme that he had to be removed from duties. I have not signed the Official Secrets Act, but I was told not talk of it, so please keep it under your hat but there is more, I think, than the religious mania. The priest was recalled to the Vatican but went AWOL and there is suspicion that Arnold has been mixed up for some time because the priest is a prominent player in a Neo Nazi group, some of whose members were trying to infiltrate the Army.

Of course, scandal is to be avoided at all costs, and the Ministry of Defence is closing ranks and they have placed Arnold where, it is hoped, he can do no harm. It is ironic that such a man has climbed the greasy pole and is now a Brigadier General; however, he was fearless when he served in the Middle East and dealt successfully with a good many insurgents which brought him his promotion.

Nevertheless, he was recently assessed by an Army psychologist, who diagnosed him as seriously psychopathic. Apparently, there are many degrees of the condition, from being difficult in a family or work place, to being harsh and needing to control others. In extremis, such a condition can lead to becoming a serial killer. It is reckoned that one in two hundred people have a measure of the psychopathic syndrome. In fact, some people rise high in life, particularly in business where they are not averse to using hard elbows and we have a great many examples of psychopathic megalomaniacs in the political sphere, such as Napoleon, Hitler and Stalin to name a few, as well as some contemporary ones across the world.

From other things the officer said, I suspect that Arnold has always had gender issues. I have often wondered if he was concealing latent homosexuality and really despised women so wanted to hurt them. I know there are many gay men who like women and particularly enjoy having older women as friends. By the way, did you know that Patrick and William are contemplating getting married when Patrick leaves the Army?"

"Yes, I had heard a whisper," said Monica, "but how does Marcus feel about that?"

"He doesn't object to gay marriage but in Patrick's case, it makes complications. He is Marcus's heir to a vast portfolio, and unless Marcus re-marries and produces another son, the blood line will die out."

"Oh, Jane, if only you were free to marry, I am sure Marcus would snap you up and you are not too old to have a child. Surely, now your husband has been committed, a divorce could be forthcoming."

"No, it isn't as simple as that because even a mentally ill patient has rights and in Arnold's case, the Pope is the stranglehold. As far as he is concerned, the Pope is God on Earth and is infallible."

"That shows he's round the bend," cried Monica, "but then most religions have a tendency to drive people insane, if taken to extremes. We see examples of it in the media every day. Oh, well, philosophy over: I suppose it is time to think about lunch. I wonder what Mrs Mackintosh is cooking up for us today. I must say, Marcus is very lucky to have such a superb cook on his staff; however, I expect he pays her well which is why she stays."

Chapter Sixteen

Although there was no easy solution to Jane and Marcus's difficulty, Jane felt better for her confidential chat with Monica, although there was nothing she could do to change Jane's situation. However, as Jane said, just having a sympathetic ear was comforting.

Marcus invited a few local neighbours to dinner before Monica left for London and Jane for the Continent. Guy and Sally even took an evening off from their labours to join them.

Patrick, Marcus's son and his friend William came to stay for a couple of nights, and Patrick took Jane aside at one point and talked to her about Arnold. Patrick seemed well informed regarding her wretched husband's incarceration and said that more alarming than Arnold's violence, was his possible connection with the Neo Nazi group. He knew that Jane would shortly be leaving for filming in Paris and Germany, and said that she had to be careful as, in her position, it could be difficult to know whom to trust. She could not understand why anyone would want to harm her but Patrick said terrorists were not predictable. The group must be furious that Arnold had been removed and feared that in his delirium, he would reveal illicit information.

Jane went back to France where Guy and the camera team joined her along with others from the French team. They began filming very early each morning and by the evening, most of the team were too tired to go on the town: instead, they had a meal in their hotel and, for the most part, chatted about the day's work. Guy often sat next to Sylvia, and realised that he was enjoying her company more and more. It was not anything specific about her; she was just a very lovely companion, with whom he felt happy.

While in Paris, Jane was asked to go to the Embassy. Due to Douglas's death, a new ambassador had been appointed, Sir Peter Layton. He met Jane and took her into his office where two men were waiting. They had come to question her about Arnold. However, as she told them, she left him right at the start of their marriage and had done her best to avoid him ever since, so she had no idea what he had been up to over the years. She was aware that he had done well in his career, had shown bravery in his service in the Middle East and been promoted several times but that was in the public domain.

"What are his political allegiances?" asked the tall, bald man, who Jane assumed to be Special Branch.

"I had no idea he has any political interests," returned Jane.

"Well, what do you think makes him tick?" he asked.

"As far as I am aware, it is his religion which is the main spring of his life, apart from the Army."

"What do you know about Father Xavier?"

"Sorry, I don't know to whom you refer."

"Oh I think you do," replied her interrogator.

"No truly, he probably has a great many Catholic acquaintances, but you must accept that I have never met any of them. I abhor fanaticism and since converting, my husband, as far as I am aware, has become very unbalanced."

Her interrogator went on, while the other man watched her closely. "It is most unusual for a bride to leave her husband on the night of the wedding so why did you run away?"

"He was violent towards me and I would not stand for it," answered Jane. "Do you blame me?"

"I am not here to apportion blame," responded the questioner. "I simply want to assess the state of your husband's mind and what political associations he may or may not have."

"Well," said Jane. "I am afraid I am unable to help you because I simply don't know."

The man was not going to easily give up and went on: "Did you ever get the impression that your husband is racist?"

"No, not specially; he didn't resent people of different races: he simply didn't appear to like humanity very much."

"Thank you, Mrs Partington. You have been very helpful, but we may need to talk to you again."

"I shall shortly be leaving for Berlin as my TV team is wrapping up our filming here in a day or so," stated Jane.

"Well, please let us know where you will be, though if we need you, it will be best if we arrange for you to meet someone at the British Embassy there."

"You have my mobile number, I presume?" said Jane. "So you can reach me any time."

With that, Jane was free to go. The ambassador asked if she would like to stay to lunch but she said that she had to get back to work as time was of the essence.

As it happened, filming took longer than expected as the setting was not only the Palace of Versailles itself, which related to the life of Mme de Pompadour, but also the Petit Trianon, the little theatre there and the Hameau, the model farm where Marie Antoinette played at being a milkmaid. Thus by the time they had finished, half of the documentary was in the can, so they packed up and travelled by air to Berlin where they met the next TV crew.

This time, their hotel was near the Olympic Stadium, and they filmed in Unter den Linden and the Tier Garten, as well as the palace of Charlottenburg, for local colour. After that, they transferred to a hotel in Potsdam, a few miles from the city. Filming at the Neues Palast did not take as long as expected but the really enjoyable part was filming at Frederick the Great's jewel of a palace known as Sans Souci, which translated to 'without care'.

From there, they moved on to Bayreuth in Bavaria; a small town made famous by Richard Wagner who, in the nineteenth century, built his Festspielhaus there to perform his own unique operas in his own unique way. It has become a place of pilgrimage to serious music lovers, but the season was over so the team did not have an opportunity to see a performance in that operatic shrine.

However, they had come for another type of theatre, the one in the Margrave's Palace, where Wilhelmina lived after her marriage. The theatre is a baroque gem; horseshoe shaped, constructed in wood, extravagantly carved and highly gilded and retains its original 18th century machinery, and the team had great fun trying out the special effects available before the days of modern technology. It was amazing though, how effective the primitive methods were and what extraordinary scenes could be set up, such as rolling waves, characters springing up from trap doors in the stage and chariots flying in from above, bearing classical gods, covered in gold paint. In addition, the acoustics were excellent and could teach many a modern architect a thing or two.

The palace is set in its own large grounds which are now a public park and the team enjoyed relaxing outside the building whenever they had a short break. Though autumn, the weather was quite warm and dry, which helped them get the filming into the can on schedule.

Last of all, they travelled to Munich where they settled into the same hotel on the Stachus where they had previously stayed and set off for Nymphenburg next day. Guy asked the team to film the picturesque garden pavilions while they were there because although they were not built until after Henriette Adelaide's death, it would be useful to have them on file. Only the central block of the palace related to Adelaide, as the rest of the building was constructed by her descendants. She was only forty when she died but her achievements were significant, and boosted the architectural, artistic and musical reputation of the House of Wittelsbach, splendidly influencing many other royal houses across Europe.

The final filming was in Munich itself, at the Residenz where she lived when in town and the ochre coloured Theatiner Kirche which she founded on the birth of her son, the next Elector, Max Emanuel; thus with the filming in the can, it only remained for editing in London and some post synch recording at Pinewood.

Although Guy had enjoyed himself enormously, it had been strenuous work so he was quite relieved when he returned home to spend a night in his own bed. Sylvia was his PA while he was at Pinewood, and he met her and the soundman, Joe, at the studios. There was a blockbuster movie being filmed on the big sound stage, so after Guy had done his voice overs, he and Sylvia took a look at a part of the business they knew little about. It was a revelation, but Guy was quite happy with his own chosen career, where he had freedom to work in the way he preferred.

Chapter Seventeen

Monica now resumed her relationship with Sally, inviting her to stay at her apartment whenever Sally was in London. She had her own flat, of course, but Monica's apartment was larger. She enjoyed staying at West Bridge Hall but now had photocopies of the original documents she was working on, so was able to come back to London in order to resume her lectureship. She had cut down her hours at the Courtauld so that she could follow her own line of research, but even so, she needed to devote some time to her students.

While staying at the Hall, she had experienced some amazingly lucid dreams, as if she was tuning into a by-gone age of which she was a part. She was aware of being a girl during the Civil War and knew that she was in love with a young Cavalier. It came as a shock though when in a dream, she met him face to face and looking into his eyes, knew that he was Guy. Well, Guy in another guise of course, but undoubtedly Guy and the uncanny experience reminded her that it was said that the eyes reflect the soul.

The young man was shorter than Guy and fairer, but his whole persona cried out that he was the man who had become Guy in the present. Apparently, he, Jeremy, as he was in the 17th century, and Hannah, the girl from the Hall, had been meeting secretly which is what made her father incandescent with rage and caused him to lash out at her. Her father's wilful lies ruined her posthumous reputation and she was buried in un-consecrated ground, which was shocking at a time of strong religious belief. Nevertheless, her mother's prayers had helped her to find the light and when Jeremy was killed in battle, their souls drifted towards each other. Now it appeared that they had returned to the physical world and to the same place in the 21st century where they had been in the 17th. Of course, she doubted that Guy was aware, although his subconscious mind must have sensed something extraordinary when Sally first appeared at the Dower House and he made love to her.

She had always wondered why Guy had seduced her without any preliminaries, or why she had allowed him to act in such a bold way. Later, she had been too embarrassed to speak about it, but since she had come to know him, she realised that he was not a womaniser at all; in fact, he treated women with great respect. However, she now believed that their subconscious minds had brought them to consummation over four hundred years after they had been denied marriage by her tyrant of a father and their untimely deaths.

Few people in western countries have knowledge of the realities of reincarnation so Sally was doubtful whether she would ever be able to tell Guy about one of their past lives. She wondered why this life in particular had come so strongly to the fore, but suspected that a deep groove had been formed in the memory, due to the intensity through which they lived, when friend became foe and danger stalked the land.

During her sleep states, Sally had the impression that she was learning things that she had never known before. She realised that because their love for each other was genuinely devoted, they had earned a reward which was now to be repaid centuries later. After all, she thought, the law of reincarnation is also called the law of compensation. It works both ways though and our evil deeds need to be expunged because the saying 'an eye for an eye' is true, but not in the way commonly accepted. We may think we get away with things but everything is recorded in our energy field and if we harm another, we automatically harm ourselves. Even our thoughts need to be monitored so that we do not send out grudges against anyone else.

She had come to understand that our actions are like pebbles in a pool and what we send out eventually returns to us for good or ill in this life, or future ones. Thus we reap what we sow, but there is no looming figure punishing us, we are judge and jury, and after death, if we have developed a conscience, we judge ourselves harshly and want to make amends. Conversely, when we have brought light to the planet through our good deeds, we are rewarded with what we call luck.

Monica told Sally that she was planning a new exhibition for Conrad Beight, but felt that she needed some respite so had asked him if he would like to accompany her to a gallery in the Cotswolds to see the work of Miranda Pointer, a young artist who exhibited there. Monica had seen some of her work on the Internet and asked Conrad to take a look. She trusted his judgement and as both thought it was worth seeing her original paintings in situ, they agreed to have a day out.

The trees presented finger like black branches entwined against a clear autumn sky, weaving a miraculous tracery. As the car sped along an almost deserted road, weak, filtering sunlight dappled the remaining leaves, now shrivelled and discoloured. When they arrived at Bourton-on-the-Water, they were quite chilled so decided to have a coffee before going to the gallery. The warm, cosy cafe and the piping hot coffee revived them, and Monica couldn't resist a visit to the model village in the centre of the town. It was amazingly realistic and full of detail, though in miniature, and made them feel like Gulliver in Lilliput.

It was only a short distance to the gallery and it did not take them long to sum up the talent of the young artist. Undoubtedly, her work had something special and Monica was sure that it would be commercial. She asked an assistant if Ms Pointer had a studio nearby and was told that it was just around the corner. Monica rang the number she was given, introduced herself and Conrad, and asked if they could visit her to see her work in progress. Miranda couldn't believe her luck. To have such eminent people seeking her out was too good to be true. She had to pinch herself to make sure she wasn't dreaming but realised she only had time to comb her hair and remove splodges of paint from her face before they would be at the door.

They told her that they had seen some of her work at the gallery and it was obvious that it met with their approval because Monica said she would like to represent her. Miranda, like most artists, was ambitious, and even today with the Internet and many media outlets, a London Gallery has kudos. Miranda was grateful to her local gallery, but knew that she would have to move on. Monica suggested that she should come up to London, and they would discuss a contract and terms.

Conrad, being Conrad, though interested in the paintings, was also very taken with the artist. She was twenty-five years old, petite, with short fair hair and a cheeky grin that set his heart racing. He mentally stripped her and thought how much he would like to paint her. Monica also thought the girl attractive, but business was uppermost in her mind. From time to time, she got rather irritated with Conrad because it appeared that he could not see a young woman without wanting to mentally ravish her.

They took Miranda out to tea at a local cafe where she was obviously well known and after they left, her acquaintances wanted to know who they were. Their sophistication stood out in such an informal setting and everyone was curious. She simply said that they were from London because they wanted to see her paintings; though she was wise enough not to tell them anything about possible representation in the capital. First of all, she had to make sure that Monica's offer was serious and then talk to the owner of her gallery because she assumed that Monica would want sole representation of her work.

Conrad was a great admirer of Matisse, and gained inspiration from his paintings and sketches of odalisques and concubines, and this led him to paint his daughter, Imogen, as an odalisque in the style of the French artist. He also knew the 19th century Indian painting, owned by Ranu Gupta, of the favourite of a maharaja. It was very beautiful, though the girl was practically naked, except for a quantity of jewellery. Conrad took this as the model for his painting of Imogen which was just as explicit and would certainly be a source of interest, if not prurience, when it was displayed at his next solo exhibition at the Gayton Gallery.

Despite his Bohemian lifestyle, Conrad had been very prolific during the past year and had produced many paintings for the Gayton exhibition. However, the picture of Imogen was the jewel of the collection. The usual suspects were invited to the private view, including Sally, Guy, Marcus, Daniel, Ranu, Emma, Jane, Tom, Ginny and Sylvia, who were all suitably impressed.

The show proved to be a critical success as well as a commercial one, not always the same thing and before the evening was over, a quantity of red dots appeared on the paintings. Ranu reserved the picture of Imogen as a companion piece to his Indian painting, the light and the dark, as it were. The next day, there was a good deal of publicity in the tabloids as well as the broadsheets and some of them daringly had a photo of the exotic painting of Imogen on the front page. The articles were full of innuendo and snide remarks regarding Conrad's relationship with his daughter, though each newspaper stopped short of libel. As one of them regularly portrayed topless girls, it was hypocritical to make insinuating remarks about the model in a work of art.

Conrad laughed it off, but it rankled; after all, he was not the first artist to paint his daughter in a state of undress, or downright nudity. However, he felt for Imogen, as it must have been hurtful for her to have her relationship with her father questioned so bluntly.

Polly, her mother, was totally unfazed by the publicity and told them to laugh all the way to the bank.

Although Conrad appeared undaunted, it obviously played on his subconscious mind because he began to have disturbing dreams involving Imogen. In one, he was a powerful man in a market, inspecting a naked girl who seemed to be Imogen. A few nights later, he was a Pasha making love to the same girl and in the third dream, he saw her as head concubine in his harem.

He did not often recall his dreams so was surprised that he remembered all three of his current dreams so clearly. However, he tried to put them out of his mind as he had a lot to think about. His sales were hitting the roof and it certainly looked as if the exhibition would be completely sold out by the end of the week.

Imogen was teased by her colleagues at Sotheby's, but in a kindly way. She had certainly become rather famous (or infamous) overnight due to the publicity the painting was receiving. She was invited to take part in Loose Women on TV and talk about her Bohemian childhood, but she declined the offer, preferring to keep her private life private. Conrad also refused offers of interviews and articles but in a way this backfired as it made people more curious about him and his daughter, rather than less.

Monica was all for publicity, good or bad, as sales always rocketed, particularly in the case of controversy. However, things were going so well that she did not urge Conrad or Imogen to change their minds about appearing in public. Let other people have their say on media outlets and arts pundits plough their furrow. Of course, in today's climate, the illusiveness of Conrad and particularly Imogen, made the clamour for interviews even louder and there was a lot of comment on social media, none of which the pair saw as they had never bothered with such sites.

One evening, Monica told Sally about Conrad's dreams and asked her what she made of them. Sally admitted that she was no expert, though she found dreams of interest and suggested that Conrad, if he was serious, should consult a Jungian analyst. She told Monica that she had recently become a member of the College of Psychic Studies in South Kensington because she wanted to use their esoteric library. Her recent research had led her to the fringes of parapsychology and she wanted to learn more.

In fact, she intended to go to the weekly lecture on Tuesday evening which happened to be about past lives.

"I know some people believe in them," said Monica, "but I have never been sure myself. If that is true, why don't we remember them?"

"I don't know," admitted Sally, "but I am willing to find out."

Soon afterwards, Conrad told Monica that he had consulted a Jungian expert but it didn't ring any bells with him so he was back to square one. Monica said that Sally was planning to go to a lecture on past lives and thought that might interest him. He rang Sally and, they agreed to meet at the College prior to the lecture and have a snack there. Sally said the lectures were always oversubscribed so it would be good to get there early, in order to bag seats.

Conrad wondered what a Psychic College would be like. He had never had any desire to explore the paranormal, but whenever he saw anything of that nature on TV, it was always portrayed as spooky and frightening. However, arriving at Queen's Gate, South Kensington, he found a large nineteenth century cream stucco house on several floors, with an imposing porch. He pushed open the heavy front door and found himself in a narrow hall with a staircase, and on the left, the reception area which consisted of a large room which also served as a library. Sally had just signed in for them both, and suggested that they go upstairs to the lecture hall and nab a couple of seats, then have a drink and sandwiches while they waited for the lecture to begin. They could look at the library afterwards if they wished, and Sally said there would also be new and second hand books on sale which might prove interesting.

Upstairs, the room was already filling up and there was a little queue at the cubicle selling snacks. Conrad settled for a baguette filled with ham and cheese, and a soft drink, and Sally, who was trying to become a vegetarian, selected a wrap filled with salad and a coffee.

They sat in a row halfway back, and did their best to juggle their food and drinks. Conrad said he was surprised to find the place so normal.

"I know what you mean," said Sally. "I was rather nervous the first time I came but it is just like any other academic establishment."

"Why did you first come here?" asked Conrad.

"I met a clairvoyant by chance and the things she told me had no rational explanation, so I asked a friend who was interested in esoteric matters, if he could suggest someone eminent in this field for me to consult. The clairvoyant was quite young and not at all well known, so I wanted confirmation by a noted expert. Anyway, my friend told me to come here and see one of their lecturers. What came up was astonishing and did indeed confirm what I had earlier been told, though the medium, Ivy Northage, knew absolutely nothing about me and I was determined not to give her any clues. It was beyond reality so I was very curious to discover what it was all about. Christine and Mrs Northage were totally unknown to each other so there was no collusion.

Anyway, the thing is that I discovered this place and began to use the library. I was staggered that so much had been written on esoteric subjects over centuries, particularly about healing and life after death."

"When was the place founded?" asked Conrad.

"I think it was in 1884 and established by the scientist, Sir Oliver Lodge, the novelist Sir Arthur Conan Doyle and Frederick Myers, among others. In fact, there is quite a scientific theme at root, and many people of good reputation have been members and lectured here over the years. In the 1980s, the novelist, Rosamund Lehmann was a Vice President and some of the people who founded Runnings Park near Malvern, have also been associated with the college.

I discovered that lectures on various esoteric subjects are held every Tuesday, so I come along whenever I am free. I have certainly learned a good deal in the short time I have been a member. Of course, there are weekend workshops and various courses during the week so it is a very active place."

Having finished their snack, they did not have to wait long for the lecture to start because soon, the Principal came in with a tall man of about fifty and introduced him as Thomas Mellor, who was making a study of reincarnation, or the law of compensation, as it is also known.

Mellor began by remarking that people often dismiss the notion of past lives because they do not remember them. However, he said that everyone remembers to a certain extent though it is not usually recognised as far memory. He advised his audience to think about places that meant a lot to them, people they had met and taken to immediately or otherwise, without knowing anything about them. He told them to consider how they are affected by intuitive likes, dislikes, talents and obscure feelings, because it is the soul that holds memories and meditation opens channels into other lives. However, he warned that exploration should not be taken lightly because one needs courage to look into the Akashic record (a memory bank) as it is not all lovely. In fact, mankind's history is full of conflicts, as well as beautiful aspects.

He explained that as we experience thousands of lifetimes, in different guises and different time scales, we sometimes change sex, and we certainly experience lots of different countries and creeds, which makes racism foolish as we are born into many different countries, although for various reasons, we may experience several lives in one country because we may need more time to assimilate.

He said it is interesting that there is now a lot of talk about people being dissatisfied with their present gender and it may well be that the soul is awakening to past memories but because reincarnation is not generally part of the Western psyche, this is misunderstood.

Mellor maintained that we belong to spiritual groups and come back, and are recycled with members of the group many times but always in different personalities. He likened it to being an actor in a repertory company who dons a costume and plays a part then lays it aside after the performance, and goes home as himself, the actor, not the part. Another time, he or she will play a different part, but maybe with the same actors, though they too will be in other guises according to the play. He said that every individual is different and there is no compunction to come back until we are ready. In fact, some people come back too soon, so bring unfinished business with them that may go badly, if they haven't grown wiser in the period away from the Earth.

He maintained that the Earth, which is a recycling plant, is also a school and we are all in different classes, some in the kindergarten; others in intermediate classes and a few in the university, as it were. In fact, we are here to learn balance and to grow conscience, which is not something we already have but which is created by our choices. When we learn our lessons well, we become harmless and generate light which benefits the planet. Like Parsifal, we begin as the holy fool then move on until we eventually reach a stage of wisdom. At first, we are pure thought but ignorant of worldly experience; so we come to Earth and make all kinds of mistakes, and turn into the Prodigal son (or daughter). However, we are given chance after chance and no one judges us except ourselves. However, everything that we have created, good or ill, has to be accounted for which is why we need lifetime after lifetime to make reparation. When we leave this planet, we see and feel all we have created in our immediate past life. Often, we are shocked because it has diverted from the original plan, but we have time in the spheres to adjust then wise ones, or Lords of Karma, help us plan a new blue print for our next excursion to Earth. However, little is preordained, as our choices will alter the plan for better or worse. The main thing is that we learn to be the best that we can be.

At the end of the lecture, Mellor took questions, but Sally and Conrad were still attempting to take on board all he had said so did not venture a question. However, he told his audience that he would be holding a workshop on Saturday and if anyone was interested, they could put their names down now.

"What do you think?" asked Conrad. "Is it worth a shot?"

"Do you know, I think it might be," said Sally. "I would certainly like to explore further." So saying, they joined the queue, paid the fee and looked forward to the weekend.

Each was deep in thought as they walked the short distance to the Underground station; next to it was a coffee bar and as it was only just after nine pm, Conrad suggested they should go in. Sally was agreeable, so they found a table and he fetched two coffees. They passed a few comments about the lecture, but soon, Conrad was back to being Conrad again, teasing Sally and asking her why she had never fallen for him.

"Oh, I don't know," said Sally. "Probably too much competition and my elbows are not spiky enough."

"Do you have a chap you keep hidden?" he asked, grinning like a schoolboy.

"Wouldn't you like to know?" grinned Sally in return.

"Yes, I would, I am endlessly curious about people and how they tick."

"Perhaps, you should have been a writer rather than a painter," remarked Sally.

"Well, I may be yet because I think my memoirs might be worth a punt."

"Oh, I think they would have to be seriously censored," laughed Sally, then she realised she had trodden on a corn. Of course, Conrad was worried about the dreams he had been having about his daughter. She quickly changed the subject, drained her coffee cup and said she had to make tracks. They went their separate ways, but agreed to meet at 9.30 am on Saturday.

In the meantime, Jane, who was staying with Marcus in Warwickshire, learned that her estranged husband, Arnold, had suffered a seizure at the hospital in North Wales and died. She was given so few details that, at first, she wondered if there had been foul play. However, she later learned that after he viciously attacked an orderly, his heart gave way and he died. She couldn't pretend to grieve as she was truly relieved to be free of him at last and she was not going to stir coals by asking questions; much better to let sleeping dogs lie. After all, she was aware that he was being investigated by Spooks, so discretion would be the better part of valour.

She later discovered that the alleged faction was not only a political organisation but had a sexual connotation involving sado/masochism. Arnold's activities had caused embarrassment in military circles and the Army authorities were doing their best to cover his tracks. There had to be an inquest as his death was sudden, but, as expected, the Coroner declared that he had died from natural causes.

Of course, Marcus was overjoyed that Arnold was no longer a barrier to their happiness and proposed to Jane straight away. She said she would marry him as soon as a decent interval had elapsed but Marcus said, "Blow that," as he had waited long enough. Jane admitted that she did not want a fussy white wedding but would be very happy to get married at Caxton Hall in London. Neither she nor Marcus happened to be religious; though for form's sake, they wondered if they should get married in church. However, it would take longer to arrange, and they simply wanted to live together as man and wife as soon as possible. Marcus had already told Jane how much he wanted children and she agreed that the time was right, so both hoped that all would take its natural course.

As for Arnold, neither Jane nor any of her friends mourned him. His family arranged a quiet funeral and naturally, there were obituaries in the broadsheets, praising his military service, but his violent, disturbed mental state, was understandably glossed over. It was merely said that he had died after a short illness.

Chapter Eighteen

Conrad and Sally met as planned at the College of Psychic Studies on Saturday at 9.30 am. Coffee and biscuits were provided, and people introduced themselves, then the workshop leader, Thomas Mellor, outlined the plan for the day. First of all, they were put into a relaxed, meditative state then taken on an inner journey where they found themselves in a library. On a shelf was a book marked 'My last life'; they were told to mentally take it off the shelf and in deep meditation, allow a series of memories of that life to unfold. After this, Thomas asked them to fill in a form about their inner experience, before they spoke to anyone as he did not want the conscious mind to interfere. There was then a break for everyone to have a warm drink and walk around for some exercise.

Next, they were told that they would experience a life of substance and were taken on an inner journey through a forest to experience that life. After they were brought out of meditation, there was another form to fill in. The next meditation session led to a life of achievement and when they returned to full consciousness, they completed the final form.

Rather than treat the whole thing as mysterious, Thomas believed that all the information that arose could be used as in any scientific enquiry. He also wanted to collate how many people felt they had been the same sex in each life, if they had changed, or if they were a different gender in their present life. He said that, at present, it would seem that there were more questions than answers as they were on an uncharted path, but he now allowed them to compare notes; some people had had lucid experiences, while others had had little in the way of visualisation: others had felt that they were making it up, still more were utterly amazed at what they had experienced. It was indeed inexplicable because some things had come up so spontaneously that there would not have been time to make them up or for them to be figments of the imagination.

Thomas made photo copies of their reports so that they could keep them and check with them over a period to see if what they had experienced was evidential. With the advent of the Internet, it was easy to research even the most outlandish matters so it would give them a grounding to continue to explore far memory.

Sally found a different personality in each life, one of which showed up as Hannah the girl from West Bridge Hall in the 17th century. Her life of substance was as a spoiled, wealthy man, while the life of achievement was that of a healer in the Far East many centuries ago.

Conrad's experiences were not as clear-cut as Sally's though he felt that he had experienced a life where he had been a Pasha and Imogen had been his favourite concubine. When she died young, he suffered tremendous grief. However, here she was in the here and now, perfectly healthy and strong, though this time, she had come as his beloved daughter; the former love link having brought them together again.

He was not at all sure about the other two lives as they were rather hazy, though he sensed that he had had to learn to exercise power wisely in the second one, as well as overcome extreme poverty in the last life. However, he felt that the sessions had been a form of therapy.

Little though Conrad knew it, he would soon feel that he was really in need of therapy, as he was in for the shock of his present life, as his wife, Polly, was about to drop a bombshell. She had taken a sabbatical from teaching and for the past six months, had been studying painting in Rome. Here she had met and been bowled over by Count Emilio de Gonzarano, a famous couturier. She had always maintained that Conrad was the love of her life, even though she enjoyed petty dalliances. She was a sexual creature who liked variety but, so far, she had not actually fallen in love with any of the men who pleasured her.

Although she had been married to Conrad for a considerable time, amazingly, she had now fallen in love with Emilio and said that she wanted to spend the rest of her life with him. In his way, he was as magnetic as Conrad and certainly more eccentric. Like Polly, 'love' had hit him hard and he asked her to marry him. He had never been married before but now thought that it was something he should try. His friends had always assumed that he was bi-sexual, but apparently, at present, his heterosexual aspect was in the ascendant.

His main business was in Milan where he had a splendid apartment, but he also had a branch in Rome. In Venice, he owned a splendid Palazzo and was in the process of opening a new branch of his fashion house in Vienna. His family was one of the oldest in

Italy, and had retained their wealth through good times and bad. However, when Emilio informed his family that he wanted to marry an English woman who was not yet divorced, they were horrified. Of course, they thought he was crazy and hoped he would soon come to his senses.

This 'English woman' who was not a Catholic nor even free to marry him, was a joke to them, and they wondered why he could not simply take her as his mistress and then cast her off when he tired of her. He was forty-five years old and the family had waited a long time for him to settle down. He could have his pick of eligible young Italian women, but trust him to be awkward. Their Catholic faith was of long standing and even if Polly obtained a divorce, it still put her beyond the Pale as far as they were concerned. It was also a case of marry in haste, repent at leisure and the family hoped that the affair would soon die a natural death.

The first thing Conrad knew of all this was when Polly rushed home and asked him to divorce her so that she could marry Emilio. At first, Conrad thought she was teasing him but soon realised that she was very serious. He had always believed that his marriage was indestructible because however he behaved, Polly accepted it and anyway, she gave as good as she got as she was never slow to take a lover if she felt like it. Conrad had accepted her, warts and all, and was grateful that he could live the life of a bachelor while being happily married. No more though, Polly wanted a change. She had been married to Conrad and living in England for many years, and now she was ready for a new husband and a new country.

Imogen thought that her mother must be having a mid-life crisis or that she had finally 'flipped her lid'. She was devoted to her father and couldn't imagine life without him so was mystified by her mother's attitude. She was also becoming fond of Daniel Brewster, though she believed that, at present, he was having an affair with Monica, but, at least, she had his friendship which she truly appreciated.

So far, Conrad had sailed through life as if without a care in the world thus Polly's appeal for a divorce had knocked him sideways. For her to actually want to marry someone else and go to live in another country, was beyond his comprehension and he began to suffer bouts of depression.

While Polly was in Italy, he and Sylvia Delavere had occasionally met at her tiny flat in Earl's Court, and he found her an entertaining companion as well as being eminently beddable. At the same time, Guy was also attracted to Sylvia but when Sally came over to dinner one night at the Dower House, she plucked up courage, and told him about her dreams and the workshop at the College of Psychic Studies where she believed she had found inner evidence that they had once been engaged, though they were not allowed to marry and had both died young. She did not want him to think that she was crazy and though he did not laugh at her, she suspected that he was somewhat sceptical.

He knew now that Monica and Sally were lovers of long standing, so he was not at all sure how to respond to Sally, even when he suspected that she was not averse to him. He happened to say how attractive he found Sylvia and how well they got on while working together. He also told Sally how much he valued her friendship and hoped that she would always be in his life. Despite this, she was rather taken by surprise as she had never considered Sylvia and Guy as a possible item, though now she began to wonder if he was falling for her. Of course, she could be wrong, but Guy was not a chap to boast of his conquests. He met many attractive women in the course of his TV work, so who knew what might be going on in the background? Sally had always believed that she was immune to jealousy, but she actually felt a pang at the idea of him loving someone other than herself. Could it be that she was carrying a torch for him? "Well, stranger things have happened," she admitted, then mentally tossed her head and began to eat her dinner.

It was out of character for Sally to be petty or unkind, but she could not help a dig as she feared that Guy was falling for Sylvia, with whom he had been closely working for a while and whom, she learned, he had taken to the opera. In fact, she had wondered if they had slept together while they were abroad as she was aware that such things happen to even the most respectable people when on tour. In fact, there is a well-known saying in the theatre, 'what happens on tour, stays on tour'. She need not have worried though, as nothing of that nature had taken place while they were away.

Though she felt mean as she said it, she blurted out, "Did you know that Sylvia is sleeping with Conrad? He is usually quite cavalier about his dalliances so I think this one must be more serious as he has not paraded it."

Her outburst took Guy by surprise as it was distinctly out of character, though she seemed to know more than he did and so it was, because shortly before she left the Hall, she had received a phone call from Monica telling her the latest rumour.

Apparently, Polly wanted out and was ready to ditch Conrad for some noble Italian playboy. Sally passed the news on to Guy and added with a slight sneer, "Well, if he gets a divorce, he can marry Sylvia, if that is what he wants."

Guy was startled at Sally's response to this latest bit of gossip because he had never known her to indulge in tittle-tattle and her relish of schaden freude shocked him. As far as she knew, he might be deeply in love with Sylvia, but the fact that he wasn't, didn't change his resentment. However, he had said too much and regretted it. He told Sally he hoped Conrad would soon sort out his life then began to talk about his work, saying, "I need to keep my nose to the grindstone at present, as we have a date scheduled for transmission on BBC Four in the spring and now is the time to make sure it is as good as we can make it. Jane Partington and Sylvia are working in an editing suite in Soho, and I pop in from time to time. Jane is amazing; she has been through such trauma, yet, she is a consummate professional and has not allowed her emotions to intrude on her work. She has not been looking too well lately so I hope she can soon begin to take things more easily."

Had he known it, the nausea Jane had recently been experiencing had nothing to do with work but had a much happier source. Although she and Marcus had not consciously been trying for a baby, when news of Arnold's death reached them, they both relaxed and made love whenever they were together. Marcus had to pop up to his Scottish estates to supervise the arrangements for the refurbishment of Drumlomond Castle during the months it was closed to the public, but he did not have to stay long as everything was well in hand.

When he returned to Warwickshire, Jane was still working with the editor in Soho. Her breasts had become even more sensitive than usual so she thought she was due for a late period. She had never been entirely regular but with the nausea, she felt it time to buy a pregnancy kit. It proved positive so she booked an appointment with her Harley Street doctor who confirmed that she was certainly pregnant. Marcus had already proposed to her but they had not yet got around to fixing a date for the wedding. He felt that, perhaps, they should push the boat out but Jane did not want any fuss, it was enough to be safely married to the lover who had waited long and patiently for her.

She was so happy that she felt doubly sorry for Conrad and his family who were not enjoying life at the moment. Marcus was over the moon at her news, and said they should get married as soon as possible and not trouble if people thought it was too soon after Arnold's death. As far as their friends were concerned though, they had long known the truth about Jane's unhappy marriage so felt her wedding to Marcus could not come too soon.

Jane told Sylvia her news and she was delighted, but told Jane that apparently, Conrad had taken Polly's desertion very badly and had hit the bottle really hard, and as he was not a habitual drinker, drunkenness was out of character. Sylvia had just received a text from Imogen who said that he had run amok: already drunk, he had barged into Daniel's studio, but finding it empty and hearing noises in the flat above, charged up there, threw open the door, and found Imogen and Daniel totally naked, and at a point of no return. He roared like a lion, berating Daniel for f... his daughter and threw a table lamp at the couple.

"Oh God," cried Jane. "Not another one; drink this time though, not religion, to turn the brain."

"I must go to him at once," declared Sylvia. "Is it alright if I leave you to it?"

"Of course," answered Jane, writing a quick text to Marcus on her phone, asking him to come up to London as soon as he could as she missed him so much. He rang her shortly afterwards to say he would catch a train as soon as possible and hoped to meet her at Patrick's mews house around 8 o'clock that evening. Patrick was away but Marcus had a key. Jane said she would finish off what she was doing then buy some fresh milk, bread, cold meat and salad, so they could eat at the mews.

When Sylvia arrived at Conrad's house in Holland Park, she found that Imogen had poured gallons of strong coffee into him and he was much calmer. He was still angry about finding Imogen and Daniel in flagrante, but they said it was his fault for barging in without knocking. Anyway, they did not deny that they had begun an affair when Monica told Daniel that she wanted to end their relationship, though she would continue to represent him as an artist.

"Yes, but what about my daughter?" angrily asked Conrad. "You can't just pick her up and toss her aside at your whim."

"I don't intend to do that," answered the young man. "I know now that what I want is Imogen. She feels the same about me and we want to get married."

"Marriage," hissed Conrad. "Do you know what you are taking on?"

"Well, it seems to have served you well, all these years," declared Imogen. "Just because Mum wants to start a new life, does not negate the years you have spent together and the fact that she gave you a daughter, can't be erased."

"I simply can't credit her behaviour," moaned Conrad. "How could she ditch me; the humiliation of it: what cause did I give her?" Sylvia couldn't help smiling at his incredible naivety; what cause, indeed! Polly had played the same game so really, it was the pot calling the kettle black, as they were equally guilty of infidelity. The thing that really bugged Conrad though, was the fact that Polly said she was truly in love with her Italian. If she had been content with an affair, Conrad would have turned a blind eye, but love, well really, what nonsense.

Chapter Nineteen

After leaving the editing suite for the day, Jane rang Monica to ask if she could pop in for tea as she had time to kill.

"Of course," said her friend. "I would love to see you and it will give me a chance to put my feet up for a while."

"I have to meet Marcus at Patrick's place at 8 o'clock," said Jane, "and I need to pick up some groceries en route, but it would be good to see you and catch up with your news. Anyway, I will be with you soon, so pop the kettle on."

When Jane arrived, Monica said, "I didn't know that Marcus was coming to town."

"Nor did he," laughed Jane. "I can't wait to see him face to face so I texted him this afternoon and told him to catch a train so I reckon he will be at the Mews by 8 o'clock."

"Nothing serious, I hope," said Monica.

"Not at all, everything is fine," Jane assured her. "In fact, now that Marcus knows, I can tell you; I am going to have a baby."

"Well, at last," said Monica. "About time too. I expect Marcus is over the moon."

"He is, indeed," agreed Jane. "But we are going to have to get a move on with the wedding. We had planned to give it a bit of time after the funeral, but blow, why should we bother what people will say?"

"No, none of their business," declared Monica, "and I think the sooner the better.

Oh, by the way, if you and Marcus want the apartment for the weekend, you are both very welcome to come and stay. You will have more space here than at the Mews."

"Well, that's kind of you, dear Monica, but we are very cosy there and I daresay we will spend quite a bit of time in bed as we haven't seen each other for a while."

"And why not?" laughed Monica. She went on, "Sally and I are going on retreat at the Seeker's Trust in Kent."

"I never heard of that," stated Jane. "What is it?"

"It's a place in the country, not far from West Malling, which has some little cottages for guests to rent but also has a conference hall, some healing rooms, a library and a rose garden, as well as permanent buildings for the small community."

"But you are not religious," returned Jane.

"No more I am, nor Sally," Monica assured her. "It is a place of respite for all comers of any religion, or none. There are extensive grounds with woods and a natural pool, and it is a great area to wind down, and enjoy some peace and quiet. However, the reason we are going this weekend is that Penny Langstaff, the Shakespeare expert, is going to give a talk and as Sally is keen on her theories, we thought it a good opportunity to beard the lion in its den."

"What a good idea," said Jane then she put on her coat and gloves, thanked Monica for tea, and set off for the nearby Pret-a-Manger shop on Piccadilly, where she bought fresh milk, a large tub of tomato soup, sandwiches and individual boxes of salad, bananas, and two Danish pastries. It was dusk but already many buildings had their lights on and as she turned into the Mews, she saw that Marcus was already there as there was a light in the kitchen. He had apparently taken her advice and come by train as there was no sign of his car.

She had hardly reached the front door when it was flung open and there Marcus stood, ready to take her into his arms. "Please, darling, let me take my coat off first and put down this shopping bag then I am all yours," she laughed.

"I can't wait," said Marcus and he pulled her towards the staircase as she struggled to take off her coat. He had switched on the bedside lamps in the guest room and turned down the covers on the double bed. Now he put his arms round her, kissed her tenderly and began peeling off her clothes.

"Stop," she called, as he guided her towards the bed. "I think we should talk first."

"Goodness, Jane darling, it's been ages since we made love."

"Not as long as all that," she smiled.

"Well, we can talk later," her lover assured her.

"Well, just take care, I am a delicate flower," she laughed, as she tumbled into his embrace. Although he was highly aroused, his lovemaking was surprisingly gentle and as afterwards they lay in each other's arms, Jane began to discuss their future. He was pleased that she had already seen her doctor and said he could not believe their luck. They had not yet tried for a baby, merely made love because they wanted to, but Jane had always felt uneasy being officially married to another man, even though they were estranged. Now, of course, she felt free to indulge Marcus's love making as often as he wished. "Well, the baby is terrific news but changes everything, my darling, and I want to wed you as soon as possible. How about if I get a special licence tomorrow and we get married at Caxton Hall as soon as there is a slot?"

"We could do that but as I am only two months gone, there is no immediate hurry and a week or two would not hurt. Get a special licence by all means, but I would love a small, intimate wedding at that picturesque little church at Wooten Wawen, near your home. It would not be too far for guests to travel as it is conveniently placed in the Midlands."

"If that is what you want, my dear love, then that will be arranged as soon as possible, and I will ring the Rev Fred first thing in the morning and book a date."

With that, they put on dressing gowns, and went down to the kitchen to brew tea and spread out the 'picnic' that Jane had brought with her.

After breakfast the next day, Marcus rang the vicar at Wooten Wawen and a date was arranged for two weeks' time. Jane had to go back to work but Marcus set off to obtain a license then bought wedding invitation cards, after which, he went back to the Mews to make a list of their personal friends and a handful of relatives.

Jane asked Sylvia if she would like to go with her to choose a wedding outfit and suggested a boutique close to Manchester Square. Sylvia thought that it was sensible to have a small wedding, though Marcus could easily afford a swanky one, but the couple had waited a long time for this moment and now that Jane was pregnant, there was no further time to waste. Fortunately, Jane had not yet begun to show obvious signs of pregnancy, so she could still look good, if she chose the right outfit.

By 3pm, she and Sylvia had finished their work in the editing suite for the day, so they hailed a taxi, which deposited them at the boutique. The shop was an elite one, with classic, expensive clothes, but as Sylvia said, "You don't get married every day." Jane chose a long, oyster coloured dress of raw silk, with a long, embroidered panel at the back in duck egg blue and silver. The sleeves were long and the neckline modest. Now, what to wear on her head? She rather liked the idea of a little veil over her face which could be raised at the service. The modiste suggested a simple gable shaped hat which beautifully framed Jane's face and the veiling added sheen to her complexion. The final touch was a pair of medium-heeled court shoes in duck egg blue.

"You will be a truly ravishing bride," stated Sylvia. "Your taste is impeccable and the outfit could not be more suited to the type of wedding you envisage."

"Well," declared Jane, "I shall need a maid of honour, so please will you be mine?"

"I shall be honoured," replied Sylvia, "but are you sure, have you not relatives or close friends who would fit the bill?"

"No doubt," answered Jane, "but it is you that I want and while we are here, we should choose an outfit for you as well." Thus the next half hour was spent choosing a suitable outfit for Sylvia. With her deep brunette hair and creamy complexion, it was decided that a soft dusky pink full-length dress, strapless but with a bolero with short sleeves would fit the bill. Matching shoes were found and a fascinator for her hair, and all was complete. Both ladies felt very happy with their purchases as they left the shop with fashionable carrier bags.

"As we are near the Mews," said Jane, "why don't you pop in for a cup of tea? I am not sure if Marcus will be there, but with all my doings, I haven't had a chance to ask you how you are and what is happening to Conrad."

As they walked up the road, Sylvia said, "Oh, after Imogen and Daniel left, I made love to him; that calmed him down because he had no difficulty in proving himself. His confidence, which was always the most amazing part of his make-up, has taken a terrible beating. He also feels humiliated to be repudiated by his wife of long standing for someone she has only recently met. He just can't take in the fact that she is serious about a divorce and wants it as soon as possible."

"But what about you, Sylvia? How do you feel about him now?" asked Jane.

"Oh, my feelings haven't changed. I am bats about him, as I have been for a long time."

"Well, you kept it pretty dark, I must say. In fact, recently, I suspected that you were keen on Guy and he certainly seemed interested in you, though being so professional, I am sure he wouldn't have made advances to you while we were abroad."

"Oh, I admire Guy tremendously and think him a most attractive man, but we can't choose who we fall in love with, and I gave my heart to Conrad from the first time I modelled for him."

"Well, I never," sighed Jane, "but what happens now?"

144

"Your guess is as good as mine," sighed Sylvia.

"If Polly does succeed in getting her divorce, do you think he would ask you to marry him?" asked Jane.

"I wish he would, I would accept immediately," sighed Sylvia.

"My dear friend, you know his reputation and there is more to marriage than sex."

"Oh, I realise that, but it is an important part of it and if it isn't right or there is no sexual affinity, it can soon spoil the best of relationships."

"Well, Sylvia, I wish you well. I wonder though who, if anyone, Guy will end up with."

"You know I think he has a very soft spot for Sally," replied Sylvia.

"You don't mean it? She and Monica go back a long way, you know. I realise that Monica is bi-sexual, but I always thought Sally was lesbian through and through."

"I reckon she probably thought she was because she had no experience with men and as long as Monica was in the picture, I don't think she ever bothered to find out what sex with a man could be like. However, I suspect something has happened to our Sally during the past year to make her think again."

"What makes you say that; do you know something the rest of us don't know?"

"Not at all, it is just intuition. Anyway, it will be interesting to see how things pan out for all of our friends."

Chapter Twenty

Although Addington Park was situated only eight miles from Maidstone in Kent, Sally and Monica decided to hire a car for the weekend rather than go by train then take a taxi to the Seeker's Trust estate. As it was Saturday, they set off early in the morning in order to escape Saturday shoppers. It was a very pleasant morning, though it had rained overnight, and pavements and roofs were still glossy in the pale sunshine.

"I gather that the Seeker's Trust is not a religious establishment," stated Sally.

"Not at all, it is based on healing and is for everybody who seeks inner calm."

"Do you know how it came about?" asked her friend.

"Well, from the publicity I read it appears that it was due to a Medium, Mr Charles Simpson who founded the Trust. In the aftermath of the carnage of the First World War, many people were looking for answers but not finding them in orthodox religion so turned to Spiritualism, which led to the more advanced thinkers setting up Research projects. Mr Simpson was inspired by a Dr Lascelles, who had lived in the 19th century and was guided by him to found a healing centre.

Fortuitously, an estate near West Malling came onto the market and a fund was opened. However, the morning Charles Simpson was due to sign the completion of sale he was still short of the asking price. It seemed that he was doomed to lose the property but suddenly, the telephone rang and a client of his asked for healing, preferably that morning. On arrival, the man noticed that he was not his usual cheery self and asked what was wrong. Charles told him about the sale he was going to lose and the man asked, 'How much do you need?'

'We are short of a thousand pounds to complete the deal,' said Charles.

'Not to worry,' said the man, making out a cheque on the spot. 'Now hurry and catch the estate agent before the office closes.'

However, it was not all plain sailing because after the acquisition, the big house burned down. It seemed a terrible catastrophe but Mr Simpson later said it was a blessing. The group who came together to administer the Seekers, could not have afforded to maintain such a large building, but the demolition of the house provided construction material for several houses for permanent residents; five cottages for guests and the rest of the buildings that now occupy the site."

"Well, what a story," responded Sally. "That's certainly what you would call Divine Intervention and the place is still going strong?"

"Never better, if the publicity is to be believed and the interesting thing is that this whole area was of sacred significance during Pre-historic times. Now what you tell me about Penny Langstaff and her theories has really whetted my appetite because I love mystery."

Their lengthy conversation ensured that the journey along the motorway passed quickly, and soon, they turned into a country lane and the hamlet of Addington Park, passing 'The Angel', an old half-timbered inn a few hundred yards from the entrance gates of the Seeker's Trust. As they approached, Monica noticed a sign low down on her right which read, 'Merlin's Brook'.

"That's odd," she told Sally. "I wonder if there is any reference to King Arthur in these parts."

"Might be," said Sally, "but then, there are legends about him all over the place and who knows if Camelot was imaginary or a real place?"

At the end of the drive, they stopped at the office where a receptionist greeted them warmly and gave them the keys to a guest cottage. They told her that they were here for the first time but that the Seekers had come highly recommended.

"Yes, many guests tell us that it is better than a health farm because here the soul is healed as well as the body.

Did you know that we have six little rooms where a group of residents on a rota, meet to send absent healing? They tune in at certain times with those who have asked for healing so that the healing energies are magnified?"

"Most people would find that a tall order," said Monica. "Is it efficacious?"

"Yes, it truly is and we have lots of correspondence telling us about the benefits that have been received by tuning in with us. You see, everything in the Universe vibrates and even orthodox scientists today use unseen energies in their work. Well, all we are doing is tuning in with the healing energy that is all around us. Computers have become commonplace, but the human mind when rightly attuned is equally miraculous.

Now, let me show you to your cottage, it's not far."

With that, the friends picked up their overnight bags then followed Kathy across the green to their home for the weekend. As they walked, Monica told Kathy that they were looking forward to hearing Penny Langstaff speak that afternoon as Sally had recently been reading some of her books.

"Yes," said Kathy, "she is a fine writer and really makes one think. She is a member of the Francis Bacon Research Trust which explores the quite remarkable story of the genesis of the Shakespeare plays, and the great mystery that lies behind the birth of Sir Francis Bacon and his hidden connection with Queen Elizabeth I."

"What is all that about?" asked Monica.

"Well, that is a very complex issue and if you are interested, you should read the books 'Arcadia' and 'Dedication to the Light' by Peter Dawkins, which can explain it much better than I can."

"Ah, here we are," said Kathy, stopping at the middle house of a row of single storey cottages. She turned the key in the lock and led them into a large open plan room, where a window, with floral curtains looked onto an area of lawn; there was also a small kitchen area, two armchairs, two divan beds, a table with two dining chairs and a small, en-suite bathroom.

"This is charming," said Monica. "I am sure we will be very comfortable here, and it shows how simply we could live, if we chose."

Kathy smiled and said, "Yes, indeed; now I am sure you would like to make yourselves comfortable but if you want to wander before lunch, I can recommend our woods and the lake. If you are interested in Pre-history, there is also a private house whose garden is just beyond our gates with a well preserved dolmen, where visitors are welcome."

"It is not my field," said Sally, "but I find the mystery of the stone megaliths absolutely fascinating and often wonder what they are all about. I rather doubt the hypothesis that they are somehow religious or just for burials. Of course, they have been used as such, but I think the original use may have been more technological than religious."

"It's funny you should mention that," replied Kathy, "but I gather from TV documentaries, that some archaeologists, scientists, engineers and pre-historians are beginning to say the same thing. It will be interesting to see what further research discovers. Anyway, I will leave you now to settle in. Our little shop supplies some basic items and is open all day, so do come in if you need anything. Penny's talk will begin at 3pm, so that leaves you time to have lunch and take a look at our library."

"Thank you so much," said Monica. "You have been most helpful and I am sure we will have a delightful weekend. We'll keep our fingers crossed that it stays dry."

"Oh, I think the forecast is good for the next couple of days, so all should be well," Kathy assured them as she let herself out.

As it was too early for lunch, the friends changed into suitable shoes for country walking and put on hooded fleeces, then set off to explore. First, they looked into the library, a large room filled with bookshelves, a carpet covering the centre of the room and several comfortable armchairs, as well as a couple of tables with lamps. At the end of the room was a tall woman with her back towards them. But on hearing them come in, she instinctively turned and Monica recognised her as Nancy Lolongo, a well-known actress of Afro/Caribbean descent. Nancy looked at Monica for a moment, then recognised her and came towards her, offering her hand. "Madam Ambassadress," she cooed, "whatever brings you to this neck of the woods?"

Monica shook her hand and introduced her to Sally, saying, "Nancy came over with a company of actors to put on scenes from 'The Merry Wives of Windsor' at the Embassy while Douglas and I were there."

"Oh, poor Sir Douglas," said Nancy. "I was so sorry to hear of his sudden death; what a delightful gentleman he was and how much I loved staying at the Embassy. Please accept my condolences."

"Are you staying here, Nancy?" asked Monica.

"Yes, but only for the weekend. I have come principally to hear Penny Langstaff, though I also welcome some rest time."

As Sally and Monica had brought a quantity of groceries with them, they asked Nancy to join them at their cottage for lunch at 1 pm; after which, they could wander over to the conference hall together to hear Penny's talk.

Nancy accepted with pleasure then returned to browsing as Sally and Monica went on with their exploration of the estate. The Rose Garden, close to the library, was, of course, lacking in flowers at this time of year, but it was interesting to read the little plaques set up by people in memory of their loved ones.

From here, they walked down to the lake, from where they could see the maisonettes where residents lived. It was quite mild for the time of year so the friends sat for a little while on a bench in the wood and imbibed the fresh fragrances around them. The trees, of course, were still without leaves, but their very skeletons appeared like beautiful statues set against the clear blue sky.

After quietly musing for twenty minutes or so, they retraced their steps back to the cottage, where Monica set about preparing lunch. Sally offered to help but Monica said that there wasn't enough room for both of them in the tiny kitchen, so Sally sat back and relaxed, thinking about all she had seen and heard that morning.

Monica was a dab hand at conjuring up appetising meals at the drop of a hat and soon, lunch was underway. Sally laid the table and Nancy arrived punctually at 12.45. Although the meal, by necessity, consisted of prepared foods, such as packet tomato soup, there was fresh salad, egg mayonnaise, and crusty bread and Jersey butter, along with a selection of cheeses, and fresh fruit. "A feast fit for a king," said the dramatic Nancy. Having cleared and washed up, the women set off for the talk, and were pleased to see that it was going to be well attended though they found three seats together.

Sally and Nancy had heard Penny lecture before, but it was Monica's first time, and she scrutinised this woman of whom she had heard so much. Physically, she was tall and slim, with white hair worn in a neat bob, and could have been any age between fifty and sixty. Her eyes were blue behind a fashionable pair of gold-rimmed spectacles and held a distinct twinkle. As soon as she began to speak, it was obvious that she held her immense knowledge and erudition lightly. She was also a giggler, and there were many amusing anecdotes in her discourse that kept everyone awake and made the lecture entertaining as well as educational.

She admitted that she had been clairvoyant from an early age, but like others with that gift, she soon learned to keep quiet about it. However, five years ago, she had decided to 'come clean' and risk the disapproval of her fellow academics. She had always been fascinated by the amount of faery lore in Shakespeare, even though modern intellectuals scoff at such 'superstitious nonsense'. Nonetheless, earlier people were not stupid and before the masses became literate, it appears that many people had 'second sight'. However, if we do not believe in something, the chances are that it will not exist for us. Not that Penny advocated blind belief, no; one had to search for the truth, but there was more residing within us than we usually realised.

It is well known that when Captain Cook sailed the Pacific Ocean, at first, the natives were totally unaware of the Europeans and their ship because they had never seen anything like it before so lacked comprehension, and it took time for the realisation to dawn on them.

Penny also mentioned the mystery of the Cottingly Fairies, which had attracted people such as Sir Arthur Conan Doyle at the time. To anyone not familiar with the events surrounding the publicity, she reiterated the story about two young girls who said they saw fairies, literally at the bottom of their garden. They had photos of them which drew a large amount of publicity and newspaper people from London haunted the family for days. Finally, it was revealed that the girls had drawn the fairies themselves then photographed them. A lot of people were bitterly disappointed because they believed that the girls had deceived them. However, other people did not see it as a con trick, but said that the girls had seen the nature spirits ethereally, but as they could not photograph the real thing, they drew them as they saw them and hoped to enable others to become aware of another realm of reality.

Later, Sally revealed to Monica that she often saw unusual things as if on an inner screen and wished she could photograph them. Penny also mentioned that human eyes are only tuned into a small section of the electro-magnetic spectrum, and though we accept that we cannot see gamma, X-rays, electricity, or radio waves with our physical eyes, we see their effects and make use of them.

Penny's talk was wide ranging and as well as mentioning the Shakespeare authorship question, she also covered the relationship between Elizabeth I and Robert Dudley, Earl of Leicester as it was relevant to the theme of the lecture. At Court, it was whispered, though never openly uttered, that they were lovers, or even secretly married, and that Francis Bacon and Robert Devereux, Earl of Essex, were their sons. There is a woodcut, seemingly of the period, but published in the 18th century of Elizabeth with two little boys sitting at her feet, one of whom is holding a rudder, (the rudder of State, as the eldest son?) and in the shadows is a third child, who may have died in infancy or been still born.

Apparently, as a young girl, Elizabeth lived at Old Hatfield Palace, with her stepmother, Catherine Parr and Catherine's second husband, Sir Thomas Seymour, Lord High Admiral of England. When she was fourteen, there were allegations that she had been seduced by Seymour and when Seymour was put on trial, Elizabeth was brought in for questioning. However, even at that tender age, she had her wits about her and gave a good account of herself. It may be that there was a child, but if so, it was a deeply guarded secret. Seymour, however, did not get off as lightly as Elizabeth but was executed for treason.

However, she was not completely exonerated as she was imprisoned in the Tower of London by her half-sister, Mary Tudor, where she met the young Robert Dudley. His father, brother and his brother's wife, the sixteen-year-old Lady Jane Grey, had been executed for high treason, but Robert had escaped with his life, though not his liberty.

As teenagers, Robert and Elizabeth lived in constant fear of their lives, but were allowed to walk on the leads for exercise, where the inevitable happened and they fell in love. Robert had been married at the age of seventeen to Amy Robsart, who later died in mysterious circumstances. When Elizabeth came to the throne in 1558, she appointed Robert as her Master of Horse, a post which gave him easy access to the Queen, as his bedroom was next to hers.

Penny said that, apparently, Sir Francis Bacon, who was born in 1561, left an autobiography in code, alleging that he was Queen Elizabeth's son by Robert Dudley and his younger brother was Robert, Earl of Essex, who, after Dudley's death, was thought to be Elizabeth's young lover; though he was really her son. He had attempted to lead a rebellion against her so she signed his death warrant. However, it appears that she had planned to rescind the order if he begged her forgiveness, but in the same way that his father, Lord Burghley had tricked the Queen over the death warrant of Mary Queen of Scots, Sir Robert Cecil, who had vowed to ruin both Essex and Bacon, acted precipitately, and when the news of the execution of Essex reached the Queen, it was too late to save her son. She was never the same woman after that and in certain quarters, it is thought that she may have been slowly poisoned by Cecil.

If Sir Francis Bacon was the editor in chief of the Shakespeare plays, it clarifies various issues; for instance, many of the sonnets are addressed to the Queen because he frequently implored her to reveal his royal birth. Also, if he was a Tudor Prince, it would explain the bias in favour of the Tudors in the War of the Roses plays. However, it was impossible for the Queen to tell the truth because for most of her reign, she had been lauded as Gloriana, the Virgin Queen, which had resulted in her becoming an icon. She was

England and seen almost as a goddess on Earth. The public had been literally brainwashed to accept her as such and there was no going back. Francis had been fostered from birth by Sir Nicholas Bacon and his wife, Lady Anne, and was brought up with their son, Anthony Bacon, at Gorhambury, close to St Alban's, the house the Queen had commanded Sir Nicholas to build, so that her son could be brought up in the Neo Platonic Academy founded by him. She called Francis, her 'baby Solomon' due to the fact that from an early age, he showed remarkable intelligence. However, when Sir Nicholas died, Francis was not mentioned in his will which surprised everyone. He had no fortune of his own but Sir Nicholas knew the truth of his birth and expected the Queen to financially support her son. She did not; he was an embarrassment to her so she packed him off with the English Ambassador to France at the age of fifteen. Nevertheless, this was a life affirming time for the young lad and where he envisioned the canon of the Shakespeare plays, his ambition being to promote English as a worldwide language, and to illustrate the whole of the human condition through drama.

The story about the Stratford lad was a construct, and considered necessary at that time because controversial subjects were dangerous and a cover was necessary. Also, Stratford was chosen as being at the centre of England and corresponded with sacred geometry. It is also significant that the plays continued to appear after the death of the Earl of Oxford and that of Will Shakespeare in 1616.

At the end of the lecture, Penny recommended Peter Dawkins's books 'Arcadia,' 'Dedication to the Light' and the 'Shakespeare Enigma' which were on sale at the back of the hall. She also mentioned two Daphne du Maurier novels about 'the Golden Lads', Francis and Anthony Bacon. She warned though that there are vested interests who do not want the truth to emerge as it would negate some reputable careers, but stuck her neck out by alleging that most of the biographies of Will Shakespeare are fictional. "However," she added, "for those who seek truth, the search is well worth the effort."

She certainly left her listeners with a great deal to think about before being whisked away by Kathy to have tea. As for the trio, they were more than ready for a cup of tea themselves, and Monica suggested that they should go back to her cottage for a pot of tea, muffins and cakes. She seemed to have become voluntary catering manager for the weekend but the other two were quite happy to let her rule the roost.

Later, they enjoyed hearty pub fare at the Angel and whiled away the evening in a very pleasant ambience. After breakfast next morning, Nancy suggested a walk over fields to the Coldron Stones, a megalithic chamber, from where there was a fine view of the Ridgeway, the Pilgrim's route to Canterbury. Having already inspected the dolmen in the private garden, they walked across open fields to the Stones and were delighted that there was no one else there.

Nancy said that they should tone together but the other two had no idea what she meant so she explained that they should each choose a note at random, and either hum or sing it to la and move about the scale at will. At first, it would be discordant, but inevitably, the sound would become homogenous and create its own blended harmony. Monica said she was no singer, but Nancy replied that she didn't have to be, merely to make a sound. Nancy was right and after initial dissonance it was just as if they had become one voice. Sally had her eyes closed but as the sound built, she became aware of crystalline geometric shapes made of light, emanating from the sound; the beams of which stretched out to the horizon. It is said that sound can create and for Sally, it appeared to be true, though it was in etheric substance, not matter.

"Well," said Nancy, who had studied singing at RADA as part of the course, "when sounds collide on the intervals of the fourth, fifth, or octave a little surge of energy is felt and it is probably significant that those were the basic intervals of early medieval music, known as Organum. It sounds strange to our ears because our diatonic music uses the intervals of the third and sixths to a great extent which is more pleasing to modern ears. However, it might be that Organum was a left over from a once powerful sonic technology."

"I am not sure I know what a surge of energy feels like," said Sally.

"Try again," said Nancy, "and concentrate." They did as asked and whether it was imagination or they really perceived a burst of energy, they were not sure, but Nancy seemed satisfied.

"Now," said Monica, "tell me what all that means."

"You see," replied Nancy, "there are legends about sound which seem to point to a pre-historic sonic technology. You have heard about the walls of Jericho being brought down by the vibrations of trumpets and the notes of a high voice being able to break a glass just by accidentally tuning in with the actual vibration of the glass? There are also stories about heavy stones flying through the air when

154

large groups of people gather and tone as we have just done, so eliminating gravity, causing the stones to fly into place."

"Gosh," said Sally, "that's a tall order, surely?"

"I am not so sure," said Monica. "Haven't you read recently about allegations that some kind of sonic power has been used against U. S. diplomats in Cuba?"

"Oh, yes, I saw a headline, but didn't read the article."

"Apparently, the diplomats became ill, and had to be flown home and tests showed that they had suffered some brain damage. It is very worrying as it has such implications for mental warfare. Like all energies on Earth, they can be used for good or ill. Sadly, our clever scientists often concentrate on the most evil aspects, which if not controlled, could have the most diabolical consequences.

There are other strange legends, of course," said Nancy. "What about a magic mirror that can show what is happening on the other side of the world? That struck me the other day when I was talking to someone on my tablet. I could see and hear her, and she could see and hear me though we were miles apart, and I thought, oh yes, a magic mirror. Then there is the saying 'open Sesame', where a door opens at the sound of a voice. Well, we experience this every day through the electronic eye that automatically opens doors in public places. There is also voice activation now.

It is true that there have been untold cataclysms on the planet, so who's to say that many thousands of years ago, mankind had not reached our level of technology or even more advanced technology than we have yet discovered? Sound is an energy that can either create or destroy, and I fear that a lot of what passes for popular music is of the destructive kind which could account for the emotional and mental difficulties such musicians often suffer.

I hope I am not boring you," she continued. "But I would just like to put a theory of mine to you, if you don't mind."

"Not at all," said Sally. "I love it; please go on."

"Well, you see, I have always been doubtful about dolmens being built as tombs. I know they have been used as such, but I think they were built by earlier peoples as part of their technology. A lot of people toning in an enclosed space would build up an energy that could be stored, so a dolmen would become a chantry, and if you think of it, every church has its own chantry. In fact, there is so much that has come down to us in a garbled form but relates back to what we call pagan times. Well, it is only a theory but it will be interesting to see if any pre-historians come up with the same theme. I know

155

that some archaeologists, engineers and scientists are questioning accepted hypotheses, and there is material on the Net to keep one up to date. I find it absolutely fascinating and it makes a change from reading scripts."

"My goodness," said Monica, "to think that I came to chill out but had no idea that my mind would be blown away this weekend though, heavens above, it really has been. I certainly have food for thought, but I shall take it in small bites lest I get mental indigestion."

"You're right," remarked Nancy, "but at least, it keeps the old grey cells active."

There was still food left over at Monica's cottage, so they returned for lunch before packing up and leaving for London. Nancy had come by train and taxi, so Monica invited her to return in their car. As they handed their keys back to Kathy, they said what an amazing weekend it had been and how much material they now had to absorb.

"Yes," said Kathy. "Penny is an extraordinary woman, but wears her vast knowledge very lightly. Did you know, by the way that she and her husband used to live here when they were first married? They also lived at the White Eagle Lodge at Liss in Hampshire, where Penny imbibed much of her wisdom. In fact, she donated the four little books in our library entitled 'Spiritual Unfoldment' which are published by the White Eagle Lodge and teach universal wisdom in the clearest way. If you get a chance to obtain them, do read them, they are very beautiful, and though they are based on the Christian tradition, they range even wider and are without dogma."

"Well," said Nancy, "I didn't know Penny is married."

"She is a widow actually," responded Kathy. "Sadly, her husband died in a skiing accident many years ago but she never remarried. There were no children either, so I suppose that is why she has devoted her life to scholarship. Anyway, I do hope you will come back," smiled Kathy.

"We hope so," said Monica, "but next time, we will come on a silent retreat and recharge our batteries."

The motorway was pretty crowded on the way back to town but they still made good time. Monica and Sally were having dinner at the Ritz with Daniel and Imogen, and asked Nancy to join them, but she declined as she had a script to memorise and it was not an easy one to learn. She was about to start rehearsals for a new production of Sir Tom Stoppard's play 'Arcadia' at the Garrick Theatre.

Monica said she had missed it when it was first produced at the National Theatre, but had seen it when it moved into the West End.

"What did you think of it?" asked Nancy.

"I thought it one of the most remarkable plays I have ever seen," replied Monica. "It is extremely well crafted and the concept is fascinating. I marvelled at Stoppard's skill in weaving two time scales spanning more than a hundred and fifty years, but occupying the same physical space. It was truly a stroke of genius. The acting was sublime, and I still remember some of the actors, namely Rufus Sewell, a very young Emma Fielding, Harriet Walter, Cherie Lunghi and Bill Nighy. However, sometime later, I saw the same play at Chichester, with a different production and cast, of course, but it did not exude magic like the London one."

"No," said Nancy, "the playwright is at the mercy of the director and the actors, as a play only lives on the stage, not in a book."

"It is the same with music," said Sally. "The dots on the page, however skilful the composer, are only symbols which do not exist in reality until the performer breathes life into them."

"How right you are," said Nancy, "and though I don't think that the public realise it; we performers are well aware of the responsibility we hold in order for a work to succeed. I am very excited by the prospect of this new production as it is being directed by Thea Constantine, who has played a large part in my career. I do hope you will come to a preview and I will be in touch nearer the time to remind you."

"I hope you will be in touch, anyway," said Monica.

Nancy had already said that she lived in the Barbican and Monica had offered to drive her home. "My nephew's great friend, William Wilcox also lives here," said Monica.

"Yes, I know him," Nancy replied. "I often meet him and Patrick, at Fund Raising Events for theatrical projects."

"I didn't know that Patrick is interested in theatre," returned Monica.

"Oh yes, he and William are 'angels'."

"Really," said Monica. "You do surprise me because neither of them ever spoke of their involvement."

"Well, without people like them investing in shows, the unsubsidised theatre would hardly exist. In fact, Monica, you might consider becoming an 'angel' yourself."

"Well, you will have to tell me how it works next time we meet."

With that, they exchanged email and phone numbers then Nancy said good night, and Monica and Sally sped off, with just enough time to get ready for their dinner appointment with their friends.

Chapter Twenty-One

The shock of Douglas's death, the discovery of his hidden family and the rift with Daniel had ruffled Monica more than she cared to admit, and for probably the first time in her life, she felt lonely. In her everyday life, she was surrounded by people, but it was an inner loneliness from which she now suffered. Somehow, it was as if an inner light had gone out and she had no idea what to do to relight it.

As she lay in bed that night, she began to assess her life and realised what a charmed one it was. She had no right to be despondent; indeed, she should count her blessings because they were many. Her health was good, she had her brother and her nephew, and lots of good friends but somehow, it didn't seem enough at present. The problem was within her. Like most people, she had been brought up in the C of E, but not since her girlhood had she paid more than lip service to it. She was certainly not irreligious; in fact, Sally's influence had shaped her belief that we are all spiritual beings living in a physical body. She knew that Sally had always questioned life and sought truth, but Monica had convinced herself that she had always been too busy to go into things as deeply as Sally did. Nevertheless, she was happy to pick up crumbs from Sally's table and she had learned a lot simply from what she heard her talk about. Now, having met Nancy, Monica realised what a lot she still had to learn. They were both on some kind of Path, it seemed and she wished that she could join them, but did not know how. Instead, she began to remember her childhood and how she had been taught to pray.

Of course, she mused, *no one actually knows what God is, yet I have to believe He or It exists because we see the effects of Divine creation all around us. On the other hand, we also see so much misery and conflict, so it is hard to be a true believer.* As she was on the verge of nodding off, she remembered, 'God be in My Head', 'The Lord's My Shepherd' and 'May the peace that passeth all understanding keep your hearts and minds in the knowledge and love of God'. *Not a bad trio*, she thought, *and tomorrow I will write them down and keep them beside my bed. I may not feel the need to go into a church or attend a service, but I need God in some form or other, and I will make a start by using the prayers I know. Doesn't it say in the Bible about being as a little child? Well, it seems I must go back to my childhood and ask for guidance. I trust that I will find it.* With that, she turned off the bedside lamp and settled down, feeling more at ease than she had done for a while. Just thinking of the prayers brought a sense of calm and she felt that she had already been guided to find something to fill the empty void in herself.

When she awoke, she felt truly rested and as she opened the curtain, a shaft of light fell on her, helping her to face the day with confidence though she decided that she would not talk even to Sally of her new resolve to find a philosophy to live by. It was her secret and if it is true that God is within, then she would make him her friend, confiding her innermost thoughts and praying that he would understand and grant her wisdom.

Sally was always so busy these days and often spent time at West Bridge Hall; the gallery ran like clockwork and at times, Monica felt redundant. Recently, she had been looking for something new into which she could pour her energies and meeting Nancy had touched a nerve. She liked the idea of getting involved in the world of the theatre, even if only as a patron. She would pick Nancy's brains the next time they met. Anyway, it would be a novel experience and she was all for that.

She had read various things about Nancy as she was a noted celebrity, but meeting her in the flesh had been unexpected. She was a striking looking woman, tall and lean but with a splendid bust, and her dusky skin was as smooth as satin. She had lustrous long, black hair, but Monica was not sure if it was a wig or not. Nancy had actually begun to write her life story and planned to call it 'Deliverance'. She was a talented writer so, unlike many so called celebrities, she would not need a ghostwriter. Her parents were of Nigerian extraction but had perished en route to the UK when Nancy was six years old. She was rescued and adopted by Dr Desmond Dorango, from Jamaica and his Croatian wife, Jarmilla. Dr Dorango was a dean at King's College, London, and Jarmilla was a full time housewife and mother to Nancy. Early on, she recognised that the little girl was highly intelligent so started her off on home schooling. She already taught three other children at home and Nancy joined them. The little girl spoke some English so that was a good foundation for learning and she made such good progress that at the age of eleven, she won a scholarship to the North London Collegiate

School. Here, she excelled in the arts, particularly drama and on leaving school, won a much-valued scholarship to RADA.

Nancy had to admit that she appeared to have been born under a lucky star because in her graduation year, she was cast as Cleopatra in Shakespeare's drama, 'Anthony and Cleopatra', and received rave notices in the National Press. This brought her to the notice of Damian Donzell, an eminent agent, who put her under contract and her first professional engagement was at the National Theatre, albeit in a subsidiary role, but at least she had her foot in an important door. Meeting Thea Constantine was another great stroke of luck as she immediately spotted Nancy's talent, however, up to that point, Nancy had only had the most casual of relationships as she was ruthlessly ambitious and felt that emotional entanglements would harm her progress. However, Thea was a force of nature, and soon Nancy and she were in a passionate personal relationship.

Monica made breakfast for herself and planned to go into the gallery to start discussing Conrad's next exhibition. However, before she could go downstairs, the phone rang and it was Imogen bursting with news she had just received from Daniel. He was still at the Biennale in Venice and Polly had joined him there. She intended to go on to meet Emilio in Vienna. However, she had received a call to tell her that he had been arrested. Polly could not believe her ears but it was also on TV News. Apparently, there had been a big Interpol round up of drugs barons, Maffiosi and money launderers, and it appeared that some dodgy money had gone into Emilio's new venture in Vienna. Interpol had been keeping tabs on some of the big boys for some time. They often picked up the minnows but rarely caught the bosses behind them. Polly was naturally concerned and upset at the thought of Emilio's incarceration. She couldn't believe that he was involved in crime but she didn't know anything about his business dealings, other than that his was a long established firm with a fine reputation and clients came from the highest levels of society.

She did not know with whom to get in touch, so Daniel suggested that as he was about to leave Venice, she should fly home with him and wait for developments. That meant she had to leave her recent paintings in Rome, but he said they could be packed up and sent to England, if necessary. The thing now was to get back and sort out her affairs. If she stayed in Italy, she would, no doubt, be interviewed by the police and it could get complicated.

Daniel was aware that Polly was a creature of impulse but so far as he could make out, she had done nothing regarding a divorce from Conrad. Thankfully, she had her passport, so a ticket was booked for her on Daniel's flight to Gatwick, and she passed through Security without any questions being asked. Had she already been La Contessa de Gonzaramo, it would have been different but as she was travelling as Polly Parsons, her professional name, she was not questioned.

It was with relief that when they landed at Gatwick, Polly again passed through customs without any difficulty but it probably helped that she was accompanied by Daniel. She had been rather quiet on the journey home, envisaging what Mafia contacts Emilio might have and how lucky she was to have been able to return home so easily. She and Daniel shared a cab from the airport, and she was dropped off at Holland Park.

A light was burning upstairs so Polly dropped her two small bags in the hall and went upstairs. She could not hear voices but when she opened the bedroom door, there were Conrad and Sylvia in bed, reading. To say they were surprised to see her was an understatement. All they could do was look on in a dazed fashion. While Polly, not at all embarrassed, greeted them as if nothing untoward had happened during the past few months. Conrad was the first to speak, "What the hell are you doing here, Polly?"

"I live here," she answered, smirking like a little child.

"Oh, no you don't," barked Conrad, "you left me, remember?"

"Well, I changed my mind," said his errant wife."

"Blast you, Polly," he cried. "You practically drive me into a nervous breakdown then pop up as if you had just been out to the shops, saying you changed your mind. Well, what about my mind; am I supposed to take you back as if nothing had happened and what about Sylvia: how do you think she is going to deal with this?"

"Oh, I am afraid I never gave Sylvia a thought, sorry," she drawled. Sylvia didn't speak because she really had no words, so left Conrad and Polly to thrash it out.

"You always were a thoughtless bitch, Polly," grumbled her husband. "I would have gone out of my mind had it not been for Sylvia, who virtually moved in here to look after me."

"Very good of her, I'm sure," replied Polly, "but she can go home now because I am back to look after you, you stupid boy."

"Don't you dare call me stupid, you cretin," yelled her husband. "I don't believe you have a rational thought in your head, you selfish tart. You should be ashamed of yourself upsetting not just me but Imogen and Sylvia."

"What has Sylvia to do with it, she isn't family?" cried the unrepentant Polly.

"I know that, but she might have been, had you gone ahead with the divorce. I could easily have married her and as she is much younger than you, she could have given me a new family of my own."

"You beast," snarled Polly, ready to scratch his eyes out. "Reminding me of my age. I'll thank you to remember though, that I am not yet in my dotage and had I married Emilio, I might have given him children."

"Well, why didn't you?" said her scornful husband.

"Because he has the smallest winkle I have ever seen in my life, and as he appears to prefer men to women, it seemed highly unlikely that I would ever conceive."

At this, Conrad laughed till the tears ran down his face and Sylvia joined in; even Polly had to admit that it sounded absurd and soon, they were all choking with laughter.

When she stopped laughing, Polly added, "Anyway, he is in jail." This set them all off again and they had to hear just what had happened to bring that about.

When they had all calmed down, Conrad said, "So, I take it that we are not to be divorced?"

"Of course not, silly boy," she assured him. "Anyway, I think Imogen would like to marry Daniel so we might have a wedding to plan."

"What makes her think he is interested in her?" queried Imogen's father. "He's been shagging Monica for some time and the last I heard, was doing pretty well with Emma while Ranu was away."

"I'll go and make a cup of tea," said Sylvia. "Do either of you want a sandwich?"

"I could murder one," said Polly.

"Just a couple of biscuits for me, sweetie," answered Conrad. While Sylvia went down to the kitchen, Polly slipped off her clothes and popped, stark naked, into bed beside Conrad. On seeing Polly sitting up in bed with exposed breasts, Sylvia wondered what was going on. Conrad told her to hand over the tea then get back into bed on his other side.

"Are we going to have a threesome?" asked the unrepentant Polly. "What fun."

"No, we are not; anyway, I should think you are too tired after your journey and Sylvia is not the sort of girl to indulge in such high jinks."

"Oh, I don't know," declared Sylvia. "Maybe I am not as unadventurous as you seem to think? I could go home, of course, or sleep in the guestroom?" she volunteered.

"No, don't do that," replied Conrad. "The bed is big enough for all of us and I promise that I will behave myself. Now if you have finished putting crumbs in the bed, Polly, I think we should turn out the light and get some sleep. We can sort everything out tomorrow. Good night, one and all."

Chapter Twenty-Two

After some initial thoughts, Marcus and Jane decided that Milton House should be their wedding venue. As it was a second marriage for both of them, they couldn't see the point of a big splash. Anyway, they wanted to be married as soon as possible and without unnecessary fuss. They had first considered the pretty little church at Wooton Wawen, which was the nearest village to Marcus's home, but he thought that as they already had a special license, they might as well use it to be married in the Yellow Salon at Milton, with the Rev Fred officiating, then have a sit down lunch in the dining room.

Thus on a bright Saturday morning, cars set off from London with Monica, her new friend, Nancy Lolongo, Captain Patrick and William Wilcox, Polly, Conrad, Imogen, Daniel, Ranu and Emma. Guy, Sally, Tom and Ginny came over from West Bridge Hall but as they were rather early, they stopped off at the Bull opposite the church and had morning coffee as they didn't want to be the first arrivals.

It wasn't far to Milton House, an attractive stone built Georgian manor, where they were greeted by Marcus, looking very dashing in his dove grey morning suit. Jane and Sylvia, her maid of honour, were still upstairs but the Rev Fred had arrived, as had a small group of local friends, including David Thornton, Marcus's best man, who happened to be the artistic director of the Royal Shakespeare Company. He and Nancy knew each other so she introduced him to those he had not yet met.

Guy remembered to warn Sally not to mention her Shakespeare research to David Thornton. "Best keep mum for the time being," he volunteered.

"Yes, I realise that," Sally replied. "Upsetting Stratfordians would make me most unpopular, and anyway, I am off duty here and out to enjoy a lovely day in beautiful surroundings."

Emma, an ambitious actress, was keen to talk to David and hoped to make a good impression on him. Of course, he was used to being besieged by attractive young actresses, so Emma would, indeed, need to impress him. Like many men, he preferred to be the hunter rather than the hunted, so was angry, one day, when a young actress came into his office; and boldly pulled off her t-shirt, offering herself in exchange for a role she coveted. With some directors, the casting couch might be a reality, but not with him. He told her to cover up immediately then concentrate on becoming a good actress, rather than a whore. As a recently divorced man, however, he admitted to himself that he would not be averse to a new romance in his private life.

Despite Emma's attempts to entice him, it was Sylvia who impressed him most when, looking ravishing in a dusty pink gown, she accompanied the bride into the Yellow Salon. Fair-haired Patrick appeared even more dashing than usual in his dress uniform and looked suitably proud to lead Jane, the delectable bride, towards a table decked with flowers that served as an altar.

In the large, elegant room, decorated with fresh flowers were placed two rows of gilt chairs with deep blue velvet seats for the guests. Marcus and David stood ready along with the Rev Fred, and Marcus thought he had never seen Jane look lovelier than she did as a bride. She was radiant and he thanked his lucky stars that all had turned out so well for them. It was a somewhat informal wedding and the service, though simple had been specially devised for them, as they were widowers who were marrying for the second time.

There were no hymns or psalms, nor a sermon, though the Rev Fred asked blessings for the couple. A harpist played before the service and for a short time afterwards, but that was sufficient, as there was no need for background music because the guests made quite enough sound with their cheerful chatter.

After a delicious lunch, many of the guests walked in the garden while Jane and Marcus changed into their going away outfits. Everyone was invited to stay on, if they wished, as there were staff in the house, then a car drew up to take the bridal pair to Birmingham International Airport en route to Jersey in the Channel Islands. The couple received a rousing send off from their guests then just before Jane got into the car, she threw her bouquet which was caught by Sylvia. Jane had not wanted to travel too far afield, but Marcus thought they should go somewhere different so they decided on Jersey, traditionally a honeymoon island and only a short flight away.

It seemed rather flat once the couple had left but some local friends remained behind, and as the weather was mild and sunny, they took advantage of the croquet lawn, though none bathed in the indoor swimming pool. Tom told his London friends that they were welcome to continue the celebrations at West Bridge Hall if they wished. It was on their way back to town so was conveniently situated for them. However, he also added that if anyone wanted to stay the night, they were welcome, as it would round off the weekend for them. Monica wanted to visit Bourton next morning, and as she had Daniel and Imogen with her in her car, they accepted Tom's invitation.

The Red Drawing Room and the library at West Bridge Hall, were particularly inviting, so most people, after admiring the gardens, settled down indoors to chat about the wedding and put the world to rights.

Sylvia and Imogen sat apart, obviously having a heart to heart. Imogen was very sympathetic to her friend as she knew how tricky her mother could be. She was also aware that Sylvia loved her father, but wondered what would happen now that Polly was back for good. Could they simply carry on as before or would Sylvia attempt to make a clean break? Polly's return was soon common knowledge and its farcical side did not go unnoticed; in fact, there were a lot of humorous comments. Naturally, they were sorry for Conrad, Imogen and Sylvia, who were surely put out by her behaviour, but the men in particular wouldn't have been human if they hadn't enjoyed some schaden freude at Conrad's expense. The only person who didn't seem at all bothered was Polly herself.

Guy felt sympathy for Sylvia, of whom he had become fond while they were working together and hoped she would be available for his next TV project which, this time would also involve Sally. Although he had now known her for some time, she was still an enigma to him. Sylvia was much easier to read and she was very attractive, beautiful, in fact. He thought that it was a pity she was so obsessed with Conrad but there was no doubting that she truly cared for him. Women were such a mystery, mused Guy, especially when the most delightful females fall for the most disastrous men. However, strong sexual energy undoubtedly plays its part and passion makes fools of us all.

Ginny's illicit relationship with Paul was over, though they had been so discreet that few others suspected that it had even started. Helen had abandoned her college course and was devoting herself to motherhood. Paul and she had settled very well into married life and parenthood; they now had two little children, and Helen had just embarked on another pregnancy. Guy joked that they seemed to be starting a baby farm.

"Well, what about you, Guy?" queried Paul. "You're leaving it a bit late, you know."

"Oh, I don't think I am the father type," replied Guy.

"Well, you don't know what you are missing," responded Paul.

"I reckon I do," smiled Guy, "sleepless nights and exhaustion."

"That's true, but it's all worth it, especially if you have as fantastic a wife as I have."

"You are very lucky, but where am I to find such a paragon?" countered Guy.

"Well, just look around you, there are lots of fish in the sea, you know."

"Yes, but I am not a Merman, so they wouldn't be any use to me," he laughed.

"Now, you just think over what I said and don't waste any time; life is short but you are a long time in the graveyard."

"Oh, well," replied Guy, "I will bear that in mind."

"Great," said Paul, "mind you do!"

It looked as if Conrad was giving Sylvia a wide berth because he knew people must be talking and laughing, no doubt, about his recent family upset, which even he admitted was farcical. Sylvia and Imogen repaired to the library to carry on their chat, but Daniel came to find Imogen, and she went off with him. While she was sitting alone, looking at a magazine, David found her.

"Hello," he said, "may I join you, pretty maid of honour?" Sylvia looked up. "There's no law against it," she smiled.

"I saw you in a film on TV the other night," he told her.

"Oh, no," she groaned, "don't tell me: Charles II."

"That's it; I found it good rollicking fun and I thought you were first rate as Barbara Villiers. What I don't understand is why you gave up acting so early?"

"I couldn't take the stress," Sylvia replied, "and you know what they say; 'if you can't stand the heat, get out of the kitchen'. I am pleased that I found out pretty soon that I am not temperamentally cut out for such an unpredictable way of life. I now prefer to be a backroom girl."

"Well, I would say it's a loss to the profession, but temperament, just as much as talent plays a large part. Anyway, Jane Partington, oh, I must remember to call her Jane MacIver now, told me what an excellent PA you are. I am actually looking for a new PA myself because my girl, who was also first rate, has just gone on maternity leave and I wondered if you would be interested in her job."

Sylvia was taken by surprise and hardly knew what to say. She was free at present because though Guy was proposing to make another documentary, it was only in the first stage of preparation. David's suggestion, therefore, seemed a real blessing. However, she told him, "You don't know anything about me or my CV."

"Well, you come highly recommended which is good enough for me," he replied. "Alright, tell me about yourself.

What is your background, apart from acting?"

"Well, to start at the beginning; my mother is Welsh and my father is French. I was brought up in Wales where my mother was a teacher and my father lectured at the University of Cardiff. I began acting in school and did rather well, so it was assumed that I would try for a drama college. Surprisingly, I won a scholarship to the Central School, but on graduation, I soon became disillusioned. I did manage to get an agent but he had few decent contacts and somehow, I slipped through the net. Then came the Charles II film but I found the whole process of filming rather degrading. I hated having to simulate intimate sex scenes with an actor I couldn't bear, in full view of other actors and technical crew, so it is a time I'd rather forget, but the fact that it is often shown on TV late at night and I still get risqué letters from fans, bothers me. I soon gave up social media as I would rather not know what people are saying about me and I have tried to get stills photographs taken off the Net. It's true I have done some nude modelling for a couple of noted artists, but that is not as stressful as filming. I invested the money from the film to take a business and computer course then looked for work as a PA. Fortunately, I was introduced to Jane and she put a lot of work my way.

I know that there are actors who can subdue their personalities to the extent that they will do anything a part requires, but I am afraid I am not one of them. You might say I am a dilettante, rather than a professional, yet, I still want to work in theatre and film, even if it is behind the scenes."

"You won't make as much money that way," stated David. "Well, I know we all need money to make the world go round, but as long as I have a regular salary and enough money for necessities, I am not worried about making a fortune."

"Do you have to get back to London tonight?" asked David, "or could you stay here overnight and come to Stratford tomorrow?"

"I think Ginny would be happy to put me up and yes, I would be free to come to see you tomorrow. I could ask her if she would be willing to drive me to Stratford."

"Good, that is fixed then. Give me your number and email address, and I will fix a time for you to come over. Now I must make tracks and say goodbye to everyone. I am so glad we have met, Sylvia, and trust that we will have a fruitful working relationship."

Sylvia could not believe her luck so went in search of Ginny, who agreed to make up a bed for her and said she would drive her to see David. She then found Imogen to tell her the news. Her friend was very pleased, not only for Sylvia, but for her family; after all, if she took the job, she would have to move to Stratford, and Imogen thought that would be ideal as it would get her away from Conrad and Polly. Although she was his daughter, Imogen was fully aware of Conrad's magnetism, and the fact that he and Sylvia had been lovers for some time, made the bond even more difficult to break, especially as he was rumoured to be such an incredible lover. Imogen had long known about her parents' sexual exploits and as a young girl, had been jealous of the other girls her father bedded. However, she came to understand that that is one of the last taboos and he would never compromise her, though some gossipmongers spread rumours that he had had an illicit relationship with her.

Fortunately, Daniel had studied with Conrad and had known the family for years so dismissed the rumours. He was aware, of course, that Conrad was an incorrigible roué but did not believe that he would foul his own nest. Imogen was only a couple of years younger than him but he had always treated her like a sister, though recently, he had realised that she was a mature woman and though not a raving beauty, was a pleasing looking girl. What's more, she was also a patient, sympathetic listener.

Unknown to her, though, Daniel seemed to be taking a leaf out of Conrad's book as he had bedded Emma during the time he was painting her picture. It was while Ranu was away but once he returned, Emma stopped seeing Daniel. Conrad and Polly had obviously always had sex addiction problems, and he soon realised that he had to exercise control over his libido if he did not want to go down the same route. He was very fond of Imogen so did not want to play around anymore. For a man not quite thirty, he was well established as a painter at home, and through Monica's gallery and her American interests, his name was also becoming known abroad. Perhaps, he thought, it was time he settled down with Imogen who, he believed, would be a good wife for him. Also, he hoped for a family and she had said that she wanted children at some point. He was glad that she was totally different from her predatory mother. However, he overestimated his will power and succumbed to Polly's lure when for a short time, she was without a sexual partner, other than Conrad, of course. There was no doubt that Polly was good fun, but also a real handful, and Daniel felt that Conrad had been amazingly patient with her because by conventional standards, she was a rotten wife and mum. Anyway, that was what he thought.

Imogen was doing well at Sotheby's, training to become an auctioneer, but she was the first to admit that she was not particularly ambitious. Yes, she wanted to earn her living and be independent of her parents, but she told Daniel that she hoped to marry one day and have children. Well, today's ceremony had given Daniel food for thought and he began to envisage proposing to Imogen when the right moment presented itself. Strangely, he did not stop to consider if he was actually in love with her.

Chapter Twenty-Three

Once they had cleared Departures, Marcus and Jane relaxed, and looked forward to a few days of respite on a holiday island. The weather stayed bright and sunny, and they had a delightful flight, seeing clearly the Isle of Wight and the Cherbourg Peninsula as they approached the Channel Islands. The first to be seen was Alderney which was the furthest out in the Channel, Guernsey and Sark were next, with small islands around them, then the largest island, Jersey, which is nearest to the coast of Brittany. The plane descended, lower and lower, until they were almost on the beach of the great sweep of St Ouen's Bay, with its Martello tower standing on a rocky outcrop in the sea. Then just a hop, skip and jump, and they were on the runway and the arrivals area. Despite its small size, it is a very busy airport, and there were several large planes waiting to depart as others were about to land, including Marcus and Jane's plane. Further to the north of the airport was the Aero Club with a wealth of small planes and executive jets parked alongside it.

The plane taxied to a stop and they were soon in the baggage hall where they picked up their small amount of luggage. There were police with sniffer dogs, but they went through the 'Nothing to Declare' section without a problem. After signing the car hire form, they picked up the car and sped off to the L'Horizon Hotel, situated on St Brelade's Bay. Here, they found a message waiting for them inviting them to dinner with the Lieutenant Governor at Government House the next evening. It was a kind gesture, but truly, Marcus and his new bride just wanted to be alone.

Nevertheless, Marcus looked forward to meeting an old Army comrade again, and introducing Jane to him and his wife. Like Patrick, after school, Marcus had graduated from Sandhurst into a Guards Regiment where he was commissioned and where he had met Martin, now General Tomkins, with whom he had served in the Gulf.

Having been shown to their room, Jane and Marcus were bowled over with the wonderful sea view from the back of the hotel and the terraces which came down almost onto the beach, so that they understood why St Brelade's Bay is famous for being the fifth best beach in the whole of the British Isles. They made themselves a cup of tea and Jane began to read out aloud from a leaflet about Jersey. Although the island is a part of the British Isles and is a Crown Peculiar, it is not strictly the UK. Unfortunately, the Crown could not protect any of the Channel Islands at the start of the Second World War; consequently, they became the only part of the British Isles to be occupied by the Germans until 1945.

Jane read that Jersey French was widely spoken until a hundred years ago and some very old people still speak it but English is now the common tongue, though Portuguese and Polish can be heard in the streets. The States are the Jersey government and most MPs, known as Senators or Deputies, are Independent, though a political party has been formed. The currency is sterling and Jersey has its own postal service.

Most of the signs in Jersey are French and many of the old families have French roots, however, nowadays, there is a cosmopolitan atmosphere though there are stringent residency conditions. Agriculture used to be the main stay of the island but now Finance has taken over and the digital age is having its effect. "Thanks, Jane," said Marcus, "that's most interesting. I assumed that the Channel Islands were like the Isle of Wight, but I see the set-up is rather different."

Having unpacked, the couple went down to the lounge, looking out onto the beach and had a Jersey cream tea then they went for a stroll in the late afternoon sun. The sea was as calm as calm could be, and they sat for a while on a bench looking out to the horizon, surrounded by early spring flowers and palm trees. On the water were some young people in canoes and a couple of jet skiers, making the most of the temperate weather. After a little while, the newlyweds walked along to the Fishermen's chapel next to the venerable old church at the end of the bay. They felt that the view across the breadth of the bay from the churchyard to the pre-historic cave of La Cotte was the equal of any foreign shore; and as they were the only visitors, the little chapel, with its early medieval wall paintings, was a haven of peace. For a while, they sat on a wooden bench holding hands and radiating happiness then they made their way back to the hotel where they had a little snooze before dressing for dinner.

So much had happened during the day that they were both ready to turn in straight after dinner. Their bedroom, which looked out on a moonlit sea, was large and comfortable as was the en-suite but soon, they were tucked up in bed together. Usually, each of them read before going to sleep but this time, they were happy to just snuggle up and give themselves up to the land of Nod. Despite her happy frame of mind and the fact that she lay in Marcus's arms, she had a lucid dream about Arnold, her late husband. She was standing on the beach with him but contrary to how he looked in life, he was bedraggled and unkempt, all his military swagger a thing of the past. He called out to her and though in life she had hated him, she now felt overwhelmed with pity. He stretched out his hand to clasp hers and in a choked voice, begged her to forgive him. Jane had a kind heart and though she was surprised at herself, she told him that in her present happiness, she was able to forgive him.

"I am in a hell of my own making," he told her. "All is dark and cold, and I cannot find a ray of light, please help me. Don't let anyone tell you that hell is hot; on the contrary, it is very cold because God's love and light are absent, but I believe that your forgiveness will generate a spark of light that will guide me."

Jane, though she had little time for religion, believed in a Supreme Being and ministering angels, so she called for help for Arnold.

She had thought little about her own mortality, but now Arnold told her that if we have not generated sufficient light during our lifetime, we will find ourselves in a twilight zone because we have to generate our own light during our lifetime. That is what the Bible means when it says that we have to show the light in our bushel. "Although I thought I was so well versed in my version of religion, I was totally ignorant of the Truth, so there were only small pockets of light where I had helped my fellow men but they weren't sufficient to lead me into the kindly light. However, it is there, I know that, even if I am not yet able to access it. When I cried, 'God help me', I found you and as you are the one I harmed most, it is your forgiveness that is so crucial to me. I have to make reparation, but you have given me the courage to begin to make amends. Thank you, dear Jane. You will never know how much you have helped me, when I always did my utmost to make you unhappy. Farewell."

The sea was a sheet of shimmering silver as he walked towards it and disappeared into the distance, draped in moonlight.

Jane had never experienced any such dream before, nor did she normally remember upon waking. However, this dream she would not forget though she didn't intend to tell Marcus about it as she considered that he would naturally be upset that she had dreamed of her unpleasant former husband on their wedding night.

Next morning, they had Continental breakfast in bed and putting the 'don't disturb' notice on the door of their room, snuggled down to enjoy an hour of conjugal bliss. Then, having showered and dressed, they got into their hired car, and set off for the little shopping area of Red Houses, less than a mile away. Having picked up the Sunday papers at Waitrose, they carried on along Route Orange then turned off at the signs for Corbiere, one of the supreme beauty spots on the island; a magical place which draws Jersey residents and visitors alike, especially at sun down. The sparkling white lighthouse on its tall granite rock overlooks the vast expanse of St Ouen's Bay with its Martello tower in the midst of the sea, though at low tide, it is possible to walk to it and along the causeway to the lighthouse. There are concrete bunkers and gun emplacements from the German occupation which tell their own story, as does the Underground Hospital in another part of the island, built with slave labour, but that was not ever used.

The couple decided to have coffee at the Phare Restaurant on the headland and skim through the Sunday papers. As there was only a mild breeze, they took their tray outside in the morning sunshine and enjoyed the sea view that stretched without interruption to New Jersey in the USA.

When they had finished their coffee, they folded the newspapers and continued their journey, making for the Five Mile Road along the sweep of the bay, with the sea to their left and an extensive area of dunes on their right. They climbed upwards northwards towards Gros Nez (Big Nose) with the ruins of a medieval castle then wandered around the wild area, taking in large gulps of the wonderfully clear air. When Jane said that her ankles were swelling, they returned to the car and took a spin before enjoying a seafood platter in the restaurant at the Phare.

Back at L'Horizon, they sat on the terrace for a while, enjoying the view of the beach where people walked their dogs, played volleyball, or rode horses into the sea. Then they popped into bed for a love-in, before getting ready to go to dinner at Government House.

The following day, they made good use of their car, touring the island. It was still rather early for tourists so they found several places closed; however, they had a good view of the Brittany coast and enjoyed a delicious lunch at the Seymour Inn on the East coast, which when the tide is out, looks like a moonscape. From there, they went on up the coast to Gorey, a picturesque fishing village, dominated by the enormous form of Mont Orgeil Castle. From there, they worked their way back along the north of the island with its high cliffs until they came to the Classic Farm tearoom, where they ate homemade cakes and drank piping hot tea. Having looked around the farm shop and bought some Jersey Black Butter, actually made of apples and liquorice, not milk, and some Jersey Fudge as presents, they drove back to the hotel.

The next morning, they rose early, had breakfast, packed and drove to the airport at St Peter where they relinquished the car, and boarded the flight to Birmingham.

Although they had enjoyed their short honeymoon, they were glad to be home. Yes, although Jane frequently stayed at Milton House, it was actually now her home, and she and Marcus were keen to renovate the old nursery for the anticipated birth of their first child together.

Patrick, Marcus's son, was not at all put out by the fact that his father was to have another child, twenty-five years after the birth of his first one. Patrick had known Jane for a long time and was devoted to her, and, as a gay man; he was pleased that the pressure to provide a future heir no longer fell to him, as he had no intention of fathering a child.

However, everyone was in for a shock when Jane's scan showed that she was carrying twins, a boy and a girl. She and Marcus were delighted but had to laugh as they likened it to the long awaited bus which is immediately followed by another one. Actually, at their age, it couldn't have worked out better as having two children for the price of one was a very special gift. Now they would have to rethink the nursery, so off they went to the shops again and had great fun choosing all the necessary items.

In the light of a multiple birth, Jane's doctor arranged for her to have a planned caesarean delivery which met with her approval. She had heard what a difficult time Paula, Marcus's first wife, had had bringing Patrick into the world, so anything that relieved a mother of such pain and trauma was welcome. Jane reflected that if the torture that most women suffer with even a natural delivery was inflicted on political prisoners, Amnesty International would be up in arms. Rather than decry women for having caesarean operations as a matter of course, it might be wise to consider such procedures as normal for the majority of women. However, for those who rely on the NHS, it all comes down to cost.

Jane was lucky as her husband had the means to arrange for the best medical team available and she was found to be in the best of health. Later on in her pregnancy, a date would be set for the caesarean and Jane settled down to await the coming of her children.

However, she was not idle as she read a lot, and was kept informed of the results of the research being carried out by Sally and Guy, principally at West Bridge Hall.

Chapter Twenty-Four

On the way home from West Bridge Hall, Monica made a detour to Bourton as she wanted to visit Miranda Pointer, to discuss a forthcoming exhibition at the Gayton Gallery. It would not take place for several months as there were other exhibitions listed before hers, but it would be necessary to see what works Miranda had ready and how many more she would need to paint in the intervening months.

Daniel and Imogen had not visited Bourton before, so were happy to accompany Monica, and were particularly keen to see Miranda's paintings.

Chatting as they drove, Imogen asked if they had heard that Emma Simson had her heart set on going to Hollywood. Her agent knew that a film about Elizabeth of Austria was in the pipeline and he felt that the part of a lady in waiting would be a good opening for her so would do his best to get her a screen test. If he could obtain even a subsidiary role for her, it would give her the all-important foot in the door. Nevertheless, she would be up against strong competition, though if she was successful, who knows where it might lead? There would be other films; or even TV series, though it was all in the lap of the gods, or rather, movie moguls, but one had to strike out to achieve anything and Imogen knew that Emma was ruthlessly ambitious.

Although Monica and Daniel's affair had died a natural death, she was very pleased that he and Imogen appeared to be getting on really well. She had known the girl since she was a child, and thought that she and Daniel would make a good match. It was important for a creative artist to have a settled domestic background, though it seemed that few of them achieved it. You couldn't say that Conrad and Polly's domestic arrangements were conventional, yet until recently, it had worked for both of them and Imogen appeared to have weathered her Bohemian childhood without becoming a nut case. In fact, she was a very balanced young woman, who was more mature than her parents.

Miranda's house was in a turning just off the main street. It was a modest, but pretty building and though it had a white painted, Georgian facade, Monica assumed that the inner core was much older. This was confirmed when they went inside and saw the large brick inglenook fireplace in the colourful sitting room, with its large extension at the back that provided a studio for Miranda. Monica introduced her to her friends and she was amazed that so celebrated a painter as Daniel had come to see her work. She offered them a cup of tea which they declined as they were anxious to see her studio and still have time for a quick look around Bourton before driving back to London.

Daniel was always on the lookout for likely competition and knew that Monica's practiced eye would not be fooled. However, he was relieved to see that Miranda's work could not be more different from his own. Her palate was subtle and she used egg tempera, rather than oil paint, which suited her strange subjects, not easy to define, yet, which evoked a haunting atmosphere.

Miranda's visitors were duly complimentary, but soon said goodbye and left to explore the model village, before their drive back to town. Monica stayed on in the studio, closely examining the paintings while the natural light lasted. She was even more impressed than she had initially been and felt that with the right handling, Miranda had a fine career ahead of her. Her work would certainly be a great asset to the gallery as it was unlike that of any of Monica's other artists. She was loyal to her established painters but always had her antennae poised to detect new talent as she was aware that to keep Gayton in the forefront of the art world, there could be no resting on her laurels.

As the light began to wane, Miranda took Monica back into her cosy sitting room. She had an electric coal effect stove in the large fireplace which gave a rosy glow, and Miranda having produced a pot of tea, sandwiches and cakes, the two women settled down to talk business. Monica asked Miranda what she hoped to achieve in the long term and Miranda admitted that she experimented a lot but was now trying to develop a uniformity of style so that her work would be instantly recognisable. Monica said that that was important if a name was to become well known, adding, "The thing about Conrad is that from the beginning, he was original almost without trying to be. Few artists are original but those that usually become successful are even if like Bacon and Freud, their work is not very pleasant to look at. Nevertheless, though both are now dead, the prices of their paintings go through the roof."

Monica said she actually preferred David Hockney, as his work was totally recognisable but also truly appealing. He was also a first rate stage designer, and Monica told Miranda that she remembered seeing his designs for 'The Rake's progress' which had been originally produced at Glyndebourne and considered them 'pure genius'. She also admired his costumes and sets for Mozart's 'The Magic Flute', then referred to Picasso 'who you either love or hate', adding that he was a first rate draughtsman and had produced exquisite line drawings. However, although his early work was delightful, it was not particularly original. She inferred that he had taken a cynical look at the art business and decided that to be noticed, he would have to be so outrageous that he couldn't be ignored. Braque was experimenting with geometric forms, and Picasso took note of what he was doing and got on the bandwagon. She confessed that she considered him rather a con artist, but it seems people like to be conned as even from the grave, he was still laughing all the way to the bank. These days, art had to be commercial and often, the worst art brought in the most money. As for the Turner prize, well, Monica wouldn't waste breath on that! Not that it hurt her gallery when Conrad won it!

Miranda turned on some table lamps and the room was even cosier than before. For an artist's room, it was very neat, with everything in its place; yet, there was something unique about it and it had a delightful ambience of homeliness.

Monica and her friends had been invited to stay the night, but when the couple came back from sightseeing, they said if Monica wished, they would drive her car back to town, or if she gave them a lift to the station, they could catch a train. She told them to take the car and asked Miranda if she would give her a lift to the station next day. Miranda agreed so after having a cup of tea and a sandwich, Daniel and Imogen set off for home. After they left, Miranda took Monica up to a pretty guest bedroom with Regency striped wallpaper and furniture, and a window with apple green curtains, which looked onto a small garden and open countryside. There was also a small en-suite bathroom which had recently been installed. Monica unpacked her small overnight case then re-joined Miranda in the sitting room.

"This is such a pretty house," said Monica. "How long have you lived here?"

"Only two years; before that, I lived with my brother in an isolated farmhouse in the Brecon Beacons."

"I suppose, it must have been difficult to promote your career from there?"

"Yes, it was for me, but my brother was a writer so it was ideal for him."

"Did he leave to marry, or did he remain in the farmhouse after you left?"

"No, he died."

There were tears in Miranda's eyes as she spoke, so Monica said that she was sorry then changed the subject, asking Miranda if there was a restaurant or pub nearby where she could take her to dinner. The artist replied that 'The Lamb' was a noted hostelry so a phone call was made and a table booked for 8pm. When they arrived, the place was already buzzing with a lively mix of locals and tourists all relishing the excellent fare for which the establishment is noted.

As they ate, Monica did her best to draw Miranda out, so told her something of her own life, hoping to encourage the girl to do the same. Monica was not clairvoyant like Sally, but she was intuitive and read people well. There was something mysterious about Miranda and she hoped to find out what it was. Jokingly, she asked the girl, "What is your story?"

"I don't know what you mean," she answered, looking down at her plate.

"Well, I see it like this," Monica went on. "When we are born, we are given a hand of cards to play and from that we create our story."

"Oh, I see what you mean, though I have never thought of it in those terms."

"So," countered Monica, "how do you think your story is going so far?"

"Maybe, it isn't for me to say. I am doing my best to become a good artist, devoting all my time to my work, but only time will tell how well or how badly my story goes," said Miranda. "So far, I wouldn't say that the story is anything out of the ordinary."

"It doesn't have to be," replied Monica. "However dull a life may seem on the surface, there is a story to be written and every human life is interesting in its own way. We also overlook the fact that we have two lives, the outer one that the public sees and our inner, hidden one."

It may have been Monica's imagination but she had a feeling that she had touched a nerve as Miranda changed the subject, merely mentioning the meal and the restaurant in general. It was almost ten pm when the women returned to the house. Miranda offered Monica a cup of hot chocolate then both of them went up to their respective rooms. It had been a delightful evening and Miranda found Monica stimulating company. She would like to have unburdened herself to her prospective patron but she had never told anyone her story and prayed that it would always remain hidden. No doubt, Monica would have lent a sympathetic ear, but the story was too bizarre and would, undoubtedly, receive condemnation, so no one must know. It was not only her story, but that of her family and had to remain the skeleton in her cupboard, though she had to admit that it would be a relief to confess the whole affair. However, she prayed that it would never be known.

She was thankful that she was not a Catholic or she would have been duty bound to confess the shameful story to a priest. She realised that to some people, it was cathartic and the priest was bound to keep the information confidential, but everyone is human and the thought that such knowledge could be used for emotional blackmail, horrified her. No, she would never give that power to any religion, or anyone else for that matter.

Next morning, after breakfast, Miranda drove Monica to the nearest railway station and during the journey, she thought a lot about her young artist. On the surface, she was a pleasant young woman with a decided talent for painting, but she didn't give much away about herself. She was a good listener and Monica had opened several conversational gambits but Miranda offered little of a personal nature in return. She was very ready to talk about art, and was, obviously, well informed regarding painters old and new. She had trained at St Martin's so knew Polly Beight slightly. However, being a shy, reserved girl, she had not really taken much part in college life, nor did she, as far as Monica could ascertain, have any romantic attachments.

The fact was that rather than looking for work when she qualified, she went back home where she dedicated herself to the solitary life of a painter. The scenery of the Brecon Beacons gave her unending delight, not only for the location but for the ever-changing play of light and the emotions evoked within her.

She had been highly influenced by the work of the painter, Ivon Hitchens, and like him, although she had painted en plein air, the results bore little resemblance to the physical world but more to the abstract, spiritual nature of the scene and its effect upon the artist's imagination.

On her return from the station, Miranda took a cup of coffee into her studio and prepared to resume work on her latest canvas, a large tempera rendering of an autumnal scene which she had started months before. As she sat sipping her coffee, her thoughts drifted over her past and what a strange one it was. She had had a happy childhood as her parents were devoted to each other, and dearly loved their children, Richard and Miranda. Richard was two years older than his sister and they were extremely close. So close, in fact, that their parents encouraged them to choose places of further education at different ends of the country in order to learn to live independently from each other.

Richard was a natural academic, whereas Miranda was artistic to her fingertips. From an early age, Richard's writing was outstanding and he developed a fascination with ancient Egypt. He did not want to become an archaeologist because that involved a good deal of physical digging. He was more interested in research so opted for a degree in Ancient History and languages. When he graduated, he spent some months at the Cairo Museum, but politically things were not good so he returned home and worked for a while at the British Museum. By this time, he had a lot of unorthodox theories which did not endear him to some of his colleagues.

Following the sudden death of their father, Richard returned home. By this time, Miranda had also qualified and was already at home, looking after their mother who had just been diagnosed with inoperable cancer of the pancreas. Peggy was soon transferred to a Hospice and the siblings were told it was only a matter of weeks, if that. They spent all the available time at her bedside and were with her when she finally slipped away. The children were inconsolable but Richard had to pull himself together and make funeral arrangements, though another funeral coming so soon after their father's death, seemed more than they could bear.

Although they were now adults, losing both parents so quickly, was a terrible blow, but fortunately, the family lawyer was a tower of strength and arranged counselling for them. An estate agent was also very helpful, as they could not envisage staying on at the family home. For one thing, it was too big and for another, it held memories impossible to erase.

His father's death triggered mental health problems for Richard. He had always been a loner, but now he dreaded having to meet people. Miranda became all in all to him. The family home was sold for a good price and they bought a remote farmhouse which stood in fifteen acres of land, surrounded by woods. They invested money left over from the sale of the family house as the farmhouse was

183

cheaper, and with the Trust Fund originally set up by their mother for them in their teens and money left by their father, it meant that even after Inheritance Tax, they had no need to earn a living. Whether that was a good thing or not, was debatable, but they weren't idle.

As far as Miranda was concerned, a lot of their difficulty came from the fact that sex education was introduced at far too early an age at their local State school. Richard, though he was a shy boy, had a good deal of sexual energy, even at the age of twelve. Miranda was in thrall to her brother and when he pressed her to enter into his sexual explorations, she fell in with his wishes.

At first, their forays were just curiosity, like many kids of that age and harmless enough.

However, by the time he was fifteen, Richard was having regular sexual relations with thirteen-year-old Miranda, though this was completely unknown to their parents. Both of them knew that what they were doing was wrong, but they enjoyed the experience. Richard had learned that ancient Egyptian royalty used to marry their sisters, so was not as bothered by what was seen as taboo in the Western world. He said it was a matter of perception and sexual mores changed from age to age. Nevertheless, Richard was sensible enough to procure contraception from vending machines and later, Miranda acquired the contraceptive pill which she took every day, though the doctor had no idea that her sexual partner was her own brother.

Miranda was always afraid of the risk of discovery and it played on her nerves, however, Richard was her lord and master, and she couldn't refuse him, even if she had wanted to, which she actually didn't. It took her some time though to realise that his mental health was deteriorating and that the only thing that seemed to keep him on track was to frequently make love, with Miranda, of course; he wouldn't contemplate having any other partner.

After their parents' deaths, Richard accidentally discovered that their father had committed suicide though it said death by misadventure on the death certificate. In a bizarre sequence of events, Jack had learned that he and his wife were twins who had been separated at birth, and adopted by two separate families who lived at opposite ends of the country from each other. They met at University but had no idea that they were siblings. Then they fell in love and married but remained in ignorance of the consanguinity.

When Richard found out, the news tipped him over the edge of an already fragile mind and he had an emotional breakdown. Sex had always played a large part in his psyche, but now, he began to expose himself in public, just in negligible ways at first, but gradually, he became more daring because he relished seeing the shocked reaction of others. Finally, he was arrested and charged with indecency. Miranda was humiliated because, of course, it was reported in the local paper. The result was that he was put on the sex offenders register. Naturally, Miranda did her best to support him, but his behaviour had ruined his life.

He received counselling and therapy but sadly, history repeated itself, and like his father, he committed suicide. He was lucid enough beforehand, however, to make a Will, leaving everything to Miranda. Somehow, he acquired a quantity of Diamorphine then booked into a hotel at Moreton-in-Marsh, where he took an overdose. Despite his state of mind, he had pre-paid by cash and ensured that Miranda was spared finding his body at home. She had loved him too well, but now she was on her own and either had to sink or swim.

In spite of her grief, she was determined to swim. She knew she had talent and that she should make the most of it. In a strange way, Richard's death freed her and catapulted her into a determined state of mind. She found representation at the Bourton Gallery; sold the remote farmhouse and bought the extended cottage close to the main street. From here, she never looked back and being taken up by Monica was the gilt on the gingerbread.

Life was good and she had no intention of wasting it. However, she felt that she had been put off sex for life, so chose to be celibate, which she found suited her fine as she could work without having to take into account the needs of a lover or husband.

Chapter Twenty-Five

Even though their affair had ended, Daniel was pleased that his relationship with Monica had not suffered. She did not hold grudges, and was actually quite pleased that he and Imogen seemed to be keen on each other. She now had two new interests in her life, Nancy, the actress and Miranda, the painter. Nancy had encouraged her to consider investing in the theatre, which would bring her into a new milieu and Miranda would allow her to foster another interesting talent.

After all the emotional upheavals, everything seemed to have gone quiet on the Conrad front and he was working hard. Monica was thrilled with his new paintings and looked forward to another blockbuster at her gallery. Sylvia was no longer in the picture as she was now living in Stratford-upon-Avon, having accepted David Thornton's offer to be his PA with the Royal Shakespeare Company. However, accommodation was in short supply in the town so she was lodging with an elderly widow in Sheep Street, opposite the 'White Swan' or 'Dirty Duck' as the locals call it. Nevertheless, she was hopeful of finding a place of her own at some point. In the meantime, she had bought a bicycle, and in her spare time was getting to know the beautiful countryside and quaint villages outside the town. There was no point in buying a car at present because she had nowhere to park it.

She had found it hard to meet Conrad at the wedding, but he acted as if she was just another friend. He and Polly were like love's young dream once more, and there had, obviously, been no further talk of divorce. No one mentioned Count Emilio, and it seemed that that episode was well and truly buried. Sylvia had once suspected that Guy was rather sweet on her, but at the lunch, sitting beside Sally, he only had eyes for her. Of course, they were working together and Sylvia was sorry that she would not be part of their team for the next TV series as she had decided to stay in Stratford indefinitely. She loved her job and felt she had really landed on her feet as she had the best boss in the world, albeit he was also her new love interest.

Of course, Sylvia knew little of David's personal background. However, she was aware that he had recently been divorced. He had said that the reason he hired Sylvia was because his former PA was pregnant and on maternity leave. What he did not say was that he had had an affair with her for a few months. Her husband found out about it but forgave her and they patched up their marriage to the extent that Marie became pregnant by him. Now David was footloose and fancy free, and was ready to try his luck with Sylvia. She was still smarting from losing Conrad, so when David invited her out to dinner and to spend the night at his apartment, she accepted and was ready to risk whatever fate held in store.

When they reached David's place, he put on the TV and saw on the rolling news that there had been a terrorist incident at the Barbican. Sylvia immediately thought of William Wilcox and Monica's new friend, Nancy, who lived there. The catastrophe had just happened but thankfully, the suicide bomb had only partly gone off and though dreadfully injured, the terrorist was still alive. There was a state of chaos but so far, there didn't appear to be any fatalities, though there were injuries, and a good deal of confusion and damage to property.

Sylvia rang Monica's apartment, knowing that Marcus was staying there. He and Jane had just gone to bed so had no knowledge of what was happening in East London. He turned on the TV and saw that it was absolute chaos; the police, rescue and fire services were on the spot, and other teams were being brought in from around London, while forensic teams were also on their way. Marcus had no idea if Patrick, Monica and their friends were safe, but it was too early yet to get any accurate information, so they watched the TV news unfold. Although there were injuries, so far, nothing life threatening was reported, however, several people had been taken to hospital.

It was with great relief that Marcus was able to text everyone with the good news that Patrick had rung and they were all safe, having arrived after the bomb went off due to the fact that they had been held up in traffic in Central London. Now they were all doing what they could to assist where necessary.

Fortunately, as more information was received, there appeared to be no fatalities and few serious casualties, more the effects of flying glass causing cuts and bruises, which was bad enough. Although there were lots of people still in shock from the blast, all agreed that it was a miracle that no one was killed and there were fewer casualties than there might have been.

Patrick was due to go to Cyprus at the end of the week and joked that he would probably be safer there than in London.

For Tom and Ginny though, who were staying in the capital for the weekend, it wasn't the end of alarms and excursions, as they received a call to say that their son, Toby, was in hospital in Edinburgh. It was too late to catch a plane, but they would be off first thing in the morning. The hospital doctor was very cagey over the phone so it was difficult to grasp what had happened. It didn't sound good so they had little sleep that night. Anyway, they had to be off to the airport early in the morning so they couldn't afford to oversleep.

The flight to Edinburgh is not a long one, but to Tom and Ginny, it seemed endless as they were both anxious to learn the worst but didn't want to alarm each other. It might be something relatively trivial; on the other hand, it might be very serious. Hospitals did not ring after midnight unless there was sufficient reason.

Arriving at last at the airport, they took a taxi to the hospital where they were met by a registrar who took them into a private room. He did not want to unduly frighten them but the situation was serious because Toby was in a coma.

Apparently, he had been at a party with student chums, which had got out of hand due to the amount of drugs and drink available. As far as his parents knew, Toby did not use drugs and was not a habitual drinker. Dr Young was trying to ascertain whether Toby had taken recreational drugs, or if anything had been put into his drink, though he could have taken an overdose, however, he thought that unlikely at a party. The police had been interviewing partygoers overnight but so far, as few of them were properly compos mentis, they were getting little sense out of them.

The main concern was for Toby to regain consciousness, though at present, it looked very dicey and Dr Young had to ask his parents if they wanted resuscitation if he went into cardiac arrest. This was a terrible thing for Tom and Ginny to face; it was as if they were living in a nightmare from which they expected to wake up at some point. Dr Young had to tell them frankly that at present, they couldn't be certain if Toby would be brain damaged even if he recovered consciousness.

The couple were assured that as they had travelled a long way, a room would be put at their disposal so that they could stay in the hospital. However, as there was a decent looking hotel nearby, they opted to book a room, but said they would be on call at all times.

Both of them were thoroughly exhausted so as they could do nothing at present to help Toby, they showered, put on their nightclothes and tried to sleep. Finally, they drifted off only to be awoken by the ring of the telephone. Toby had regained consciousness, could they come at once? They certainly could and lost no time in throwing on their clothes.

Toby was sitting up in a private ward when they arrived. He looked very pale and drained, but he could speak to them, which was the main thing. Both Tom and Ginny were close to tears with relief at seeing their son conscious once more.

By lunchtime, Toby was returning to his old self. He was even able to eat a little lunch and the police agreed with the doctor not to try to interview him until later in the afternoon.

His parents sat with him, neither of them wanting to go to lunch. Instead, they popped to the outpatients' café, and bought sandwiches and tea in plastic cups, which actually tasted like nectar as they suddenly realised how thirsty they were, and even enjoyed the packaged sandwiches eaten at his bedside.

Toby saw the police alone while his parents went out to a local park for some fresh air.

They were still anxious to know how the crisis had come about but the doctor told them to wait until the next day before they plied their son with questions. When they received the message in London, they had been so startled and anxious that they had not thought of ringing Paul and Helen at that late hour as with young children, and Helen being pregnant, they tended to go to bed early.

Thank goodness, Toby was conscious and they hoped he would soon be released from hospital so they could take him home to West Bridge. Tom rang and Helen answered. He told her that Toby had been at a party but had had a bit of an accident and had ended up in A & E. He made as light of it as he could and she accepted that they would be back, with Toby, as soon as possible. Not to worry, as he was going to be alright and they would ring before they left Edinburgh to let them know that they were on their way.

Toby told his parents that he had been a silly young fool and had taken a pill. He didn't normally take drugs but was feeling down because his girlfriend had just left him for his best friend so when a partygoer offered him a coloured pill, he had thought, *what the heck,* and took it. The fact that he was not used to such things had a devastating effect on him and caused the coma. It had been a stark warning to him and once was enough. He was just thankful to be alive as his condition could well have proved fatal. He had never been in trouble with the police and assured them that he certainly wouldn't take anything ever again, party or no party. He was given a telling off, but was not charged, which was a great relief all round.

Dr Young said they would like to keep him for another night to make sure his kidneys were not affected, but then his parents could take him home. The brain scan showed no harm had been done but Dr Young insisted that he was a very lucky young man, because he had been right on the edge. Many other young drug takers had not been so fortunate.

Ginny wanted to talk seriously to him but Tom suggested that they leave it until they were at home. Fortunately, he was released the next day and they all flew to Birmingham. Paul came to collect them, and they were soon safe and sound at West Bridge. Tom said he had never been more pleased to see the old place, and was thankful to be home and dry. It remained to be seen though, how soon Toby recovered his customary good health and natural buoyancy.

Helen came to see him and brought her little ones, but realised that their boisterousness was more than their uncle could cope with at present so soon took them back to The Gables. She was getting near her time now, but didn't seem fazed as she had delivered her previous babies like shelling peas.

Chapter Twenty-Six

Finally, Tom and Ginny had a heart to heart with Toby, and he confessed that he had not been happy studying Theology. He wanted confirmation of eternal truths, but found none in his forays across several different religions. In fact, he had even more questions now than answers and the last straw was when in his studies of Greek temples, he came to the Holy of Holies shrine and found that it was empty. It was all symbolic, of course, but it mattered greatly to Toby and cast him into a dark depression.

He had suffered a terrible crisis of confidence and experienced the dark night of the soul. "It was dreadful," he told them. "There was a long dark tunnel without a light at the end and I was on my own in a cold, empty universe."

Tom took his hand, looked into his eyes and said, "This is not unknown, old chap, but it is the beginning of wisdom. You may not understand it now, but you will, in time, I assure you."

Ginny then asked about his private life, "Did friends not compensate for the disappointment in your studies?"

"They should have done," replied her son. "I had a delightful girlfriend, but just before I had that experience, I found her and my best friend, Angus, in a very compromising situation. I felt betrayed by two people I trusted, and when I was invited to the party and offered that drug, I thought, 'what the hell' and threw caution to the winds. Well, I paid for it and will never be so stupid again."

"Now," said Tom, "what are we going to do about University?"

"I suppose it would be stupid to waste three years of study, so I will buckle up and take my finals, then with your approval, Dad, I propose to sign up for a course in estate management?"

"That would suit me just fine, my lad. I never understood why you wanted to study Theology in the first place. As far as I can see, it is a rather inconclusive sort of course. Religious belief is a private matter because no one knows what God is, or can confirm any of the accepted stories and myths that have hung around for so long. Some people take the Bible literally but it has always struck me as being largely allegorical, with the odd bit of ancient history thrown in. However, what do I know? I cannot claim to have studied it."

"So," said Ginny, "all's well that ends well and thank Heaven for that."

"I didn't think you believed in Heaven, Mum," laughed Toby. "Oh, Heaven's all right; it's just the rest of the clap trap that I can't stomach. However, we do our bit going to church on Sundays, just to keep the locals happy."

During the night, Helen went into labour. Fortunately, Nanny Betty and the nursemaid, Rose, were on hand while they waited for the midwife. Up to now, Helen's labours had been unusually short, so everyone was forewarned that this time it might be the same. They were not disappointed: Helen was young and fit, and within forty minutes, the new arrival, a little girl, was in her arms. Paul was with her, and hearing all the coming and going, the younger children woke up so he brought them in to see their new sister. The first little boy, Monty, was disappointed that it was a girl, but Simon, the younger one, said he was pleased and would help Nanny look after her.

Paul rang Ginny and Tom, and they came over but left Toby sleeping. Sally had returned so they invited her to join them. Piers, the archivist, also woke up so they said he was welcome to come over to The Gables. Soon, there was a party atmosphere in Helen's room but presently, the midwife shooed them all out as Helen was about to feed the baby. Rose put the boys back to bed, and Nanny took charge of Mum and the little girl. Ginny took the guests into the kitchen, made a pot of tea and handed out mugs then having drunk hers, the midwife bade them all good night but said she would call in tomorrow to make sure all was well. Nanny would now rule the roost, of course and that suited her down to the ground. She was a first rate nanny who adored the children, though she was not a push over with them, so Helen never interfered with her. However, Helen was delighted that she could go through the baby stage again, and looked forward to playing with her little brood while Nanny, Rose and Ginny did the hard work. Paul, having already bred two sons, was now delighted to have a little girl to spoil.

Back in London, Conrad's 'little girl' Imogen, was wondering why Daniel was not around so much. He was in the studio each day, of course and working hard, but where he went in the evenings, she did not know. When she asked him, he made excuses, or looked furtive, so she was none the wiser. She was also aware that whenever she tried to talk to him about their relationship, he prevaricated or changed the subject. Finally, she told him she had changed her mind and didn't think they should marry after all. Rather than being upset, she thought that he actually looked relieved. Of course, her parents and friends were sorry because they hoped that the couple would tie the knot. However, it was better to sort things out now rather than later.

Imogen was working hard at Sothebys and said there was so much to learn that she wondered if she would ever make an auctioneer, though she meant to come out on top. She loved the work, but it was certainly not easy and she knew that she would have to build up her personal confidence in order to handle such an onerous job which involved dealing with very large sums of money. She happened to mention her lack of confidence to Monica, one day and as ever that resilient lady had the answer, telling Imogen to buy a bottle of Larch, from the Bach Flower Remedy range because it promoted confidence. However, it would be some time before Imogen qualified and longer still before she stood on the rostrum.

Now that Daniel had become elusive, she often joined her parents for a meal in the evenings. They were getting on well and just wanted to be allowed to put the Emilio business behind them. Nevertheless, Conrad was well aware that his wife was a nymphomaniac who needed a lot of sex, not only with him, but with lovers for variety: so, bless her, with the best will in the world, she would, no doubt, continue to have her cake, as it were; however, as long as she didn't fall in love, he could cope with the fall out. He had never loved anyone as he did Polly and was glad when she acknowledged that Emilio had been an aberration, a stupid infatuation that should never have gone as far as it did. It was a mystery to her why it had got out of hand, because with hindsight, she realised that he was more gay than straight. What a sillykins she had been. Still, it was all over now and she would never contact him again. Thank heaven, Conrad had forgiven her and taken her back. He was her loadstar and she did not know how she would function without him. Love was very different to lust and much more rare. Well, she enjoyed lust, but it was love that really counted.

Imogen had not looked for another flatmate after Sylvia left as she had begun to enjoy her own space. Although she counted Daniel as a really good friend, she found him unreliable so she decided that it was time to spread her net and make new friends. There was a chap at Sothebys who had asked her out once before but she had declined because she was with Daniel at the time. Now she reappraised him and thought that an evening out with him might not be a bad thing. His name was Rod Whittacker and he specialised in Russian paintings. Imogen knew little about him, other than that he was in his late twenties and single.

One evening, she was at home when the bell rang and when she opened the door, found Conrad standing on the mat. He rarely came to visit her so it surprised her. However, he said he had been in the studio all day and felt like a change of scene. He had not phoned so took a chance on finding her in. She was delighted to see him, especially as he was alone and hoped they could have a comfortable evening together a deux. He told her that he had been working himself into a frazzle and looked forward to having his furrowed brow soothed. She asked if he had eaten and he said he hadn't but hoped she might rustle up something for him.

"Well, I have pizza and salad with ice cream to follow, so you are welcome to share that," she told him.

"Fine, couldn't be better. Shall I put some music on?"

"Yes, why not, there's a recording of 'Carmina Burana' on the CD player, let's have that."

"Right you are; do you want me to lay the table?"

"Well, Dad," she laughed, "you are suddenly getting domesticated and not before time."

"Yes, that's what your mother says."

"Where is she, by the way?" asked his daughter.

"Lecturing, I think. I rarely ask as I can't keep track."

After they had eaten and cleared up, Conrad changed the CD to Beethoven's Emperor Piano Concerto, and both of them relaxed in comfortable armchairs in front of the glow of the artificial coal effect fire, sipping their drinks and letting the exquisite second movement carry them away to goodness knows where. It was perfect; an oasis of calm in a busy world.

Suddenly, there was a ring at the doorbell and Conrad silenced the CD. Imogen opened the door and there stood her mother, Polly, with Daniel.

"We went to Holland Park," said Polly, "but finding it empty, we thought you might be here."

"Where have you been?" asked Imogen.

"Oh, here and there, here and there," she answered nonchalantly. Daniel looked down at his shoes. Surely, he and her mother were not at it?

Oh, dear, sex again, she thought, *it really is getting rather boring.*

194

Had she known it, Daniel was in a real quandary because his love life was becoming too hot for him to handle. At the Biennale in Venice, even before news of Emilio's arrest reached her, Polly had been making a play for Daniel. He and Imogen were more than just good friends at that time, but he found it impossible to resist her scintillating mother. The fact is that Polly could not exist without sex and as Emilio had been away for a couple of weeks, she needed someone to take his place. Daniel felt as if he was on a merry go round from which he couldn't get off.

When she returned home, she set her sights on Daniel as a stopgap until her next adventurer appeared and such was her sexual power that he had become putty in her hands. She was not a bad person, just a confirmed hedonist, who put her own desires before that of anyone else. Despite the fact that Daniel and Imogen had been in a relationship, she never stopped to consider that she was hurting her daughter. She was forty-four, still attractive and a cosy armful, but insatiable and as rampant as a barrel of monkeys where sex was concerned. She never let up, never got bored or ran out of energy. She loved Conrad, of course, but he was familiar territory, and she loved change and variety. Daniel reckoned that her libido would kill her in the end and probably him too, if he did not extricate himself from her clutches.

The way his sex life was going, it was a wonder he had time and energy to paint at all, and it was not as if he was trying to let off steam, he had more than enough to occupy him, so why did he think of sex all the time? He and Imogen were good mates but had not made love very often; in fact, he was not sure that she really liked sex. She had said that she would like to marry one day and have children, but now seemed in no hurry to change her single status. Anyway, she was intent on becoming an auctioneer so that was her focus at present.

Another complication had arisen due to Daniel's developing friendship with William Wilcox. He and Patrick had been an item for as long as Daniel had known them, but Patrick's career often took him abroad, and William, tied to the City, was frequently at a loose end after his working day ended. He believed that Patrick was faithful to him; anyway, Army discipline made it difficult to carry on homosexual affairs, so really, it was not so much that Patrick resisted temptation as that he had little opportunity to do anything about it.

William, on the other hand, though he never admitted it to Patrick, did occasionally enjoy some light dalliance, nothing serious, just a little mutual pleasuring. He had never gone in for cottaging or overt promiscuity but after Patrick went to Cyprus, he invited Daniel to a play at the National Theatre, where they bumped into Nancy who had been rehearsing and they all agreed that they had been very lucky to avoid injury when the bomb had gone off at the Barbican. None of them were hurt and their flats were undamaged, so they were truly thankful, as it might have been very different. After the show, Daniel and William had supper then went their separate ways. A few evenings later, they went to the cinema together, and William invited Daniel back to his flat for a drink and a snack.

It became obvious to Daniel that William found him attractive but he had no thought of getting involved in a gay triangle. They talked about sex in general and the bottle of fine wine went down pretty quickly. William asked if he had ever had any homosexual experience and Daniel had to admit that something like that had got him into trouble at school. One day, thinking they were safe from prying eyes, he and another boy were experimenting, just touching and fumbling with each other; nothing too heavy, when a young master found them. He appeared angry and told them they deserved to be punished. He demanded that they bend over, then picking up a ruler, he whacked them several times on their bare buttocks. They were only twelve but both of them had erections and it seemed that the teacher was just as excited as they were. He then pulled down his trousers and pants, and told them to do the same to him as he had done to them. He was beside himself, shrieking with either pain or delight; the boys couldn't tell which, when, suddenly, the door opened to reveal the headmaster. When he saw what was going on, he was incandescent with rage. He instantly dismissed the teacher, telling him to collect his P45 from the office at once and threatened the boys with expulsion if they mentioned anything about this shocking affair.

They were truly sorry at having been caught, and for being the cause of the young man's dismissal, but they had tasted forbidden fruit and decided that they would carry on regardless, only in a more private environment. Often, they went to the woods and enjoyed themselves in peace; however, by the time they were fifteen, they had discovered girls and switched their allegiance to them.

"Don't you ever feel like experimenting again?" asked William. "Funny you should say that. When I first studied with Conrad Beight, I had a terrific crush on him and he only had to come into the room for me to get a hard on."

"Did he know?" asked William.

"I doubt it; anyway, if anyone is truly heterosexual, it is Conrad. He wouldn't have been interested in sex with a callow youth like me. In any case, girls were around him like chocoholics in Cadbury's."

Daniel was never quite sure what happened next; maybe it was the talk of sex that led him and William to the bedroom. William began caressing him, taking off his jacket and nudging him little by little towards the bed. By this time, Daniel was already aroused, and William laid him down, pulled off his tee shirt and began to stroke him. Daniel knew he ought to resist but didn't seem able to do anything except give himself up to sensuality. William then took off his own tee shirt and unzipped his jeans, revealing the most beautiful rod Daniel had ever seen. No wonder Patrick had fallen in love with him. However, William said that he and Patrick had never had anal sex as neither of them fancied it; anyway, there was plenty they could do to pleasure each other without that.

William then began to show what he meant and Daniel was raised to astonishing heights of passion. The upshot was that he stayed the night. Of course, William asked him not to mention this to anyone, in case it got back to Patrick; he did not want to be disloyal or unfaithful, but excused himself by saying that the sexual urge in those of high libido is so strong that even with the best will in the world, it is terribly hard to resist. Daniel agreed to keep quiet, not just for William's peace of mind, but for his own, as life was complicated enough already.

He said that he had recently been seeing a married woman and needed to extricate himself. William admitted that he and Patrick had long intended to marry once Patrick left the service then they would go to Scotland, where Patrick would administer his father's Scottish estates and William would be financial advisor.

He told Daniel that he believed that love and sex were not necessarily compatible. You could have a strong desire for someone you were not in love with which was simply chemistry; body calling to body: whereas truly loving someone was on another plane entirely, more in line with the soul than the body. He could understand why people took lovers just for sex, but it was sad when a truly loving relationship broke down because the other partner could not forgive what was perceived as infidelity. To William, it seemed wholly ridiculous to throw away a genuinely loving relationship for some sexual peccadillo. However, emotions were unpredictable and sex was not just a game; indeed, it could be deadly. Although he had always endeavoured to be faithful to Patrick, he did not believe that human beings were meant to be monogamous, which is what made fidelity so difficult.

Daniel said that with that attitude, how could he contemplate taking marriage vows to be faithful for life to one man? Would it not be better to just enjoy a loving relationship without the ties of matrimony? William said there were pros and cons but Patrick was set on it; nevertheless, they would have to see how the land lay when Patrick was no longer a serving soldier.

Chapter Twenty-Seven

Patrick was in Cyprus for a six-month tour of duty with his battalion, wearing blue berets as they were allied to the UN, in order to maintain the integrity of the buffer zone between Greek and Turkish Cypriots under the auspices of Operation TOSCA.

The island has always been strategically important to the British, but never more so than today because it is close to Syria and other areas of Middle Eastern conflict. Patrick, as an Intelligence officer in a signals' regiment, was well placed to keep an eye and ear on insurgencies, but it was not all work and no play as far as the Brits were concerned; the beaches were readily available, and there were all kinds of sports facilities, as well as excursions to the capital, Nicosia, which made it a desirable posting.

Patrick had taken a young second lieutenant under his wing as it was his first foreign deployment. The lad was twenty-two years old, intelligent and very good-looking. Although Patrick was fair, Robert was fairer still and had the bluest of eyes which held a very frank expression. He was shy, but not unfriendly and when he asked Patrick if he played chess, Patrick agreed to give him a game. Robert was very skilful and easily beat Patrick, but as the senior man knew he was outmatched, he accepted the result with good grace.

They often had a drink together in the Officers' Mess, but as Patrick was the senior officer, Robert kept his distance. However, one day, finding themselves with time on their hands, Patrick suggested they drive to the beach and Robert agreed. The sun was beating down so they were glad of the shelter at the mouth of a cave when they reached the beach. They had brought water with them and sandwiches, so lay on the sandy ground just inside the cave, enjoying the pristine view, and listening to the plash of the waves and the cry of the gulls, diving and swirling white against the brilliant dome of blue.

Patrick asked Robert about his home and was told that he came from Ripon in Yorkshire. He had gone to a local grammar school where he had been in the Army cadets. On leaving school, he applied for Sandhurst and was thrilled to be accepted. He had thoroughly enjoyed his time there and his parents were duly proud at his passing out parade. He planned on making the Army his long-term career and was determined to go to the top of his chosen profession.

"What about your personal life?" asked Patrick. "Do you have a girlfriend?"

"No," replied Robert, "nothing like that."

"What?" queried Patrick. "A handsome young chap like you, I'll bet the girls are queuing up."

"I never seem to have had any interest in girls," replied the young man.

"Oh, do you bat for the other side?" smiled Patrick.

"Not that either, I am afraid."

"Well, what do you do for a sex life then?" asked his interrogator.

"I suppose, you would say I am an Onanist."

"No, I wouldn't," Patrick laughed, "because I don't know what it is."

"It is in the Bible," Robert told him. "Apparently, there was a chap called Onan who dropped his seed on the ground and was chastised for it."

"Well, there are some rum coves in the Bible, so I wouldn't worry about him."

"I don't, I have accepted that it is the best thing to keep me out of trouble. I have never dared come out to my parents because it would floor them and I don't want them to be upset. In fact, I have become very adept at pleasuring myself. I place a mirror in front and seeing myself naked turns me on. I also found an old Polaroid camera that still functioned so took some photos of myself and they turn me on when there isn't a mirror."

"Well, you seem to have sorted yourself out pretty well, old boy," retorted Patrick.

"Yes, but I would hate my private life to become public knowledge, so I rely on your discretion."

"No problem, I am no blabber mouth."

The shimmering sea looked most inviting so Patrick suggested that they should go for a swim.

"I don't have trunks or a towel with me," said Robert.

"No worry," returned Patrick, "there's no one around and the sun will dry us off."

"OK," said Robert, peeling off his shirt and shorts. "Let's go."

Patrick did the same and both men, as naked as the day they were born, appeared as beautiful as any classical Greek athlete, lithe and strong, without unsightly tattoos, which Patrick had always considered to be bodily abuse. In fact, he could not credit that something that had always been identified with low life should have become fashionable for women as well as men.

He was four years older than Robert, and had a light covering of hair on his chest and pubes. He also had some pale scars, remnants of military exercises, though he had thankfully been spared actual battle injuries. Robert's body was pristine, absolutely without blemish and had very little hair. Patrick was taller and more muscular but Robert was also beginning to develop his muscles by working in the gym.

It was so hot that it was a delight to run splashing into the sparkling water. Swimming was a special delight in such a hot climate and Patrick took every opportunity to get to the beach, though he was usually alone. There were always lots of people at the military base so it was good to sometimes have one's own space. However, he was enjoying being with Robert, as they tussled with each other in the water, pushing and wrestling; then struck out for a good long swim, after which they returned to the beach.

Again, they settled into the shade of the cave, lying full length on their backs, recovering from their watery exertions. Both men were well endowed where it counts, though the water had somewhat diminished the dimensions. However, they soon became warm again, and it was Robert, not Patrick, who made the first move, nestling up to him and caressing him all over. Patrick did not move; he simply let the youth explore his body; relishing the sensations he aroused. They were starved of sex and for the next half hour, they were lost in each other, until, finally drained of passion; they were overcome by sleep.

The sun was sinking fast as Patrick began to stir then was horrified to find that they were cut off by the tide. The cliffs were too high to climb so their only hope was to swim around to the next bay. He woke Robert, who was naturally dismayed to discover their plight. However, both stayed calm and plunged into the sea again.

When they did not show up at the base, a call was put out to see if anyone knew where they had gone. No one had any idea but when they had not returned by midnight, there was general alarm.

There was still no sign of them next day though Patrick's jeep was discovered on the cliff top but it didn't look as if they had been kidnapped, as there had been no ransom note and there was no sign of a terrorist incident on the island, so what might have happened to them was a complete mystery. Of course, when they arrived at the beach, they had been wearing shorts, tee shirts and sandals, but these must have been carried away by the tide.

After forty-eight hours, the Commanding Officer of the base contacted Patrick's father to inform him that his son and another officer were missing. Marcus was naturally deeply worried. Jane had just gone into hospital for the caesarean so it could not have come at a worse time. However, the CO told him there must be some rational explanation, and not to panic as he would keep in touch and let him know as soon as there was news.

Fortunately, the next day, the men showed up, dressed in fishermen's togs. They had not been able to make the next bay as the current was too strong for them; exhausted, they had floated on their backs, and, luckily for them, were spotted by a fishing smack and hauled aboard. It was not possible to land them immediately and as the radio on the primitive little vessel was on the blink, they just had to sit tight until the fishermen returned to shore.

Of course, the news was flashed to Marcus straight away and everyone on the base was relieved, though the chaps were ragged no end for being AWOL. A bond had sprung up between the two officers, but both agreed that they should cast a veil over what had happened before they were marooned. It had been delightful, but was too dangerous and they did not want to face military censure if the truth became known.

From that time on, although their friendship developed, there was no sex between them. Patrick was delighted when the CO gave him the news that his stepmother had been delivered of twins, a boy and a girl, and mother and children, not to mention father, were all doing well. Somehow, it deepened his sense of independence and removed a weight from his shoulders regarding the inheritance.

Life though is always ready to throw a curve ball and shortly after Patrick's escapade, he was introduced to a young woman by the name of Petra Dubrovska. She was ghost writing an autobiography of a general who was about to retire (or so she said), and had come to the island to soak up the ambience and to see life on the base for herself. Patrick was assigned to be her escort, and found that he enjoyed acting as a guide to this delightful and obviously intelligent young woman. She was intensely interested in the military and asked all the right questions. Over lunch, she told him that her parents were originally Polish but lived in Stourport-upon-Severn, where she had been born twenty-four years ago. She had wondered about joining the Army but after reading English at

Cambridge, she decided that her career lay in journalism. She had never ghosted a book before but saw that it could prove a lucrative sideline for her.

After escorting her around the base after lunch, they ended up having tea together in Nicosia and discovering that an operatic concert was to take place that evening; Patrick rang his commanding officer and asked for the evening off as he wished to take their guest to a concert. Permission was given and the couple booked tickets, had a little look around the town then turned up for the concert. The singers were based in Athens but were on tour and Cyprus was their last port of call before returning home.

Contrary to popular belief, not all operatic singers are huge; in fact, the four before them were all young and attractive. They had just graduated from the Conservatoire, experiencing their first professional tour, and were keen and fresh voiced. The soprano was Bulgarian, a slim, petite girl with fair, probably dyed hair, but the mezzo's looks were very sultry and exotic, with dark skin, lustrous dark eyes and hair, and a voice to charm the gods. The tenor was typical of the type, medium height, sturdy and broad shouldered with a round face, and a shock of dark, curly hair; however, his voice had real quality and a vocal range that reached into the stratosphere without losing its beauty. Finally, the bass, a tall, slim, fellow with dark good looks and a sublimely dark voice to match, completed the quartet. Although singing in concert in evening dress, his body language and facial expression proved him a natural actor, and Patrick told Petra that he could see him developing into a fine, comic Leporello in Mozart's Don Giovanni as he matured.

There was no orchestra, but the female pianist provided excellent accompaniment and the concert began with the divine quartet from Fidelio; then came a duet for the bass and the mezzo from Cosi fan Tutte, followed by the exquisite trio from the same opera sung by Don Alfonso, Fiordiligi and Dorabella. The tenor sang Il mio tessoro, then the bass delivered the comic aria, La Calunia, which made everyone laugh aloud. The first half then ended with the delicious duet for soprano and mezzo from Lakmé by Delibes.

At the interval, Patrick expressed his delight at the quality of the performance and said that he hoped the young singers would have luck because all of them deserved to go far. However, many are called and few are chosen in that most difficult of careers, so they needed luck and the right professional support in order to be truly successful.

The second half was as delightful as the first one, with well-known potboilers such as Rudolpho's aria and that of Mimi from La Boheme, and O Soave Fanciulla, the duet that closes the first act. The mezzo then dazzled everyone with her rendering of the most dashing of Princess Eboli's arias and the bass touched all hearts with Gremin's aria from Eugene Onegin. The concert ended with items from the Merry Widow, including the soprano's Vilia and the duets; Jogging in a One Horse Gig and Love Unspoken, finishing with a rousing quartet arrangement of the Champagne Chorus from Die Fledermaus.

It was quite late when the audience emerged into a balmy, windless night, with a sky full of diamonds, and a moon riding high, as Patrick and his guest drove back singing snippets of the melodies they had heard during the evening. Captain Patrick McIver was very knowledgeable about classical music and he was delighted to find that Petra matched his enthusiasm. He said he could not understand how the rock and roll era had lasted so long, to the detriment of quality music. However, Petra said that most of the populace enjoyed the atmosphere of pop concerts and festivals because they could join in, jumping up and down, and shrieking in unison with the pop wallahs, whereas at a classical concert, the joy was to sit quietly and absorb the beauty of the music, whereas in the commercial field, it appeared that ugliness reigned over beauty.

At first, Patrick had assumed that he would find it tiresome showing a visitor around, but on the contrary, he had thoroughly enjoyed himself and the concert was the gilt on the gingerbread. When it came time for Petra to say goodbye, he was truly sorry to see her go. Although he liked women, he had never been as drawn to any of them as he was to Petra. He could hardly believe it and felt that he had to see her again, if only to find out if on further acquaintance, she had the same effect on him. Thus, they exchanged numbers and as Patrick hoped to be back in London before long, Petra said she would be very happy to meet up again. In the meantime, they would stay in touch.

What Patrick didn't know, even though he was in Intelligence himself, was that Petra had been recruited by MI6 when she was at Cambridge and was doing the same kind of work which he did. She had actually been trained as a honey trap, using her female wiles to tempt men who were being investigated. As far as Patrick was concerned, she soon ascertained that he was not a ladies' man, but had no evidence that he was a practising homosexual.

She had signed the Official Secrets Act, of course and was under cover as a writer. As in the case of Arnold Partington, there were always subversive elements trying to infiltrate their way into legitimate military units, so the Army itself was not immune from coming under the scrutiny of Spooks.

Petra told Patrick that she was ghost writing a book, but actually, she was investigating Arnold Partington and as his widow was now Patrick's stepmother, she had been assigned to find out what he knew privately about the general. Actually, he knew very little as Jane was totally in the dark about Arnold's exploits herself, thus Petra learned nothing of any importance. Nevertheless, she enjoyed a few days paid holiday on Cyprus and fell under the spell of the delightful Captain McIver. However, Patrick was no fool and began to wonder if Petra had a hidden agenda. She certainly had a good cover, but as he thought the matter over, he was aware that she undoubtedly had a seductive way with her when she plied him with questions. She was charm personified but then; he told himself, he could not afford to give her the benefit of the doubt and, after all, discretion was the better part of valour so he would not be keeping in touch with this Marta Hari when he returned to London.

Chapter Twenty-Eight

The news of the birth of the twins soon spread among the friends, and Jane was inundated with cards, flowers and presents for the babies. She and Marcus were over the moon with their darling offspring, who were bonny and healthy. They decided to call the boy, James and the girl, Victoria, after Marcus's grandparents.

They spoke to Patrick on the phone, and he told them of his exploits and said how delighted he was to have a brother and sister, though it had taken his father twenty-six years to get around to it.

Tom, Ginny, Guy and Sally were among the first of the visitors to take a peek at the twins. Helen and Paul sent their love and presents, but were busy looking after their own new arrival as well as the toddlers. Tom brought photos and everyone admired the charming little family.

Helen would like to have come, but she was breast-feeding, so it was not easy to get away; though, of course, she could have brought the baby with her. Anyway, she did not want to interrupt the child's routine as Nanny ruled the nursery with a rod of iron.

Everything at Milton House was much more flexible, with a delightful Nanny named Evelyn, who already doted on the twins. Jane was pleased to find that she too was able to feed them herself. She had wondered if it would be possible but with Nanny's help, she soon got the hang of it, though feeding two babies at the same time took a bit of juggling.

Naturally, everyone had to hear about Patrick's exploits, and all were heartily thankful that he and his comrade had been rescued from what could have been a fatal accident.

"That will teach us all not to fall asleep on a beach," laughed Marcus, "especially when there is no one else around."

Marcus added that Monica frequently emailed him with the news of the London pals. Apparently, she had been seeing a lot of Nancy Lolongo who was now in repertory at the National with 'Arcadia' and had a part in a new comedy. She knew that Daniel had become friendly with William who was missing Patrick and they were often at the theatre, concerts or cinema together.

However, Daniel did not seem to be seeing so much of Imogen these days. Polly, it appeared, was up to her old tricks again and apparently, bedding a Spanish postgraduate student, named Pedro Gonzales. Conrad seemed past caring but definitely missed Sylvia, though Imogen did her best to keep up his spirits by taking a great interest in his current work.

While Marcus was telling them all this, the phone rang and it was Monica to say that Conrad had just won the Turner Prize. The rules had been changed so artists of any age could win the award. It was a great fillip for him and he was over the moon, so was Monica.

For the past two years, some critics had begun to down play him as rather out of date, but it seemed that with the new rules, he was in the right place at the right time and would begin another trend in the world of art. To be frank, she was not a fan of the prize which she considered too gimmicky and not really about art per se. However, she would not complain, as it would surely lead to higher prices for his work. She hoped that Daniel, who assumed he was Conrad's successor, would not feel that his nose had been put out of joint.

Tom and Ginny said they had to get back but told their hosts that they had had a most enjoyable afternoon, and it was great to see Marcus and Jane looking so well, and to meet their adorable twins. Tom said it was a relief to see a happy family because he could not take any more alarms and excursions after Toby's hospitalisation, and Patrick's disappearance but appreciated that all's well that ends well.

Sally and Guy stayed for tea, and Jane, having seen the babies settled, came to join them and Marcus. Jane said that although she was thrilled to have the twins, and was kept well occupied, she had missed her work and hearing how the new project was developing. She was delighted that their 'Ladies' documentary series had now been shown, and had won critical approval in the UK and the States, and was also selling well further afield. She longed to hear how Guy and Sally were getting on with the new project that dealt with mysteries of the era of Elizabeth I. They said it was a labour of love delving into the documents of the period, and researching prints and portraits that would enhance not only the TV content, but the book that Guy was writing to accompany the series.

He said he was very grateful to Sally for pointing him in the direction of Piers Gambourne, who was now permanently at West Bridge as archivist, and a great help to them, particularly in transcribing old hand writing and translating Latin texts. The exciting news was that they had unearthed what proved to be a diary. It was in code but Piers had succeeded in deciphering it. He was making an English translation which he hoped to publish though he said it was pretty startling and might offend some Catholics. Jane was very curious and wanted to know more so Guy said that it appeared to have been written by a young priest, just prior to the Dissolution of the Monasteries, and would raise eyebrows. Now she was more curious than ever but had to be patient a while longer.

It seemed that everything had settled down at West Bridge. The workmen had now left, and the atmosphere in the large old house with its twenty-two bedrooms was warm and welcoming so the family appeared contented with their lot. Toby was soon to take his finals then would begin a new course of study, but in the meantime, he was helping a friend in hospital radio. He had enjoyed his time at home, recovering from his 'accident' and the little ones were lovely. Of course, they did not live at the Hall as their parents were resident at The Gables. Helen was now a full time Mum and loving it. Sally may have had her suspicions about Paul and Ginny, but had never voiced them, and now she was glad because they seemed to have settled into a comfortable relationship without any erotic overtones.

Dear patient Tom was an interested observer, but never interfered. Some husbands would have simply gone over the top, had they been in his shoes but he knew the side his bread was buttered and did not intend to do anything to overturn the apple cart. He loved Ginny so much, and if she was happy and contented, then he was too. She certainly deserved the best. He was very grateful that Piers had come into his employ, as he was a first rate scholar and a delightful companion.

Piers made no secret of being gay and Tom was very relieved because he was the kind of attractive chap who would normally have delighted Ginny. However, Piers teased and flirted with her, feeding her amour propre, but he never gave her any reason to think he was serious. Actually, he was more interested in her husband than herself due to their collaboration on the ancient documents, and history of the house and family, which both were finding ever more fascinating. Tom was a solid, reliable type and gave Piers a feeling of security which he valued. He was still recovering from his last tragic affair, so was not ready at present for any romantic adventures. However, he now had a family around him, and was grateful that he had been so warmly welcomed and taken to its bosom.

Sally learned that Monica had a new, significant other in her life, in the delightful form of Nancy Lolongo. It was always Monica's friendship that Sally valued, rather than mere sex, and as long as she could keep that friendship, she wished her well and even had the grace to bless their union. For Monica, it was no longer a case of dalliance; she was truly in love with Nancy and now knew that Nancy fully returned her love.

Although many people are eaten up with jealousy when another is preferred, Sally had tempered her ego over the years and believed that to understand all was to forgive all. Anyway, she was in the privileged position of knowing that Monica had been the mother who tried to protect her in her 17th century life when she was Hannah and that they would no doubt be together in many other guises in the merry go round that is life.

She and Guy had become good colleagues over the past couple of years, intellectual equals who valued working together on fascinating subjects. Although Guy had never referred to it, she sometimes thought of the seductive afternoon when she first visited the Dower House. It was not as if she had suddenly fallen in love with Guy; she felt that she had always loved him, not just in this life but in many others, including the one she knew about in the 17th century and it was remarkable that they were together again in the same place four hundred years later.

The phrase 'the eternal now' was not unknown to Sally but over the past six months, she felt she had begun to understand the strange concept to which it alluded. It was as if we have one life that stretches throughout eternity, but we keep playing different roles, like actors. Each age puts its etheric imprint on places, like on film and each film fits on top of the previous one, ad infinitum. Thus everything is NOW.

Guy had recently seen the first episode of David Starkey's TV documentary series based on the Churchill's. He admired Starkey greatly because as well as being a distinguished scholar, he had the common touch so was able to express complicated subjects, clearly and simply, pleasing experts and laymen alike. Starkey began with the Seven Years War and its comparison to the Second World War, and the connection between Sir Winston and his ancestor, the Duke of Marlborough. He also likened Hitler to Louis X1V, both of them demonising certain people, Louis, the Huguenots and Hitler, the Jews.

Sally had not seen the episode but was interested in hearing about it. She said it would not surprise her if the British wartime leader was the reincarnation of Marlborough, which would account for his deep interest in him, leading him to write several significant books about the general and his times. She also said that she believed that it was possible to be born into the same family in more lifetimes than one.

Maybe, Louis XIV had returned as Hitler. One lifetime was not enough, so souls returned to carry on what they had already begun, though, sadly, they often fall into the same patterns and cause further trouble, rather than learning from their mistakes. She, however, had sometimes wondered if Napoleon had returned as Hitler. Of course, it was possible that he had followed on from the two previous megalomaniacs bringing even more disaster. It was a horrible thought, but what if such people were instruments of the Lords of Karma working to teach humanity through suffering? Sally did not believe that we are meant to suffer, that is one of the reasons that she could not commit herself wholly to Christianity, with its concentration on sin and suffering; requiring a divine source to free us from the results of our actions. Why could not humanity learn through love and joy? As the writer, George Bernard Shaw, stated, "Christianity is a great idea; what a pity it has not been tried." Well, she had no answers, so it was time to put philosophy aside, and concentrate on the here and now.

The drive back to West Bridge was a pleasant one and Sally took several surreptitious glances at Guy's handsome profile as he drove. If he had stopped the car and taken her into his arms, she would have melted, just as she did the first time he embraced her. However, he was rather silent as he negotiated the traffic, but she wished she could have had a penny for his thoughts. Had she been able to read his mind, she would have been gratified to know that he was thinking how lovely she was and wondering how he could break through the invisible barrier that had existed between them since he had made love to her. It puzzled him why she had never referred to it, but then, he hadn't mentioned it either so she may have thought that he was trying to forget. He knew that he was falling in love with her but felt like an inexperienced schoolboy, not knowing how to act. She gave so little away, yet, she was warm and friendly, and had a most ravishing smile. At some point, he had to become daring and find out how she really felt about him. He had learned from Marcus that Monica and Nancy Lolongo had embarked upon an affair but Sally gave no sign of being upset; indeed, she seemed very content with her lot as she, Guy, Piers and Tom were having a great time uncovering the most fascinating material at West Bridge. Perhaps, she had just consigned his seduction to some backwater of her mind, glimpsed merely as a novel experience.

As Sally thought about him, her whole body tingled with yearning and she longed for his hands to caress her, sending her into a state of bliss just as before. Unless they were actually working together, there seemed to be a shyness which, somehow, neither of them could overcome. Sally knew how she felt about Guy but she was still in the dark as to how he felt about her. He had been so bold when they were first alone together and he had certainly appeared to enjoy their encounter, so she failed to understand why neither of them could resume what had formerly begun.

Now she had to go back to the Hall and pack a case as she was due in London tomorrow, so couldn't spare more time to fantasise about Guy. Her seniors at the Institute were very understanding as they had allowed her to rearrange her schedule so that she only taught two days a week, leaving the other five to her research and writing activities. She was not experienced as Jane was in TV production but Guy was glad to involve her in the documentary series as a back room academic.

He, sometimes, thought of Sylvia too. He really liked the girl and was pleased that she had settled so happily into her work at Stratford. He was quite aware that in common parlance she was 'shagging' her boss, but was surprised at the speed at which she had separated from Conrad. He couldn't look into her innermost heart though, or know that she would always love Conrad. However, with Polly's return, she knew that she had no future with him. He was not as good looking as David or as personable, but she was devoted to him. There was no rhyme or reason, she just was and always would be. She felt that the relationship with David would always be impermanent, mainly because she could not commit herself: she was a practical person though and felt that a glass half-full was better than one-half empty.

Although Guy could not approve of Conrad's seemingly uncontrolled sexuality, he could not help liking him and appreciated that most other men liked him as well; that is until he came too close to their women. Nevertheless, everyone has free will and his affairs were always consensual. Guy would not presume to preach to anyone but people seemed to accept bad behaviour if it was committed by a genius: for instance, Picasso, Gaugin, Francis Bacon, Lucien Freud, Eric Gill, Stanley Spencer and Augustus John for starters.

Notwithstanding, he thought, *it appears that the sexual climate is changing, and such men might find themselves in hot water if they didn't exercise control over their personal desires.*

Chapter Twenty-Nine

When Guy and Sally returned to the Hall, Tom met them, and said that Piers wanted to see them all in the library as he was ready to reveal the contents of the diary. Sally said her packing could wait, as she was longing to know what Piers had found.

The code had not been a difficult one to break but obviously, the young priest, Father Stephen, had not wanted his writings found, so had hidden his diary in the safest place he could find and disguised the text by using code. How it came to end up at the Hall was not known; in fact, until a few weeks ago, no one was aware of its existence, but hopefully, it would provide fuel for Guy's book and the documentary.

Father Stephen began by outlining the history of the convent which had occupied the site of West Bridge Hall at the beginning of the thirteenth century. It was not originally intended as a religious house but as a refuge for a group of Cathar women led by a Parfait, Jeanne Doucet, who escaped persecution and death in the Languedoc, in the South of France. Two hundred Cathars had been rounded up and set on fire at Montsegur, but thanks to a local resistance movement, a few of them, notably Jeanne and a band of young girls, had been spirited away in the face of great danger.

After a long journey and many adventures, the group boarded a ship and sailed to England; however, prevailing winds drove them westwards, and finally, they made their way to Oxfordshire and the area now occupied by West Bridge Hall. The women were granted a piece of land where they built a modest shelter and began to cultivate the plot in order to grow their own food. Jeanne Doucet could read and write both in her own tongue of the Languedoc and in Latin, though none of the other girls were literate until she began to teach them. All were young and strong, and they helped the old and sick, acted as midwives and laid out the dead.

Consequently, they were hailed as good women, though they were not nuns, just simply trying to live a good life and to help others. Their Cathar philosophy was based on the cult of the Bogomils, which is why they had fallen foul of the Catholic authorities who destroyed them in large numbers, and even instituted the Inquisition to hunt, torture and kill them. To the women, England was sanctuary and for a long time, they were left to their own devices, but finally, as the original women succumbed to age and died, the Church began to take over, and a convent was founded on the basis of their humanitarian work.

By the early sixteenth century, the convent had become an established arm of the Church, coming under the jurisdiction of a priest and his assistant, Father Stephen. This young man, unusually for his era, was a free thinker who disliked many of the religious practices of his day. He knew that there was corruption in some religious establishments, including his own and was not surprised that the Reformation had taken place on the Continent in order to remedy perversions in the universal religion.

England was not immune either and Father Stephen believed that it was time for the Augean Stables to be cleansed. He accompanied Father Innocent, the senior clergyman, when he visited the convent; however, much of the senior's involvement was corrupt and he relished taking the nuns' confessions which, even though they were meant to be confidential, gave him a handle for emotional blackmail.

The novices had to present the convent with a dowry when they became members of the community, and they also had to go through a ceremony where they gave up the world and became brides of the Church. The whole process was meant to be symbolic, but had become mixed up with pagan fertility rites. Each novice in front of the congregation was stripped naked and her own clothes were taken away, then she was ritually deflowered by Father Innocent. The ceremony was a travesty but was considered a great honour for the novice and her family. After the ritual, the girl was clothed in the habit of the convent then led through a grill into an inner sanctum. Most novices took final vows and never saw their families again. It must have been a great ordeal for the girls, though some of them may have believed that they had a vocation, though many girls were consigned by their families, especially where there were several daughters to support. To give a daughter to the Church was considered the highest honour for a family.

Father Stephen said that however corrupt the Church may have been at that time, the nuns were some of the finest women to be found. They believed that prayer was important, they also contributed in practical ways to the community as Jeanne Doucet and her girls had done four centuries ago.

Soon after the young priest finished writing his secret dossier, the Dissolution of the Monasteries took place. Like all revolutions, it went too far, yet, there was a reason for the split, apart from Henry's break from Rome in order to marry Anne Boleyn, because the Church had let down, not only the people, but the founder of the Christian religion itself. Part of the convent was demolished and the nuns sent back to their relatives, while the rest of the building fell into ruin, only to be used as a source of building materials when a splendid new house arose on the site.

Later, the de Giffard family were ennobled and given the estate by Elizabeth I, enabling a new chapter to begin. What happened to the young priest is unknown, but hopefully, he converted to the Protestant faith and escaped the dreadful fate of many of the clergy who would not recant.

When Piers finished speaking, his listeners were stunned by what they had just heard. Tom and his brother knew something of their history, but had not even heard of the Cathars. Piers already had some knowledge of them but said that until about fifty years ago, they were completely unknown as the Catholic Church had expunged them from history. Theirs was a philosophy rather than a religion, and they believed that the world was in the hands of what they called the Demi Urge, a tyrannical being that caused death and destruction. However, they also believed in the teachings of Christ but not the dogma that was being doled out by the Roman Catholics. They trusted that by living exemplary lives, they could escape from the wheel of reincarnation.

"Well," said Piers, "that is how I understand it, though I am no expert. They had no clergy or hierarchy, but at about the age of forty, those already married and with grown up children, would become Parfaits, and embark on a teaching mission. Their only ceremony was the Consolamentum which they received on their death bed."

Piers continued: "It is still difficult to obtain information about these people because all the records we have of them were written by their oppressors and are stored in the Vatican Library. However, even their enemies admitted that they were good people. They made such a success of their lives that the Catholic Church and the King of France became jealous so trumped up charges of heresy against them, imprisoned or executed them and stole their lands.

Only a few French scholars of modern times knew about the Cathars, but Professor Nelli was first in the field and the psychiatrist, Dr Arthur Guirdham, through two of his patients, began to learn amazing things through the dreams and far memory of the women. These patients did not know each other, nor did they come to the doctor at the same time and neither of them were scholars; one had not learned French and the other only had limited schoolgirl French, though she wrote poetry in the tongue of the Languedoc like the troubadours."

"Tell me about the troubadours," said Sally. "Of course, I am aware of them but I would like to know more."

Piers nodded, "Yes, they are interesting and I think it is time for an in-depth study of them. They were, of course, itinerant performers, who travelled widely, entertaining, and teaching through music, song and story. As for Dr Guirdham's patients, there is no logical explanation for the quality of the information they were receiving but later as more historical evidence came to light, Professor Nelli said that the women should always have the benefit of the doubt, rather than the scholars, because their information was proving accurate, whereas the academics were still feeling their way in the dark."

Piers recommended Dr Guirdham's books, 'The Cathars and Reincarnation' and 'We Are One Another' as they opened up further avenues of historical mysteries.

Sally asked why they had been so persecuted and Piers answered, "For the same reason the Jews were annihilated by Hitler and his cohorts; jealousy and greed. However, Dr Guirdham had discovered, though he had no personal memory, that he had been a Cathar too and that several patients who had come to him at various times, appeared to have been reincarnated Cathars, born into a relatively small area in the West of England, working quietly in the background to raise consciousness in the hope of improving humanity."

Piers said that in his estimation, things had not altered that much and the Catholic Church was still an unhealthy organisation. He put a lot of the perversity and abuse down to imposed celibacy. "It is against Nature," he declared, "and denying sex simply makes it more desirable, just as being on a diet makes one think of food."

Sally asked what had brought it about, and Piers said he believed it was more to do with money and property than religion because if a clergyman or nun was allowed to marry, their first loyalty would be to their family, instead of devoting their lives to the Church.

"I long ago formed the opinion that the Church, though purporting to have been founded by St Peter, was actually a power construct of Constantine the Great and his mother, Helena, and had little to do with the teachings of Jesus Christ, though the worship of the Virgin Mary has kept the divine feminine alive in an otherwise patriarchal establishment."

"You know," said Sally, "I can't understand how anyone allows themselves to be controlled by a religious organisation, but then, if it is their free choice and not through oppression, I suppose it gives them a sense of belonging or of identity, though apparently, monasteries and convents are having to close down because of the lack of recruits."

Chapter Thirty

Ranu Gupta had now returned to London and as Emma was in America, Monica assumed he would be at a loose end, so she invited him over for a meal. He had accompanied Emma to Hollywood and seen her settled into a pleasant hotel in Beverley Hills then flown to India for the birth of his third child.

Over the meal, he brought Monica up to date, and said that Emma was glad to have him with her because everything was so new and strange. She was also very wary of the film moguls she met. A Hollywood agent, Bill Blitzen, was appointed to look after her interests 'and his own' retorted Ranu ironically. He was an old hand and certainly knew his way around the film world so was good at pulling strings, and in no time, Emma was given a couple of screen tests but was, naturally, rather nervous. However, contrary to some actors, once in front of a film camera, she came to life. It felt the right place to be and the camera loved her, as she did the camera.

However, when she first arrived in Tinsel Town, she was upset because the film she hoped to audition for, had been shelved. Nevertheless, she was assured that if the rushes of her tests were approved, they would find something else in the pipeline for her. Nevertheless, she wondered what was going on when Archie J Ponder, one of the most powerful men in the film world, said that he would like her to take two screen tests, one fully dressed and one in the nude, and perhaps, think about having a boob job. She was insulted and let him see it. Her agent though, sheep that he was, looked uncomfortable as he knew that if actresses wanted to get on in films, they had to be prepared to comply with what was asked of them.

Emma was nothing if not feisty and started as she meant to go on, declaring that she didn't see how that would prove whether or not she was a good actress.

"Your boobs are rather small, young lady, are they not?" asked Ponder, a tall thin man with dark glasses and a disdainful mouth. "What has that to say to anything?" she responded with a sneer. She was so angry that she felt fearless. If they did not like her, it would be their loss; she would go back to England and make a killing in the theatre. "I am not applying to become a Glamour model. I am a serious actress and I expect to be treated as such." The men looked at each other as if they couldn't believe their ears; for a newcomer who had yet to make her name in the States, to bear such an attitude was beyond them. They were more likely to be met with fluttering eyelashes, seductive smiles and obsequious looks. Emma's agent was decidedly uncomfortable and tried to shush her, but she would not be brow beaten.

"I have to tell you, I aim to be in this business for the long term. I do not want to be thought of as sugar candy. I want to play a variety of roles, and to go on acting into old age like Maggie Smith and Judy Dench, who are my heroines."

The men could not help but smile and one asked, "How do you know that you will live that long?"

"I don't," she answered, "but there's nothing like being optimistic."

Ponder thanked her for coming and said they would be in touch with her agent.

"Gosh," said Bill when they were outside. "I don't think they will forget you in a hurry, but whether you'll be offered work is something else, you could just be a write off. They don't like difficult, know all actors, so you may never get a chance to film in Hollywood. It's a small place and word soon gets around."

"I am sorry if you think I behaved badly, and I know you want me to succeed but I am not a lap dog and I won't be pushed around. I would rather go home with my tail between my legs than submit to their lack of respect."

"Respect don't pay the rent," he retorted, his Bronx accent thicker than usual, which made Emma laugh.

Whether she had really burnt her boats or not, she would never know because one of those amazing strokes of luck which often accompanied her career, came out of the blue with newspaper headlines the next day accusing the tall thin mogul, Archie J Ponder, of alleged sexual depravity with a number of young actresses going back two decades. Because he was powerful and could ruin careers, there was tacit agreement to keep quiet, but finally, enough was enough, and two courageous actresses came out and declared that he had raped them when they were in their teens. He categorically denied it, but there had been too many incidents of sexual blackmail so others also found the courage to reveal that they had also been exploited by him, though they had been too frightened to speak out as it would have been his word against theirs. As someone remarked, "even in cases of wrong doing, money and power talk."

However, two days later, Emma's agent was called into the Front Office and greeted with warmth by Hal Jubbwell, a junior executive. "Sit down; would you like a coffee, or a Coke?"

He declined a drink and asked if they could get down to business.

"Well, your girl is certainly a one off, but I expect it's because she's English and don't know the ropes in Hollywood. Anyway, we have seen the tests and she is a knock out. She is fair but she has the allure and figure of Audrey Hepburn, and that's pretty unique in Hollywood today so we think she will be a box office smash."

Bill couldn't believe his ears but asked what kind of roles she could play.

"Anything, I reckon with the right director."

How much Emma's tests really led to her being awarded the leading part in a forthcoming film, or if they were afraid that she would add to the list of actresses coming out of the woodwork with tales of sexual harassment or blackmail, was a moot point, but neither she nor her agent questioned it.

Later, another mogul was alleged to have made overtures to young male actors as it was routine for him to ask them to strip for a screen test. That certainly put a nasty taste in the mouth as it gave the impression that sexual mores were still questionable in Hollywood.

Hal was now in full flow: "I'll tell you what we have in mind for her. We have bought the rights to Donald Hart's book, 'A Demon God'. The title may change for the film but we can imagine your Emma in the lead role. The character is an English girl, fair as a rose, who converts to Islam and becomes first a Jihadi bride, then an enforcer of suicide bombers, mainly women. It's a sort of Joan of Arc role in reverse. Do you think she would be interested?"

"It sounds a meaty part and that's what she's after for her Hollywood debut. The subject is certainly a current one and should, by rights, get a good deal of publicity," replied Bill. "So yes, full steam ahead."

"Welcome to the ship; we start filming in a month and I suggest that she stays in town to be on hand to find her way around the studio, and get used to life here. We will hire an apartment for her near the studio and a car will be available for her. Does she drive, by the way, or will she need a chauffeur?"

"Oh, she drives, no problem, though she will need some practice in a car with left hand drive and getting used to your roads."

"By the way," said Hal, "from the way she reacted yesterday, we got the impression she would buck at nude scenes. There is one in particular that is necessary to the plot but we can film it in shadow or get a body double for her."

"That surprised me," answered her agent, "because I know she has modelled for a well-known artist who specialises in nude paintings."

"Well, it would be more authentic if she could do it herself."

"Yes," said Bill, "but I think we will keep quiet on that score for the time being. She was not happy about the boob job comment though. Most actresses have to slim but she is a naturally thin girl who finds it hard to put on weight. A big bust on her slim frame would look stupid, don't you think? Also, if you are going to promote her in the Audrey Hepburn mould, she doesn't need a big bust. Audrey did very well without it."

Soon, Emma was caught up in the Hollywood machine and a lawyer, as well as Bill Blitzen, was brought in to oversee the contract. Naturally, she urged Ranu to stay on for a couple of days longer to make sure all was above board but he said that he doubted he would be allowed to interfere and anyway, his wife's time was drawing very near, so he had to get to India as soon as possible.

He endeavoured to make their last night together very special as they knew it would be some time before they saw one another again. He promised to keep in touch and she said she would do the same, though both of them realised that if Emma was successful, it was likely to be the parting of the ways because their lives would go in different directions; especially if Emma became a famous face.

After his time in India, Ranu returned to London pleased that all had gone well with his wife and baby, but admitted that he missed Emma tremendously. Monica asked him how he could bear to be apart from his Indian wife and family, not just Emma. He told her that his children were a delight and his wife was the best in the world.

"Then why don't you live with them?" asked Monica, with a furrowed brow.

"You may well ask," he sighed, "but you see, I am between two very different worlds. I am Indian and am proud of my culture, but I was born in London, so I belong in the West. I love the freedom and the tolerance that are endemic in Britain because there are no people as respectful of free will as the British. London is my home and I have become used to living like a shuttle cock between two continents; now it looks as if I shall be including a third one with Emma in America."

"How complex your life is, dear Ranu," replied Monica. "Surely, no more than yours was when you were married to Sir Douglas, and lived and travelled all over the world," replied Ranu. She laughed, "Of course, you're right, but I am jolly glad not to have to be on the move any more, unless I choose to be.

Tell me about your wife; how can she be content with you away most of the time. Surely, she gets lonely."

It was Ranu's turn to laugh. "Not at all, she is surrounded by family and servants, and has her darling children."

"But," Monica went on, "to put it bluntly, what about sex?"

"She has staff who will obey her every whim and if she is randy, her maid knows what to do. Unlike the West where it is sink or swim; our women are taught the techniques of pleasuring and whether it is with a man or a woman is a matter of circumstance. My wife is intact, as we Hindus have never stooped to genital mutilation as some Muslims do even today, though it is a barbaric and totally unnecessary practice."

"What is the reason for something so utterly cruel?" Monica asked.

"Oh, purely for the subjugation of women," he answered. "It is comparable to your medieval knights locking up their women in metal chastity belts while they were away from home. However, the belts had keys, so the women could be freed but the operation, usually carried out on young girls is savage and cannot be reversed. One pities the poor creatures who must suffer terribly during the sex act or in childbirth."

"It is difficult to understand why their mothers, who were also victims, are complicit in the mutilation of their daughters," Monica observed.

"Even in the so called civilised UK, this practice goes on behind closed doors, or the girls are tricked into going abroad for the cut, yet because there is the fear of offending minorities, no charges are brought by the police. They call it tradition and much that is not agreeable, is done in that fearsome name. However, as I said, my wife and other women of our culture are safe from such disgusting practices. Many terrible things still happen through misplaced ideologies, even though we are now in the twenty-first century, so we can hardly claim to be truly civilised. Animals suffer too, and Halal and Kosher killing should have been banned a long time ago, but they are cultural and neither Muslims nor Jews must be offended, though the animals, of course, have no say in the matter. Food laws were instituted many centuries ago because the ancestors of these people lived in deserts where there was little water and great heat. Consequently, meat went off very quickly. However, it shows the tenacity of the human mind because even now that refrigeration is ubiquitous, old habits die-hard. Of course, if you also add a religious context, it is doubly difficult to enforce reforms. Dear Monica, I am sorry, I have been on my soap box for too long, but I think you understand how strongly I feel about any kind of cruelty, especially to youngsters and animals."

Changing the subject, Monica told Ranu that she was going to the Cotswolds again and wondered if he was free to accompany her. He said he was ready for a little diversion and would welcome the chance to see some beautiful countryside.

"You will also see a beautiful young woman," laughed his friend.

"Well, two birds with one stone, hey? It can't be bad. Who is she?"

"She is my new protégé named Miranda Pointer. At present, she exhibits with a small gallery in Bourton, and has a house and studio close by. I discovered her on the Internet and took Conrad to see what he thought of her work. Well, he was actually blown away and practically begged me to sign her up, before someone else did. She is ambitious and though grateful to have been able to show at the provincial gallery, she has her sights set on London, as you may imagine."

"Well, I am all for backing new talent, as you know, so when do we go?"

"Would the day after tomorrow suit you?"

"Yes, the sooner, the better, chocks away!"

Since winning the Turner Prize, Conrad had taken on a new lease of life and rather than rest on his laurels, had thrown himself into his work and was producing incredible pictures. He knew that Polly was seeing a good deal of the student, Pedro Gonzales but was actually quite pleased because he wanted to concentrate on work and was grateful that there was someone to keep Polly amused. He thought he must be getting old, though he was not yet fifty, because he no longer wanted to bed models and painted them less often in the nude. His work had actually taken on a much more esoteric aspect, certainly more fantastic than his earlier work had been.

He wished that Polly would settle down but she became more manic as she grew older and he began to realise that she had certain mental health issues. Neither he nor Polly took drugs, though they tried cannabis as students. However, they did not care for it, preferring to be in their right minds rather than out of them. Now Conrad wondered if Pedro had given her anything suspect, as she was always so full of beans. She was an energetic woman but her present state did not seem natural.

Of course, he could not call the kettle black, as he had certainly sowed a good many wild oats too. It was as if both of them were stuck in adolescence, yet, he really did believe that he was now growing up. He felt sorry for the way he had cast Sylvia off, but she seemed to be doing alright and there was no future for them as he was married. Now, at last, he wanted to have a settled home life as 'ordinary' people did. He was aware, of course, that several of his friends had rather offbeat personal lives too, but none as outrageous as that of Polly and himself, and he felt guilty that Imogen had grown up in such a Bohemian household. Well, it didn't seem to have done her any harm. She was a balanced young woman, and looked set fair to make a success of her professional life and hopefully, her personal one too.

Both of her parents were amoral; but never knowingly harmed anyone. They laughed at life and took everything in their stride. They had both been blessed with good health, as was Imogen and tragedy had never darkened their door, though a terrible event was shortly to devastate them.

Chapter Thirty-One

Since returning to London from Italy, Polly had settled back into her old life without any trouble, mainly due to Pedro, a young virile man, who was happy to indulge her, gave her a real shot of energy, equal to a powerful drug so that now she thoroughly enjoyed her teaching, and was thinking of writing a book, a compilation of her best paintings with hints and tips for amateur painters. She realised that she had become stale as an artist and teacher which was what sent her off to Italy, and meeting Emilio seemed the gilt on the gingerbread at the time. She, suddenly, saw a totally new way of life unfolding if she married him and felt ready for a major change. Conrad was happy with Sylvia and Imogen was independent, so why shouldn't she enjoy pastures new? She would join the jet set and have lots of new, glamorous friends. However, once Emilio was arrested, the scales fell from her eyes and she was keen to return home. Not all who become filthy rich do it the legitimate way but, thankfully, Emilio was exonerated and released without charge, but despite this, it brought Polly down to Earth with a bump, and she resolved to be more cautious in future.

Emilio accepted that their little idyll was over, and had all her paintings packed up and sent to her. At present, they were in Conrad's studio, but she decided that it would be a good idea to make over a room in their large Holland Park apartment as a studio for her own work.

Pedro, however, had a bedsit in Soho which was handy for their meetings. It was a large room in a tall, seventeenth century house, once owned by Huguenots. There was a tiny shower room en-suite and the room itself was as well organised as a caravan, with a bed which came out of the wall, a kitchen comprising a compact unit with sink, cooker, fridge and cupboard, concealed behind tall wooden shutters; and a sofa, an armchair, a chest of drawers, small table and two dining chairs. For an art student, it was surprisingly tidy, though his clothes were visible as they hung on a metal frame.

Polly never thought to ask him what the rent cost in such a central part of London, but she was now aware that his father was in a good way of business in Madrid so he was not short of money. She also learned that he had the use of a box room along the corridor which served as his studio, thus, for a student, he was doing pretty well.

On the day in question, the weather was warm and pleasant so Polly suggested her class should go to St James's Park to paint or sketch en plein air. Of course, there were tourists and people cutting through the park, but it was a large enough area for them to find a more secluded spot where they could work in peace. Some of them settled near the lake but others found nearby buildings a challenge which they were happy to sketch. Polly made her rounds, encouraging and coaxing, and showing how to improve perspective, doing all the things a good pedagogue does. All in all, it was a very pleasant way to spend the afternoon, which resulted in some attractive works; ready to be finished in the studio.

After they packed up for the day, Polly, Pedro and two other students were leading the way to Trafalgar Square, when, suddenly, out of nowhere came a heavy lorry at an alarming speed that plunged into them, and the group behind them, throwing bodies far and wide. The speed and force was so great that those at the head of the group died instantly, while those behind them were horribly injured. There was utter pandemonium as all the traffic was stopped, and the shrill shrieks of police cars, ambulances and fire engines soon rent the air. At first, it was not clear whether it was a tragic accident or terrorism, but it soon became apparent that the devastation was planned. Drivers, tourists, pedestrians, all were totally in shock and though they wanted to help, were too paralysed by to be of immediate assistance. The Rescue Services were quickly on the spot and quickly put their expertise into practical use. Polly and her three students were beyond help, lying in a large pool of blood, together in death as they had been in life. The other students were in urgent need of help and paramedics sprang to their aid, getting them off to hospital as speedily as possible. The lorry had hurtled onwards finally crashing against a wall, causing utter mayhem, and more fatalities and injuries. The young driver and his companion were bruised but largely unhurt, and a police team of marksmen dragged them out at gunpoint. It was a miracle that the police did not shoot them on the spot, but they were more useful alive. It was obviously a terrorist attack and these men would, hopefully, lead them to the rest of the cell as it was unlikely that they were working alone.

The first Imogen learned about the catastrophe was when someone came into Sothebys having heard about it on their smart

226

phone and told everyone what was happening near Trafalgar Square. Of course, she had no idea that her mother and her students could be involved as she knew that she was teaching at the time, but tragically, they were lying dead in their own blood, less than a mile away.

It took a little time for the victims to be identified, but the police were very sensitive in the way they gave the terrible news to Conrad and Imogen. Of course, it was like the bottom falling out of their world. Polly, who was always so full of life and vigour suddenly puffed out like a candle, it was beyond belief, but showed the fragility of life, yet, how very precious it is.

Of course, all the friends rallied around the bereaved pair. However, Conrad, normally the most peace loving of men, lost his temper and raged in a way never seen before. He cursed and swore at the insane criminals, who had devastated the lives of many, not just his wife and her students.

"Where are the decent Muslims to condemn these vicious sods?" he wailed. "The monstrous, blackest of blasphemers who have killed their god and put a bloodthirsty demon in its place? What an ideology that can brain wash to such an extent and the wretched false prophets who teach that killing Infidel will lead them into Paradise where they will have seventy two virgins at their disposal. That is utter, utter evil and yet, weak minds believe it. No, they will rot in hell for all Eternity. The bible prophecy in Revelation warns of wars, and rumours of wars and false prophets; well, we see the reality of that every day on our TV screens.

As for mosques, I'd raze them all to the ground because who knows how much sedition is planned there, and as for putting offenders in prison, I would put 'em in a plane and drop them over the sea. That would be better than putting them in prison where they just infect other minds. Damnation to all ideologies; we have enough evidence from the twentieth century to show what they cause: religious cults, Fascism, Communism, Nazism and now Jihadism. Well, I reckon that black force that fuelled the Nazis is alive and well in Daesh." No one had ever suspected that Conrad was a racist, nor indeed was he. He just lashed out in shock and grief; bewailing the fact that toleration had gone so far as to be stupidity: now look where it led. No, enough was enough and zero tolerance was the only way in the face of such murderous acts.

He carried on shouting, cursing and damning the Muslim invasion of the west. He moaned that he could understand European migration, but not the virus of an alien creed, and ended up in a welter of tears of anger and despair. Imogen was so concerned about him that she called their doctor who came and gave him a sedative to calm him down. He slept for twenty-four hours but remembered little about his tirade. Monica came round and gave him the Bach Flower Remedy, Sweet Chestnut, which is for extreme mental anguish, hopelessness and despair, as well as Star of Bethlehem for bereavement.

Polly and her students were now in the Police Morgue, and it was terrible for Conrad and Imogen to have to identify her. They did, but she was no longer Polly. The undertakers had done a good job of restoring the body to the best of their ability, but after such a catastrophic killing, they could not perform miracles. However, awful though it was, Conrad and his daughter were glad to have seen what remained of Polly because though it was terrible, it gave them a sense of closure. Polly, like a bird, had flown away leaving only a broken shell. Conrad now knew what Sally meant when she said that the body was merely the instrument of the soul and when the soul disappeared, the body was simply an empty carton. Naturally, there were a lot of formalities to go through, including an inquest, but finally, the bodies were released so that funerals could take place.

The perpetrators of the crime were in custody, and the police and MI5 were working round the clock to discover who else was involved. They picked up one or two young men, but finding no evidence, had to release them. Nonetheless, the search would continue until sufficient evidence was available to put an end to the cell that must exist, and bring all of the perpetrators to full and summary justice.

Monica and Ranu, like the other friends, wanted to be there for Conrad and Imogen, so put off their trip to Bourton until the following week. Sally and Guy were still in London so rushed to give moral support, but Conrad shut himself in his studio and painted like fury. Imogen also preferred to go back to work, though anyone who tried to express sympathy was given short shrift. She appreciated their concern and sympathy but it just made things worse. Also, she could no longer watch TV because the news was full of the incident. At least, the police had two men in custody but no one was convinced that that was the end of the story. However, what was a term of imprisonment where they would just become more radicalised or infect others with their insane ideology, compared to the lives of the innocent individuals they had so wantonly destroyed?

"If I had my way," declared Ranu, "I would take them up in a plane and throw them out from a great height over the most inhospitable part of the planet."

"Or," said Monica, "dump them on an uninhabited island in the Arctic Ocean and let them die of exposure. Don't look at me like that, Daniel. It would be cheaper than prison and save humanity a great deal of grief."

"Well," said her friend, "include the megalomaniacs who opened 'Pandora's Box' in the Middle East out of pure hubris, causing untold suffering to thousands of innocent people, yet who are still walking Scot free, making money hand over fist." The others nodded in agreement as it was a mystery to them that after three judicial enquiries, none of those responsible for invading Iraq had been brought to book, even though at least two million people had marched in protest again the aggression at the time. Yes, Saddam Hussein was a monster but then the world is full of abominable dictators and Britain cannot destroy them all. It is up to the populace in each country to monitor their leaders and keep psychopaths at bay through the ballot box.

After the inquest, Imogen persuaded Conrad that they needed to get away to neutral territory. He agreed, so they hired a cottage on the Isle of Man, where they could lay low and not draw attention to themselves. The cottage was quite isolated but though they had to go to the shops from time to time, so far, they had not been approached. Sothebys were very sympathetic, and allowed Imogen paid leave so she and Conrad sought solace in nature in a beautiful place but which so far, was unknown territory to them.

Their only consolation at that desperate time was the fact that the paintings Polly created in Rome were the best she had ever done and Imogen said that it would be wonderful if she could have a posthumous exhibition at the Gayton Gallery because that would be her best memorial.

The island did indeed bring them some peace of mind and painting was always their best therapy. After three weeks, they were ready to return to London where Monica helped them to organise a memorial service for Polly at St Paul's church in Covent Garden. Conrad was delighted when Monica, unbidden, offered to host an exhibition of Polly's work as soon as she had space at the gallery. Imogen expressed the view that those who write or paint are fortunate, as they have a posthumous identity whereas those who leave nothing concrete behind are often forgotten after a couple of generations have passed.

Chapter Thirty-Two

While Sally and Guy were in London, they went to see Nancy in 'Arcadia' by Sir Tom Stoppard. Both of them agreed that it was one of the most remarkable plays they had ever seen; a veritable masterpiece, in fact. Guy acknowledged that this work is truly extraordinary and beyond doubt one of the foremost dramas of the twentieth century. Stoppard's use of two time lines at the same location is formidable, and lends mystery and even magic to the whole play. With Sally's experience of living between different levels of reality, it was bound to appeal to her even more than to Guy, who despite being highly intelligent, did not have Sally's psychic gifts.

After the shocking terrorist attack which had claimed the life of a friend and some of her students, the couple felt the need of the solace that beautiful music brings and went to hear an afternoon recital by the baritone, Giles Davies, with his accompanist, Nigel Foster, given under the auspices of the Schubert Society. The programme opened with the short song cycle, An Die Ferne Geliebte, by Beethoven; sung by a beautiful, mellow baritone voice with musicality of a high order, along with the poetry and sensitivity that the work requires. It was sheer magic and truly touched Sally's heart, making her weep as she thought of Polly, the friend who was now far away. The programme also included songs by Schubert and the Liederkreis Op. 24 by Schumann, which touched a deep vein of humanity, and brought catharsis because as Sally said, music was the best therapy she knew. Guy, to whom music had always meant a great deal, was delighted to discover that she loved music as much as he did and hoped they would have other shared musical occasions in the not too distant future.

The next day, they were back at West Bridge, where Sally took up her studies again, assisted by Tom and Piers. Guy was in contact with the BBC who put forward some names for an Executive Producer to take the place of Jane, now the Countess of Drumlomond. She had indicated to Guy that when the twins were older, she would like to work with him again but in the meantime, she hoped that she could help with research or as a consultant, working from home. Bringing up twins was exhausting, even though she had Nanny, but she would not be able to relax if she left them too early. However, by the time they went to kindergarten, it would get easier, at least, she hoped so.

At last, Ranu and Monica were able to go to see Miranda at Bourton. As she was a pretty girl, not unlike his Emma, she immediately took his eye. He preferred his girls slim and petite, as was Miranda, though she did not have the sparkling personality of Emma. In fact, she was rather quiet. Ranu did not know of course, nor was Monica aware, how very withdrawn the girl had been when her brother was alive. She was always afraid that people would find out about their unconventional relationship so became extremely discreet, as indeed did Richard until the last few months of his life.

Now with Monica's encouragement and support, Miranda was discovering her own individuality, allowing her innate personality to emerge without fear of scandal. Monica introduced Ranu and he said how much he was looking forward to seeing her work as Monica had told him how much she admired it. The girl took them into her studio and Monica was delighted to see how much painting she had done since her last visit. In fact, it appeared that Miranda was living the life of a nun, totally immersed in her work; her only respite was occasionally popping down to the pub for an evening meal. Her painting was taking on a surreal quality, yet, she copied no one, everything was original to her. She found other artists inspiring but even had she wanted to copy, she could not as she had no talent for impersonating the style of another artist.

Monica indicated that she would like Miranda to come to London to work and offered to hire a live-in studio for her. Actually, this came about quite incidentally, because Pedro's former bedsit was advertised and Monica went to see it. It was ideal, especially as Miranda could have use of the small room that Pedro had used as a studio, so when she came up to London, she was thrilled to be presented with a place to live in cosmopolitan Soho. Everything would be very different, of course; she was used to a country town and had previously lived way out in the Brecon Beacons, so to be part of the artistic London scene was beyond her wildest dreams. However, if the noise and bustle of the capital became too much, she could pop off to Bourton to recharge her batteries.

Shortly after his visit to Miranda, Ranu flew to Hollywood to see how Emma was getting on and found that she had taken to the place like a duck to water. She had thrown herself into the part of a female terrorist, but was devastated to hear of real life terrorism in London that had taken the lives of Polly and her students, as well as injuring many more, two of whom had since died of their injuries.

America was also suffering gun incidents which claimed many lives, but no politician had yet succeeded in limiting the supply of guns. They were endemic to the States as the Second Amendment of the Constitution gives the right to individuals to carry arms to protect themselves and their families. It beggars belief that after one of the worst incidents which caused a large death toll, shares in gun manufacture actually rose.

It was understandable for those living in remote areas to have guns for protection when the country was first opened up but is very outdated in the twenty first century and proves that violence just breeds violence. However, although against her will, Emma was persuaded to buy a gun for her own protection and keep it handy at all times.

Despite manmade chaos, the elements were also hitting hard at the continent through devastating hurricanes and now extensive fires across California that were made worse by savage winds. It was hard to understand why it was happening, but vast areas were being destroyed and thousands of people made homeless, as well as those who lost lives. Nevertheless, life had to go on and Emma, as an optimistic girl, trusted that somehow things would improve. As she said, "Look at Europe after the war where bombs had divested great cities such as London, Portsmouth, Liverpool, Birmingham, in the UK; and in Germany, Hamburg, Munich, Berlin and Dresden, as well as cities in other countries, yet, tons of rubble had been cleared and all were now thriving. Mankind caused the problems and it was up to mankind to solve them."

On the face of it, in the short term, it looked pretty hopeless. Yet, hope was what was needed and for the American Dream to be visualised again.

Emma was certainly finding fulfilment, though she had to fight her corner from time to time. Sexual harassment was not the least of her worries, but she managed to keep her cool. The good thing was that after extensive adverse publicity, film moguls and directors were becoming wary, and realised that they could no longer enjoy having carte blanche with young, ambitious actresses. Emma was set on stardom on her own terms and was taking acting classes when filming allowed. However, as a lead character, she appeared in at least three quarters of the film so on rare days off, she just wanted to sleep, but alone, not with someone just to promote her career.

Her relationship with Ranu was of some duration, and used as she was to her suave, beautiful coffee coloured man with his mop of silken black hair and darkly gleaming eyes, she believed she had been spoiled, and as he was also kindness itself, she was not about to lower her standards. There was little enough time to renew their sexual relationship, though they did occasionally have some private time together in Emma's smart apartment. If truth were told, Ranu regretted that Emma was so obstinately ambitious, because he could see that it was inevitable that as her career took off, their relationship was bound to wane. However, he was also very ambitious so had no right to criticise her. He would keep in touch with her and visit as often as he could but it was not much fun when she was filming, as even if he was allowed on set, they were surrounded by other people. Sad as it was, he had to accept that their enjoyable life in London was fast drawing to a close.

Time fled so quickly, that all too soon, Ranu had to return to the City where he had business meetings lined up. He was planning to set up a new factory in an area near Bangalore, which would give much needed employment to women and girls but the conditions must be right. He was not an exploitative employer; on the contrary, he paid well and though he never cut corners, productivity in his concerns was high, so he still made a handsome profit, which meant he could continue to expand, giving work to those in areas of high unemployment. He also set up training centres to teach computerisation and ensured that his workers had a good knowledge of English as, like it or not, it was accepted as the universal language, without which workers were hampered in the global market.

It was an emotional moment when the lovers parted as they did not know when they would meet again. If all went well regarding investment, Ranu would fly to southern India though he had no knowledge of how long he would be required to remain in the sub-continent. Nonetheless, he trusted that the right venue for his factory would be found and setting up a competent management structure would enable him to delegate from London, via technology.

All went well in the City when he returned to London, and with reputable investors on board and a good business plan, he was assured that the project would succeed. He had good people on the ground in India so he felt he could relax and recharge his batteries before he had to leave again. In the meantime, he lost no time in visiting Miranda, this time without Monica. He took her out to lunch and told her that he was willing to invest in her work. She could hardly believe her luck; to have two patrons, Monica and Ranu, was incredible for a young, unknown artist.

Ranu was already missing Emma, so was tempted to begin a relationship with Miranda before he had to go away. However, there was a lot of water to go under the bridge with all the myriad aspects that go with entrepreneurship so he expected to still be in London for considerable time. He had originally hoped to invest in Bangladesh but due to monsoons causing extensive floods and the influx of Muslim refugees from the Miramar region, he and his backers decided it was too risky so settled for southern India instead.

Miranda had told him on the phone that she would be living in London, thanks to Monica's kindness, but when she said she already had a bedsit all lined up in Soho, he was pleasantly surprised. Accommodation, not only in central London, but in every other area of that great city is in short supply, so she considered herself tremendously lucky. A bedsit would not equate with her Bourton house and studio, but one could barely afford more than a cupboard in central London, so she was fortunate to have a bedsit in a very large room. She had no intention of selling her Bourton house because she knew she would always need a bolthole; however, her London bedsit would provide a convenient piéd ã terre.

Ranu, however, could appreciate that if his relationship worked out as well with Miranda as it had with Emma, he would be setting her up in style. He did not want a casual relationship and had never been a chap for one-night stands. He was also fully heterosexual, so needed a woman in his life, someone who would share his bed on a regular basis. He also wanted someone to be companionable, as well as providing regular sex and loved talented women. Miranda certainly fitted the bill; she was lovely and talented, what more could he desire?

However, he hadn't reckoned with Miranda herself who was enjoying her freedom and did not want any strings attached even with the most dashing of men. Her work consumed her and though she would appreciate Ranu as a patron, if it came with strings then she wasn't interested.

He and Emma had had a delightful life together. She had never complained about him having a wife and children in India. Her only concern is that all should be well with them, and she knew how generous Ranu was and how much he valued his family, even if he didn't want to live with them in the home of his forefathers. He had become thoroughly westernised and could not imagine living there indefinitely. However, his family wanted for nothing and his wife was content, so all was well.

If Emma had still been living in London, Ranu would not have thought of taking another mistress, but she had indicated that if things continued to go as well as they were at present, she could envisage making Hollywood or even Los Angeles her permanent home.

Of course, Ranu was totally ignorant of Miranda's history. He assumed that in her teens, she had boyfriends but now lived the life of a nun because she was dedicated to her painting. Had he been aware of Richard, who knows what his thoughts would have been? Miranda was determined never to spill the beans however close she became to someone. There were some things that always had to remain secret because even though a lot of taboos have broken down, incest was still considered a heinous sin as far as society was concerned.

Since Richard's death, Miranda had put all thoughts of a sex life behind her. She was privileged to have a talent for art because that had become her strongest passion and it took up most of her mental space, waking or sleeping. She found that she had so many ideas for paintings that she would not find time to produce all of them even if she lived to be a hundred.

However, she would have been less than human if she had not found Ranu attractive. It was not just his good looks, but his appealing personality. He was special and she felt that he was someone she could trust, though never with her closely guarded secret. Over lunch, he told her something of himself, and of his wife and family in India. He never mentioned Emma though. The fact that he had a family made Miranda feel comfortable and she began to relax with him. He was charm personified but did nothing to alarm her so she felt that she had found a friend. When they parted after the meal, he shook her hand and did not even attempt to kiss her on the cheek. She thought this a bit odd, as most people now do it automatically; anyway, she was pleased that he, obviously, saw their connection as that of artist and patron, which suited her down to the ground.

On the drive back to London, Ranu sensed he must be missing Emma even more than he thought as he felt decidedly randy. If he had been able to seduce Miranda there and then, he would have done so, but he was a man of principle so made not the slightest move to embarrass or frighten her. She, obviously, regarded him merely as a patron and would have been startled, and probably very alarmed if he had attempted to make love to her. In fact, it could have ruined their business relationship before it started. No, though she really appealed to him, if he intended to make her his mistress, he had to go warily. He was not a despoiler of females like Conrad. He truly respected women and would do nothing to harm them. When he was first married, he had lived in India, and he and his wife had a good relationship, but he soon got itchy feet, and he was fortunate that she understood that he needed to live in England.

It is said of East and West that never the twain shall meet, but Ranu and Ranee seemed to have found the key. She liked her life the way it was and though her husband was undoubtedly attractive, she had never actually been in love with him, but had simply obeyed her parents and married the man they chose for her. She grew fond of him over the years, especially once the children were born, and she realised that he was happy to come home and impregnate her when she wanted another baby. Although she kept her innermost thoughts from Ranu, she actually preferred women to men, though of course, they were necessary for procreation. The fact that her husband was away so much also gave her the excuse for her lesbianism, though it was not called that by her or any of her ladies. Ranu was a very sophisticated chap, of course, but even he might have been somewhat fazed if he knew of his wife's predilection. As far as he was concerned, the fact that she turned to other women to pleasure her was simply a case of convenience.

The last time he was in India, curiosity had got the better of him regarding lady boys and he had gone in disguise to see a live sex show. He felt rather guilty, yet, it was beautifully staged and was quite in the uninhibited tradition of ancient Hindu sexual mores. It had excited him so much that he had gone home and passionately made love to his wife, who, to her great delight, soon discovered that she was pregnant. That actually pleased them both, thus enabling Ranu to overcome his guilt at becoming a voyeur, even for just one evening.

In London, even though Patrick would soon be home for good, Daniel was still seeing William who had been thrown out of kilter when he heard that Patrick had disappeared. Therefore, it was with great relief that he received the news that he had been found and was little the worse for wear. Of course, he had no idea that Patrick had been in a compromising situation with a fellow soldier; some might have assumed that, but there was no actual evidence that they were other than comrades enjoying a swim when off duty.

William wondered whether to tell Patrick about his relationship with Daniel when he returned from Cyprus. However, Daniel said it would be better to keep quiet about their little forays, although, they did not have to keep their friendship secret as long as it only involved going out occasionally for meals, as well as the odd visit to an exhibition, a film, play or concert.

"What I think," observed Daniel, "is that what the eye doesn't see, the heart doesn't grieve over. Confession might be good for the soul, but it's often painful for the recipient and does no good at all. Let's agree that 'silence is golden'."

"I am sure you are right," sighed William.

Much to his surprise, though, Daniel had become passionately attached to William. He yearned for him as he had never yearned for a girl and was in a quandary as to what to do about it. He wanted to see Imogen again, but as a good mate, rather than a love interest. He knew he could never marry her now that he acknowledged that when it came to sex, he liked men rather more than women.

He had no intention, though, of coming between Patrick and William, if they wanted their affair to continue but it would take a lot of self-control on his behalf to overcome the feelings that he had for William.

Patrick, no more than William, gave any evidence of a change of heart and William had no evidence to show that Patrick had changed his mind about marriage. Indeed, William was as keen as ever, despite his casual affair with Daniel. He wanted to put down roots and have more structure in his life. He knew Patrick so well and was sure that they could make a go of a same sex marriage. It was getting easier all the time, despite pockets of resistance in certain quarters. However, that should not affect them. Patrick was keen to do as Jane and Marcus had done, and looked forward to a quiet, intimate family wedding at Milton House. They could go to the Highlands for their honeymoon then settle down at Drumlomond Castle to begin their married life and new careers.

Nevertheless, the plans of mice and men do not always go as they might. William was horrified and shocked when he read a newspaper report about a couple of gay men who adopted two children. One of them agreed to keep working but the other became a househusband. That was another thing, the fact that they both referred to each other as husband sounded bizarre. Nevertheless, there is no appropriate vocabulary for such unconventional relationships. The trouble started when the stay at home husband found it difficult to cope with an eighteen-month-old girl. Although babies and toddlers are small creatures, they require a good deal of care and attention; they are vulnerable so rely on the adults in charge of them to an inordinate extent. Jane had said how difficult it was to care for babies as a first time mother even though she was privileged to have a nanny and nursemaid.

Well, the stay at home husband became frustrated trying to cope with childcare, but it also seems that he had mental health issues as he said the baby was a devil child and began to seriously ill-treat her. Finally, her injuries were so severe that she died and her so-called carer was arrested. William did not know what happened to him, but suddenly, the whole thing struck him as being totally bizarre and unnatural.

Perhaps, so many people had become gay because Nature had decided that the population needed to be culled as people were living longer and war was to be avoided. However, the whole thing was turned upside down by gays wanting to be parents but not by normal means. Procreation was debatable; IVF, surrogate mothers, abortion and so forth. Fostering and adoption were acceptable, but ideally, William felt, the carers should be a heterosexual couple. Of course, children were sometimes abused by conventional couples, but even so, giving a baby girl to two fellows seemed totally wrong and he wondered why, even if not ideal, a baby boy had not been assigned to them.

He also felt instinctively that abortion was wrong, though he would never deny the right of a woman to undergo the procedure if circumstances demanded. However, with contraception widely available, he couldn't understand why it wasn't extensively used. It would certainly save women a lot of grief.

William admitted that were he in the position of those two gay men, he would be wildly at sea. Nevertheless, it made him think twice about same sex marriage. He and Patrick had never discussed children. He knew that Patrick was against having a child with a woman in the normal way, but had never mentioned wanting to adopt or foster. In fact, they would both be too occupied with running Drumlomond Castle to have time for parenthood.

Family life and society, in general, had become fractured, so many methods were being tried to redress the balance. A free, tolerant society is an ideal, yet, freedom comes at a price and the emancipation of women had not necessarily made them happier. In fact, many women were struggling to cope with children, work and sometimes elderly parents, causing them to be continually exhausted. Also, the fact that many men had abandoned their families and left women to cope singlehandedly, added to their suffering. Selfishness had become endemic and there was not enough consideration for the children whose lives were turned upside down by the dissolution of the family. In single parent families, money was usually in short supply, despite welfare for those worse off, but responsibility and duty had been ignored in many cases. Of course, many women were keen to have careers but there were even more who, if they had been financially secure, would have preferred to stay at home and bring up their children themselves. Latch key kids, once a rarity had become the norm in present day society, and the results were plain to see in lack of discipline, gang crime, depression, self-harm and even suicide. William was the last person to want to live under a dictatorship, but he felt that public consciousness should begin to promote better values. Education was a good thing but with so many people not coming out of further education until their early twenties, adolescent attitudes carried over into their thirties or later.

Like Daniel, William was in a quandary. He had always been a thoughtful man but suddenly, he became more aware. It had taken the tragic murder of a baby to wake him up, and realise that he needed to examine his own life and principles.

Of course, he admitted, there were no simple answers, every case had to be judged on its merits and the world was a minefield, a mixing pot of every type of person. All might be equal in the sight of God but not in the amount of wisdom derived from living on Earth, even if, like Sally, you believed in reincarnation.

He had always assumed that the world would improve from age to age but history did not bear that out. How did you account for all the good people in the world as well as those 'mad, bad and dangerous to know?' Sally reckoned, it was like a huge school, and we are all prodigal sons and daughters. Some have learned their lessons well and are en route to the university, while others are still in the kindergarten stage, though the majority are in the middle school. Lifetime after lifetime, we are given the chance to improve but sometimes, we return very little different to what we were before, and make the same mistakes so have to go round and round until we make progress. What was it Shakespeare said about good being interred with their bones; and what about the sins of the fathers? Well, William had never studied psychology or philosophy, but one couldn't help picking up snippets along the way.

Now he had to get to work and start playing monopoly in the City, buying and selling commodities. There would be time when

Patrick came home for good to get down to brass tacks. They would have to be truly honest with each other because subterfuge lies and misunderstandings always lead to trouble.

Chapter Thirty-Three

Daniel had had time to think about his life and aims while Imogen had been away, and decided that he was ready to propose marriage to her. He was no longer an adolescent hell raiser so it was time to put his infatuation for William into perspective. It was hard because he was still in thrall to a very attractive chap. However, he knew that in time, even the most intense infatuation wanes, though he hoped that their friendship would last, but without any sexual connotation.

He decided that he now wanted a more balanced way of life, and looked forward to a wife and children, and a settled home life, though he would not let domesticity get in the way of his creative work; on the contrary, he hoped it would enhance it.

Imogen had always been a good chum and they had grown ever closer over the years. He had also begun to look at her work more objectively; she had always been dear little Imogen, but he realised that he had taken her for granted. On seeing the paintings she had brought back from the Isle of Man, he appreciated that he had previously underestimated her as a painter. Of course, she had lived under the shadow of her famous father and of her mother, who though not in his class, was an artist of considerable worth, so Imogen's work had gone largely unnoticed. She had not thought much of her painting either, but she wanted to be part of the art world which is why she had begun her apprenticeship at Sothebys.

Although he had not yet reached a conclusion as to how Imogen might react to his proposal, he was sure her father would not be at all happy about it. Conrad was a charming chap, but had the ego of a dedicated creative artist. It was as if Imogen was not just his daughter, but his possession. The fact that he had just lost Polly, was a bad time to confront him with the fact that he was about to lose Imogen to another man, albeit one he looked upon as a surrogate son.

However, fate was about to take a hand once more in the affairs of the little group of friends. Sylvia had certainly been enjoying her job in Stratford and was not indifferent to David's loving attentions; however, as soon as she learned of Polly's death, she wanted to get back to London. She knew in her heart that she would never truly get over Conrad. He was her soul mate, she felt and there would never be anyone else like him.

Throwing caution to the winds, she gave her resignation at the theatre and nothing that David said could persuade her to change her mind. He had got used to having her around; she was not only vividly attractive, but a fun person too, and they had certainly had some memorable sexual encounters, but Sylvia was adamant; she was needed in London and to London she would go.

In the meantime, Daniel proposed to Imogen and was refused. As he thought, Conrad was not in favour and Imogen did not want to add to his distress at such a time of bereavement. However, unknown to Daniel, Imogen had been seeing Rod Whittacker, a colleague, who had been appointed to a senior post with Sotheby's New York branch. He wanted to take Imogen with him as she could train there just as easily as in London. She was tempted to accept, that is, if she could get around Conrad, who would undoubtedly baulk at her living so far away.

As soon as Sylvia arrived in London, she went straight to Holland Park. She had not let anyone know that she was coming but Conrad greeted her with open arms.

"How did you know how that I was calling to you, my dearest, dearest love?" he asked.

"My soul must have heard you," she laughed, "because I just knew that I had to drop everything and rush to your side. I was so sorry to hear about Polly; it was unbelievably tragic, but I didn't know how to approach you, other than sending my condolences, then I heard you had gone away. Well, here we are together again and unless you send me away, I am here to stay."

Imogen was delighted to see Sylvia and indeed, her father looked like a new man so it seemed that his recovery would be sooner rather than later. She felt that with Sylvia's return, fate was taking a hand in her own affairs, and next day, she went to see Whittacker and accepted the New York position.

After work, Imogen visited Daniel at his studio. He was covered in paint and had obviously been working with a will. He was not a neat artisan like her father, in fact, at the end of the day, there was often as much paint on Daniel's work clothes as there was on his canvas. He was experimenting with abstracts and Imogen was amazed by his exquisite colours, quite ravished indeed.

"You really are in fine form," she told him. "I absolutely love these paintings which are much larger than your others."

"Yes," he answered, "but they may be more difficult to sell because of their size."

"I can imagine that there are few private houses where they could hang but I think you are onto something with corporate organisations and art galleries so do plod on. Has Monica seen them?"

"No, I was keeping them as a surprise until I was sure in which direction I was going."

"Well," replied Imogen, "I think you should get her round right away as I am sure she will be thrilled. Oh, by the way, Daniel, I have accepted a job with Sotheby's New York Office and will start in a month's time."

"Good lord, does your father know?" he queried.

"Not yet, I am biding my time, but I think it will be OK because Sylvia is back and he is cock a hoop, so won't miss me too much. Anyway, I think Monica has been putting out feelers to get him a New York solo exhibition, so we may meet up at some point."

Actually, quite a lot was happening behind the scenes as far as Monica was concerned. Firstly, she was in the process of buying the New York gallery where Guy had worked many moons ago; also Nancy Lolongo was going to Broadway with 'Arcadia' and Monica was planning an exhibition for Conrad as soon as the purchase of the gallery was completed. She had been keeping her cards close to her chest, so even Sally did not know what she was up to.

Sylvia had moved in with Conrad and Imogen plucked up courage to tell him about her plans to go to America. He said how much he would miss her, but would not stand in her way. Then he told her that he had proposed marriage to Sylvia and she had accepted. They were both deliriously happy but still wanted her blessing. Imogen could not have been happier herself and wished them all the happiness in the world.

Although Polly's death was relatively recent, they did not want to waste any time, so set a date for a quiet, registry office wedding the following week, with just Imogen and Daniel as witnesses. After that, life continued much as it had before, with Conrad painting, and Sylvia looking after the apartment and modelling for him from time to time. She told him, however, that if Guy asked her to act as his PA for the Elizabethan documentary, she wanted to accept. In fact, if she worked as a freelance, she would be able to pick and choose when, or if she worked. He agreed that he would be quite happy, as long as she was not away for long stretches at a time. He had just learned about Monica's plans, and added that if he went to America when she was up and running, he would naturally want Sylvia to go with him.

Chapter Thirty-Four

In Cyprus, Patrick had had his suspicions about Petra confirmed and he now realised that she was, indeed, a honey trap who had kept close tabs on him. Well, it didn't work with him. He was quite aware of the way Spooks operated but wondered what could possibly have led her to him. No doubt, she was MI6, but he had done nothing wrong, other than having a little dalliance on the beach a few weeks ago with Robert, but that was not known.

He had been quite taken with her but not in a sexual way, so was she trying him out to see it he was homosexual? Perhaps, his preference was common knowledge though he didn't think so, as his only affair was with William who was not remotely connected with the Army. Well, times had changed and it was no longer illegal even if the Army was not comfortable with such relationships.

He began to look closely at the things she had said when they were having a coffee or a meal together and gradually, he realised that it was all to do with the late Brigadier General Partington. Of course, his father had now married the general's widow so maybe they thought that Patrick was party to some illicit information. Well, they could stuff it because there was no information to have. Jane was no more a party to such information than he was. In fact, she had done her best, ever since the ill-fated night of her wedding, to stay as far away from her estranged husband as possible and took absolutely no interest in his affairs.

He reckoned that the Spooks were trying to establish his alleged links to a Neo Nazi cell, but had failed so far to ascertain the extent of infiltration into the military.

Well, much as he hoped such scum could be weeded out, he had no information to give, so when Petra packed up and left, he assumed that she had been recalled because she had nothing to report.

It was ironic, anyway, that a serving soldier, even one as bonkers as Arnold, should have become mixed up with such a group. In fact, it was unthinkable that anyone whose grandfather had fought to destroy Hitler and his insane crew, should even contemplate resurrecting such a diabolical ideology. The interesting thing is that when he and Petra first met, they said they would keep in touch, and meet when Patrick returned to London. However, she had left without making any such arrangement, so he realised that her friendship was not friendship at all, but purely professional. Well, he had to admit, she was good and so young too, but, of course, she was an undergraduate at Cambridge in her teens so was probably recruited then. At last, the penny dropped, what a fool he was, the general whose story she was 'ghosting' was Arnold, not a retired general but a dead one.

A couple of weeks later, he was back in London and hanging up his military hat. His term of service was over and he was about to be launched onto civvy street. William was delighted to have him home but both of them felt they needed breathing space. They had a heart to heart over a meal at the mews one night and both of them said that they had been seriously reconsidering marriage, as it was a big step. Unknown to each other, they had been shocked at how easily they had become enamoured of a new love interest, William with Daniel and Patrick with Robert.

Now neither of them thought it would be a good idea to rush things. They knew they would always be the best of friends, but marriage was something else and may not be such a good idea after all. It would be better to have the freedom to stay together because they wished to, rather than be compelled to by a slip of paper. However, William was keen to have a change of occupation so was still hopeful that he would be engaged as financial advisor at Drumlomond Castle when Patrick took up his residency there. In the years he had been in the City, he had made quite a financial killing, so money was no object to him.

Marcus, Jane and the twins were very happy in Warwickshire, and apart from visits, had no intention of living permanently in Scotland.

Sylvia and Conrad appeared to be enjoying married life, though their friends were disappointed that it had been so secret, just in a registry office, without guests. However, they booked a room at the Ritz and invited all their friends to a reception. Sylvia even invited David, with Conrad's permission, but her new husband could afford to be magnanimous because he was the one she had chosen to spend the rest of her life with.

Of course, David was not over the moon when he heard that his former lover and PA was married, but though he and Sylvia had enjoyed their time together, neither of them had pretended to be in love. It had been a pleasant interlude, but Sylvia had no illusions that David would be single for long.

There was nothing much that anyone could tell Sylvia about Conrad because she had known him for long enough not to be surprised, although she and no doubt he, would have been taken by a great deal of surprise to find out that Helen Dainton was his daughter by Lady Virginia Torrington. Nevertheless, Sylvia had been devoted to him from the first time she met him, and despite his peccadilloes and faults, her love for him was unconditional and total. She had never tried to change him; in fact, she didn't believe that anyone had the right to forcefully change another person. If changes were to be made, they had to come from the individual concerned. Now, although she had never envisaged being married to him, she thanked providence that her years of devotion had been well and truly rewarded.

Monica and Nancy were also devoted to each other, and looked forward to being in New York together. Both of them would be busy, of course. Nancy would have rehearsals during the day, and Monica would be involved with lawyers and gallery staff, but once 'Arcadia' was in performance, Nancy would have her days free and gradually things would ease off for Monica, although there would then be the proposed exhibition of Conrad's latest works.

Truth to tell, Monica felt rather guilty about Sally, but had she known it, she need not have worried, because though it had taken her a long time to realise it, Sally was now hopelessly in love with Guy. Nothing of a personal nature had happened between them, but they were enjoying a very compatible working relationship. Guy had even suggested that Sally should co-present his new documentary series with him. She was very photogenic, really knew her stuff and with his coaching, he was sure she would make a first rate presenter. However, she did not warm to the idea because she preferred to be a back room girl, like Jane and Sylvia. Guy, she told him, was born to present, and she feared letting him down by her lack of experience and confidence. He was disappointed but agreed that there are horses for courses.

He had been drawn to Sally right from the start but having learned of her long-term relationship with Monica, did not think he had a hope in hell of winning her. Instead, he made the most of working with her, though he sighed in vain for want of a deeper, more personal relationship with her. He had the grace to blush when he thought how he had behaved the first time they were alone together and feared that it had set up an impenetrable barrier between them. It was his misfortune that he had fallen in love with a lesbian when the world was full of hetero women. Indeed, until he met Sally, he did not know that he had ever met a woman of her kind. He had known Monica for years, of course, but she was married and it never entered his head that her women friends might be more than friends. Now though, he realised that both women had been extremely discreet, and there was a tacit acceptance by their friends of the status quo. However, meeting the darkly beautiful Nancy Lolongo and seeing her on stage, had completely overwhelmed Monica who was now delightfully in love. It was not just Nancy's looks, though these were undeniably exceptional, nor even her magnetic presence that held Monica captive; it was her warm and loving personality, and her zest for life which Monica found irresistible.

However, when they first met, Monica feared that she had competition from Thea Constantine, because of the important part she played in Nancy's life. It was true, of course, that Thea had given Nancy a great start in her career, but Nancy had more than proved that Thea's belief in her was justified. Thea gave her a foot in the door, which was invaluable but Nancy still had to walk out on the stage alone; and character, confidence and tenacity are as important as talent.

The next time Monica and Nancy were alone, Monica broached the subject of Thea. Nancy did not deny how crucial meeting the director had been. She had taught her so much, not just in theatrical terms but in life. When Nancy first met Thea, she was not long out of drama school and hardly knew where she was going. As to sex, she had never given it a lot of thought. She was ambitious from the word go and had been offered the casting coach but she resisted as politely as possible. However, Thea made no bones about being interested in her personally as well as professionally. She saw her potential as an actress but on another level, to put it crudely, was as randy as hell, when she thought of Nancy. Up to that point, Nancy had never been truly confident of her sexuality, but she was soon overwhelmed by Thea's sexual energy. The director was not at all feminine, indeed, everything about her was masculine but she knew how to pleasure another woman, and soon, she and Nancy were entrenched in a deeply erotic affair.

Thea had a lot of clout in the theatre and their relationship did Nancy's career no harm; in fact, it set her feet firmly on the rung of the ladder which she speedily began to climb. Thea had first seen her in her graduation performance at RADA. She played Cleopatra in Shakespeare's 'Anthony and Cleopatra', and her reviews were more than any debutante has a right to expect. Thea was immediately aware that here was a major talent to be watched and when she was asked to direct the play in the West End, she opted for Nancy as the female lead. She took a calculated risk because Nancy was a mere beginner, but again, the reviews were amazing and this led to the novice actress going straight into the National Theatre in a significant role.

However, Nancy was now well established and Thea had another protégé, a young woman by the name of Marianne Chernikova in her sights. Her parents were Ukrainian migrants but Marianne was born in London. When Thea met her, she had just left drama school and had a student boyfriend. However, Thea soon put a stop to that and before you could say 'knife', Marianne was sharing Thea's bed. Of course, Nancy was very grateful to Thea for all she had done for her, but with the knowledge that Thea had a new love interest as well as a new talent to nurture, Nancy felt emotionally free and able to express her love for Monica.

She did not want to have any secrets from Monica but Monica also felt the need to unburden herself to Nancy. She told her about Sally, and said before they went any further with their own relationship, she should tell Sally about it and hope she would not take it too hard.

"Mind you," said Monica, looking thoughtful. "I have long had a feeling that she has a soft spot for Guy Giffard. I have never known Sally to have a relationship with a man in all the years I have known her, though she has been aware that as well as having a husband, I have also had minor affairs with other men. Throughout my student days, I thought I was lesbian, but circumstances alter things and with marriage on the cards, I did give myself to Douglas. He was totally hetero, but I never let on that I wasn't and in fact, with my various experiences in life, I am convinced that I am bi-sexual. If you can accept that, dear Nancy, then all is fine but if you can't forget my past, there will be nothing further to say. I want to be faithful to you and as I get older, I see no reason to make myself available to men. Can you accept me as I am?"

"I love you, my dearest Monica, so, yes, I accept you as you are, warts and all, and trust that you will love me just as I am." Monica smiled and drew her close as they kissed, and pledged themselves to each other 'from this day forward'.

Guy knew that Monica was buying the New York gallery, but also saw in a magazine that Nancy Lolongo was going to Broadway with the Stoppard production. He had long suspected that the two women were now an item, and he was anxious about Sally and her reaction. However, she greeted him very cheerfully and said she had known for a few weeks but had been asked to keep it secret until it appeared in the national press. He did not, at first, realise though that she was talking about Monica buying the gallery.

By this time, Patrick and William had finally decided that they were now truly ready to commit themselves to marriage so had asked Marcus if they too could marry in the Yellow Salon. Of course, he agreed but said that he might as well become a registrar as his house seemed to have become desirable for weddings.

Three weeks later, the boys tied the knot, surrounded by their relatives and dearest friends then flew out to Cape Town for a honeymoon, before embarking on their new life in Scotland. Guy and Sally returned to West Bridge in the late afternoon sunshine, and sitting under an arbour in his garden at the Dower House, they discussed the sound tracks they thought appropriate to accompany the film of the new documentary. Guy was very sensitive about the music that was chosen for his sound tracks but many programmes have a constant barrage of drumming because that is what people are used to in their everyday lives. However, it is an imposition and causes irritation, especially when the unwanted sound is louder than speech. Guy thoroughly disliked what has become a cliché, and said that sometimes, it would be pleasant just to have the picture and silence, though it seems that is not allowed in these days of 'sound design' but which to him were more like 'noise design'.

As the programme was set in the sixteenth century, Guy planned to have music by composers of that era such as Byrd Tallis and Campion, just as he had insisted on having Gretry, Handel, Haydn and Mozart for his 'Gracious Ladies' series. Because the Wilhelmina episode was set in Bayreuth, some crass individual said they should have Wagner. However, he was shouted down because Wagner was not born till 1813.

"Really," said Guy, "it is about time the British populace were properly educated regarding quality music because there has been too much emphasis on the head banging stuff for too long."

Sally laughed but said that prejudice against classical music could be put down to Left Wing bigots who declared it was elitist and not for the proletariat. "Yet audiences are there," she added. "You have only to look at the Proms at the Albert Hall and the Proms in the Park each summer to see that is the case. However, tons of money is put into the commercial pot, while orchestras and classical performers are always struggling to make a living."

They were lying on a tartan rug, under a spreading oak tree with golden beams of sunlight filtering through the leaves, creating a halo around Sally's gorgeous hair. As Guy looked admiringly at her, he remembered the first time she had come here and how he had made love to her without any resistance on her part. Now, he longed to take her in his arms again and cover her naked body with kisses. Believing that Monica had a new love, he gambled that Sally might again welcome his advances so plucking up courage he said, rather quietly, "Marry me."

Sally could not believe her ears and asked him to repeat what he had just said. This time, he spoke louder and she gave him a quizzical look at which he nodded his head.

"Well, what took you so long?" She chuckled. "Of course, I will marry you; haven't we been engaged for the past four hundred years? You know, it really is time you made an honest woman of me."

His answer was to passionately kiss her then he drew her to her feet and rushed her into the house. "It's time for the next instalment," he called over his shoulder, as he quickly pulled her up the stairs into his bedroom, where he was about to initiate the love making of which they had been cheated four centuries ago; but now well aware that life is truly everlasting.